MW00944538

THE OATH

A fictionalized life of Hassan Bey O'Reilly of Damascus

SARAH B. GUEST PERRY

Copyright © 2015 Sarah B. Guest Perry

All rights reserved.

ISBN: 151979391X
ISBN-13:9781519793911

DEDICATION

For my parents

Thomas Whipple Perry

1925-2013

And

Helen B Guest Washburn Perry

1928-2003

CONTENTS

PROLOGUE

It was 1848. A momentous year when revolutions lit up the political sky in a broad arc like a string of exploding firecrackers.

Running across Europe it stretched from Dublin and its Young Ireland in the west to Paris, then Berlin and Vienna and south through Hungary into Serbia.

Its principal city, Novi Sad, controlled by Austria, was situated at an international border and Danubian crossing northeast of Sarajevo, which was firmly under the control of the Turks. Sarajevo would become considerably better known when the Balkan powder keg ignited World War I at the beginning of the long summer of 1914 when the Archduke Franz Ferdinand, heir to the Viennese throne, was assassinated here.

1848 was a year similar to our Arab spring, but with a difference. Each revolution was staged independently of the others, not seeded by outside Great Powers seeking to increase their influence by attempting the overthrow of leaders to be replaced by ones more to their liking.

One rebellion inspired another in a domino effect. In the end, most rebellions failed to accomplish their worthy goals, as so often is the human condition. The French overthrew their king and concessions were won elsewhere, but many citizens were displaced. Germans fled to the United States and Hungarian civilians and soldiers fled the armies who had defeated them, crossing over the Danube to Vidin and elsewhere in the northern reaches of the Ottoman empire.

Dislocated people everywhere changed the face of Europe as individuals were forced to leave one place and flee to another to make new lives for themselves.

One of those individuals was our main character, Eugene O'Reilly of Dublin, son of a prominent solicitor and his wife.

Eugene was forced into exile after the collapse of the 1848 rising and was saved from transportation to Tasmania because of his minor role. Through Lord Palmerston, the Foreign Secretary in London, he found a position in the Levant in the land of the Turks and their sultan.

Fleeing one rebellion he found himself a soldier of fortune in a time when that was acceptable. He was viewed as a Western military advisor who could bring the local cavalry up to snuff for an expected war with Russia in the eastern Ottoman provinces northeast and across the Danube from Belgrade.

He watched his Austrian opponents and saw the occasional civilian flee them, heading south. He could not have known that among those in flight was the Hungarian mother of his future wife, Mathilda Solomassy, who was heading south unaware of her future as an odalisque or white slave to be sold to a ranking Turkish gentleman.

Eugene served in the Crimean War and he rose in the Turkish command. He was given the title of Hassan Bey or "beautiful lord", the first westerner to hold the title, its previous holder having perished in the war.

Once peace had been restored in the Danubian sector, he headed for Constantinople or Istanbul, affectionately known as Stamboul, and its Golden Horn or harbor filled with ships and caiques darting to and fro.

The city, built of brightly painted wood, showed blank walls to the street with latticed windows overhanging the doors so the ladies in their haremliks could see and not be seen, shadows playing behind them in the evenings when one could attempt to guess the ages and number of the ladies in residence.

Perched high above the Golden Horn on the European side was the Pera or foreign quarter. As dull colored as the Ottoman quarters were bright, it was filled with westerners doing their best to live a western life under an exotic sun.

Soon Colonel O'Reilly was off to Damascus for a new post in the province of Syria in the southern and western reaches of the empire. In his time, you could travel from the Danubian border and Sarajevo, south along the coast to Stamboul, and then westward along the sea, all the way past Gaza nearly to the Nile, without seeing a single border post. All was as one.

Syria, as it was then, extended east through the Circassian mountains nearly to Yalta and the Crimea, southeast nearly to Kabul, south through the Arabian desert to Yemen and west to the edge of the Sinai. It encompassed the twenty-first-century nations of Lebanon, Syria, Jordan, Israel, the West Bank, and Gaza. The latter three constituted the Palestinian *eyalet* or provincial subdivision ruled by viceroys in Gaza and Jerusalem.

Damascus was a sleepy little place, far different from its commercial partner, Beirut, two days ride away. It came to life as caravans of pilgrims from the northern half of the empire traveled to Mecca and Medina and as Bedouin tribes emerged from the desert in summer in search of grazing land.

Colonel O'Reilly rose higher in his career, attracting an international following eagerly consuming what news they could glean of his exploits from their local newspapers.

Making a life for himself in Syria he rose to be head aide de camp to the provincial governor and dear friend of the high living French envoy Count Bentivoglio on the coast.

Finally overreaching himself after decades under the Turks he was sent into exile in a Europe he had left behind. Accompanied by his loving wife Mathilda Solomassy, a pasha's daughter who had yet to learn how terribly she had been wronged, he headed into an uncertain future.

Two decades after 1848 an echoing boom from the western hemisphere as the American Civil War erupted.

Different reasons for war but the same effect, people fleeing and forced to make their way in a new culture having been born and raised in a culture that was no longer there. Southerners were forced to flee their homeland and head north as job opportunities shrank as the Southern economy collapsed.

Among them was our third main character, James Bankhead Guest, born to a Baltimore cotton merchant and his second wife, raised to be a tobacco planter in western Virginia and forced to adapt to a new life in New York City as a cotton broker.

Through a friend, he meets the widowed Mathilda Massy, who, haunted by a pain that can never leave, has been driven far from her home and remade herself, becoming a Worth trained dressmaker. Together they make a life.

A common theme really, three people all born and bred in one culture, pushed out and then forced to remake a life in another as best they can.

Now they can haunt your dreams as they have haunted mine for nearly ten years.

To view a carefully curated slideshow of period artwork illustrating various points in the narrative, please visit sarahbguestperry.com.

Much is owed to the librarians at the Boston Public Library reference section, Widener Library at Harvard University and Boston College, who eased the research involved greatly. I thank my wonderful editors, Ann Matranga and Scott Anderson of imaginary forests.com without whom the books would never have come to exist, my friends Jacqueline Dunn and Tim Sullivan and my endlessly supportive children, Jonathan, Margaret, and Juliana Correia.

Sarah B. Guest Perry
Brighton, Massachusetts
August 29, 2015

1 DUBLIN & CORSTOWN

On August twelfth, 1826, in the master bedroom of a house on Lower Gardiner Street in Dublin, Ireland a baby boy was born. His mother was Emily O'Reilly, daughter of Michael and Catherine McConnell. His father was Matthew O'Reilly, a prominent city attorney. The baby's older brother, James, was about to turn five.

The boy was named Eugene after his father's cousin who was a parish priest stationed in Navan, a town in County Meath just north of Dublin.

The family was very proud of their new baby. They hoped that he would enter the priesthood or perhaps follow in his father's footsteps and become a lawyer.

The O'Reillys lived in a large granite townhouse. Six steps went up to the front door. An areaway led down to the kitchen and its sculleries and pantry. The dining room and library were above on the ground floor along with the drawing and morning rooms.

Upstairs was a master bedroom with dressing rooms down the hall. The boys' domain, the nurseries, was up another flight on the third floor.

The servants lived at the very top of the house in garrets under the eaves. In back there was a yard paved with cobblestones and a carriage house where the family horses resided along with James' shetland pony.

Most days it was just the two boys, Eugene and James, with their nurse Polly.

Their father, Matthew O'Reilly, did his best to come up and see them once a week. Glad shrieks filled the air when he appeared, followed by loud footsteps.

He would run through the nurseries and into the schoolroom. Letting each boy take a turn on his shoulders, he pretended to be a racing horse tearing along the road in County Meath.

Both boys laughed, wishing they could do it every week. But that was impossible as their father was often called away on business.

His father's games sparked Eugene's interest in horses. He insisted on being taken to tour the stables behind the house far more often than Polly wished.

When he was two, he went to his mother and said, "Mama, I must go visit the horses today. They are lonely and miss me."

His mother put him on her lap, saying, "Eugene, my darling, of course.

"But since it is raining perhaps you can go tomorrow, or on Saturday when Papa can take you. Or perhaps next week when Uncle Jarleth is here. I think that would be more fun than having our stableman Tom show you around."

Jumping down, her son replied with a stamp of his small foot.

"No Mama. I need to go every day so the horses know me and will let me pet them. I don't want to wait until Papa can come."

It was an odd request for a two-year-old, but a sweet one. His mother smiled for she had loved animals nearly as much as a child.

"Maybe we can arrange a short visit today," she said,

"and a longer one later."

Eugene ran into the hall and waited while the maid fetched his raincoat and boots. Out the back door and across to the stables he ran, hand in hand with Polly, an umbrella over their heads.

Standing still in the yard, he sniffed. There was a reek of wet horses and hay. Another sniff and he reached the stable entrance.

Tom came out and peered down at Eugene for he was very tall.

Leaning down towards the little boy, he said, "Young master I am glad you have come to visit. Would you like to see the horses? That must be your intent. Otherwise, it is a nasty day, better spent by the fire."

Polly smiled.

Eugene responded, saying, "Yes, Tom, I want to visit them. I thought of waiting until Papa came. Since he is away, I asked Mama instead."

Tom gazed at him.

"Sensible," he said, "for you love horses as much as your uncle. Here, come with me. There are sugar lumps in my office. A treat shall help them remember you."

Polly sat down to wait.

Setting off with Tom, Eugene clutched the bag of sugar lumps. When they reached the first stall, Tom put a lump in Eugene's hand.

Telling Eugene to hold his palm flat, Tom pushed his fingers down. "So you won't get nipped," he explained.

They visited all six horses in turn, the pony last. Tom told Eugene to learn their names.

"Next time I shall have somc carrots, their favorite," Tom said. "They love carrots even more than sugar."

Eugene looked up in surprise.

"Carrots aren't treats," he said. "I hate them."

Smiling, Tom said, "They are good for you, Master Eugene. In any case, the horses think they are treats."

Eugene laughed. "Oh, that is too funny."

When he asked to be put up on a horse's back, Tom glanced at Polly over Eugene's head.

Looking down, he decided to let the young master try. Better to give him a chance than bring on a tantrum by saying he was too small.

Plucking Eugene off the floor, Tom settled him first on a carriage horse and then on Star, James' pony.

Eugene sat on the blankets, pulling Star's mane while the grooms who were standing round came to watch. A treat, it seemed to Eugene, even though James rarely came to the stables at all.

When they walked through the stable Eugene spotted his father's riding horse, though Tom had tried to sneak past.

Piping up, Eugene asked, "Why can't I sit on him?"

"Riding horses are skittish and are not safe without a saddle. Star is small and more accustomed to children.

"If your father agrees we can saddle up Star as your feet should almost reach the stirrups. Still, you have to be a bit taller to ride astride. We could put a basket on her side but that I don't think you'd like."

The young master agreed.

"That's a baby thing," he said. "Can I see the saddle instead?"

Heading for the tack room, Tom smiled. His young charge was chatting with a groom about Star and insisting on seeing every bridle.

Polly ran to get him just as cook finished dinner. Eugene had been in the stables all afternoon. Tom apologized for keeping him so long and explained that Eugene had wanted to see everything.

Polly nodded.

A long time, yes, but the little master had been happy.

Eugene reached up for Polly's hand.

Nodding, Tom said goodbye. "Master Eugene, you

need to go back now, but you can come whenever you like. Tomorrow I shall have carrots."

James and Eugene took their meals at a table in the corner of the nursery. Eugene sat in his high chair on one side with Polly and James on the other.

Water for tea was boiled in a kettle on the hearth, just to the right of the coal scuttle. Everything else came up from the kitchen. Peace and quiet reigned.

James was well behaved by nature, listening to his nurse and almost never showing a temper. He greatly resembled his father and grandfather Eoghan.

Eugene was just the opposite. Taking after his adventurous Uncle Jarleth, his mother's brother, he had a feistiness that led him into mischief despite his intentions to be a good little boy.

Leading Polly on a merry chase all day long, Eugene tried not to trip over his petticoats for he was still in dresses as he was too small to be breeched.

By the time he turned one, he had what seemed to be a death wish or, in any case, a wild streak. Somehow he had acquired a liking for running full tilt across the nursery and somersaulting head first into the coal scuttle.

Getting stuck, he had to wait until Polly yanked him out by the feet, head and shoulders black with coal dust. It took endless washings from the pitcher to get it off of him.

The maids took to bringing several pitchers at a time. Otherwise, he would not have been presentable at tea.

Eugene also liked to play cavalry charge with James' toy sabre. All the more fun it was since as James wanted to be a soldier when he grew up, he did not want anyone to touch it.

Charging straight at the fireguard Eugene knocked the blankets onto the hearth. At least once it took all the water in the pitchers to put out the fire.

Eugene's mother and Polly dressed Eugene in navy blue so that the dirt didn't show. They knew white would stay white for less than an hour.

The boys spent hours on the hearthrug spinning their tops. On rainy days, Eugene tried to roll hoops with a stick. Polly tried to stop him because it was an outdoor game, not meant for the nursery.

Baths took place twice a week, first Eugene and then James, using the same water since the maids could not come up twice. Their father's tin tub from Corstown was painted with white enamel and repainted every year.

The maid brought hot water up in brass cans up the back stairs from the kitchen. Polly added pitcher water if it was too warm.

Bathing in front of the fire the boys were cozy and warm. Using Pears soap for washing Polly scrubbed their backs with a sea sponge. Nightclothes and towels hung on the fireguard.

A warming pan was kept under each of the beds. There was no fire in the night nursery, and the children could be cold even with eiderdowns.

In summer, they bathed before the window hoping for a breeze.

Eugene, though mischievous, was a merry and loving little boy.

Polly loved him dearly. He spent most of his time with her except when he was in the stables with Tom or downstairs with his mother. He slept in the night nursery with James, with Polly's bed in the corner by the door.

There was a chamber pot under each bed, and a candle and candlestick apiece for light when it was time to pull them out. The candles were beeswax for the boys and even for Polly, not tallow like the maids upstairs.

An oil lamp sat on the round table by the fire, not to be touched by little fingers because its chimney was very fragile. The reservoir in the base was filled with thick, sticky oil, not to be knocked over for it would take days to clean up.

The lamp burned all day in winter. There was not much direct light as the house was on the shady side of the street. Without the lamp, the boys' mother and Polly could not have sat and read, even in the morning.

The boys often fell asleep watching Polly knit stockings. Eugene, the more imaginative of the two, gazed at the shadows on the wall, looking for recognizable shapes.

"James," he whispered, "do you not see that the shadows look like a pig or a kite?"

James, with his rather stolid and unimaginative nature, whispered back.

"Hush Eugene," he said. "Polly shall hear you. I see nothing but shadows and our nurse by the fire. I don't know why you think you can see anything. Hush before she tells us to be quiet. It's time to go to sleep."

James would turn over, crawling under his covers.

Sometimes Eugene would continue, and Polly would have to come in.

Still the shadows comforted him. When he was tired or bored, he always looked at them.

Unlike James, Eugene was often bored. He much preferred being outdoors where there was more to look at and no one to complain if he messed up his clothes.

Still, he could be comfortable even if he had to stay indoors. There were red Turkish carpets and a rocker where he could sit on Polly's lap. An overstuffed armchair with cretonne floral upholstery stood in each corner where he could curl up with a small toy.

There were shelves for toys, picture books and James' dominoes. A large oak table with battered legs too, kicked by generations of children while they sat and painted.

Like much else in the nursery, the table had been handed down, having been kicked by the boys' mother and Uncle Jarleth in their nursery.

A large window seat with a soft cushion looked out over the street because the day nursery was in the front of the house.

Both boys spent hours by the front window. Sitting, they watched passersby for hours along with street vendors who sold matches, flowers, milk and nearly everything a home required.

The family had a much-loved cat named Mittens with black fur and white paws.

Loving all animals, not just horses and his father's wolfhounds, even Eugene treated her kindly. He spent hours sitting with her in the corner by a mouse hole as she waited to see a mouse emerge.

Only once or twice did he hurl a buttonhook at her during a tantrum. That showed real love because the buttonhook flew in James' direction every time Eugene got mad at him.

Polly took the boys out each afternoon to the park to get some air.

When Eugene was tiny, she carried him which did not go well for he could not look around as he wished. There were no prams, so he had to confine his gaze to Polly's arms.

Like all babies, he was dressed in a petticoat and skirt so long they would have reached Polly's hems had he not been wrapped in a shawl.

He had much the same view once he could walk, as it was a half mile to the park, but he squirmed less. His skirts stopped at the tops of his black button boots, and he wore drawers underneath over white stockings.

Getting down when they arrived, he ran around.

"No Eugene!" Polly would call as he ran through the mud after his ball.

Polly was happy on the bench with her friends. She got up if Eugene was very naughty but otherwise not.

He tried to behave and had to sit on the bench watching the others if he didn't. It was worse than sitting at home on his little chair watching Mittens because he could see the others having fun.

Polly, growing tired of his questions, would soon give in. Easier it was to put him back down and let him play.

Polly visited with the other nurses and governesses. James played tag and hoops. Eugene kept busy with his ball, kicking it with other boys.

There were fights when he pushed boys on their stomachs into the mud, and he had to sit on the bench again. The boys always called him back. He was a natural leader, and they wanted to play with him no matter what their nurses said.

Once an hour had flown by, Polly stood up, saying that it was time to go.

Rubbing Eugene's face with a wet handkerchief, she did her best to make him presentable in case they ran into his mother's friends on the way home.

Picking him up, she carried him home, James trotting alongside.

Whisking them up the stairs, she cleaned their faces and hands. Special clothes went on for teatime. Wool in winter and linen and cotton in summer. Tunics with matching drawers underneath and white stockings with flat sloped strapped shoes.

Suitably attired for tea with both of their parents, or just their mother if their father was away, they headed downstairs to the drawing room. James and then Eugene got hugs from their mother as they entered in their teatime outfits, Eugene with the occasional smudge.

His mother said nothing. She knew that he loved being in the stable and at the park even on rainy days. A childhood memory that made her smile having spent hours outside with her hoop in all sorts of weather.

The boys saw their mother only twice a day during the week, for an hour in the morning and again at four for tea.

Both boys drank cambric tea and had a plate of cucumber sandwich wheels rolled in mayonnaise and parsley. They finished with their favorite biscuits and cakes.

When their father was home, they would sometimes play word games.

Sitting on the carpet, their mother helped play dominoes if he was out. Sometimes she had a storybook, and they sat in the big armchair, Eugene on her lap, James by her side.

Afterward, the boys sat on the hearth on child-sized ottomans, red for James and green for Eugene, playing with Bible blocks or looking at picture books.

When dusk came on, the head housemaid came into the drawing room to light candle sconces and the candelabra on the mantelpiece.

A flame burned at one end of her long brass rod, and there was a snuffer at the other end. The boys took turns holding the rod while she lit the candles.

Always being lit last, the spermaceti candles were used only when necessary. They were one of their father's economies since they were very dear.

Spermaceti oil was made from the heads of whales he said, killed by Nantucketers and then shipped all the way to Dublin. A fact that Eugene found fascinating and James found disgusting.

Chatting happily with his mother James played with the blocks.

Eugene was always a little restless. He rose to trot around the room and raced over to the windows to look at the houses across the street.

Then he tore back to his mother's lap, climbing up while she covered him with kisses and held him close.

She loved both her boys but Eugene was her favorite though she tried not to show it.

Eugene had her brother Jarleth's dark Irish looks, without his height it was true, but that would come later. James looked rather more like her husband with his light brown hair, a little twin almost.

The boys lived from one Sunday afternoon to the next.

It was Polly's afternoon off, and their mother would come up to look after them herself. In summer, she wore a dress with a shawl over her shoulders. Her dress was always in colors, never white, for it would get dirty when she picked the boys up.

Sitting in the rocking chair, a boy on each side, she read or told stories about her childhood in a village not far from where their father was born.

Both children clamored to hear her country tales of fairies and wee folk. Eugene was sure they were real. James as always had his doubts.

All three of them sat down on the hearth to spin tops.

When naptime arrived, Eugene snuggled in his mother's arms in the rocker and fell asleep, waking up under his eiderdown.

With James, she read books for older children or talked with him as they waited until Eugene woke up.

While they waited for Polly, their mother took out the animal blocks.

James liked building and Eugene liked the animals. Their mother helped, talking first to James about her cousin who was an engineer and built bridges. With

Eugene, she talked about animals, especially camels and lions and others not to be seen in Dublin as their zoo was too small.

The boys had riding lessons with the stable staff once a week. Eugene was always ready early. Much to his delight, he got a pony because his father and Uncle Jarleth felt he was ready.

Eugene's father came home early one Saturday, and he and Jarleth took Eugene to see some ponies that were for sale.

There were two that were the correct height. Saddling both up, they chose the spotted one and named him Spot.

Eugene wanted to ride him home. Uncle Jarleth explained that first they needed a saddle as he had not liked the ones that were available.

Eugene said goodbye to Spot, petting the pony's mane with gentle strokes.

The next day Spot arrived. Eugene helped take him to his stall, giving him some hay. To no one's surprise, he sent most of the afternoon admiring Spot, so long that his mother had to fetch him to go to the park.

She changed her mind about that since Eugene was helping the stableman with the water, taking James instead.

She merely asked Tom to bring Eugene back in time to get ready for tea. She could tell Eugene had a natural affinity for horses that James did not share. Indeed, James barely went except when forced.

Each boy now had his own shetland pony. Their father had Uncle Jarleth find a trained instructor. Going to the park once a week, they often visited the elegant one downtown instead of the one nearby.

Dressed in jodhpurs and riding boots, James managed his own reins by the time he was six.

Wearing a blue dress Eugene held children's reins for

instruction, not the actual reins that the instructor held to control the pony. Spotting the difference Eugene complained but got nowhere.

The boys missed their father.

A prominent solicitor, he had connections and work in London and spent much time away. He sent letters from London or cards from Edinburgh and Manchester. Sometimes he visited his brother Andrew, a newspaper reporter in Paris.

When he was home, he took his boys out for long rides. His two wolfhounds ran behind, a treat because the boys did not get to play with the wolfhounds every day.

When the boy's father was home tea was always more fun. More interesting too, for he had grown to like steak and kidney pie.

Even James found it better than the nursery food upstairs.

Nurse liked boiled mutton and baked apples but no pie. Their father allowed wedges of pie along with teacakes and other good things that grownups had for tea.

Sometimes their father let them sit beside him in his big leather chair, one boy on each side, talking to them about where he had been.

Eugene loved hearing about other places. Sometimes his father read them Uncle Andrew's letters from Paris. He described the River Seine and the parks that lined its banks.

Looking up Eugene squeezed his father's hand. A sad look had come over his father's face.

His youngest son gave his father's hand another squeeze and asked why his uncle never came to visit.

Matthew O'Reilly returned the squeeze, saying, "Because he cannot, Eugene. Please. I have told you before."

Eugene thought about it. An uncle in Paris was exciting.

"Can we go see him then," Eugene piped up, "if he can't come here?"

"Yes, but it would be expensive and far for you to travel. I have only been to Paris twice. It was a long way. You have to take the packet boat and the coach from Cherbourg. It takes several days and would be hard for you, James and Mama. But no, he can't come here. I wish he could."

Eugene sat quietly. His mother looked at her husband over her son's head.

"Maybe you should tell them something they can understand," she said.

"As they grow older, they shall have more and more questions about Andrew than they do now when they have only one or two. They are both curious. If you say nothing, they will ask at your mother's and that shall upset her. I think it would be better to say something now, so they don't get confused."

"Perhaps you are right," her husband replied. "Eugene's questions are getting more and more frequent. It's hard for me, but I am grown and understand. Boys, can you come here for a second?"

Both of them ran to him.

He picked them up, one on each knee.

He explained, saying:

"When your Uncle Andrew was young, he was in a rising against the king. Not the king we have now but his father. Perhaps he should not have done it. But it is hard to be governed by the English, so we are not mad at him because he had to try. No one, not even your grandfather, was angry though your Grandmama was afraid he would get hurt.

"The English won and the rebellion ended. I was not very old when it happened. Your uncle is much older than me. But I remember how upset my parents were.

In the end, he had to leave Ireland and never return. It broke your grandmother's heart and my father's too though he tried not to show it.

"Andrew worked for newspapers. So he went to Paris and found work as a journalist and has been happy. He cannot come here or to London. It has been hard on all of us, for he would love to see you. But he had to do what he thought was right."

Concluding, their father said:

"I am sure that you don't entirely understand, but he can't come here. Maybe when you are older, we can go there and see him."

The boys ran to the corner of the room.

Whispering to each other, they tried to make sense of it.

They ran back to tell their father that they understood, but their parents were talking. The boys went back to their blocks on the hearthrug because they knew not to interrupt.

Their father looked so sad that even Eugene remembered not to ask about his uncle. He thought he would ask his mother instead, but she looked sad too so he learned not to raise the subject at all. Better to say nothing.

Time went by, and Eugene turned six. He no longer wore dresses, drawers, and tunics. Instead, he had a skeleton suit like his brother, along with jodhpurs and riding boots.

The riding instructor allowed him to take Spot's reins instead of leading him. He even had a small crop that he could use if Spot failed to respond.

Eugene began feeling grown up, and so content he could almost purr.

The boys and their mother escaped from the Dublin heat to Corstown in County Meath most summers. They went to visit Grandmama since she had retired there after Grandpapa Eoghan had died.

As they rode in the coach, Emily O'Reilly and Polly squabbled with James who kept asking how much longer it would be till they arrived.

Having lunch at an inn, they traveled on. At last, they arrived at a shop just outside of Corstown near the house.

There they alit because their mother would let them have a treat of their choosing.

Candy was forbidden at home, but their mother never said no.

She only said, "Boys, that will ruin your supper," as they clambered back in.

They traveled a few more miles in the coach. Looking exhausted, the boys' mother fanned herself as James and Eugene licked the stickiness from their fingers.

They were so excited to see Cousin Maureen and Grandmama that when the coach stopped, they ran towards the house, not waiting for their mother. Neither stopped to talk to the horses, not even Eugene.

They spent the next day exploring.

The house was quite large, with many rooms like their house in Dublin.

It was lit only by candles since Grandmama thought lamps were too modern and was especially good for a game of hide and seek on rainy afternoons. There were dark corners everywhere for cousins to hide.

Running up to the attic they played with everything in the old trunks. They wrapped up as goblins and ghosts in Grandpapa's old capes. They pounded with mortars from the Harold's Cross apothecary, for Grandmama had brought enough things to fill twenty or thirty trunks.

The cousins had as much fun with the trunks

themselves as their contents. Climbing in, they pretended the trunks were beds. They pushed them like sleds down the length of the attic to the little window.

Calling up the stairs, the boys' mother and Auntie Mary said they were too loud, but that didn't stop the fun.

When darkness fell, they went downstairs. Grandmama would allow no candles. Too boisterous, she said. Candles would be knocked over.

They were allowed to play for hours, leaving more time for the grownups to socialize in peace. Once the children descended, there was no quiet. They wanted to be taken to the woods, the river and everywhere else.

On a rainy day, the boys' mother or Aunt Mary would ascend the stairs to retrieve everyone for tea doing their best to ignore the mess. Everything from the trunks was scattered around the attic.

"Children," Emily O'Reilly would say, "I am glad you are having fun. It is a good place to play, but you must put the things back in the trunks."

Maureen, the eldest cousin, would reply, saying "They need to help me, Auntie, especially Eugene. He likes to try on the uniforms, and he takes everything out of the trunks so we can ride in them."

"Mama, can I please just go downstairs," asked James, "because Eugene and Patrick made most of the mess?"

Knowing that was true his mother answered, saying:

"You need to help for ten minutes, James, and then all of you need to come downstairs for tea. With the four of you helping, it won't take much longer than that. You don't have to put the trunks back where they were under the eaves. You'll just pull them out next time, and no one else comes up here."

Most of the time they were outdoors all day on the ponies with the wolfhounds tagging behind. Eugene and

James ran through the woods with Uncle Edward's son Patrick.

Uncle Edward had been gone since 1830 when Eugene was just four. Both boys loved Patrick, who came up every summer with his older sister Maureen and their widowed mother, Mary. They lived in Harold's Cross near Grandpapa's old shop, too far away to visit much over the winter.

Sometimes the cousins pretended to go fox hunting with ponies for horses and wolfhounds for beagles.

Eugene, who was always in the lead despite being youngest, would pretend to scare the fox into the open since he had the loudest yell. Wearing jodhpurs just like a real hunter, he jumped over obstacles and creeks, Cousin Maureen right behind.

Tiring halfway through the wolfhounds would head back to the house. They were not inclined to obey Eugene. That and the ponies tended to brush the dogs too closely and make them yelp.

They bathed in the small river that ran behind their grandmother's house.

The older ones were allowed to swim alone.

Eugene had to come with Polly because he liked to wade out until the water was over his head in the middle of the river. The current was stronger there. He would start drifting downstream and have to be fished out.

He did it anyway. It was far more exciting than wading in the shallows looking for small stones and trying to catch tiny fish with his hands.

He missed Maureen, who liked being in the middle as much as he did, but she had to stay and practice the piano or embroider. The boys swam naked, and she was not allowed.

Eugene watched as the neighbor boys raced with James and Patrick, swimming and running along the bank.

There were contests to see who could run fastest and who could pick up the most rocks in five minutes. In stone skipping contests, Patrick always won as he could skip stones furthest.

At noon, the boys headed back to the house for a large lunch and rest.

Grandmama, like the boys' father, didn't confine meals to nursery food. There were dried red and green apples along with pears, apricots, and greengage plums.

They ate berries as they came in season. Strawberries first, followed by blackberries and gooseberries.

Sometimes they were for dessert. At other times, they were snacks to be eaten right off the plants while they were playing outside. Sometimes they ate so many they had no room for supper.

Eugene loved picking and eating. Often he ate more than was good for him.

When that happened, he was put to bed for a day or two with a bilious attack. He wept in frustration doing his best to lie still because his room being near the woods he could hear the other children having fun.

The boys stayed with their mother for the entire summer leaving their father at home to work. They were very excited when he came to visit, always managing to arrive by coach unless Tom could drive him in the carriage. It was a special Sunday when he was there, the only time they could relax with both parents.

The boys watched while cook prepared a picnic for the wicker basket. Meat and sandwiches, fruit, lemonade and a small flask of Irish whiskey for their father.

Running outside as the dogcart was being brought around Eugene was lifted in with James. Driving out into the woods to eat, the boys' father always took the reins. Sometimes with their cousins and Aunt Mary, other times with just the four of them.

Eugene would stand watching as his mother spread out a blanket on the ground when they reached a good spot. He helped her take the food out of the hamper.

After they were settled, Eugene would run to catch up with his father and James. He followed them into the woods to go mushroom hunting. Matthew O'Reilly put mushrooms into a small basket lined with a tea towel.

Later, back at the picnic site, he made a small fire. The boys' mother sliced the mushrooms and gave them to her husband to cook in a pan. As he was finishing up, the boys' father smiled. He loved the outdoors as much as his boys.

His wife, who loved the outdoors but not the woods, pulled Eugene onto her lap. She came for her husband's sake, and because the boys loved it so.

When fall came, the boys' mother packed everything up to go back to Dublin for the winter. The boys always complained. Even the air felt freer in County Meath.

They loved Grandmama's attentions, the time they spent with their cousins and walks with their father in the woods. Still, once home again, they welcomed their routines and the chance to be back with their friends.

Routines changed as first James and then Eugene went off to study at Mr. Hall's, a boarding school outside London. But each summer included a Corstown holiday.

2 DUBLIN, LONDON & CORSTOWN

When James was five, his mother gave him daily lessons in religion, arithmetic and reading. Leaving the nursery every morning he went downstairs. When he turned seven, he began lessons with tutors. The schoolroom, down the hall from the nursery, looked out toward the stableyard. Globes, maps, and blackboards were spread around.

The room was quiet until Eugene burst in. He missed his brother and he didn't like being alone with Polly.

Giving him a tablet and pencil, the tutor allowed Eugene to sit down for a lesson.

Irritated by his arrival, James often said, "Little brother, you need to go back to nurse. These are my lessons. You need to play with your blocks."

Eugene glared, first at James and then at the tutor.

"I'm bored," he said. "I want to stay and learn like you."

James came back for lunch.

He said, "Little brother, it is all your fault. You come in so much that the tutor saves all the harder lessons for after lunch when you are off riding, and then I am sleepy."

James had lessons for two hours before dinner and another two after. It was much the same for Cousin Patrick. Scribbling at the other end of the table when he was allowed to stay Eugene did his best to be quiet.

Eugene turned five in the summer of 1831.

He danced up and down in the nursery because he was finally old enough to have lessons with his mother in the morning. He hoped it would be as interesting as James' tutoring.

He had another jolt of joy when his father announced that he could ride Star, Spot having become half a hand too small.

Eugene worried because he loved Spot.

Shaking his head his father said that Eugene shouldn't be so sentimental but he let it be since he knew how much Eugene loved animals.

Eugene begged for a riding horse so he could sit as tall as James in the park.

Uncle Jarleth said his legs had to grow and his feet had to reach the stirrups so that he could control his mount. Promising that there would be a horse when he was taller, Eugene's uncle added that he would be such a good rider he would even be able to ride out without an instructor.

Feeling a little better for his legs were getting longer every day, Eugene piped up and asked, "When will I be old enough to have the riding horse?"

Uncle Jarleth, having been in the cavalry, made all the decisions around Eugene's riding.

"When you are nine," he said. "Maybe earlier, as you are tall like me. It depends on how fast you grow."

"I hope I grow very fast," said Eugene. "I want my own horse. I want to go riding when I want instead of waiting for someone to go with me."

Laughing, Eugene's uncle looked down at him.

"Just like me, you are. Personality and curls along with the rest. I'm sure at the rate you are growing you shall be taller than your mother by the time you are twelve. Perhaps you'll be ready for a riding horse when you are eight. But you do have to wait until you are that old to go out alone. If the horse gets spooked on the street, it is better for now if someone else is there."

Eugene frowned.

"All right," he said. "I hope I grow fast."

Uncle Jarleth and his father, who had just entered the room, broke into peals of laughter.

"How like you, my boy," said Eugene's father.

"Your first thought is of Star and not the lessons you will be starting with your Mama next week. But for now, you can run and play. Or maybe your uncle can be persuaded to accompany you to the stable, even though it is raining and doesn't seem like a good day to ride."

Eugene headed for the back of the house with Uncle Jarleth.

His father turned, running into his wife in the back hall. Overhearing Eugene heard his father say that he didn't understand him.

Squeezing his uncle's hand, he felt better when he heard his mother say "He is more like Jarleth and James is more like you. But they are both good boys."

Eugene's mother made lesson plans, starting with religion for that was very important to her. Next came letters, geography, and a little arithmetic.

Eugene got better at paying attention after his father found an illustrated Children's Bible near his office. His mother searched for verses that spoke about animals or had pictures of them to hold the interest of an animal-loving little boy.

One week he asked about geography after a boy in the park said that he didn't study geography at all.

With a smile she replied.

"It is fun to find all those countries where your Uncle Jarleth has been posted. Your Papa is looking at the bookseller's for a good map so we can tack it up and mark each place."

Eugene loved his lessons. He was always happy with his mother and he wanted to learn to read like James. That's the way it was for him with everything, being a little brother.

His mother was wreathed in smiles every time he came down, tablet and pencil in hand. In him, she saw her favorite brother with his dark curly hair and bright blue eyes along with Jarleth's feistiness.

Sitting quietly after the lessons Eugene listened to stories of his uncle's adventures with the British army in India.

His mother told him about tigers and elephants and all sorts of things, that and a wild polo match in 1829.

She told him how Uncle Jarleth had helped seize Ghazni when he fought against the Afghanis. Listening to one story after the other, Eugene loved them all.

Eugene dearly loved both his uncles. He was close to Jarleth because of his help with riding. But he also loved hearing about Uncle Andrew and the way he fought for Ireland.

He learned to ask his mother or his Auntie Mary up in Corstown about Andrew because it upset his father and Grandmama so much.

When Eugene turned seven, at first, he was pleased to have a tutor and study upstairs in the schoolroom. But by the third day, he missed having lessons with his mother.

Running downstairs, he burst in on her and hugged her around the knees.

"I miss lessons with you, Mama," he said. "The

tutors won't let me talk about geography as long as I like. They say it's time for my other lessons, but you let me talk longer about what I want to learn."

"My little son," she said, even though he was quite tall and up to her shoulder already.

"The tutors know more than I do about all the things you need to learn. You are a big boy now and you have to learn Botany and History so you can go to public school in England, just as James will in a few years.

"We also want you to learn Gaelic since your cousins' father wrote a Gaelic dictionary. The tutor shall instruct you in Irish History too. He knows a great deal."

"Yes, Mama, but they don't teach like you. And I don't like French. Could I not just learn Gaelic?"

Eugene's mother shook her head.

"No, my little son," she said. "You need to learn French along with Gaelic. French in many ways is more important to your future, as it is for all educated gentlemen. I know it's hard, but you need to do your best. I can barely understand it even though I had a few lessons. You need a tutor for that."

She continued, saying, "I miss our mornings together too. Maybe you can go riding at two, right after your lessons are done. Then we can spend time together until tea is ready. How would that be?"

Her son smiled and his eyes began to dance.

"I like that idea. I love spending private time with you. I don't love French. But if you and Papa say I must learn it, I must."

Explaining, she said, "The French is for your future. You need it to go to a school near London, and then on to university, maybe Cambridge or Trinity here in Dublin."

"London sounds far away, Mama," Eugene observed.

"It is, but you will be older then. James shall go and then you will go, and I shall miss both of you very much. But let us not think about this now. Run along and let me finish the letter to my friend. We can see each other later. Come here. Give me a kiss first, please."

Eugene kissed her, blowing another kiss from the doorway as he went back upstairs to the schoolroom.

Slipping back into his chair, he picked up his pencil to be ready for the rest of the morning. Now that he could look forward to being with his mother later, the lesson did not seem so bad.

A few months of peace having followed his parents had a new idea.

Papa told them at tea, dancing lessons at an exclusive school downtown.

Complaining about being "trussed up like little chickens" James and Eugene said that they did not want to meet young ladies.

Begging, James said, "Please, Mama, I don't want to go. I'd rather have another Botany lesson though I hate Botany. Eugene and I can learn to dance later."

"Please, Papa," added Eugene, for he had just come into the room.

"Why do we have to learn to dance? I would rather be with the other boys in the park or out riding Star. Other than Mama, Grandmama and Maureen, I don't like girls."

Drawing himself up to his full height Eugene's father adjusted his tie.

"Boys," he said, "knowing how to dance is as important as riding or your school lessons. And that was not a nice remark about girls. One day you shall feel different and want to go to dances. If you can't dance, the girls won't like you.

"This is a good dancing school. We are going to a lot

of trouble to send you. You will need to take the carriage and your mother won't be able to use it for her visits. There are schools nearer, but at the one we chose you will meet a better class of young people."

Eugene frowned, looking so comical his father nearly laughed in spite of himself.

Emily O'Reilly smiled.

"Boys, perhaps you will like it. Your father is right. One day you shall like girls even though you can't stand them now. In any case, a gentleman must know how to dance. Maybe you will like the clothes too after you wear them a few times."

Clothing arrived in the morning from the finest children's shop in the area.

Eugene ran down the stairs just as the housemaid took them in. Helping her carry them to the morning room he watched as his mother opened the parcel.

He had misread the address and thought it was a toy from Grandmama. When velvet short pants emerged instead, he screeched with disappointment, pounding his heels on the carpet.

Tossing the short pants and jackets around the room, he hurled black dancing pumps through the air, just missing Mittens, who ran under the piano.

He tied silk stockings in a bow around his neck like a scarf. He ran around the room until his mother managed to catch him and take him on her lap.

She said that he had been very naughty. Even if he did not want the clothes, he should, at least, look at them. A kiss for Mittens, too, she added, for he had scared her.

Looking up into her face, her son said, "I am sorry Mama. But I don't want to dance. I want to go riding instead."

"I know, child," she said, "but you must be civilized. I shall help you clean up. Your father will be very angry if he comes home and sees things like this.

"We can look the clothes over. Maybe they won't be so bad after all. The short pants are like the linen ones you wear in the summer. The jacket is like your father's. The dancing pumps are different from button boots, but you told me only yesterday that your boots were too tight."

Looking up through his dark curls Eugene said nothing. He helped her pick up the scattered clothes and lay them on the sofa now that he was calmer.

Eugene apologized.

"I was angrier about dancing school than the clothes," he said. "I think I will like them. The velvet feels nice. The stockings do too, less itchy than my wool ones.

"I'm not sure about the pumps since I am used to boots, and I can't walk in them outside because it is too muddy. But let me try them on to see how they fit and how they look with the jacket."

James ran in and Eugene recruited him to try everything on.

Sitting down on the sofa, both boys put on the jackets and pumps.

"The jacket isn't warm enough and the shoes are very tight," said James. "Can't we wear our boots instead?"

His mother shook her head.

"Boys," she said, "the shoes will feel better and the jacket will be warm enough in the carriage. In any case, this is what boys wear to dancing school, along with a big white handkerchief for the quadrille, a dance you will learn.

"But hush. Papa will be here soon. He doesn't want to hear about this for it has been decided. Let me call the maid so you can take everything upstairs."

Picking up his pumps Eugene looked over at his mother.

"Riding in the carriage with James will be fun," he allowed. "The clothes are all right, but we still don't like the idea of dancing with girls."

"Enough, the two of you. Time to go upstairs for dinner."

Eugene followed James out the door and up the stairs to the nursery, saying nothing. Once their parents had decided on something and had spent money on it, he knew they had to do it.

Dance lessons started the next Thursday.

The quadrille was the worst of it, four movements, all with the same girl.

They had to ask young ladies to dance, signing their dance cards with a tiny pencil. Eugene felt more distressed at this than James since his handwriting was not as good.

Things got better bit by bit.

They learned which girls were less likely to foot stomp or trip. They had Tom take them a few minutes early so they could be first in line to ask those specific girls to dance. Since many others lived much further away and arrived later, they had their choice of partners.

It was fun talking with boys they did not see otherwise because all of them had tutors at home.

Pushing boys he didn't like onto the floor Eugene earned reprimands from the dancing mistress. Sometimes he was knocked off the bench, getting his clothes dirty.

Neither boy liked the dancing, but still it was better than being home. Winter had arrived and it was hard to play outdoors.

Their mother occasionally asked how the lessons were going. Even Eugene had stopped complaining, a surprise, far better than she and her husband had hoped.

James explained that Eugene embarrassed him by

pushing boys onto the floor. Asking girls to dance had gotten easier, he reported. Still it was hard. He would rather do something else.

"I was once a girl," said their mother. "Sometimes girls don't like to dance with boys. It will get better. But one day you will be glad you can dance, I promise you."

When James was twelve, he gave up skeleton suits for small versions of his father's suits. Long pants in light colors, dark ties and cravats, boots to wear outside and black pumps for inside the house.

Complaining to his mother Eugene said that he wanted to dress like James though he would have ruined any light colored pants or short boots in five minutes at the park. He received a new skeleton suit instead. The sailor collar, a new style, appeased him for a while.

The next new thing that came along proved harder to bear.

Eugene knew something was coming. Many letters arrived. His father went away in the summer instead of coming up to Corstown. His parents talked for hours in the drawing room, stopping when he or James entered.

In August, Eugene found James sitting in a corner of the schoolroom looking very distressed. He asked him what was wrong.

"You were right, little brother," said James. "They were talking about us. Papa told me this morning that I have to go to Mr. Hall's School outside London in September. He said that it is like Eton and that I would like it. Many of the sons of his business friends go there he told me."

Eugene started to cry and James hugged him.

"You are too old for that," he said. "Don't worry, I shall come back in between terms. Otherwise, nothing will change for you until they send you in a few years."

Stuffing his hands in his pockets as he always did

when he was nervous Eugene shook his head.

"I don't want to go either. But if they can make you go, they can make me. I would rather stay here with my friends, but Papa always seems to want us to find new ones. Maybe it won't be so bad James."

"They are sending me partly because it is not far from London and Papa can come out to see me when he is there," said James. "That is all right.

"The bad part, at least for me, is that I shall have to take riding lessons and learn to jump. They have a fox hunting program, and there are competitions and gymkhanas with other schools."

Eugene's eyes got big as saucers when he heard about the riding.

"Jumping lessons? Oh, I wish I could go now instead of later. That's much more fun than lessons upstairs."

Looking at him James scowled.

"I know you love riding. I dislike it and am much worse at it than you. Mama and Papa wanted to find a school you would like so we could go to the same one."

"I am sorry," Eugene said. "But jumping is not that hard and maybe you will like fox hunting. Anyway, I will miss you very much. We have been together always."

James gave him a hug, saying, "I shall miss you too. Perhaps on one of his trips Papa can bring you and you can visit.

"I have to be there September fifth. Mama said that she will need about a month to buy everything including a trunk. When Papa goes to London in September, I shall go with him and he will take me to school with my things. I don't mind going away to school. But to leave Ireland is hard. I have only been to London twice when we went at Christmas."

Chatting a little while longer about the new school the boys settled into a game of dominoes. They were interrupted by their mother who fetched James to be measured for the outfits he would take.

They talked about Mr. Hall's a bit more after supper while Polly worked on her knitting. They knew their father's mind was made up, and they had to do what he wanted.

Eugene's mind filled with visions of jumping lessons and gymkhanas to come and he did not want to jeopardize anything.

Emily O'Reilly finished packing the trunk as the great day arrived. They had dinner the night before with their parents, a rare treat that included roast beef, James' favorite.

It was a bittersweet occasion for James would be off to London the next day. But still it was an important family occasion. Uncle Jarleth came to say goodbye, along with Patrick and Maureen, who had come from Harold's Cross with their mother.

Eugene stood in the doorway the next morning with his mother, watching his father ride off with James towards the harbor and the packet boat.

His mother clutching him, he waved as they went around the corner and out of sight.

"I am glad I have you left, my little imp, to keep me company," she said. "Your father is gone so much and now your brother is off to school."

Looking up Eugene saw tears in her eyes.

"Don't worry, Mama," he said. "James shall be back soon. I am right here."

With that, they turned to go back in the house. They spent most of the day together, riding in the afternoon.

Emily O'Reilly noticed that Eugene was so accomplished he was almost another Jarleth.

Trying not to let Eugene know, she finally explained when he had a jump that she did not want to try. Eugene laughed in a kind way before they turned around and went back home in the late afternoon.

James arrived at the pier with his father. Standing in line, they waited until Tom got James' trunk down. Tom waited until they sailed out of sight so that James could wave at him.

The crossing went smoothly, as did the rest of the trip.

Five days later they got off the coach in the small village where Mr. Hall's School was located. Mr. Hall himself was waiting to greet them and transport them to the school.

James felt a little surprised as they got closer. The school was further out in the country and much bigger than he had thought.

Asking Mr. Hall how many boys there were he was startled when he was told:

"Two hundred, ranging from eight to eighteen. Many are your age. Some of their fathers are members of parliament. You will have no trouble finding friends. Most of them are new, too, including your roommate whom you shall meet shortly."

James turned to look out the window because Mr. Hall was making him nervous. He saw lots of orchards that reminded him of County Meath.

Buildings rose up over the trees. They looked like Grandmama's house with its dormer windows and large chimneys.

Ignoring Mr. Hall and his father who were discussing how many fathers were in trade and how many were lower aristocrats he kept busy watching two dogs race alongside the carriage.

They pulled up before the main door and an assistant showed them to James' room.

Nodding his head, his father murmured that he was glad the room was large, with two windows and a stove.

The assistant introduced James to his roommate who took him down the hall to see the washroom while the porters brought up the trunk.

His father hugged him when they came back, shaking hands with his roommate. He helped James unpack and then went off to talk to Mr. Hall again before he left for his dinner engagement in London.

He had promised not to leave until they had said goodbye and kept his word. James stood looking forlorn as the carriage rounded the curve of the drive.

James felt happier once he had settled in and became fast friends with his roommate. Missing everyone back in Dublin, he lived from one of his father's visits to the next.

His courses went well. History was a struggle, but Geography and its globes came easier than he had thought it would.

James never got in trouble and rarely interacted with Mr. Hall.

Riding was very hard, harder than in Dublin, his mother having allowed an extra lesson upstairs instead of a riding lesson sometimes.

Knowing the school was focused on riding James tried hard. Fox hunting was mandatory, including learning to jump logs and creeks.

Every six months a real hunt would take place with beaters and dogs. It reminded James of Eugene's games back in Corstown, and he had hated it even then.

He fell a few times as he had feared. Indeed, back home he had barely been able to ride around the meadow while the others jumped over the logs.

Plucking up his courage, James told the master.

"I hate riding," he said. "My brother is very good at it. That is why my parents chose this school, as he will be following me here. Please, I have already fallen twice and sprained first one ankle and then the other. I need to skip some of the lessons."

"But riding is a vital part of our program. I am afraid that unless your father allows it, you shall have to continue. Even Mr. Hall can't change this without a word from Dublin. The school was founded in part to promote equestrian skills. So there may not be much that can be done."

"Are you sure?" James asked.

"When my brother arrives he shall make up for all my lack of skill around horseflesh. Are you sure Mr. Hall can't help me? I was hoping he would. I am not sure Father will agree with me."

James tried to get his father to give permission on his next visit.

His father said no.

It was too much work to find two different schools for his sons. Plus, riding and fox hunting could be useful at Cambridge or Oxford to help him meet a proper sort of person.

Clearing his throat, he added, "James, I know it's difficult. Eugene can outride anyone in the family except for your uncle. He may end up following Jarleth into the cavalry.

"I shall speak to Mr. Hall about letting you skip the gymkhanas. I know some of the jumps are scary for someone with your skill level or mine. But you will have to keep on with the fox hunting and the lessons. If you can skip the gymkhanas, it will help. That I shall endeavor to arrange."

"Thank you, Father. I am happy here otherwise. But yes, the gymkhanas have big jumps. I am afraid of a bad spill. A friend broke his arm in the last one."

Agreeing, his father said, "Don't worry. After we come back, I'll speak to Mr. Hall."

They went to the village for lunch. It was better than

the school's food, though not as good as cook's at home.

Afterward, James' father went to speak to Mr. Hall, who granted his request, saying he was impressed by James' behavior. He never snuck away or stole fruit like the other boys, and only joined a snowball war once.

After five years at school, James decided he would like to follow his father's footsteps into the law. He was accepted into Oxford University since he had high marks. One of his father's business contacts was the brother of one of the deans, too, which helped his chances.

There was much joy in Dublin that fall when the acceptance letter came.

James took a year off before commencing his study of law. He spent the fall visiting English friends, including a month with his roommate's parents at their estate in Yorkshire.

Things went well until he was taken on a tour of the coal mines, a major industry in that part of the world. The mines looked dirty and mean up close, something James had not anticipated.

After heading south for one more visit, he turned west to take the packet boat home.

James had wanted to start at Oxford when the next term began.

His father dissuaded him, writing that the Season would be a good investment with many useful people for him to meet. James could spend the winter in Dublin and start Oxford in September instead.

Running to the front door, Eugene met James when he arrived.

His mother and Polly waited to greet him in the hall. They hugged him and he hugged them back. Their effusiveness making him nervous, he fled, running up the stairs to his room.

His room had been redone, at his mother's request, red and blue as he had wanted with a new suite of furniture shipped all the way from London.

Making a visit to the tailor, Eugene in tow, James ordered everything. His brother watched, turning green with envy when James charged it all to their father's account.

James got two pairs of cashmere pants with straps on the bottoms where they tucked into his evening slippers so the pants would not wrinkle. He ordered white muslin shirts with pleats and detachable collars. Diamond patterned cravats to be fastened with one of Father's pearl pins, and a fitted black double-breasted tailcoat with brass buttons.

Standing still as he tried on the samples, James said, "Little brother, I feel trussed like a chicken, as you used to say back in our dancing school days. The slippers are just as tight as our old pumps. The tailcoat is too tight to use the pockets."

Eugene laughed.

"I like the clothes," he said. "I'll have my own when it's my turn to go to the ball. But it may feel less trussed once they are all your size. At least, you won't be like the fellow down the street who is so large he has to wear a corset underneath."

Laughing, James nodded and then looked serious.

"But really, Eugene, how do I look? If I can find a girl, it would make up for all those dance lessons."

His brother laughed back.

"They will all want you to sign their dance card."

They calmed down as the tailor's assistant tried not to smirk. Checking the list, Eugene made sure everything had been ordered.

At home, Eugene listened to James' tales of pleasant

suppers in the company of Dublin friends he hadn't seen since before his Mr. Hall's days. The dancing stories fascinated Eugene most.

As his brother was waiting for his lesson James came into the schoolroom one morning.

He told Eugene "On the way home I thanked Father for sending us to dancing lessons. I am much in demand as a partner because of them. I can pick up steps quicker than some too. Many of the girls have become quite pretty. They remember us and ask me to take a dance on account of it. Indeed, little brother, I think you need to go back for more lessons."

"Why? You look exhausted. You must be dancing too much."

"Too many glasses of champagne at the ball yesterday. I didn't get home till four. But seriously, Mother was right about the lessons."

"Are you sure? I'd have to give up a riding lesson to take dancing again."

James hesitated.

"Yes, I am sure. You were good at the quadrille. I think you will be good at the new dances, especially as they don't involve the white handkerchiefs you kept dropping on the floor."

"Thanks a lot, big brother. I stomped all over one of them and made Mother mad."

"At the time, it seemed amusing. But seriously you should ask her about sending you. Once you get to Mr. Hall's, sometimes there's a dance master but it would be better to do it now."

"All right, all right, I shall ask her. But you need to take a nap so you can go out again. I can see that the Season is tiring. Have you found any pretty girls yet? That's the most interesting part."

"Not yet, but tomorrow evening is the grand cotillion ball. I've been told quite a few young ladies will come. They are bringing a small orchestra from London that is all the rage."

They were interrupted as the tutor came in, lesson book in hand. James headed downstairs for a nap. Eugene opened his Botany book. Afterward, he went out for a ride, nodding in passing to James as he headed down the stairs, looking resplendent on his way to a dinner party.

The next day passed in much the same way.

Standing in the hall after dinner Eugene watched as James swept off to the cotillion, dressed in his elegant clothes with a cashmere opera cloak hung over his arm.

Swallowing hard Eugene said nothing. The pain of being younger and having to stay home with their parents was almost too much to bear.

He waved as James drove off and went into the drawing room and then up to bed. He read for quite a while, thinking about what James was doing and envisioning himself there.

Meanwhile, James arrived at the cotillion. Its mere size made him nervous. Running into some of his friends in the cloakroom he made his way into the ballroom. He watched as debutantes in white dresses were presented to the solicitor general.

The rest of the evening was devoted to dancing and flirting with the eligible young ladies of Dublin society. But try as he might, despite the number of events he had attended, James had yet to meet a young lady who might be able to capture his heart.

He stared into his champagne glass at supper.

Coming up behind him a cousin introduced him to a Miss Susan MacDonnell, who had been presented earlier by her father.

Whispering, his cousin said, "Her father is a colonel, commander of the Enniskell Dragoons. Very fashionable."

James turned and took the young lady's hand.

He was glad to see that she was petite, with lovely red hair. She wore a white gown in the new fashion with trim ankles that peeped out from under her ankle length skirt.

Carrying a nosegay in her kid glove covered hands, she was the prettiest girl he had ever laid eyes on. Her quiet personality and graceful carriage added to her charms.

James felt delighted when Susan sat with him at supper. They shared three dances when the orchestra started up again after the interval. He sat chatting with her on the gilt chairs that were scattered around the edges of the ballroom.

The young lady began to fascinate him.

When he asked how she knew his cousin, Susan said, "I know his sister. We went to school in Belfast together. She had visited for several weeks before we came into town with our mothers. They have taken a house for the Season."

"I had forgotten she went there," said James. "I should have recalled since I wrote to her."

Laughing from behind her fan, Susan said, "So you should. I don't remember meeting you before. Maybe your school was further away, too far to visit."

"I was at Mr. Hall's just outside London, and only just got back. I'm off to Oxford in the fall to study law. I intend to go into practice with my father in the city."

He watched her lips turn down and then go back into a smile.

Rapidly, he added, "But I shall be going back and forth. I have missed Ireland and all my family and friends so much that I could not spend month after month in England and not come. I can hardly wait to be done with my studies and be able to stay."

James gave an inward sigh of relief as the lady

smiled, saying "Will you be in Dublin from now until you leave for Oxford?"

James nodded.

"I was thinking of going to Corstown for a few days to visit my grandmother," he said. "But for now, I am here. She is quite elderly but insists on staying there for the winter."

James tried to think of what to say as people began putting on their wraps and coats.

Finally, he asked if she rode.

He said that he intended to go riding downtown the next Saturday. He was afraid she would not be at the dinner he was attending a few days later. Granted, he'd have to have Eugene take him riding. But he had to see her again.

"Yes. As a matter of fact, I am going riding with your cousin who introduced us and one or two friends," Susan said.

"We shall be there at ten. Could you meet us at the gate?"

Nodding, James replied.

"Yes, I can. I shall look forward to it."

Seeing her mother by the door holding her coat, Susan rose to her feet. Bidding James farewell as he headed for the cloakroom she made her way out.

James emerged in a few minutes hoping to say goodnight but found that she and her mother were gone.

The next morning, he slept through breakfast.

At lunch, he mentioned Susan. His father murmured in an uncertain tone that she might be suitable.

James continued on.

"The colonel, her father, was reared Anglican but converted in his youth. She is a nice girl with impeccable manners and spoke of her parish priest several times. Her father must have converted before she was born. Might it be a problem Father?"

His mother answered instead.

"I am sure she is a very good Catholic. What your father means is that he was in line to command the dragoons when he converted. No one was able to learn whether it was an honest conversion or to enable him to get the command. An old story that hopefully does not matter now."

Putting his water glass down, his father added, "You may be right, my dear. Hopefully, it was a true conversion, but it matters not until we see how things progress."

James looked at both of them.

"I have only seen her once," he said, "although I shall again on Saturday. Her family is suitable enough for her to have been presented, and she is good friends with our cousins.

"More important to me is the fact that I told her I was an excellent rider and invited myself to accompany her and some others this weekend. I am going to have to have Eugene take me out this afternoon and each afternoon until Saturday."

At that, Matthew O'Reilly smiled.

"I am not sure you can ride like Eugene by Saturday," he said. "But I'm sure he shall be willing to coach you. That will have some effect."

Eugene came home, erupting into gales of laughter when James explained.

"I understand," said Eugene. "You need to see her again. I'll try. Let me go up and change into my clean boots while you do the same. We can pick the mount you need to keep up with a country girl. You need the calmest horse possible. You don't want to lose your seat."

James wanted to respond to his brother's remark about the calm mount, but biting his tongue, he said nothing. Without Eugene's help, he knew he would make an idiot of himself in front of Susan.

Following his brother upstairs to change he ran back down and met him at the stable door. Once they were inside James was further embarrassed when Eugene told him he should take their mother's riding horse. He didn't want to be seen on a mare.

James started to argue, then stopped as Eugene continued, adding that he needed a mount that was rarely skittish and not too large. Their mother's horse was the only one that met all those requirements.

Grumbling James thanked his brother. He followed Eugene out into the road and down to the park where they stayed until sundown. Riding along the paths, Eugene showed James how to use his crop and imparted other skills.

Though he wanted to gallop the horses for a while to exercise them, Eugene kept their pace to a canter. He knew that James was terrified of falling off into the mud.

They rode out each afternoon. James felt more competent by Saturday morning. He was nervous about seeing Susan again, but not about the riding, which he thought he could handle.

When he got to the park and met her, he rode slowly enough to chat. He felt fortunate because she could not see how tightly he was gripping the reins in his gloved hands.

After that, James saw Susan as frequently as possible, taking care to accept invitations to all the parties and dances that she would attend.

They were together at a number of other social occasions over the remainder of the Season, including two theater parties where they sat in the same box.

Giving up their rented house at the end of the

Season, Susan and her mother returned home. In late spring, there was a burst of excitement when house party invitations arrived. One was for James and his mother for the Glens, the MacDonnell home in County Antrim.

It would be several years before James finished his studies and was advanced enough in his career to ask the colonel for permission to marry Susan. In view of that, their parents allowed the young people to correspond and occasionally meet but nothing more.

By mid-July, James was busy getting ready to leave for Oxford.

Getting together with his friends he ordered new outfits from the family tailor. Despite his fondness for Susan, he became so busy he forgot to send her his weekly letter. A domestic catastrophe nearly ensued when she wrote, questioning his fondness for her.

The mothers managed to patch things up. Emily O'Reilly wrote Susan's mother to explain that her son's intentions were good. James wrote twice to apologize.

He was on tenterhooks for a few days until a letter came back from Susan. Forgiving him she put his mind at ease. It was a blessing. Otherwise, he had not been sure he wanted to leave for Oxford.

James headed off to Oxford and his mother turned her hand to outfitting Eugene for Mr. Hall's.

This followed an entire summer's worth of conversations as Eugene was very worried about his studies. He loved History and liked French better than Geography. But Gaelic was his favorite and best subject.

Three weeks before his departure his mother told him that Gaelic would not be taught. Her son shook his head.

"Then I want to stay here," he said.

"First, it is good your father is not here," said his

mother. "He very much wants you to follow James' footsteps at Mr. Hall's. He would be upset to learn that you don't want to go. I know Gaelic is important, but it is more important for you to be in England. Since they rule us, they will never teach Gaelic.

"Still, it is wonderful that you are so interested in languages. Over the next few years, you need to use that skill to perfect your French. Your marks in French are higher than in all your subjects except History."

"I shall miss Uncle Jarleth. He doesn't like it in England."

"You can study Gaelic on Easter break and whenever you are here," his mother said. "And yes, my brother doesn't like England, but still it is a nice place and it will be good for you.

"You forget about the riding program. You shall love that, and it is half the reason your father chose the school. I am ordering two new riding outfits in the school colors of black and white with three new pairs of boots and a top hat. You shall look very handsome I am sure."

At that, Eugene smiled.

"New clothes are always fun, especially new boots. If you can let me learn more Gaelic when I am here, it will help. I shall love the riding but still I will miss all my friends. Father didn't go away to school in England. I don't see why I have to."

"It was unusual to go to school in England when your father was a boy. But it is something we want for you. Even though I will miss you terribly, it is still a good thing for you to go. You will not be very far away you know. The packet boat comes here, and there will be a break before you know it. Your father will see you when he is in London. We shall write every day. I shall miss you as much as you miss me."

Eugene watched as a tear came into his mother's eyes. He saw her blink it back and his own eyes were glistening.

Dabbing her eyes, she said, "You will be able to ride more than you could in one of the Irish schools, none of which has an equestrian team or fox hunting and jumping lessons as Mr. Hall's does. You shall be able to compete in gymkhanas.

"I am sure you will make the riding team and go out on real fox hunts. There is a gymnasium where you can toss Indian clubs on rainy days. Athletics is encouraged. You will like that."

Eugene listened.

"Yes, Mother, I will like that but don't want to leave," he said. "Still, making new friends will be fun and I promise not to make mischief."

Reaching out his mother held him close, knowing that when he was off to school, it would be hard. She was used to seeing him every day and the sadness in her heart was distressing. She hoped it did not show since he was not her little boy anymore.

The next day Eugene went downtown to the tailor for measurements. Once the new trunk was delivered, the packing commenced.

The great day arrived.

"Growing up at last," he thought.

Running upstairs for his jacket he paid a visit to the stables to see Star and his riding horse after breakfast. Tom promised to look after them both.

His mother was on the front step waiting to give him one more hug.

Then he was up into the carriage with his father and off down the street. Making the same trip James had taken five years earlier, he arrived at Mr. Hall's in the same amount of time.

When they arrived, Eugene followed the master

down the hall to meet his new roommate, Rex Crotty.

Frowning because the room was not quite as large as James', Matthew O'Reilly turned and smiled. It was big enough and Eugene's legs sturdy enough to handle the extra stairs.

The master took them on a tour, starting with classroom buildings and the dining room. Eugene smiled when they arrived at the gymnasium he had heard about.

The stables were left for last at Eugene's request.

The master, at first, refused to go to the stables for it would take too long. But remembering that Mr. Hall had said the second O'Reilly boy was a much better rider than the first he agreed, Mr. Hall having mentioned that he hoped the lad's riding skill would help improve the school's equestrian reputation.

Eugene followed the master in for an extensive tour while his father waited outside on a bench.

Eugene's father knew that when his son was near horses, it would take a while before he emerged. Settling himself in with his *London Times* and a copy of the *Dublin Illustrated News* he relaxed while his son chatted with the stablemen.

Eventually, Matthew went inside, finding his son in the last stall raptly talking about types of hay while stroking one of the horses. He told Eugene he was off to meet with the headmaster.

Smiling, Eugene asked, "Must I go, for I am having fun?"

The master shook his head.

"No," he said. "You can stay here with the horses. But remember that dinner is at five."

The stableman offered to let Eugene know when dinner time arrived.

Matthew O'Reilly and the master walked across the school grounds to where Mr. Hall was waiting.

Mr. Hall greeted Eugene's father as he came in. He asked how James was faring at Oxford, for he had been one of his favorite pupils. He asked about Eugene's personality since he had not heard much other than about his riding skill.

Eugene's father was loath to say how mischievous and feisty his youngest could be for fear he would be discharged before he began.

Explaining that Eugene was very bright and gifted at languages, Matthew said he was nearly fluent in French and Gaelic but said no more.

A glass of port having been shared Mr. Hall headed for his private quarters while Eugene's father rode back to the inn in the school's carriage.

Eugene was in the dining room where he had already gotten to know several boys.

Eugene's first few weeks in the schoolroom went well. The fox hunting lessons went even better. A happy letter headed home after only a month. He had been elected co-captain of the riding team.

Still, stories of Eugene taking apples from a neighboring farm made their way to Mr. Hall.

He was surprised since James had been quiet and studious. Even though he knew that personalities could vary between family members, the contrast usually wasn't as dramatic as it was between these two.

Doing his best to be sedate Eugene's mischievousness came out around the edges.

He got hungry and hooked apples from the orchards that belonged to the surrounding farmers. Their description of a tall boy with dark curly hair ended up on the master's desk.

Eugene's natural leadership ability rose up. He had no trouble recruiting fellow students to go hooking with him. He even managed to form teams to have apple fights with the local boys, or the Irish boys versus the English in an apple war.

It might not have been so bad if they had thrown the apples that had fallen on the grass instead of picking them off the trees.

In that case, it cost the farmers money and this made them angry. They had no trouble bringing this up to Mr. Hall every time they spotted him in a local shop or at Saint Michael's, the parish church where he was warden.

Another few weeks passed. With the farmers beginning to wish the school was in a different town Mr. Hall shook his head. He feared he had paid too much attention to Eugene O'Reilly's reputation for horsemanship.

He wrote to Matthew O'Reilly at his law offices. Eugene's father wrote back that his son would settle down, offering a sizeable amount to make up for the stolen apples.

Mr. Hall let it be.

Already Master O'Reilly was excelling in the equestrian program and had led the school's way to their first gymkhana win.

Eugene and his roommate and now best friend Rex Crotty organized races down the passageways of their dormitory on rainy or wintry days.

Using candlesticks for hurdles, they raced two or three abreast down the hall, which made a considerable racket below.

The masters who lived in rooms on the first floor said nothing. They knew the boys couldn't go outside to run around and work off excess energy in the rain. That and what they were doing was noisy but harmless.

Never coming up to check, they never learned that sometimes the candles were lit to make the hurdlers jump higher.

Eugene's high spirits and pranks disturbed Mr. Hall

more and more as time went on. Even when he wrote Dublin, it did no good. The master tried to keep an eye out to deter him from drawing other students to his side, but Eugene was irrepressible.

Most of the pranks were confined to the school. But Mr. Hall learned of one in the village. The confectioner told him that Master O'Reilly had decided to run away, persuading a friend to go with him. He said:

"They came into the village to buy some candy and chewing tobacco from my shop. As they arrived, they saw a local boy who had spoken to you about their plan to run away last month. They had just begun to thrash him when I came out and stopped them."

Summoning Eugene the next day, Mr. Hall said, "Why are you trying to run away? You seem happy enough here and your brother never tried to leave."

"My friend and I wanted candy and tobacco to chew behind the stables. If that boy hadn't seen us, we would have been fine. I didn't know the confectioner was watching out the window. I am sorry and won't do it again."

"Come here," said Mr. Hall.

Inching over, since he was sure he was going to be thrashed, Eugene looked up at Mr. Hall who was very tall, though not scary. He had a head that looked like an old potato and he was very fat.

Mr. Hall looked angry which worried Eugene.

The last thrashing had not been fun. Afterward, he had had to eat his mutton standing up with no dessert for a week too.

Steadying himself for the blows of Mr. Hall's cane Eugene was surprised when nothing happened.

Looking up quizzically into Mr. Hall's face after a minute, he heard him say, "I am not going to thrash you. That doesn't work because you are one determined, mischievous boy.

"No, I am going to have your riding stopped for two weeks. I have tried all else, but you have put a major blot upon the school. The running away and the candy are bad. But chewing tobacco is worse, especially because the entire village must know by now."

"Please. I need to ride and there is a practice tomorrow. I won't go into the village again or buy tobacco."

The master came in just then. He had been talking with the other boy. Both men told Eugene to wait in the corner by the bookcase while they spoke at the other end of the room.

A nerve-wracking hour passed, or so it seemed, before they called Eugene over, saying:

"We are trying to be kind and understanding. We want to avoid some of the punishments used at Eton. But we need to check your playful exuberance, which is why you may not ride for two weeks. You pay no mind to anything else."

Balling up his fists as he always did when he was upset Eugene said "Yes sir."

Having to give up riding for even one day was hard to imagine, especially since he had not meant to thrash the boy where anyone could see him. That and he knew the master hated tobacco but since all the stablemen used it he had thought they would say nothing.

"You may leave now and go study, Master O'Reilly," said Mr. Hall.

"I shall think about whether to write your father. As he is coming in two months, I may not. No more tobacco or leaving the school, and don't even go near the stable for two weeks. Now you may go."

Eugene turned on his heels.

Walking out the door, he went straight back to his

room. He astounded his mates with the news that he had not been thrashed. A surprise, he said, for since school had started he had been thrashed more than anyone else.

Eugene told them Mr. Hall might write his father or talk to him when he arrived. He explained that the sad part was that he had been forbidden to ride for two weeks, even in the meet he had thought he would win.

Consoling him his mates went back to their studies. Eugene worked on his arithmetic, the bane of his existence ever since he started lessons with his mother. No matter how hard he tried numbers just never added up right for him, unlike James, who could add whole columns without a mistake.

Looking forward to his father's visit as always, Eugene's joy was tempered by the fear that his father would learn of his escapade with the tobacco. Still there would be a nice dinner in town, perhaps just the two of them or with Rex.

Occasionally his mother appeared, having traveled to London to attend a special social occasion.

Eugene would attach himself to her the minute he saw her, staying by her side for the duration of her visit. He would run into her arms when she cried "Eugene darling" even though he was too old for that. He missed her so much that he couldn't help it.

Mr. Hall often thought of speaking to Mr. O'Reilly about Eugene's behavior. More, he realized, because his pupil inspired other boys to make mischief than because of what he did by himself.

In the past, it had seemed more sensible to say nothing. Eugene was a smart boy who did his schoolwork, and he was a riding team captain who led the team to victory at many meets.

One night Eugene went too far, and his father had to be told.

Everyone was asleep on the second floor in rooms off of a long hallway. Just after midnight, a loud moan came from the hall. Doors opened and faces peered out, seeing nothing as it was pitch black.

Lighting his candle, the master carried it up the stairs. He illuminated two large calves and a donkey stampeding up and down the hallway, baaing, and braying. Eugene and Rex laughed along with the others.

Mr. Hall came up with his candle. Standing in his nightshirt with his cap sticking straight up in the air over his ears he was clearly angry. He ordered the boys and the staffers to grab the animals, glaring as they managed to do so.

The animals galloped, trying not to be caught as he glared even more. Staffers ran down the hall to avoid the calves while the boys shrieked, plastering themselves against the wall.

The animals were captured.

The headmaster glanced in the corner. He noticed a long rope that appeared to be the same one that was tied to the great bell in the bell tower. Suspiciously, it was tied next to an open window big enough to admit the donkey and the other animals. Making it clear, he thought, that boys had assisted the animals in their ascent to the second floor.

His voice growing louder Mr. Hall asked who had helped the animals. There was no response of course. Eugene tried hard not to laugh, stuffing his nightcap in his mouth.

Mr. Hall had his own ideas about who could have organized such a thing. Staring straight at Eugene with an unfriendly expression on his face, he said, "Eugene did you do this?"

Shaking his head, Eugene replied "No sir."

Mr. Hall kept asking, and no one admitted to anything.

The headmaster looked tired and the master who had joined him did too. They rang for the porters to come lift the most obstreperous calf and carry him out. Watching as the calf was tied to their backs, Mr. Hall stared as a white cloth attached to its foreleg appeared.

Gulping as it came into view, Eugene leaned to his left and whispered to Rex, asking "Did you forget your handkerchief? Old Hall is going to be very mad."

Noticing them, the master glared hard at Eugene, who straightened up and stood still, his hands trembling as he held his candle.

Mr. Hall told the porter to remove the cloth. It was a school handkerchief. Several students looked alarmed as it was untied. Mr. Hall read the number written in the corner in India ink. Each student had an assigned number and Mr. Hall knew them all.

Pulling his nightcap down over his ears, he said, "It is the number twenty-nine. The student whose number that is should come forward."

No one said anything. Eugene tried to hide. He knew Mr. Hall knew number twenty-nine was his.

Mr. Hall walked forward. Standing halfway down the hall from Eugene he glared at him.

"How dare you do this Eugene?" he asked. "You are a graceless scamp, incorrigible. I shall write to your father this time, Master O'Reilly."

Eugene replied, saying, "I didn't do it, Mr. Hall. It is too hard a prank for me to think up."

He balled up his hands as he always did when he was nervous. Horror came over him for his handkerchief was missing.

Walking down the long corridor, he tried not to laugh at the spectacle of Mr. Hall yelling in his nightshirt, cap, and slippers.

Once in front of Mr. Hall, Eugene said that he did

not know who had used the rope to help the calves and donkey get upstairs. He added that since he had been sound asleep, he did not know which boy had tied his handkerchief to the calf's leg though he had ideas.

"I lose handkerchiefs all the time and I lost this one last week, I believe," he said. "I went to bed at nine. I was so tired that I did not hear the calves and donkey running up and down the hall. When I woke up, it scared me. I am afraid of donkeys and their long ears and braying."

Eugene continued in the same vein while Mr. Hall kept yelling.

One of the other members of his apple-hooking gang agreed that he always lost his handkerchiefs.

His roommate Rex said, "I know he had nothing to do with the calves or donkey for Eugene went to bed early with a headache. I was up hours longer, while Eugene slept in his bed."

Mr. Hall looked even more tired.

Saying he had enough for one night, he yelled only a little while longer. Adding that Eugene and his friends must have done it and that he would prove it in the morning, he sent everyone back to bed.

Eugene went back to his room and lay down on his bed, fear gripping his heart. His roommate lay down on his and they listened for Mr. Hall's steps on the stairs.

Once he was gone, Eugene's friends came in one by one and tried to figure out what to do if their fathers were notified. They had never seen Mr. Hall so angry.

Mr. Hall wrote to Matthew O'Reilly in the morning.

He asked Eugene's father to come to the school on his next visit to London to speak to his son about his behavior. He said that his attempts to discipline Eugene were not working.

Finding out that the letter was mailed Eugene was

upset since he did not want his parents to be angry. His independent life at school was fun and he had made good friends there.

He did not want to have to go to another school, make new friends, and lose his spot as riding team captain. The big gymkhana, too, as he had a very good chance to collect several prizes.

Eugene's father wrote back to say that he had a business engagement in the city in two months' time. He said that his wife was more inclined to be lenient, but that they intended to get to the bottom of it.

They had taken a great deal of time to choose the school he wrote. He hoped that Eugene could remain and that like his brother James he might be admitted to Oxford after graduation.

With two months to wait, Eugene became very quiet, quieter than he had been since he arrived. Smiling, Mr. Hall said he had turned over a new leaf and would be an honor to his school.

The six-week Easter break arrived. Eugene's father come the week before, riding out from London on the railway.

Taking a cab to the school, he took Eugene into the city on the new train.

He wanted to speak privately and try to find out what had happened. Eugene's father knew his son was high spirited. But at the same time, he did not mean to go too far, for he wanted to make his family proud.

Matthew O'Reilly was not sure Eugene and his friends could have made so much trouble on their own though somehow it had been done. The task was to find out whether Eugene had been part of it.

The fact that a handkerchief with his student number had been tied to the calf's foreleg made it seem likely he had been involved. But it was not clear that he was the ringleader, as Mr. Hall thought.

Eugene's father ordered a nice dinner at the hotel restaurant. Roast beef with Yorkshire pudding and gravy, peas, rolls and butter, and an apple custard for dessert.

After dinner, they went upstairs to Matthew O'Reilly's suite. A parlor set in red, turkey carpet and velvet draperies like the drawing room back home in blue not green.

Two bedrooms, one much larger than the other with a double bed with a red eiderdown. The other, intended to be a dressing room, had a narrow spool bed and green eiderdown.

Eugene stabbed the coals over and over with the poker as his father began to speak. He made the flames leap up with a loud hissing noise. Cinders fell with a small plop until his father told him to stop.

Eugene's father asked his son if he had organized the prank or played a part in it.

Clearing his throat, he said, "I don't think you organized it. That would be very complicated. But it does seem that if your handkerchief was tied to the calf's leg, you must have had something to do with it."

Eugene balled up both his fists, jamming them into his pockets. His father went on for ten minutes until Eugene finally broke down.

"Father, I knew about it, but I did not plan it for I hate donkeys. I did not tie my handkerchief to the calf's leg. I lost it about a week before when I chased a dog through the swamp behind the school. I think a boy who is my enemy picked it up and tied it to the calf."

His father talked for most of the evening about the prank.

Eugene said no more. His father grew tired of lecturing. Even when he threatened to box his youngest son's ears it got him nowhere.

Sitting down, he said, "We can talk more tomorrow. I am not sure this is the entire story. Perhaps someone did find the handkerchief and wanted to get you in trouble. So we can skip the ear boxing. You can go to bed instead."

They returned to school in the morning. Matthew O'Reilly was to meet with Mr. Hall in his office.

Heading back to his room Eugene sat down and played cribbage with a friend, a pastime they both liked.

Two hours passed in this manner until there was a knock on the door as they were rising to get ready for dinner. An assistant had come to fetch Eugene and take him downstairs.

Giving Eugene a secret handshake for good luck Rex watched as his friend clutched a lucky sprig of heather in his fist.

When Eugene walked in the office door, Mr. Hall was seated behind his huge desk. There was a brass lamp on it and bookcases filled with books behind.

His father sat across the room before a roaring fire. He and Mr. Hall were looking very stern and unhappy which did not seem to bode well.

Inching over in Mr. Hall's direction Eugene listened as the headmaster started in.

He explained that since Eugene had admitted to leading numerous apple and snowball fights he had probably led this prank as well. Before Master O'Reilly's arrival, Mr. Hall added, there had been no fights with the local boys.

Mr. Hall caught his breath. Coughing, he went on.

"I am positive it was you because your handkerchief was tied around the calf's leg. Since James was so popular here and your parents do not want you to have to leave I will allow you to stay, albeit with an additional punishment."

Eugene drew a deep breath.

So far it was not too terrible though so far it had been his worst hour since coming to the school. Still, he wondered when the cane would come out as he had felt its end only the week before.

Standing on the hearth rug for what seemed like hours Eugene listened as Mr. Hall and his father lectured.

He needed to concentrate on his schoolwork, they said, stay out of trouble and stop encouraging other boys to be incorrigible.

He might have been asked to depart that very afternoon, Mr. Hall added. But because his riding was so good and because his father had begged that he be allowed to stay he would be allowed to remain.

Standing still, Eugene said nothing, fists in his pockets twisting his handkerchief into knots.

His father recognized the gesture and wanted to hold him close. He understood what his boy was going through, but he said nothing. Eugene needed to learn a lesson instead of leaving for a lesser school.

"I am sorry," Eugene kept repeating, as he didn't want to leave his horse and his friends.

He wished his mother was there. Surely she would take his part. She understood him while it seemed his father only understood James.

Standing on the same spot on the carpet for what seemed like eons Eugene waited until the lecture ended.

Mr. Hall said the same thing his father had at the hotel, that he wasn't sure Eugene had organized the prank. He shared the master's doubts about whether he could have done it.

Concluding, he said, "So you can stay until you finish and head off to university."

Breathing a sigh of relief for his reprieve Eugene barely heard what Mr. Hall said next.

"You shall not be allowed to captain the riding team for the next term. The boy next below shall take your place. Also, you cannot compete in the big gymkhana with all the other schools."

As Mr. Hall's last sentence sank in Eugene began to plead.

"I have already been punished by not being allowed to ride. I love riding and am proud of captaining the team. I know I can make a big difference in the gymkhana and perhaps win it for the school."

His father replied.

"I know it will be hard, son, but perhaps you'll learn from it. You are lucky that I don't have to take you back home to your mother today. You will be allowed to ride and next term you can be captain again. This hurts the school as well as you. Without you, the odds on winning the gymkhana are not as good."

"Yes, you can ride Master O'Reilly," Mr. Hall said, "and hang around the stable when you don't have lessons. This will no longer be forbidden. Maybe in the end you will have learned something.

"Perhaps you shall continue to behave as you have since the prank. I have heard no complaints from the locals about snowballs and apples since then."

Eugene was exhausted from tension. His handkerchief was torn to shreds inside his pocket.

"You can leave," said Mr. Hall, "and go back to your room to get ready for dinner. Tomorrow the riding master will tell the team about your demotion and that you're not allowed in the gymkhana. You are dismissed."

Running out the door, Eugene went back upstairs. All his friends were sitting on the beds as he walked in eager to find out what had happened.

A great shout of joy filled the air as he explained that he was allowed to stay, followed by a group embrace as everyone hugged him at once.

Asking if he had been thrashed Rex looked shocked when Eugene shook his head for they all had been for some offense or other.

A sad look came over his friends' faces when he explained that he couldn't ride for the gymkhana and couldn't captain the team, followed by disappointment for they knew that it meant they would probably lose. Eugene's horse was a great jumper but wouldn't even trot for anyone else.

But then there was smiling all around. The main thing was that Eugene could remain. For that, they were all pleased.

The dinner bell rang ten minutes later. Trooping down early everyone was pleased for the meal was better than usual. Roast beef instead of mutton, that and for once it had not been burned.

Whispering in Eugene's ear Rex said that Mr. Hall must have thought Eugene's father was staying so he had made sure dinner was good.

Eugene felt a little afraid lest Mr. Hall make him wait by the side watching everyone have their pudding, but the headmaster said nothing.

After dinner came vespers. As usual, Eugene rested his head on the pew and fell asleep as even the sermons were boring.

Waking up as the last hymn ended Eugene followed everyone out and went back upstairs.

Rex and the others were in his room when he entered. Sitting down, Eugene told them about his trip back and forth on the railway. It was so new he was the first pupil to ride it.

He told them how the compartment had looked. Almost like a carriage, he explained, with two seats opposite.

He described how he had stared out the window watching the world go by while his father read a book.

People walking along in the lane, a lumbering coach, and even laborers with rakes building haystacks out in the fields.

Railway workers had shoveled coal into the coal car in London until it was full as the train was to go fifty miles past the village station. Even his father had had to cover his ears when the hiss came as the water finished boiling just before they got into their compartment.

One of the boys who knew a lot about coal because his father owned two collieries asked how much coal the trainmen had used.

Eugene told him that it was a lot but that he didn't know how much they used for the return trip.

Eugene finished in the spring of 1844.

It had been six long years but the great day had finally arrived. His entire family came to see him graduate, James on the train from Oxford and the rest on the packet steamer.

It was a big day for the O'Reilly household, partly because Eugene's parents had worried about whether or not their youngest would do something else that would force Mr. Hall to dismiss him.

Fortunately, this hadn't happened. Having become far more adept at covering his tracks Eugene had made sure Mr. Hall never heard the worst of it.

Had he found out, not even Eugene's skill at leading the riding team to victory would have kept his place in the school. Indeed, he and his gang had moved on from hooking apples to taking chickens along with numerous sneakings out in hopes of meeting girls.

Taking every prize connected with horsemanship, Eugene went up on stage four times. Towards the end, he went up again a fifth time to collect the team trophy.

Mr. Hall's attitude began softening as he watched his pupil run up the steps again and again.

Granted the rector had said something about Eugene

hitting him with a massive snowball in the back of his cassock during a graveside service. Still Eugene had done so much for the equestrian team that Mr. Hall had been able to raise the school fees by five percent.

Mr. Hall shook Eugene's hand when he gave him the first place trophy for riding.

"Congratulations Mr. O'Reilly," he said, looking oddly as though he would become sick.

"Thank you, Mr. Hall," said Eugene. "I have enjoyed winning, but I think you will be glad when I am gone. There will be no more pranks and chasing of girls."

He had his diploma and his Trinity acceptance, and he was not afraid of the headmaster anymore.

Overhearing this last remark Matthew O'Reilly did his best to look stone-faced.

Patrick and Maureen sat laughing because they had heard how good Eugene had been. They had been afraid he was forever changed but no. His stripes were the same under his new coat.

Looking distressed Mr. Hall shook hands with the new graduate before Eugene stepped back to his seat.

The O'Reillys headed back to Dublin as Eugene traveled north to Leeds, Rex's parents having invited him for a month's day. Being fond of the Crottys Eugene's parents had approved.

They felt that a month with them might encourage Eugene to tame some of his wild ways.

If they had known more of all the races and escapades Rex had instigated instead of the other way round, they might have said no.

Meanwhile, back at school Mr. Hall breathed a sigh of relief. Packing up a few things, he took a walking holiday so he could ease Eugene's pranks out of his mind.

There would be no more reports of mischief, at least

not until someone else like Eugene came along. That Mr. Hall intended to do his level best to prevent.

Feeling sorry for whoever ran the school the O'Reillys sent him to next the headmaster rejoiced.

He had seen the last of young Master O'Reilly. At last, he could breathe free.

Eugene had not been admitted to Oxford, which made him smile.

He knew that if he had been accepted, his father would have made him go. Its social connections would have won out over any republican thoughts in a heartbeat.

He was happy too to have a broad smile from his mother. She he had missed most of all. Better downtown, he thought, than far away.

In private, James said, "You have to ignore negative remarks. The connections are there to be made."

Eugene replied.

"I can see everyone more easily at Trinity. More opportunities for fox hunting, too, several each year. If I had been accepted to Oxford, I would have had to borrow mounts. Father refused to take on the additional expense of shipping my riding horse, Mr. Moonlight. That alone is enough reason to be glad Oxford didn't want me. The girls, too, though that I did not explain."

He had become a tall, handsome fellow with a shock of dark hair, a very pleasing countenance and a great deal of charm.

Far more young ladies to meet in Dublin than in Oxford because of the Season, that and Maureen's friends too.

Granted he had not been allowed to tarry long enough to chat with anyone. But now that they were done with any luck it would be allowed.

Eugene's summer did not go as he had thought. Far too much time spent looking at rooms, hardly enough time to ride let alone meet anyone.

He had to spend entire afternoons in his mother's wake looking at one suite after the other. All the students needed rooms and they all wanted to be near the campus.

The summer frittered away. One place was too small and another too far away.

Wishing she was in Corstown Emily O'Reilly finally found something that might suit. Two rooms, furnished with a spool bed and decent parlor suite and only a block from the library.

Eugene rode downtown on Monday afternoon to look at the rooms.

Sitting down on the sofa, he said, "Mother, the wool is itchy. I need to find a different place."

His mother, who by then was tired of looking at rooms, said, "Eugene, please. You don't know how many places I have seen. I have to help James when he finishes and I have no more energy for this.

"I shall get you a cashmere shawl to drape over the sofa and it will not be itchy. If it is not big enough, I shall get a cover made, but it's not a reason not to take the rooms. This suite comes with a maid to clean, and the dining room where you will take your meals looks nicer than most."

A smart remark sat on the tip of her son's tongue, but he held back.

Looking over at the hair that had escaped from her hairpins Eugene realized how hard she has been working to find him a place.

Apologizing, he said, "I know how hard it has been. Other than the sofa I do like it. The bed is very comfortable. I can walk across the street to read Gaelic, which is what I have wanted to do ever since I left for

Mr. Hall's."

"Eugene, you do not know how bad some of these suites are and in what a mean condition. This one has nice bookcases and a decent sized desk. The armoire is huge. Just having the maid will be a big help."

"Mother please don't worry. I can see how tired you are and it is a nice suite. I am afraid someone else will want it, so can we let the landlady know I would like it today?"

His mother sat down on the sofa to rest her feet.

"Yes, we shall," she said. "The housemaid said the landlady was in her office downstairs. Please help me up. I am exhausted."

Extending his arm, Eugene stood and held the door. They went downstairs to take the suite.

Breathing a sigh of relief, they climbed into the carriage and headed home. Eugene gazed out the window while his mother worked on her lists of what he needed, adding bedding since the eiderdown had not looked new.

Eugene's father was home when they arrived.

Looking relieved at the news, he smiled. A true relief, his wife having looked more exhausted with each passing day, unable to even think of Corstown until rooms had been found for Eugene.

All three headed to Corstown for a fortnight's stay. Eugene's mother spent much of her time resting with her husband on the terrace.

Eugene rode out with Patrick in between sentimental trips to the attic. Very strange it seemed that he had ever been small enough to fit into one of the trunks.

They returned home the day before James arrived for a brief visit. He was going to London to apprentice with a friend of his father's for a year before he took his place in the family firm.

The week passed well. Despite their differences, the O'Reillys were happy to be under one roof.

Ending all too soon Eugene and his mother stood on the doorstep with a last embrace as Matthew took James down to catch the packet steamer for London.

Father and son were very excited. Once the apprenticeship was finished, they would be able to begin practicing together as they had longed to do for so many years.

Eugene's mother began packing up her younger son's things, filling up the huge trunk that had come back from Mr. Hall's. Eugene had acquired so many outfits that a second trunk was required to hold them all.

His first trunk was immense in his mother's eyes. But it was not large enough to hold his collection of custom-made riding boots, jodhpurs, and crops.

Calling Eugene into the library, his father said, "You are going to study, not fox hunt. Maybe you can get rid of some of the crops and boots. It just makes more for your mother to pack."

Eugene replied, saying, "I am going to study. But I need all my riding things so I can come up and exercise Mr. Moonlight. You told me how hard it has been for Mother and the stablemen to do it for me."

"You do more than just exercise that horse, but since the trunk is already purchased, you might as well take it along. Better it be at your lodgings than here. As long as you can come up on Saturdays that will be fine. Hopefully, you will greet your mother when you do. She has missed you these past few years when you were away at school."

Nodding Eugene agreed.

"Of course, I shall visit. I have missed you and Mother and Polly and shall be back to visit more than you like."

"You can never be here too much for your mother," said his father. Then, changing the subject, he asked, "Do you intend to ride downtown as you did in the past?"

"Yes. I am used to the bridle paths and I hope to run into my old friends. Though Patrick told me about a different park a little further from Trinity with some hedges to jump. I might look at it."

"Be careful. Jumping makes your mother nervous."

"She knows I won all those awards."

"I know, I know. Just don't tell her. She loves you so she worries. Your uncle rode like that when he was young and it made their mother nervous, something she has inherited."

"Grandmother did tell me that. I shall be careful so she doesn't worry and will ride downtown for the most part in the park that has no jumps. Even James rides there."

"That's true. Why don't you ride where you want? We'll let your mother think what she wants. Agreed?"

The conversation shifted to talk of his courses and the professors he would have. There was no more mention of his large collection of riding gear.

A grand celebration took place on August twelfth, Eugene's eighteenth birthday. His parents wondered how it could be 1844 already. Somehow it seemed like only yesterday that he had been small.

In two more weeks, on September first, Eugene got up early.

Both parents helped him move into his rooms. Breathing a sigh of relief as the door closed Eugene smiled as they departed.

He was glad to be home, but it was hard living in his old room with less independence than he had had at school. His mother had not been able to stop asking when he would be back and which friends he was seeing.

Eugene settled into his new routines, enjoying his course in Gaelic, which he had missed the whole time he was in England. He liked his History course nearly as much and his Mathematics not at all.

His French course went very well, much to his surprise.

Having learned more at Mr. Hall's than he had realized, he had become entirely fluent. His marks kept him at the head of his class.

On Saturdays, he rode out on Mr. Moonlight and dined with his mother.

As the weeks went by he rode longer, dining only when he was directly asked. It was partly because of his studies. New friends took up much of his time, which made sense but was hard on his mother.

Eugene spent hours during his first term deciding which of the numerous eating clubs he would like to join. Important it was, he realized, as much of the school's social life happened within their walls.

Two clubs had banquets twice a year, huge dinners followed by copious Irish whiskey and Irish songs. It was hard to choose. Applying to both, in the end, he hoped to be accepted by one.

Eugene persuaded his mother to purchase the new clothes he needed as a Christmas gift.

He created a wonderful scene as he opened the packages, recalling the opposite scene when he had tossed his dancing clothes around when he was small.

He opened package after package from the family tailor. White shirts and stocks and black frockcoats emerged. Red and green vests along with trousers with black low-heeled pumps reminiscent of his dancing school days.

Jumping up after everything had been opened Eugene hugged his mother and thanked her effusively.

"I shall look so fashionable in them," he exclaimed.

"I am sure you shall, Eugene," his mother said with a smile.

Matthew grumbled about how expensive they had all been, saying the money might have been better spent on books.

Turning to him, Eugene smiled.

"Thank you, Father. Other than studying I will only attend my club. Don't worry, I am doing my work."

"I think you are, Eugene," his father said, "but students at Trinity are not fashion plates."

Breaking in, his wife said, "But dear, the Season shall be starting soon. He will be attending balls and dances as his brother did. Granted, they were also purchased so he can join the eating club that interests him. But Eugene has been very careful and spends long hours in the library so he has earned them."

As Eugene started dusting his new dance slippers, his father said, "That is true. We did buy all those things for James and of course, Eugene should do the Season.

"He has not lived here for a long time. He needs more of a social life than there is to be found on the Trinity campus. Still, what with his studies, he can't go out every evening as James did for those few months."

Eugene looked up.

"I want to go to many of the events but mostly the dances," he said. "I am hoping to avoid the dinner parties although a theatrical party would be fun. I have too much to do to go to as many parties as James because he was not in university at the time."

"You have taken so many dance lessons I am sure you will be very popular," said his mother.

Remembering his dances with his wife when they

were young Matthew O'Reilly smiled.

"Just be careful to manage everything. You need to do the Season. Never any question of that. It just made sense for you to start at Trinity now instead of waiting another year."

Eugene agreed he would get everything done and absently thanked his father.

The main thought running through his head was about his first choice club. It was having dinner in a fortnight on a Friday that was set to run into the next morning. The club leader had managed to snare an orchestra that would be brought in from Paris to play the latest songs.

It would be a tragedy to miss it, Eugene thought. His new clothes saved him. Without them, he could not have dreamt of attending.

Now he could go to the dinner and have clothes ready for balls with his cousins later.

Things stayed much the same for the rest of his first year and into his second. Occasional visits to his family, hours spent studying in the library and Mr. Moonlight with evenings at the social clubs for he had joined both.

The family felt very small without James. Everyone was relieved when his apprenticeship in London ended.

His mother went back to looking for lodgings before he arrived.

Searching closer to downtown, she tried to find something near her husband's law offices. Unlike Eugene and Matthew, he had no horse or carriage. He was afraid of the first, and the second he could not afford.

After her hunt for rooms for Eugene, Emily O'Reilly had a much better idea of how to go about it.

Indeed, she was able to find something only a week

after James arrived. It had the same number of rooms as Eugene's but was more elegant. A leather parlor set instead of wool, she was happy to see, a thicker mattress and only a ten-minute walk to the O'Reilly law offices.

Once everything had been delivered the packing commenced. James' law book collection proved easier to pack than Eugene's riding paraphernalia.

Still, it was harder to move.

Once packed in a second trunk it proved impossible to lift. Not even Eugene and the new stableman could pick it up. In the end, the books had to be moved in stages in the family carriage.

Following his books downtown, James began to see more of Susan since he had not forgotten her sweetness and her blue eyes.

The two had managed to keep corresponding all the years he had been in England, combined with occasional visits when James came home on holiday or when Susan stayed with cousins in town. They were serious and thought of marrying as soon as James was doing well enough to ask for her hand.

Spending his extra pounds and pence on theater tickets, James attended with Susan nearly every week. Often he and Susan went with a set of parents or else their cousins, with an elderly cousin to chaperone.

James and Susan journeyed out for dinner at the O'Reilly townhouse when Susan was in Dublin.

By now James' parents had come round and they were fond of her. Though whether it was due to her sweet self or the possibility that they hoped Eugene might be allowed to join the Enniskillen Dragoons was impossible to divine.

3 DUBLIN, CORSTOWN & PARIS

After the thrill of attending banquets and musical evenings at his clubs had worn off, Eugene became more interested in politics. He had often pestered his mother to tell stories about his Uncle Andrew, asking so many times that both his parents became uneasy.

Though their only contact was through letters, uncle and nephew became close.

Andrew saw himself as a young man in Eugene. They shared an adventurous streak the Dublin O'Reillys did not possess.

Checking the boards where notices went up Eugene found nothing. Indeed, the locations were not publicized for the solicitor general did not approve.

One Friday evening he was lucky.

At a banquet at his eating club, he was seated next to a Richard O'Gorman, a Trinity student of whom he had heard, rumored to be a regular attendee at the secret meetings Eugene had been trying to find a way to attend.

Doing his best to conceal his excitement for fear of scaring off his new friend, Eugene chatted throughout the evening.

He offered Richard one of the fine cigars that James had given him a week before.

Then he managed to steer the conversation to the last rising as Richard's uncle had played a role in it, one that had ended in hanging instead of exile.

"How interesting," Eugene said, "to be randomly seated next to someone whose uncle may have known mine but who paid a higher price. No one here wishes to speak of it."

Mr. O'Gorman smiled.

"Yes, it is a small world. I had not intended to come to the dinner since I am just over a cold. But here I sit enjoying your cigar and conversation."

He saw Richard again the next week at a dinner held by his mother's cousin. Retreating into a corner, they discussed politics until they were pulled away to dine.

The musicale went on and on afterward.

Standing by the door, Richard waited as the last note was played. To Eugene's delight, his new friend invited him to a meeting the following week.

Eugene connected with more of Richard's friends after the first meeting. He found himself attending several meetings each week.

He did his best to keep his father from knowing. Surely his parents would not approve.

Things went well for several months.

Finally, his luck ran out.

His father appeared one day, unannounced, his hair sticking up and tie slightly twisted. His son braced himself as this was a sign of the senior O'Reilly's distress because he was a stickler for proper attire.

Letting him in, Eugene offered his father the sofa.

"Good morning, Father," he said. "How are you?"

His father could be upset over any number of things, from drinking to the meetings so he sat ruminating over anything and everything.

Finally, his father spoke.

"I have come to ask about your attendance at those meetings," he said. "If your mother finds out she will be worried. It's not because your cause is wrong as you know we don't think that, but out of fear you will end up like my brother. What must seem exciting to you makes her worry.

"You do know by now how hard it has been on all of us never to see Andrew. Indeed, I have seen him only three times in all these years."

"I am careful Father," said Eugene. "I have only been to a few meetings. Mostly I go to class or my clubs."

"It started that way with Andrew and then he got swept up. I was too young or I might have ended up in Paris too and then there would have been only one of us to look after our parents. You are a wonderful young man, but I can see you are attracted to your uncles' exciting lives."

Continuing, his father said, "Granted I am the most conservative of my generation, but I am proud of our ancestor who fell at Drogheda. Will you please endeavor to limit your involvement so that you don't end up like my brother, forced to leave, never to return?"

"I am careful," said Eugene. "I don't want to have to go away. Still I hate the English."

"Don't hate the English. Hate the government they have imposed upon us, and that is not the same thing. Lord Palmerston is as much of an Irish patriot as anyone, but he is in the queen's cabinet."

"He is working to make things better, but it will take too long."

"'Tis always like that when you are young. It will get better, I promise you. In the meantime, you must avoid these meetings as much as you can so that there will be no sad news going to your mother. You are her pet and I am not sure she could bear it."

"I promise," Eugene said.

Rising to his feet his father said, "I have to go home in a minute. Your mother does not know I have come and she will wonder where I am.

"Please try to concentrate on your studies. Perhaps you will meet a young woman or two during the Season and that will give you something else to think about. Come here, my boy. Let me hug you before I go."

Eugene helped him up, embracing his father as he left. He was stiffer than he would have been with his mother but close just the same for he loved them both.

Once his father had gone, he went to lie down. Waking later, he thought about what his father had said and decided to skip a few meetings and see how it went.

Over supper at the tavern with Richard they talked of girls since the Season was near upon them.

Richard said, "I had terrible luck last year. But my country cousins are coming into town which should help with the invitations."

Giving up their political meetings they strived instead to be included on the dowagers' official lists.

To Eugene's delight, all his dancing lessons were finally paying off. Word of his skill with the steps managed to proceed him. He was vaulted along with Richard to the top of the lists that all the mamas consulted before sending out their invitations.

They were very curious as the first invitations came in.

Wondering how to make a good impression, they asked James to come round and explain it all.

Eugene poured a glass of port for his brother and sat down.

James said, "Well, little brother, let me see what I can remember about the Season. That is other than drinking champagne, dressing up and sleeping late, all of which you know to do. Don't sound too desperate because you might get taken off the lists. First, you need to be suitable. As you are already included, that hurdle has been met.

"Dancing well is the next thing. Otherwise, the young lady you dance with first will erase your name for any later dances and let word get around to her friends. That's the kiss of death as then you will be allowed no dances at all."

Breaking in Richard asked, "What do the dance cards look like?"

James laughed again.

"You are babes in the woods."

Eugene glowered, saying, "Remember those riding lessons, after you met Susan and told her you could ride?"

"I remember and thank you," James said, responding in a quieter tone. "The dance cards are cardboard with the dances printed on them. They come with small silver pencils attached by a silver cord. Each girl is given one on her arrival.

"Once everyone is in the room you walk over to whomever you would like and ask her to write your name in for a specific dance. A popular girl will have her card filled instantly. So you have to try to be among the first to arrive. Otherwise, there will only be dances with plain girls left."

Continuing, James said, "You will need an opera cloak and the right clothes. The tailor will know. Black and white now, no navy blue or green. Granted, Eugene, you always know what's in and out."

Richard, knowing that Eugene's tailor bill was the largest in their class, chuckled to himself.

Laughing, James teased Eugene, who had turned beet red.

"As if he needed an excuse to visit the tailor. He is our fashion plate."

Growling, Eugene collapsed into a fit of laughter as he remembered his row of riding boots that took half the bottom of his armoire.

Richard offered to take everyone to lunch. Agreeing for they had worked up a good appetite, the O'Reilly brothers followed him down to the tavern on the corner for sandwiches and ale.

Afterward, James went home and Richard and Eugene went to the tailor. Using the line of credit his mother had set up so that her husband would not complain, Eugene bought what he needed.

With James' coaching, the Season went well for both young men. Both were so busy they could barely fit in their eating club activities, let alone anything political.

Arriving late the first evening, they were forced to dance with wallflowers who stomped on their feet as James had warned. After that, they made it a point to be among the first to arrive.

Word spread of Eugene's dancing ability and charm and his friend's good looks and the girls came up to them instead of the other way round.

They were exhausted by the end of February as the Season finished up. But they had met girls they liked, or, at least, Richard had.

Eugene was trying to arrange an introduction to a Miss Elizabeth Sullivan, a beautiful blonde he had seen at several dances. She had tapped his arm with her fan during the cotillion quadrille in a most electrifying fashion which was most encouraging.

Great frustration had set in the next day. He had not been able to find anyone within his circle who was acquainted with the lady or her family so he could be properly introduced.

Racking his brain, he tried to think of an intermediary despite James' and Richard's amused glances as they told him to find someone known to their own circle instead.

At Sunday dinner, his father sat at the head of the table staring off into space as Eugene went on.

Finally, Matthew said, "This is how I was after I spotted your mother at church one Sunday."

"I am trying to find someone to introduce you to her, Eugene," said his wife. "Don't give up."

Glaring straight into the centerpiece as Eugene could talk of nothing else James said, "Please, little brother, you are too young."

Emily, looking at them all, said, "He is fond of this girl. But Eugene you are trying even my patience. One more story and we shall have to shift subjects before your father flees the table for his office and your brother for the conservatory."

"I am trying not to think of her," Eugene said, gazing around the table.

"I was having some success until she tapped my forearm during the last figure. I can't forget her now and can hardly think of anything else."

Relief arrived when Eugene found a history fellow whose sister had been at school with Elizabeth. He was introduced at supper just ten days before the end of the Season.

They went with the group to a grand ball after. Eugene was not Elizabeth's supper partner, but he took all of her dances except for the first and the last waltzes.

A chaperone glared, perhaps thinking he was holding Elizabeth too close.

But Elizabeth did not mind. After the supper interval, she confided that she had been taking secret lessons. A Dublin dance master, she said, who had studied in London with a Frenchman, who also taught at the French court.

Whispering back, Eugene said that he had studied too. The truth was that he had been practicing in Richard's lodgings. One leading and then the other, they were guided by diagrams from the dance classes they had been too exhausted to attend.

Eugene was in raptures on Sunday.

Saying nothing, James sat still as Matthew and Emily looked relieved. One son was apparently settled, and the other was on the right path.

Daydreaming through his classes for a week Eugene was preoccupied with visions of Miss Sullivan. It seemed to him that he had made a good impression.

When Monday rolled around again, he got a message from his mother asking him to help her shop for a birthday present for James the next day. Eugene wrote a note and agreed.

They stood on the corner waiting to cross to a tea shop in search of refreshments.

Suddenly Elizabeth appeared at his side with her sister and her aunt. They were engaged on a similar errand, she said, searching for a gift for their younger sister who was at school near Belfast.

To his relief, she took his hand even though they had only been introduced once.

Smiling past his nervousness, he was glad to see that her outfit was as stylish as his own. The length of her skirt was as current as the pleats on his shirt.

Looking down at her, he smiled even more broadly. Her blue mantlet made her skirt sway in a most attractive manner. Her reddish gold hair looked even more golden under her bonnet with its crown of roses.

Eugene was so happy to have Elizabeth by his side that the introduction to her younger sister Lucy passed in a blur. Noticing that Lucy's petticoats peeped out, he was glad Elizabeth's did not show.

He bowed to their aunt. Turning to face his mother he found that she required no introduction since she was already embracing Mrs. Sullivan. The ladies explained that they were schoolmates, having attended the same convent school, but had not seen each other since.

Eugene watched the ladies embrace. They exchanged butterfly kisses in the middle of the sidewalk, something that Eugene had never seen his mother do.

Finally, he said, "Mother, why didn't you tell me you know Miss Sullivan's aunt?"

"Because when I knew her she was Catherine McGregor. We

were at school together but after my wedding we lost touch. How exciting this is. How glad I am that you have been introduced to Miss Sullivan or we might never have met again."

The young people stood in the cold air chatting for what seemed like two hours as the ladies became reacquainted.

Ten more minutes passed. Eugene's mother looked over. Her son was shifting from one foot to the other as the young ladies clutched their mantlets closer.

"Catherine, since it is almost tea time, could we retire to the new railway hotel?" she asked. "The young people are freezing and no doubt hungry. We can have a good visit."

Glancing at her charges, Mrs. Sullivan said, "Girls, I am sorry. Too much chatting. Let us go eat. Their high tea is supposed to be wonderful. It's not too far to walk but I think cabs would be easier."

Eugene nodded, followed by the girls. High tea with its kidney pie, sandwiches and cake sounded like a wonderful idea.

All five of them piled into two cabs. There was room enough in one, but it would not have been proper since the young people would be on each other's laps. It was a ten-minute ride, not far but exciting.

Arriving, Mrs. O'Reilly led the way.

Doormen opened the double doors so they could proceed in.

The décor took the young people's breath away. Elizabeth and Lucy had never been in a hostelry so stylish. Eugene had not stood in a hotel lobby since his father had taken him to London.

Standing on a very large cabbage rose in the center of the carpet, they glanced around.

There was hand carved woodwork everywhere and a potted palm in each corner. Guests walked up and down the grand staircase with bellboys trailing behind.

Eugene's mother led them across the carpet toward the dining room, feeling a little embarrassed as the young continued to gaze round.

The dining room was most impressive with large chandeliers and Wedgwood service plates at each setting.

Eugene hurried to pull out the chairs.

High tea was ordered between embraces. Listening to his mother tell her friend about when he had been little in Corstown Eugene felt embarrassed.

"You cannot imagine how darling my little Eugene was," she said. "He would sit in the trunks in the attic while his older brother pushed him around as though he were on a sled. One day he terrified me when he nearly drowned in the river."

He talked with Elizabeth about dancing and music.

Hoping to distract her from his mother's stories, especially the one about when he had been small enough to fit in Grandmama's trunks, he spoke a little louder.

Soon the three of them were having a merry conversation about plays they had seen.

New bands too, since several had been brought over to play at the different dances and balls. Elizabeth talked about one band in particular that played the best waltzes.

Eugene spoke in a more and more animated voice until Lucy noticed that their elders were giving them disapproving looks.

Elizabeth's aunt began saying something but stopped as Emily whispered in her ear. She reminded her of the convent school and how they were now reduced to matrons on gilt chairs. Older, she added, than they had thought they'd ever be, but not forgetting.

Tea having arrived both ladies poured. Three plates were covered with cakes. Some filled with strawberry jam, others with brandy flavored cream shaped like horns.

Several plates of Eugene's favorite watercress sandwiches disappeared, earning him a severe look from his mother.

Still she only said "Eugene" because she knew he was consuming them to quiet his nerves.

Her son looked down at his plate. To his horror, he saw that there were only a few left.

Thinking Elizabeth had noticed, he offered the plate first to her and then her sister in case they wanted the few sandwiches that remained.

His nerves recovered as he glanced over at the other's plates. Feeling relieved, he noticed that they were both covered with toast and scones. Then he reached for the last sandwich.

Surprising the young people, the waiter arrived with the savory course, a large beef and kidney pie. They politely clamored for some though they had already eaten nearly all the sandwiches and toast.

Lucy finally asked. "Can we have some, Auntie, or is it for you and Mrs. O'Reilly?"

Emily O'Reilly looked at the empty plates, laughing for the young were always hungry.

"Yes, you can have some," she said. "We have had such a good time visiting. We owe it to Eugene and your sister. The pie is large and we have managed to eat a few cakes ourselves."

The ladies chatted on after they were done while the three young people went to collect their coats. Helping his mother with her coat Eugene followed her across the lobby.

The steps were a little slippery and he was happy the minute Elizabeth's gloved hand grasped his forearm.

Descending the stairs, the ladies blew a last set of butterfly kisses.

Eugene wondered when he might see Elizabeth again. Relief swept over him as he heard her aunt say:

"Dear Emily, we must see each other again soon. When is your next visiting day? I want to continue our visit and bring my sister in law to meet you. I know she will be delighted we have found each other again," followed by his mother replying "Oh do. Please come."

Opening her bag, she added, "Eugene, please ask the Sullivans' cabbie to wait a minute while I give Mrs. Sullivan my card."

There was a brief flurry. The cabbie looked irritated as he stood waiting. Eugene stood by his mother, waving as the Sullivans departed.

Eugene thanked her the minute the door closed.

"Oh Mother, thank you," he said. "I didn't know when I could see Elizabeth again. I hope you liked her."

Replying, his mother said, "Dear, had she not asked me I would have asked her. We were very dear at school. Miss Sullivan seems like a nice young lady. I can see why you like her. She has a lovely manner and appearance. I think they will come next week though I expect you will be busy with more manly activities."

Eugene felt rather shocked.

"Mother, I am planning to come home on Wednesday to visit

Polly, but maybe I will come downstairs in the afternoon."

"All right," his mother said.

She laughed, saying, "We won't tell your father since he will twit you about it. You can come, though I warn you that you will find it boring, sitting and sipping tea while one's friends come and talk about their children."

Eugene went to his parents' home on Wednesday after his Gaelic class. Wetting his hair down each time he heard the door open, he breathed a sigh of relief when he heard the Sullivans announced.

"Mrs. Sullivan, Mrs. Edward Sullivan, Miss Sullivan and Miss Lucy Sullivan," the maid called, opening the drawing room door with a flourish.

Eugene was barely able to keep himself from leaping up and running over to Elizabeth. So ecstatic was he that she was standing before him breathing the same air that he nearly failed to take her hand in greeting.

The ladies sat down as the maid brought out fresh tea. Elizabeth walked over to Eugene, asking to see the ferns as she had heard that several were quite rare.

Eugene walked her to the windowsills where the ferns were kept in individual pots. They came to the last fern and he didn't know what to say next as his nervousness was getting the better of him.

Just then Mrs. Sullivan called them over. She asked Elizabeth to play her new song, explaining that her niece would like to sing for her old friend.

Emily wanted to shake her head but nodded. She was a very good pianist and could hardly bear listening to bad playing, but Catherine was her friend.

Turning to Elizabeth, she said, "Please play Miss Sullivan. We would all like to hear you." Her remark surprised her son because she never let anyone else play.

Elizabeth nodded in thanks.

She sat down at the piano. Leaning over the keys she played the opening notes of a piece from Wallace's *Matilda of Hungary*, singing in a bell-like soprano voice.

The look on Eugene's mother's face turned from resignation to a broad smile as the second verse began.

Clapping when the song was done, she exclaimed, "What an exquisite aria my dear. How did you happen to choose it?"

"My cousin saw the opera when she was in London and told me about it," Elizabeth said.

"It has only just arrived here. Auntie found the sheet music downtown and I have learned the song from that. I am glad you like it, Mrs. O'Reilly. I have a few more songs I would like to play, as my aunt has not heard them all. Perhaps you and Eugene would like to hear them too."

Grinning as the last words left her lips, Eugene gazed at the fireplace instead of Elizabeth's face. His smile might have been a cause for alarm in Catherine Sullivan's mind since the young people were barely acquainted.

The young people managed to see each other a few more times before the Season ended. In spring, there were picnics with friends when Elizabeth came to town to stay with her aunt. But Eugene fretted for the summer when Catherine Sullivan would be away.

Fortunately, he was relieved of all his fears over Sunday dinner at the house.

His father put down his fork.

"I know you are both sad about selling the Corstown house even though you understand," he said. "What would you think about having a grand house party there with your cousins this summer? I know you have barely seen them since all of you went off to school.

"We were together when Maureen married Oscar, but there was not much time to chat. The fact that they live in Belfast does not help matters though it's good for her husband's medical practice. Your mother and I have not seen much of them even though they named their new son after me. It seems better to be together so Little Matt can be introduced to us all."

Grinning, James said, "Father what a wonderful idea. It will be grand to have a last family party there."

"Eugene, what do you think," asked his father. "You have kept eating while we talked about it. Not surprising, roast chicken being your favorite, but would you like to go?"

Eugene took a sip of wine.

"Very much so," he said. "Like James, I understand why you are selling it, but I would very much like to see it one more time."

Teasing his brother, James said, "I will try to remember old times by stuffing you in a trunk."

Eugene glared back.

"If you do I will stuff you in another one and get Susan."

Their father waited while the maid brought round the mashed potatoes.

"Boys, you are too old for that," he said. "I don't think either of you could fit in those old trunks. I had forgotten you had fun up there on rainy days. I remember our picnics and Sunday rambles better. But I am glad you both want to go.

"We are thinking of the last weekend in July. The court docket will be fairly empty and Eugene will be between terms at Trinity. In fact, your mother has already written Patrick and Maureen. She has yet to hear back from Belfast, but Mary has approved the date so it should be all set."

James spoke up.

"Father, I have one question," he said. "Might Susan come along? It is a large house and there will be chaperones. I want her to see the house as I have told her about my childhood visits. Maybe Eugene would like to bring Elizabeth as well."

"I shall have to ask permission, but I think it will be fine since your Aunt Mary and I will be there," said his mother.

"If need be, Susan's mother and Catherine Sullivan could be included. I was thinking of asking Catherine to come. It is such a lovely old fashioned house."

Eugene broke in.

"Oh Mother, could you do that, please? I would like to show Elizabeth everything and have her meet Patrick and Maureen."

His father nodded, saying, "My dear, I think you should invite both young ladies. Squiring them round will give James and Eugene something to do. The house is so large there will be enough bedrooms to go around."

Both sons spoke at once, begging their mother to agree.

Finally, she spoke.

"Yes, Matthew, we shall have room. Don't worry boys, I will write to their mothers today."

James thanked her, followed by Eugene.

Everyone scattered after dessert. Mathew and his sons headed upstairs for a game of billiards. Emily went to her desk to continue working on her lists.

She waited anxiously for a reply from the Sullivans as she was not sure Elizabeth's mother would allow it. She started a list of foodstuffs but was unsure of the final count.

It was a relief when Mrs. Sullivan's note arrived. It contained an acceptance, not the decline Eugene's mother had been fearing.

With her sister in law's help, Emily began to sort everyone into the available rooms.

Taking the coach up both ladies made sure everything was aired out. The preparations were so tiring that it was a welcome moment when the weekend finally came.

All five O'Reillys traveled up on Thursday. Maureen and Oscar met the coach with Little Matt because they had come down the day before.

Giving the baby a kiss, Emily ran off to speak to the cook while everyone else sat chatting. She returned to find Eugene and James admiring the baby in between less complimentary observations about his appearance.

Little Matt was the first baby born into the family since Eugene's birth twenty years earlier. Neither of them had much experience with infants.

Maureen looked distressed. Though she had not expected much interest, she had hoped they would, at least, be polite.

Her Uncle Matthew came to her rescue. He explained to his sons that at that age they had not resembled any living relatives either but that Little Matt soon would look much more like one of them.

Embarrassed the brothers apologized to their cousin.

Laughing, she said, "You two have never even seen a family baby before. I am sure Elizabeth and Susan will think he's adorable when they arrive tomorrow."

Eugene and James went upstairs to see the attic a few minutes later.

As they made their way up, James asked, "What do you think she means about Elizabeth and Susan and Little Matt?"

"Ladies are more interested in babies," said his brother. "I think he's handsome. But he's so small that when they handed him to me, I was terrified I would drop him on the carpet. Father was right to put the towel over his shoulder before he picked him up.

The baby did get a little sick. Look what he did to my shirt."

Eugene and James were dispatched to collect their guests from the coaching depot when they arrived the next day. Having tea on the terrace there were charades after dinner, a Corstown tradition much loved by all.

As dusk was falling, they collected their lit candles and oil lamps from the hall table.

Elizabeth, looking confused, said "My dear Eugene, why are the lamps so old fashioned?"

"Grandmama refused to buy any newer ones. She wanted to keep it as it had been before."

Elizabeth smiled.

"My great auntie is like that too," she said. "She has old lamps and fireplaces instead of stoves and for a few days it is fun. We shall be outside most of tomorrow, which I am looking forward to because I can see all your old haunts.

"You must be sad to see the house sold. For that, I am sorry. But I am happy to be here so I can meet everyone and share a few days of holiday with you before you go back for classes."

Eugene smiled back.

"We shall make sure you and Susan have a good visit. You can play with my baby cousin if you like after we look around. I must warn you that he spat up on me yesterday. Perhaps he will be better behaved tomorrow."

He leaned down to give Elizabeth a brief kiss on the cheek. Straightening up as her aunt was right behind them, he kissed her hand instead. She blushed and then he was gone.

Elizabeth gazed after him while her aunt opened the door. Eugene turned to wave as he reached his room. Her aunt having gone in, Elizabeth waved back.

The weather was glorious the next day, warm with a bright blue sky.

Taking Elizabeth out after breakfast, Eugene showed her the woods where he had shared picnics and gone mushroom hunting before heading for the river.

He omitted tales of his stone skipping days and similar exploits since she seemed a quiet girl who would be unlikely to approve of such goings-on.

Walking arm in arm they crossed the lawn and walked towards the house.

Luncheon was served on the long terrace table, with the baby in his nurse's arms. There was roasted chicken and beef, plain and corned. Baskets of bread and rolls to butter, wine, and cakes and fruit for dessert.

Afterward, the gentlemen retired inside with their cigars. The ladies remained outside. Taking turns holding the baby who by now had gone to sleep they talked of days past and those who were gone.

Eugene and James emerged from the house, as the conversation in the library was a little dull.

To Eugene's relief, Elizabeth looked fascinated rather than bored.

Whispering she said that she was glad to learn of the summers in the house.

His mother mentioned all the fun up in the attic, but she did not go on about the trunks or the kitchen tray races down the stairs into the front hall.

The trunk story might have been too much. Eugene had been careful to portray himself as very quiet and well behaved, a description that fit James far better than it fit him.

A grand dinner was served later, with a gala cake for dessert. Matthew O'Reilly sat at the head of the table offering toasts to everyone present for the last of the wine cellars needed to be consumed.

Later the older people retired and the younger ones retreated to the drawing room. The girls took turns playing the piano while everyone danced.

Wonderful aromas drifted up the stairs, waking Eugene up at dawn.

Following the scent of bacon down to the dining room, he was greeted by a sideboard covered with chafing dishes. Like Christmas, he thought. Kedgeree, bacon and sausages instead of just one and even a compote of stewed prunes as a centerpiece.

Guests drifted in, serving themselves, and sat down at the long walnut table.

Matthew put down his napkin once the guests had left for the morning room.

As the last story ended, he led his family out into the hall and then through the house, telling them what they could choose to take away with them. The more valuable things would be sent on to Dublin or Paris or sold with the house, he said.

Starting at the library, James took some books and a chair.

Moving on to the drawing room, Eugene wanted some of the Wedgwood, saying, "I used to look at these pieces with Grandmama whenever I visited." He also took his silver christening mug from the mantel.

Heading upstairs to the linen closet, Eugene wanted his red eiderdown, tattered though it was, for he had always used it when he was little.

His mother asked "Dear, why would you want that? I remember your carrying it around, but it is about to disintegrate."

"I know Mother," her son said, "but somehow it means Grandmama to me."

Emily nodded.

Laughing her niece said "It's not as though either or you want it, and others have taken a few things that seem odd. Patrick, you have an old inkwell and James a fountain pen."

"You are right," said James. "Each item is a sentimental memory to the one who wants it. Eugene if you want your tattered old eiderdown I'll say no more, and I promise not to tell Elizabeth."

Meeting their friends on the terrace, they left the things they had chosen in a heap in the middle of the passage.

Eugene and James drove all the guests back to the coach depot. They returned to the house for an early tea before driving to Dublin, with enough hours of daylight to avoid lighting the torches to see their way home.

For the first time that weekend, Emily and Matthew sat down to chat once their sons had gone back to their lodgings. They were sad, and yet it was a delight to have been together and meet the new baby.

Once lemonade had been rung for the conversation turned to talk of their sons and their young ladies.

"Glad I am that Miss Sullivan was here," Matthew said. "She has a good head on her shoulders. Very determined, too, which shall counterbalance Eugene's impulsive notions."

His wife laughed.

"Well, at least, some of them," she said. "I do believe he will always be more like Jarleth than you. He seems to have the same adventurous spirit."

Her husband laughed back.

"I don't mind that, but I am worried about those meetings. Once or twice when we were on the terrace, I heard him mention *The Nation*."

Emily frowned.

"The newspaper? My friend's son reads it. I understand why the young people are concerned. We understand better than most. Still it worries me. To have Eugene caught up in it would be hard. We have only two boys and I love him so much. I am sure he is not going to meetings. He would have said something to me.

"Oh Matthew, he is so young. I am not sure we can get him to understand the consequences if he gets involved."

"All we can do is try," said Matthew. "He can't get *The Nation* in Corstown, but I'm sure it's available near his lodgings. I know Patrick reads it. That is why it was mentioned. Bless them. I want freedom for Ireland too, but being old, I think it would better to wait. When I see Eugene I shall ask him about it.

"As proud of him as you are, but just as worried about what could happen. Andrew was sure he would be fine. But when he wasn't able to attend Father's funeral it was very hard."

Emily nodded.

"He shall be here next Saturday for lunch before he goes riding," she said. "I shall try to discuss it with him then. And yes, the Corstown apothecary only carries the *Illustrated Dublin News*, so I am sure he was not reading it on the sly."

They were blissfully unaware that their second son had a copy of *The Nation* stuffed in his pocket as the family carriage rattled downtown. He had purchased it before he caught the coach the week before.

Fascinated by Elizabeth as he was, he found Irish radical

politics even more intriguing.

Eugene didn't take the paper out until he reached his sitting room. If James learned of it, he would surely tell their parents.

Opening it up to check the meeting listings, he found one only three blocks away. A pity public meetings in the library had been banned, as it was just across the street.

One meeting followed another. Eugene and his friend Richard attended as many as possible in hopes of wangling admittance to a secret session.

Success arrived after several weeks of scheming.

To their delight, they managed to meet Thomas Meagher, William Smith-Brien's aide.

It was not as exciting as meeting the great man, but close. Eugene was electrified when he shook his hand, nearly as much as when he met Elizabeth.

He put so much time into organizing help for the August special election that he fell behind in his letter writing. Elizabeth wrote to ask what was wrong since she had become accustomed to two letters a week.

Eugene wrote back to apologize. It would be better in September he wrote though that was not likely. Becoming president of one confederated club he was elected to run a second.

At the end of July, he finally met the great man as Smith-Brien had been away in London for weeks.

When early September rolled around, Eugene had more time for Elizabeth. He felt dejected just the same, for none of the Young Irelanders had managed to gain a seat.

Attending his lectures, he wrote to Elizabeth late into the night, happy with the second but tired of the first.

He was happy he would be done with school in January. But it was bad in another way. He would have to give up his lodgings and go back home. Not only would it be hard to give up his independence but there were all his meetings too.

Going to his father's office, he asked if Matthew would be

willing to continue to pay for his rooms so he could stay downtown.

No luck.

Staring at him, his father shouted "What! I have paid for your lodgings so you could be near Trinity. Once you finish you shall have to move back home, hard as it may be for all parties. At least, it will encourage you to do something with yourself."

Eugene pleaded.

"Please Father," he said. "Just for a little while."

"No, but I have been investigating what you might do. I'm corresponding with Susan's father to see whether anything is available with the Coldstream Guards. I think a military life might suit you. I have not heard back yet, but as he knows their commander I am hopeful there will be something."

"That might suit me though I would rather not fight for the queen."

"Finding a different army is very complicated," said his father. "Why don't you think about this, my son? Don't think of asking your mother as she is partial to you. It's good we are in my office where she can't hear and take your part. It is a large expense. Had we lived closer you would not have had lodgings.

"It shall be uncomfortable for all of us until everyone adjusts, although I suspect you will not mind the food. It will be all right. We will be glad to see you more. We have missed you ever since you went off to Mr. Hall's. You can have your old position back exercising the horses. With you downtown the beasts have suffered."

Eugene smiled at that.

"I shall be happy to exercise the horses," he said. "And I will be glad to see you more too."

His father looked at him.

"Something will turn up. You can keep your mother company until you go with the Guards."

Leaving as his father's clerk arrived Eugene headed off to another meeting, feeling buoyed up as he arrived.

There was excitement in the room. Thomas Meagher had decided to stand for the Waterford seat.

With messages needing to be sent out to other clubs in Cork and Minster so they could assist, a discussion of various strategies began. They talked about what to do in January if Meagher did not get in.

Christmas came and Elizabeth and her aunt arrived for the Season, a most welcome distraction. Worries about the past and future elections had crushed Eugene's spirit and by extension had half crushed his mother from worry over his state of mind.

Seeing Elizabeth at midnight Mass on Christmas Eve he saw her again at supper on Boxing Day.

There was a dinner party to bring in the New Year at the railway hotel. Eugene spent the day before choosing his outfit as he always did. He ignored the remarks a neighbor made while the door was ajar to the effect that his sitting room resembled a jumble sale.

He attended so many dinner parties that his vests started getting tight.

Buoyed up again, his feelings on an optimistic curve, he put thoughts of a Waterford loss out of his mind and counted on a win.

In late January, distress rose up and Eugene's depression was palpable. Meagher did not take the seat.

Doing his best to seem all right, Eugene headed uptown to see the ladies so they would not know. Elizabeth because her father was a staunch Old Irelander, his mother because sensing that his involvement ran deep she feared for his future.

He did his best to keep up an optimistic front into mid-February. Even Elizabeth wanted to know what was wrong.

Explaining was too complicated, and he began to lead almost a double life. An uptown one with Elizabeth and his family, the other downtown with his more radical friends. No one having managed to gain office every plan had collapsed after Waterford.

His mother came to his lodgings to help him pack as his studies came to an end. She left early on the third day, the last book having been packed.

Once she was gone, Eugene pulled out the draft of his speech.

There was crosshatching in places. Adding a few lines, he tried to calm himself. He found it very difficult since it was his first time chairing a secret meeting and only his third speech.

He debated what to put in and what to take out. Smith-Brien's plans stayed in of course, but the paragraphs about Dublin Castle he scratched out since the solicitor general would be very angry. Better a small rising than a life spent in jail.

He had a sandwich and some ale at the tavern. The meeting went well but to his mother's dismay, she was ignored when she arrived to do his shirts.

She called, "Eugene! What's wrong with you? I asked you to bring me your shirts. Is it Elizabeth? Did she write you? Eugene!"

Her son jumped.

"I am sorry Mother," he said. "I am fine and so is Elizabeth. I am worried about my friend."

"You are very distracted these days," she said. "I hope you are not reading that newspaper. You know what happened to your Uncle Andrew. Proud as I am I pray you are not involved with the radicals. If you are, please stop, as only trouble can come of it. Promise me my child."

Eugene's mother was far too upset to notice his hands ball up as he responded.

"No, Mother. I did go to a few meetings with Richard, but I stopped. Still, I am upset, as it is moving awfully slow."

Taking his hand, his mother looked into his eyes.

"I know it needs to change," she said. "I just don't want you to get hurt. We won't talk about it anymore now as the carters shall be here shortly to move your things. Come help me. If it takes too long, we won't be able to meet Elizabeth and her mother for tea."

Eugene sprang into action as the last words left her mouth. He carried things to and fro at a trot and they finished at three. Rushing downstairs, they sailed off in a cab, only to arrive five minutes late.

He graduated the next week, much to the relief of his parents who had not been sure he would finish. The carters brought up everything in the morning. Following behind in the carriage Eugene sat with his winter cloaks and boots piled high around him as they had not fit.

Feeling very much at loose ends once Elizabeth had left the city Eugene led his meetings.

If he went round to the back door on his return and took off his boots, he could sneak up with his parents none the wiser. With the stairs oiled nothing squeaked.

The maids said nothing. They might have been sound asleep he thought or maybe they were protecting him.

The meetings and Mr. Moonlight didn't fill up enough time, and melancholy started seeping its way back. He was a man of action. Having nothing to do but think did him no good.

He shopped downtown with his mother and wrote letters to Elizabeth, spending entire afternoons with a pen. A letter went out every other day.

Susan's father wrote, saying that a spot in the Coldstream Guards would not open up until later in the spring.

Eugene spent hours lying on his bed, staring at the ceiling and looking for shapes as he had in the nursery.

Finally, he decided to write Uncle Andrew in hopes of an invitation to visit, because that his father would approve. Hopefully, he could go with Richard. It would be fun to see Paris with a friend.

A more sympathetic ear could only help. Surely his uncle would understand.

Perhaps the French army had a spot. More interesting than the guards that would be and with better uniforms.

Then too Paris would be a good place to learn to build barricades, a skill that would be vital if Meagher managed to take the castle.

Going downstairs while his mother was out, Eugene borrowed her fountain pen and wrote:

18 February, '48
Dublin
Dear Uncle Andrew,

I hope you are well and that the winter has not been too bad in Paris.

I would love to see you for I have heard so much about you over the years. I have not been able to see you and I would love to do so. I know you are working, but I am not asking to be entertained.

I know it is presumptuous, but the Season being over, my beloved Elizabeth has gone back to the country.

I am hoping you shall allow my Trinity friend to accompany me. He would like to meet you since I have told him so much about you.

We wish to visit the cafes and such places and have a holiday from our schooling.

Most of all I hope to see you as I have wanted to get to know you better all these years. Uncle Edward having died when I was little, I have been sadly without time spent with my uncles. I will bring funds to pay for what we spend so you need not worry about that.

Please reply soon. I truly need a change of scene,

Your loving nephew,

Eugene

Hearing his father's voice in the hall, Eugene used his mother's red sealing wax and the seal his father had given him for Christmas. He jammed the letter into his coat pocket and went down to the corner shop for the post.

Waiting for his uncle's response, he wrote Elizabeth so often that she was impressed.

Much to his mother's distress, he even offered to accompany her on some of her visits. With a distressed look, she agreed as many times when he had come to ride he had not even come in to greet her.

A letter addressed to Matthew O'Reilly arrived from Paris two weeks later.

Spotting it as he passed through the hall, Eugene nearly reached out to take it as the maid went to put it in the library for Matthew was in London.

Once the maid had gone down to the kitchen, he sat down at his father's desk. He wanted to know his uncle's response badly. He would have steamed the letter open had it been possible without breaking his uncle's seal.

Days ticked by until his father returned. He spent hours staring at the envelope whenever his mother was safely upstairs or had left the house.

Eugene's father returned home.

Sitting in the drawing room, Eugene listened to his father's footsteps as he went upstairs with his grip and then came back down. Disappearing into the library Eugene's father closed the door while Eugene ascended the stairs to his room.

Eugene paced up and down before the fire, jamming his hands into his pockets with the door closed so no one could see.

One of the maids knocked on the door just as the clock struck the half hour and told him that his father wanted to see him in ten minutes.

A flurry ensued. Rushing to the washstand to freshen up Eugene patted his curls down. When he was nervous, his hair stood nearly as straight up as his father's did.

His father embraced Eugene again as he entered the library and offered him a seat.

"A letter arrived from Andrew while I was gone. He enclosed one you sent to him asking if you could visit."

Eugene nodded.

"I thought it would be nice if Richard and I could visit for a few weeks," he said. "I have been feeling melancholy and have little to do until I can start with the Guards."

"You are the sort of young man who needs to be active. In any case, Andrew writes that he would be glad to have you and your friend stay for a month. He is working so he cannot amuse you, but the two of you are old enough to go around by yourselves in the afternoons.

"Your melancholy worries me," Eugene's father added. "A change of scene would do you good."

"I hope by getting away for a few weeks I shall feel better when I come back," Eugene said. "I very much want to go. Paris is supposed to be a wonderful city."

"It is glorious, especially in the spring. I shall write Andrew back today and accept his kind invitation. He wants you to come but wanted to know if I approved. He is worried about your state of mind, as am I.

"You will not be away long, and you can see your young lady when you return. You can write her and purchase a small gift. Ladies like small things from Paris, my son."

At dinner, they talked about the lectures and plays Matthew had attended in London, as he seldom spoke of business affairs with his wife.

Then he shifted to talk of riding, saying that Eugene was doing a splendid job exercising the family mounts, even the carriage horses.

Eugene thanked his father.

Not mentioning that he exercised the carriage horses by having the coachman take him back and forth to his confederacy club meetings he nodded his head.

The coachman passed the time at a nearby tavern, waiting for Eugene to emerge for a final pint. His parents would never find out what he was doing.

The meeting the evening before having run very late, Eugene retired to his room after dinner to read.

As his parents came up the stairs he heard his mother say "At least in Paris he will make different friends. It's sensible to send him, Matthew. I hope he gets this nonsense out of his head. I trust your brother, but our son finds odd companions."

His father started to reply as their bedroom door closed. Eugene felt encouraged since she had agreed.

Getting out of bed he said a brief prayer. More than anything else he did not want to hurt his mother.

Walking over to the window, he gazed out at the moon. It was scary, yes. But Smith-Brien was sure there would be a rising. Surely he would know for he knew Cork and Waterford well. Like Corstown, Meagher said.

All that was needed was some dry tinder and a match. In twelve months, there would be a free Ireland, and he would not be in a prison cell as James predicted.

Eugene slept in the next day. The rain came down in sheets.

Starting another note to Elizabeth, he bathed and went downstairs at ten in search of breakfast.

He was surprised to find James in the morning room with their mother.

Running over James gave him a bear hug and told him the news. He had proposed to Susan and she had accepted.

Eugene walked into his mother's open arms. There was a huge smile on her face as she left a few tears of joy on his shoulder. Tearing himself away he went to get something to eat since he was starving.

Plate and teacup in hand, he listened between bites.

Explaining, James said, "I asked her three weeks ago, but the colonel needed asking before it was announced. We think perhaps we'll get married next fall.

"I have felt terrible that I couldn't tell you. Nothing I could do but wait. I was nervous talking to Colonel MacDonnell, but he was terribly kind. He said that my career was going well and that I could have her, for they know I shall be good to her."

Jumping up his mother hugged him.

"When you were here last, it looked like you were bursting with something you couldn't tell us," she said. "Oh James, what wonderful news. Don't you agree Eugene?"

Eugene nodded, his mouth filled with the crusts of his toast.

He swallowed. Taking a sip of tea, he agreed.

"Yes Mother, it is wonderful. My brother, I am sure you will be very happy since she is a great girl."

Eugene wanted to leave at eleven. His mother had already begun speaking of the wedding trip and other ladies' details.

But he had to stay. His father had been summoned home to lunch to hear James' news.

There were more embraces as Matthew came through the door just ahead of Aunt Mary. Hot meat was served for lunch with sherry after.

By two o'clock Eugene had managed to sneak back up the stairs while his father and brother retreated down the hall to the library.

His mother sat with her sister in law in the morning room enthusing over the bride's gown, reception, wedding trip and everything else. Since Maureen had been wed only a few years before the ladies could compare notes.

Shutting the doors behind him, Eugene overheard them say, "The Lake Country shall be perfect for their wedding trip. Quite lovely that time of year."

Eugene sat down with Elizabeth's note and shared the news.

Lying down, he stared at the ceiling.

Sitting up with a start he remembered Meagher's speech at the last meeting. He had spoken of a delegation to Paris to visit the revolutionaries. Maybe he could arrange to be included. Thoughts running through his head, he fell asleep.

The next morning Matthew took Eugene into his library.

"You need to be cautious," he said. "You should resign from your clubs, not just the offices. Think of what happened to your uncle. That was mild. They hung many men who did little more.

"While I was in the City I heard of a new bill making its way through Westminster. They are trying to make possible sedition enough to lock someone up. I am sure you don't understand. I don't have time to explain. I must hurry to my office.

"Changing the subject, between you and me, I am excited about James' engagement. Susan is a wonderful young woman from a fine family. She will be a wonderful addition to ours and I look forward to having a daughter. But I cannot spend one more day listening to the ladies' chatter of gowns and veils.

"I suggest that you go riding often, and when you're home, do your best to listen. In any case, I have written to Andrew to accept his invitation. What's more, the colonel wrote that you can start with the Guards in mid-May. So I told Andrew you will be there from early April to the first week in May. Does that suit you?"

"Yes Father, it does," Eugene said. "And thank you. Afterward, I can drill with the Guards until the wedding. I don't mind hearing about the wedding clothes. Talking about food is nearly as good as eating it, but I shall try to ignore the talk about the wedding trip."

His father replied, saying "Good for you, just listening is almost more than my nerves can stand. But your mother is having great fun. She has a right since she has missed having a daughter.

"I'll get your packet boat tickets when I buy my own ticket back to London. Promise me you will end or, at least, curtail your revolutionary activities so we need not worry. I am asking Andrew to keep an eye on you so that you do not find more meetings in Paris."

"Thank you for the approval and the tickets," Eugene said. "I do not think many revolutionaries will be in the Paris cafes, so it shall not be hard to avoid meeting them."

Looking at his son hard, Eugene's father smiled and said, "I love you, my son. Much as Ireland is in need of reform, it is better to wait. But I don't want to fuss anymore. I am glad you wrote Andrew. What better time to go on a trip than before you start to work like me and have trouble getting away."

Ten more days inched by. Eugene got goodbye kisses from

Polly and his mother. James took him and Richard down to the docks, waving as they sailed east on their grand adventure.

The trip began uneventfully, and then a squall blew up as they were exiting the Solent.

Eugene and Richard wanted to stay on deck but thought better of it when the captain ordered them below.

Looking rather green for he had only sailed to England twice before Richard sat with Eugene in the salon.

Eugene tried to calm his friend.

"We won't sink," he said. "This is normal my friend. We are still in a channel."

Then he rushed for his berth in a fit of seasickness, leaving his friend not entirely reassured.

The next day they sat on the deck and enjoyed the sea air, catching their first glimpse of France as they steamed into the harbor at Cherbourg.

Standing towards the bow, they watched tugs steer the steamer into its berth.

They looked on as sailors jumped out of nowhere, swarming like mice around a cheese to secure the fore and aft ropes.

Going in for a minute they ran back out. They watched the gangplank swing out, followed by a second further aft for the baggage.

As they walked towards the customs shed, Eugene nearly had his foot run over by a longshoreman dragging a trunk.

After much pulling out of papers and reuniting with their baggage they boarded the boat train and headed east.

Eugene walked into Andrew O'Reilly's open arms the next day in Paris. Just as his father had told him, Andrew looked like an older twin to Patrick with the same light brown hair, though he was thinner and taller.

Both young men were so exhausted by the time they got to the flat that they could barely sit upright.

Chatting with them in the drawing room Andrew finally had the maid show them to their room since neither young fellow could keep his eyes open.

Andrew followed along.

Apologetically, he said, “I hope you don’t mind sharing. I have only one guest room and it’s a small flat.”

Eugene answered, saying ”No uncle, it is fine. I am glad just to be here. We had roommates at school and we are used to it.”

Smiling his uncle said, “I am glad you don’t mind. Matthew, I know, has an entire townhouse. I was not sure how you would feel.”

They walked into the room. There were three windows overlooking a park, a day bed on each side and a carpet that matched the drapes.

Turning to Andrew, Richard said, “It’s bigger than my room back home. All I want to do is lie down and take a nap if that’s all right. I am sorry you had planned an outing, but perhaps we can go later.”

Andrew nodded, quietly closing the door as his young guests’ heads hit the pillows.

He spoke to cook about dinner and sat down to work on his story for the *London Times* because he was their Paris correspondent.

Awakening at five both boys came out for a few biscuits before they went off to bathe and dress for dinner.

Andrew chuckled to himself as they emerged. His nephew had inherited his Beau Brummel ways. His shirt front pleats were of the latest mode, unlike those of his friend.

Conversation halted as the boys devoured their steak and potatoes.

Once the maid had brought dessert Eugene’s uncle mentioned that there were many cafes nearby, for he had to be gone all day.

Saying that they could go to Versailles on Sunday and see its gardens he added that he had bought tickets for two operas. Verdi for the first evening, he said, and Halevy’s *Valley of Andorra* for the second as it was supposed to be quite funny.

“I hope you two like opera,” Uncle Andrew said.

Eugene nodded.

“Thank you, uncle. Mother read that the Halevy work is excellent and a trip to Versailles would be wonderful. I have heard so much about it, especially from Cousin Maureen, who loves art. As for the days you will be gone, we shall be fine. If you can just show us where the nearest cafes are, we will be all set.”

Richard agreed and Uncle Andrew responded.

"I can see that you two are old enough to find your way home, "he said, "even after a few glasses of wine. A terrific city this is, especially when you are young."

Eugene nodded, followed by Richard. The port came round. Uncle Andrew asked about Dublin. He spoke about the United rising, but only in general terms, for Eugene's uncle could see that his guests' eyes were as big as saucers.

Awakening early the next morning Eugene joined his uncle over croissants and coffee, as Richard was still asleep.

His uncle spoke of Corstown.

Then, clearing his throat, he said, "How are you, Eugene? It's a delight to meet you after all this time, but like your father I am concerned about your melancholy."

"I am trying to cheer up," said his nephew. "I had hoped someone would win so that we could try in Westminster. I helped with the campaigns, first in August and then I worked on Meagher's campaign in January.

"I'm not sure what comes next. Mother and Father would like me to stop and I'm trying hard to do less. If I do more, Elizabeth will not approve. Very conservative her father is. Not like us."

"It's rather muddled, I can see," his uncle said, "Ireland and the girl. Eventually, it should straighten itself out. Your mother told me about the girl and she sounds wonderful.

"But I can see the difficulty. No one has taken a seat. The old blood is hanging on as it were. I know. As a correspondent, it is my job to keep up. Meagher's loss was the worst of it as he was best prepared. Nothing for it now but wait till Downing Street calls the elections again."

Continuing, he said, "Certainly I hope you do no more. Not because I would not be proud, for that I already am. In that sense, you're more my boy than Matthew's. But I have paid quite a price. Minor as my role was, they were angry and drove me out.

"Your grandfather was terrified I would be hanged since many were. I only helped organize and did not fight, which is why they didn't take my life. But even so I was detained for two horrendous months. I get chills just remembering when your Grandmama came to see me there.

"And of course, in the end, I was exiled for life. I have been happy here, but all of us suffered when I could not even return to bury your grandparents. Nor could I help Mary when Edward died. It nearly killed my mother. She never got over it."

Scratching his knee, Eugene's eyes started to glaze over as Richard appeared in the doorway.

His uncle fell silent for a moment till Richard left to have his coffee. Uncle Andrew asked if he was republican. Eugene nodded.

Uncle Andrew was quiet for a moment.

Starting up again, he said, "At any rate, I think a month away will do you good. When I leave, I shall tell you where to find the café, and I'll give you some money for your brandies so you can pass a pleasant afternoon.

"You need to rest. Try to put all of this behind you. It makes sense that Ireland's condition upsets you. Still you must try to think about better things. Your young lady maybe. Please rest, though. Your mother is most worried about you, and even to me you look nervous."

"I'm here because I know I need a change," Eugene said. "Besides, I am only happy when I have something to do. Nothing to do in Dublin now but wait for the Guards to start. That and sit with Mother while she chatters of Susan's wedding. I have too much time to reflect on Ireland's fate."

Reappearing, Richard said "Good morning, sir," as he balanced a cup of coffee on his knee.

Andrew greeted him.

"I have been having a talk with your friend about his goings on," he said. "He tells me you too have played a part. Indeed, our king was overthrown in February but that need not concern you.

"As I have told Eugene, I think you should enjoy the cafes. We can see a few points of interest on Sundays."

Uncle Andrew went on in the same vein for a while. His visitors did their best to look fascinated, as older people always seemed to talk that way.

Eugene's uncle finally glanced at the mantel clock and, rising to his feet, went off to get dressed and be ready to leave.

His guests relaxed when he headed down the hall. Leaning back against the cushions they breathed deep. It seemed there was a lecture around every corner.

When Andrew reemerged, frockcoat and hat in hand, they sat back up. Eugene accompanied him down the stairs and to the end of the block so his uncle could point out the café right around the corner.

Andrew gave Eugene a hug which he did not like and a handful of francs which he did.

Eugene retraced his steps as his uncle climbed into the cab. He spent the rest of the morning reading the Paris newspapers while Richard snoozed in an armchair.

Setting out for the café after lunch they took an outdoor table, as the day was fine and rather warm.

They ordered absinthe instead of brandy, with its accompanying spoons and lumps of sugar. On the packet boat, they had heard that absinthe was the fashionable drink to have in Paris and they longed to try it. They found it was a most interesting shade of green, and rather bitter without the sugar.

They whiled away the afternoon as young women walked by in twos and threes, barely having enough energy to walk back when the church bells struck four.

Returning at six Uncle Andrew found both houseguests splayed out on his sofa. When they told him about the absinthe, he smiled broadly and said little for if he was their age he would have tried it too.

Eugene and Richard managed to rise when dinner was announced. They consumed a fair amount of chicken and then sat playing euchre in the drawing room until it was time to retire.

The next few days passed in the same fashion, sleeping late and afternoons spent around the corner.

Eugene did his best to puzzle out why his uncle said nothing. Must be that his uncle thought watching girls was better than thoughts of Ireland.

Whispering, Richard replied with his best advice.

"Don't ask him," he said. "If your uncle knew you were less interested in girls than in finding a barricade building tutor he would send you home."

They went to Versailles on Saturday to see the chateau and its gardens. The next day another week began.

Over dinner, Uncle Andrew said, "Eugene, your father would want you to do what you are doing. Rest and have fun. It will be a good memory when you are an older gentleman with your own children and townhouse."

Eugene and Richard went downtown on Wednesday.

Meeting Andrew at his newspaper office, they went on to the opera house. The fun was counterbalanced by another lecture, but they agreed to every word. Better to let it all go, for they didn't want to go home.

To Eugene's joy, they managed to meet some acquaintances of Richard's on Thursday. Thrills washed over him like a waterfall because these men had been on the front lines against the king and they knew the ins and outs of street fighting.

Friday and Saturday they slept and went out. Their days were punctuated by Mass every other morning, for Andrew was pious.

The third week, they went to *The Valley of Andorra* on Tuesday, finding it more amusing than the Verdi of the previous week.

On Wednesday, a messenger arrived with a note for Richard from Smith-Brien. Fortunately, it was after Uncle Andrew left for work, as only that morning he had lectured them again.

Just the name on the envelope was exciting. Richard handed it to Eugene to read:

My Dear Richard,

I hope you are having a pleasant holiday. Meagher and I have decided to follow through with our plan to approach the French. Hopefully, they can be persuaded to help as they did at Gantry Bay in '96.

We are at the hotel mentioned on the envelope and would like you to meet us tomorrow so you may accompany us. Just send a note with the lad.

Sincerely,
William

Eugene read the note.

"That address is not far from the Opera Comique. You can get there and back without uncle finding out, for he will be very angry if he does. You need to hide the note as he knows who Smith-Brien is. But why did they only write you?"

"I don't think they know you are here," said Richard. "I gave them the address before we left but didn't say we were visiting your uncle. Just that I was going on a trip. Don't look so upset. I am sure they will be happy to see you."

Eugene tried not to look angry, but he felt terribly insulted.

His friend said, "Too late to go now since it is nearly five. But we can go tomorrow. Now where is your foolscap? I need to write a note for the boy. I know where your uncle keeps his, but I am not sure we can use it."

"I am not sure either," said Eugene.

Walking down the hall, he returned with his new writing portfolio, for the boy wanted to leave.

Taking it from his friend's hand, Richard said "Very nice. Morocco leather."

"A graduation gift from Father," Eugene murmured as Richard wrote his note, folding it in half before he handed it to the messenger.

Changing into their dinner attire, they sat in the drawing room. They waited for Uncle Andrew to return, doing their best to disguise their excitement after he arrived.

Pleading exhaustion, they went to their room immediately after dinner. It was becoming near impossible to control their jubilation as broad grins spread across both their faces.

They barely slept.

Eugene ate so little for breakfast that Uncle Andrew was concerned he might be ill.

Going back to their room until he was gone, Eugene and Richard soon emerged in their best outfits. Hiring a cab at the corner, they headed downtown.

Eugene was so excited he nearly pushed his friend into the gutter in his eagerness to depart the cab.

His fists were balled up so tight his pockets began ripping. He had only once been in the presence of both leaders.

Richard tried to calm him as they approached the desk.

Ascending to the third floor Eugene knocked on the door. Smith-Brien let them in. Richard explained that since he was staying with Eugene's uncle he had brought Eugene along.

"Eugene, I am glad to see you," said the great man. "But you look very nervous and we haven't even gone to pay our call on Mr.

LaMartine yet."

Eugene managed to squeak out "I'll be better by then. I promise."

Thomas Meagher crossed the room.

Giving Eugene a brief embrace, he said, "Glad you could come. Had we known you were there, your name would have been included. In any case, we are all nervous about paying our call. But yes, we'll be calm once we arrive."

They ate in the dining room and then went to get ready, as Thomas had been anxious that they not spill on their best frockcoats. Eugene did his best not to cut any capers for fear he would be sent back.

Ascending the stairs when they arrived they announced themselves as they sank into armchairs, their palms covered with sweat.

"A meeting in five minutes perhaps," said the aide.

Smith-Brien muttered.

"Might have been longer had Mr. O'Reilly contained himself," he said.

Eugene overheard but managed to stay mute.

The door opened and everyone filed in. Meagher and Smith-Brien stepped forward, extending their hands which Mr. LaMartine politely shook. Richard nodded politely. They began to speak of their need for acknowledgment and help.

Much to their relief, the French leader heard them out, but they were dismayed that his response was far more tepid than they had hoped.

Instead of offering aid he merely said:

"I shall think about it, gentlemen. Once we have decided, my aide will let you know. We have just driven out our king and have little energy for overseas adventures."

Looking startled Smith-Brien said, "If all you can offer is an acknowledgment of our efforts, we shall still be happy. Our efforts are inspired by yours."

An aide cut in as he began his next sentence.

"At the conclusion of our meeting, we shall take up the matter. Maybe we can do something, but nothing can be decided today."

Turning Smith-Brien faced the others who stood, all in a row, hands jammed in their pockets as the aide saw them out.

"Thank you for seeing us," Smith-Brien said. "We look forward to hearing what you decide. Hopefully, it will be favorable. We are true revolutionaries in the same spirit as you."

They sat silently in the cab on the way back to the hotel in a state of shock since they had expected better. So much hope and energy had been expended.

Piping up, Eugene said, "I don't know why we left so fast. Perhaps we could have persuaded them."

Meagher gave him a stern look.

"No, I don't think we could have," he said. "It seemed that their minds were made up before we got there. We shall have to go back to our planning now since all else has failed."

Richard muttered something from his corner of the cab.

Smith-Brien turned.

"It did not go as we wished. We may stay one more day in case they decide for us, but no longer. We will be more useful in Dublin. I bet the British ambassador spoke to him first. It makes me hate them all the more. Or perhaps Lamartine is loath to offend, but their minds seemed made up, I must say."

Back at the flat, Eugene and Richard played desultory hands of whist all the rest of the afternoon, one listless round after the other.

Arriving Uncle Andrew inquired about their melancholy, for a miasma had settled over his guests' heads.

Eugene managed to distract him, but a sinking feeling settled in. Surely it would be only a matter of days before his uncle learned of the failed mission and their part in it.

They took their usual seats at the café the next day. A note from Meagher had come just before they left, sent from the train station for he and Smith-Brien were headed for Dublin. The French had written, declining to help.

Much to their relief, Uncle Andrew returned home that day in a good mood.

The next day he arrived early, just as they were going out.

Stomping up the stairs, he burst in on them with his hair sticking up, a sure sign of distress in an O'Reilly.

Seeing Eugene begin to put on his frockcoat he demanded,

"Where do you think you're going?"

Eugene stammered, saying "Only to the café, uncle. We shall be home for dinner. But why are you home now instead of at your office?"

"You know why. Now take your coats off and sit down. I have to write Matthew and let him know that you shall return on the next packet boat. Really, Eugene, I trusted you and your friend to behave. But no, you joined the president's mission."

Richard spoke up.

"We have been trying to behave as you ask, Mr. O'Reilly," he said. "But William Smith-Brien is my friend, so I felt obligated to visit. Then, before we knew it, they were off to pay their call and they asked us to come."

Eugene broke in, saying, "That is all we have done, Uncle Andrew. The rest of the time we have been in the café."

"Yes. I know that's where you've been. No one minds that. It is a normal thing for young men on holiday to have a drink and watch the world go by. But I was charged to keep you from your radical friends and this you have done anyway. You shall have to go home."

"But I was to stay another week. That and our call did not accomplish anything."

Andrew O'Reilly looked his nephew in the eye.

"Do you not realize that they don't want to anger Westminster?" he asked. "Being your age you probably don't, but that's the way of things in the real world. I understand this and your father does too.

"That's how I found out. A dispatch came from the president's office describing you two, along with the leaders of the Young Ireland group who paid a call on the new republic's leaders, to no avail. I could have told you it would not work. But of course, you failed to ask. Now I have to answer to your parents for what you have done."

Concluding, Uncle Andrew said, "I understand. At your age, I thought the same way. I suppose I would go into exile again for Ireland, but it has been hard. You two need to stop before the same thing happens to you."

Richard cleared his throat.

"Do I have to leave too," he asked, "or just Eugene?"

"You have to leave my flat, yes, but I cannot make you leave France if you can find another place to stay.

"Eugene, I have sent your father a message with one of the Times carrier pigeons which he shall have tomorrow. So you are leaving then. I shall take you to the station and give you enough money for the packet boat."

Richard said nothing.

Eugene asked, "Not even one more day? For Father may be in London when the message comes."

His uncle shook his head.

"If you had not met with your radical friends, you could stay longer," he said. "But by going to the palace with them, you have managed to get written up in the Times and no doubt the Dublin papers too. So my hands are tied. If I don't send you home, your father shall come and fetch you."

Eugene swallowed hard at his uncle's last remark.

"All right, I will pack my things. Though I want a bottle of absinthe to take along. We cannot get that in Dublin."

Uncle Andrew laughed.

"I have one," he said, "a gift that I have not opened. But don't say anything, as Matthew will think I am corrupting you. He's strictly a brandy and bitters kind of fellow. I wish this had not happened. I have much enjoyed having you and your friend here. Go and start packing up. If you get it all done, I shall let you go off to the café."

Both young men went down the hall with their tails between their legs to pack their grips.

Eugene, feeling rather shaky, complained to his friend, saying "I thought I'd have a few more days at least."

Everything was packed. A message was sent to Richard's cousin in Paris. Uncle Andrew kept his word about the café. But to their dismay, he came along to make sure they did not get into trouble.

Richard's cousin appeared in the morning and Eugene wished he had a Paris cousin too.

Taking a cab to the station together, Eugene got out and the others went home. The only bright spot was the extra francs Uncle Andrew put in Eugene's hands to buy absinthe in Cherbourg.

All too soon Eugene was standing at his parents' front door in

Dublin praying that Polly would answer because she never yelled.

But it was his father that appeared, his hair as straight up as his brother's had been in Paris.

Matthew gave his son a hug and then a tongue lashing that was almost as bad as his brother's.

"Fortunately, your mother is visiting Susan's mother. If she was here, she would be lying prostrate upstairs. It's not Andrew's fault. You are too old for a keeper. We did know that your friend goes to the same meetings. But no one knew about Smith-Brien's scheme until it broke in the papers. Truly I thought your judgment was better."

Eugene tried to speak up for himself. His father marched him into the morning room, for the library was being repainted.

Sitting his son down in a chair, he continued his lecture and Eugene let the words wash over him. At school, it would easily have merited a thrashing from Mr. Hall, but since he was now three inches taller than his father that was not possible.

He tried to listen.

Matthew went on and on, saying, "We knew nothing of your goings on at Trinity. But you are upsetting everyone with fear of what could occur.

"If anyone could dissuade you I thought it would be Andrew. I was small then but I remember how fearful it was when your Grandmama went to visit him. He was held in a terrible place, a dungeon really, built before Kilmainham, which replaced it."

"Of course, I wish Ireland was free," Eugene's father continued, "but I am old and have the patience that goes with age. I do believe the Repeal Association will yet prevail. The Sedition Act you appear to have forgotten about. It's not signed yet, but it passed the House of Lords.

"They can far more easily put you in a cell once it's signed. They shall be able to detain whomever they like with no real proof of anything. You're taking an even greater risk than Andrew, perhaps.

"But at least you need not unpack. I have heard from Colonel MacDonnell. A spot has arisen early with the Coldstream Guards at their Aldershot barracks. I have already procured your ticket."

"I need to rest first and see Mother, James, and Elizabeth," Eugene said.

"That I am sorry about. James, you can see. He shall be here for dinner. But you need to be somewhere where your friends aren't. This is all I can say. I am at my wit's end. I love you my child and I am trying to help you."

"I love you too, Father. It's just that I'm so afraid change will never come. But maybe I'll like the Guards. They have wonderful uniforms with lots of braid. I remember the uniforms from Mr. Hall's. My friend's uncle was a Guard and he would visit."

"That I hadn't known," Matthew said. "You can leave in the morning. But go up and change. I can see you are tired. If you have the energy, you can take out Mr. Moonlight.

"The Guards should suit you well. It will give you something to do. Lots of riding at Aldershot and that you will like. Perhaps you shall make it your career. That or you would make a good cavalryman with your fondness for horseflesh. I would have been terrible, but you would do well.

"Come, hug me, for I am glad to see you, and then go up and see Polly. She is so worried about you."

Eugene found himself on another packet boat in the morning, heading for the southern English coast as his father had refused to let him wait an extra day.

Eugene hated his new commander on sight. The commander felt the same way about him because Eugene appeared to lack any discipline and would not take orders. Indeed, he spent all his time riding while refusing to do the drill.

He reappeared on his parents' doorstep two weeks later. As luck would have it, his father had left for work, and he fell into the loving arms of his mother.

Life was difficult in the O'Reilly home for the next few weeks. Matthew and Emily did their best to watch their youngest born like hawks.

The object of their concern did his best to be reassuring, but he had no independence. He searched for more oil to quiet the squeaks on the back stairs when he came in late, having snuck out to a meeting.

"My child, you do not understand," his father said when he found Eugene in the hall, boots in hand. "Because of my work, I know what the British are thinking. You are on thin ice. They aren't sure whether you met Smith-Brien in Paris."

Eugene said, "I am careful."

His father's hands gripped his shoulders.

"Your mother is weeping into her pillow. Please stop going to meetings. The police would have come to question you, but because I am the law agent they have not appeared. They know I will not allow any radical meetings under my roof. You are turning my hair gray, my boy."

Eugene watched his father go off towards his bedroom before he went into his own.

He felt terrible, for both leaders had been at the meeting. He did not want to lie, but his parents were so upset.

Meeting locations were switched so often one forgot where they were. They had not been held in the same place twice since he got back from Aldershot. Surely no one was following him. He could outride them all.

Drifting off to sleep, Eugene woke near noon and went downstairs for breakfast. A deep sense of foreboding settled in as he waited for his father to return.

With fear in his heart, for he was tired of his father's tongue lashings and his mother's tears, he appeared in the dining room at the stroke of six.

At first, things went well because Matthew spoke only of Corstown. Being glad to be left in peace his son said little.

Just after the trifle was served, his father lifted his fork, announcing, "After dinner we shall have a little talk in the library about the need for you to be cautious."

Eugene stared hard into his water glass.

Looking at him his mother said, "Eugene, are you paying attention? Your father is trying to help you. Put your fork down."

Eugene shifted his gaze, as his mother rarely corrected him at the table.

"Yes Father, I know. The laws are hard for me to understand. It's easier for me to concentrate on riding and Elizabeth and leave legal matters to you and James."

"I know and that's fine," said his father. "It makes sense, for your brother has no riding skills. Indeed, you can take jumps no one but Jarleth would try. But we are straying far from the subject."

Matthew rose and kissed his wife.

"If you can excuse us, my dear."

In the library, they waited for their brandies. Matthew took out two cigars, bestowing one on Eugene. It was a surprise as cigars were his great luxury, rarely shared.

"What is sedition?" Eugene asked. "I don't even know that."

His father looked shocked.

"Treason," he said. "An act against the crown. What they convicted Andrew on. Until last week, a judge had to approve the warrants. Now the queen has signed the new law. Someone who is merely suspected of sedition can be held. They need not prove anything.

"You can't be held forever, but truly you don't want to see the inside of Kilmainham. My criminal law friend has been there many times. He tells me it is far better than the old dungeon, but still not a place where I want you to be."

Eugene smoked a bit and started on a second brandy.

Then he said, "I thought we had rights that can't be changed."

"Yes and no. Since the law has been signed, your rights are limited. The papers and I weren't the only ones to learn of your escapade. The queen was quite displeased, as Lord Palmerston wrote to tell me."

"The good part is that the death sentence is gone," Eugene's father added, "as they cannot get a conviction from an Irish jury. You get years in Tasmania instead, and two years of hard labor for a lesser charge. When I think of such a punishment in connection with you, it is painful beyond belief.

"Smith-Brien is safe because he is a member of parliament, but in this house, that's cold comfort. So you must promise to stop."

"I think many are as sick of the British as we are," said Eugene. "But I understand about the law now, and will try to be more careful. Uncle Andrew told me about his dungeon. I don't want to be there."

His father answered.

"It was terrible," he said. "The price to be paid can be very high. Your friend Richard can visit you, but no one else. If Thomas Meagher crosses this threshold, you will have to deal first with me and then the authorities."

"That I would not allow for Elizabeth would be most upset if she heard. In any case, Meagher is way above me. He would not even want to come here."

Chuckling, his father poured a little more brandy.

"Here, help me up. My rheumatism is bothering me. We can rejoin your mother."

The next few days passed peacefully.

Meeting friends for a pint of bitters when his father was due to come home Eugene managed to stay calm.

To his surprise, on Thursday after lunch his father appeared and asked him upstairs for a round of billiards.

As soon as he picked up his cue, Matthew launched into another lecture.

Eugene's brain glazing over, he listened.

"The authorities know where Meagher and Richard are staying. They intend to go out and pick them up to be questioned at the Castle because Smith-Brien's paper is getting worse every day. You may not leave the house tonight."

Eugene picked up the chalk.

"But I was going to go have a pint later."

"You are having a pint now and you can have another if you wish it," retorted his father in a short voice.

The first game was over. Another started. Matthew won because he was a better player. His son asked, "Do the British really know where they are? It is all kept secret."

"Yes. An informant has told them. The new law will let them pick up Meagher. Now that they have Smith-Brien in their snare they can take him too. It's one thing to be a theoretical radical and quite another to be a real one, at least in the eyes of the Crown."

Eugene muttered something.

Cringing, his father said, "You sound like Andrew. Maybe you can avoid joining him in exile. In the meantime, you can stay put and keep your mother company. You are better at listening to her wedding chatter than I am."

They played euchre after dinner.

Following his wife up the stairs, Matthew retired at ten while Eugene sat in the drawing room with a book and a fan.

There was a quiet knock on the door at eleven. A messenger boy stood on the doorstep with a note from Richard:

Old man, the British are on our trail. They have learned of our whereabouts. We have received a warning.

We need help and somewhere to hide. By the time you get this, we shall be in the darkened streets. No moon tonight, only the occasional torch which we will do our best to avoid. Headed for your crescent and will arrive in an hour or so.

Yours,
Richard

4 DUBLIN

Eugene sat back down with his book, watching the small hand on the mantel clock make its circuit around the dial. He thanked his lucky stars. If James had not gone back downtown, he would still be up.

Creeping down the back hall, he unlocked the stable yard door. His father always locked it after dinner and a quick exit might be needed.

As the clock chimed midnight, he sat back down with a yawn for he had been up late the evening before.

A loud banging made him jump. When he opened the door, Thomas Meagher was revealed slamming the brass knocker with both hands.

Eugene pulled his friends in. Rushing to slide the pocket doors closed he heard his father's voice calling out "Who is there?" followed by his father making his way down the front stairs in his nightshirt and cap.

Eugene did his best to push everyone into the drawing room. Richard his father recognized and Meagher he knew from the papers.

Eugene smiled weakly as his father stepped onto the

carpet. Matthew O'Reilly looked angrier than his son had ever seen him. His hair was sticking up as straight as a candle.

As he pushed past to lock the front door, Eugene's father said, "You two are not going to escape the British so easily. Mr. Meagher and Mr. O'Gorman, you are not welcome in my house. I will not harbor revolutionaries."

Eugene stood by the door trying to figure out what to do.

He was stunned by his father's appearance since he had thought all were sound asleep upstairs.

It was all he could do to manage a whispered "Father, please. They shall be gone soon" as his friends cowered in the shadows.

Eugene's father called for the stableman who arrived rubbing the sleep from his eyes.

Looking rather startled by the tableau of his employer in his nightshirt and the young master with his friends he asked what was needed.

"I need you to go to the police station and ask them to come for these two gentlemen. Do not stop to saddle up but run instead. Not far, only three blocks."

Putting on his cap, the stableman headed down the hall into the night.

Matthew O'Reilly stood watching him and then turned towards Richard.

"I am willing to put up with a lot from my son," he said, "but I will not tolerate you young fellows in my home. Eugene I shall deal with you tomorrow. But for now I shall stand here until the authorities remove your friends."

Meagher started shaking as he contemplated spending the night in the local holding cell.

Rushing over to his father Eugene moved so quickly that it seemed to create a draft. He forced his father down and tied him to the tall chair by the door. Once he had fished the keys out of his father's pocket, he unlocked the door and let the others out.

As Eugene closed the door, he did his best to ignore his father who was shouting like a Brahma bull. A sigh of relief passed Eugene's lips as three minutes later the police arrived.

Eugene's mother crept down the stairs in her wrapper and mules just as the police were untying her husband, the noise having awakened her. All of the servants followed her down. The commotion had awakened the entire household.

"Mrs. O'Reilly, it appears your son was harboring two of the radicals we are out to seize," said the police. "Your husband had locked them in, but young Mr. O'Reilly restrained him and let them out. They are out in the night leaving your husband in much distress."

Looking at her son, she said, "Oh Eugene, it is too much. What will we do with you?"

She hurried to her husband to make sure his hands had not been injured.

Trying to calm him she stroked his arm while he said in a broken tone "I told him not to bring his friends here but he did."

The police soon departed in hopes of catching their prey. Eugene said very little.

Eventually, he asked, "Can I go to bed now? I am tired."

"After you help me up," his father said.

"I am too exhausted to deal with you now. You have jeopardized all of us. Not only yourself but your mother and I as well. You should have thought of that. Your friends having to hide need not translate into your letting them in."

"Just give your father your arm," said his mother. "With his knees walking up is hard. How could you have tied him up? You have manners. Much as we respect your need to foment a rising this should not have occurred."

The atmosphere downstairs was unpleasant the next morning. Eugene's father breakfasted at one end of the table while his son did his best to shrink into a little corner.

To his surprise, his father said nothing until he had finished eating.

Launching into another lecture that was much the same as the last one Matthew glared at his son.

Eugene did his best to say nothing as he didn't want to upset his mother.

Beginning anew, his father took a new tack, saying, "You shall lose Elizabeth if you continue. The Sullivans are of very conservative stock."

Eugene erupted.

"She won't leave me. I am sure of her love," he shouted. "Even though we disagree once we are free I believe the Sullivans will embrace me."

"I don't think so," said his father.

"Wrong you are on another account. You would throw away all I have strived so hard to arrange. Advantages that have been so hard won. Your expensive schooling and your spot with the Coldstream Guards. I had to pay for that you know. You could have made all sorts of connections there.

"I have done well for an apothecary's son. You have the ability to advance further since you were born to us here and not in County Meath over a shop. Dancing classes and clothes for the cotillion your mother was not invited to debut at.

"Your brother's engagement to Susan too. Just her father's command would have helped you. Maybe you could have enlisted there but no. You are on the verge of throwing it all away and this you mustn't do."

His son bit the inside of his cheeks hard for he had known how angry his father would be. He was unable to think of what else he could have done.

A sputtered response escaped his lips.

"Father," he said, "I am sorry about the chair, but what else could I do. They would have been arrested. Good men who don't deserve Kilmainham because the laws are wrong."

A shocked expression creeping over his face, Eugene's father said, "They may think they are too good for jail but the British won't. Praise God you don't end up there with your poor mother weeping over you. Thank God your grandmother did not live to see this day. It would have been the death of her."

"Grandmama would have loved me anyway."

"Of course, she loved you. In many ways, you were her pet. A staunch republican lady. She would have been proud but sad at the same time."

Eugene stared down the length of the table.

Losing his temper, he shouted:

"Yes, Grandmama would have understood. No friends in Parliament to help. They put that damnable yoke on us with the Act of Union. I have chafed under it for my entire life. I cannot bear it. I would rather die than live out my life under them."

His father stared back.

"I am doing my best. I don't want you to leave Ireland. Hard enough losing Andrew let alone you. King George signed the Act when I was small. Better now for Catholics can hold seats. You need more patience, something even you will agree you lack."

"Yes, Father," his son responded for adding anything would not help.

"I am trying to become more patient with everything. Not just with the British."

Matthew O'Reilly left to go downtown.

Heading upstairs to hide in his room his son was

waylaid on the stairs by his mother. Following her back down he listened as she begged him to find friends that were more like James'.

Eugene swallowed hard. The notion of having friends as boring and prawn-like as his brother's was painful.

Nodding his head, he said, "Yes Mother, I know you are worried. I apologized to Father about yesterday. I don't think James' friends would like me very much. But I shall try if it will make you happy."

His mother smiled as she came round the table and gave him a kiss.

"Not the same friends, my dear, just quieter ones that are more sedate."

To Eugene's intense relief, his mother dismissed him so she could work on her correspondence. Her son headed upstairs to take a nap since his father had forbidden any riding for fear that even with a stableman in tow he would manage to see his friends.

As he fell asleep, he had no way of knowing that a note was being composed downstairs to send off to Jarleth.

A reply arrived two days later by return post, saying:

22 April, '48

Dearest Emily,

First I am sorry to hear that Eugene's difficulties are continuing for I had hoped that his experience in Paris would have taught him something. Of course, I shall come.

I am as fond of you as I am of him. In some ways, I have always thought of him in some ways as mine since I have no son.

We all understand his concerns for our beloved country. He is too young to understand the peril he faces. Maybe he can be taught some patience which I shall attempt to do.

Matthew knows I might have followed Andrew into exile or

worse had I not been a mere lad of twelve when the '96 occurred. To our mother's relief and my distress, I was far too young to join them.

But do not fear. I shall be at the station by nine and in Dublin by one.

Your affectionate brother,
Jarleth

An initial thrill washed over Eugene that turned into distress. It seemed his uncle had come to deliver another lecture instead of more exciting stories about chasing ladies in Paris and India.

Bracing himself for another tongue lashing, he watched the door close.

"My beloved nephew," said Uncle Jarleth, "first let me hug you as even in the country I have heard of your exploits. That and I am glad you are not the worse for wear. I hear you had a lovely time with your friend and several bottles of absinthe in Paris. But you cannot tie your father to the furniture so your friends can leave."

Eugene replied, saying, "We had a lot of fun in Paris. Uncle Andrew took us to see Versailles and two operas. He even gave us money to spend in the cafes."

"And watch pretty girls, no doubt," said his uncle. "What better way to spend a holiday at your age. If you had only stuck with the absinthe and the girls all would be well."

Eugene gazed at his uncle looking shocked.

"How did you hear of that?" he asked.

"Surely you knew," said Uncle Jarleth. "Your mother told me. In any case, it was in all the papers. I knew it was you. You are just like Andrew and me, not wanting to wait to right our wrongs.

"Not here because you want your own path. About that I do not give a fig. But rather because if you continue you may be in Paris too and never allowed to return. You forget. I was once you or you were me. Had

I been a few years older, I might have ended up in Paris myself. Certainly not India."

Standing still, Eugene let the words wash over him. He needed a whiskey but as no one was offering it seemed unwise to ring.

His uncle caught his breath.

Embracing his favorite nephew, he said, "I have gone on longer than I meant to as I am not used to it. I understand but am worried about you. Your mother would want me to continue, but it's more comfortable upstairs. Perhaps we can go up to your father's billiard room and talk over a few pints."

They played the rest of the afternoon away. There was no tea because it was Eugene's mother's day to receive.

Continuing on till dinner, they did their best to stay quiet and not shout when a good shot was made. Much to Eugene's relief, no one ascended the stairs or remarked on the lack of angry voices filtering down.

At five thirty they headed downstairs, making sure to leave everything where it had been.

Poking Eugene in the ribs as they walked down, Uncle Jarleth said, "Are you sure the coast is clear and the ladies gone? Much as I love your mother, I am as tired of these bridal discussions as your father is. I am glad for James, but it is getting tedious."

"Mother's hours end at four thirty, so all the ladies must have left by now. The talk of clothing doesn't bother me, but I have heard much more about the Lake Country than I ever wanted to."

Just as they reached the second-floor landing, Eugene's uncle said "Very pretty there but that's all you need to know. Good for you to listen to it all. Very lucky too. My poor sister would be in floods of tears over you more often otherwise.

"That is why I am worried. Your mother is more delicate than you know. We shall speak no more of that. You have heard enough lecturing already and it has made as far as I know no difference. The billiards may have helped more."

"It was fun. Thank you. I am trying for I don't want to distress her."

As they reached the guest room doorway, Jarleth turned to embrace Eugene. "I know you don't want to, but try. Here. We can go down together and brave the ladies should there be any left."

Side by side they entered the drawing room where to Jarleth's relief all the visitors had gone home.

Dinner was extra special with roast mutton because it was his uncle's favorite.

Eugene rose afterward and began following his mother back to the drawing room since his father only allowed James to linger.

To his delight, he was called back for the after dinner ritual of port and cigars because his uncle asked him to stay. Turning to take his seat, Eugene looked at his father who said not a word. Too worn out to argue with his brother in law it must be.

Peace reigned in the drawing room afterward. At least in the minds of the adults Eugene had been cured of his foolishness and revolutionary ideas.

Eugene's ennui settled back in when after a week's visit Jarleth went home. Staying in his room all morning he sat downstairs with his mother in the afternoon.

He went riding with one of the stablemen in tow. Somehow it was not as amusing what with a chaperone on his tail. Granted the man was fond of him but he appeared to care more about keeping his job. Still the occasional shared glass of bitters at the local tavern on the way home was fun.

Sunday was the only bright spot. He was allowed to attend Mass with Elizabeth at her parish as she had decided to spend the spring and summer in Dublin with her aunt. That and his new door key for as he got home earlier than his parents he needed to let himself in.

The weeks passed albeit very slowly. Not even an outing to the shore, stuck upstairs and barely able to breathe what with all the questions his parents insisted on asking.

Managing to sneak out each Tuesday Eugene chaired the meeting he was still president of.

On the second Wednesday in June, he did his best to keep his excitement hidden.

Choking down his breakfast behind as blank a face as possible, he managed not to smile for Richard had come to update everyone. Plans for Newport and Killahoe with speeches on market day to enroll new members. Perhaps Meagher and Smith-Brien both.

As June crawled by, he became more optimistic. Surely if the case was made before more people, the peasants and farmers would understand.

Time passing so slowly it dragged. Towards the end of the month, a copy of the morning paper was waved under his nose.

As he sat down, his father said, "Your friends have had bad luck."

Once the paper had been tossed in his direction, Eugene unfolded it to find headlines and a three column engraving. Skimming the article, he listened with one ear as his father carried on.

Something about Smith-Brien and Richard having gone up to Killahole. On an inside page a quote from a Limerick correspondent. Three sentences about Smith-Brien standing on a tree stump trembling like a leaf while Richard worked the crowd.

Newport after, it said, but much the same reception.

An anxious speechmaker and very few that wished to join.

Eugene's father glared as his son handed the paper back.

"Well, they didn't do anything illegal," said Eugene.

Sputtering, Matthew O'Reilly managed to reply.

"They can't detain them because Smith-Brien is a member of parliament and your friend is also higher up. But do you not see that they were more scared of the authorities than anything and in any case only a few joined them."

Eugene finished his toast.

"The next speech shall go better. Newport isn't fertile ground. I think there will be better luck elsewhere. But Father, why are you lecturing me as I was not there. I haven't been there in three years."

"With you penned up in the house you can't. Even now you don't seem to grasp the danger you are in. These two are safe for now. But with the Habeas Corpus Suspension coming into play tomorrow anyone can be detained. Be careful, my child. If your mother was not indisposed and sleeping upstairs, she would be begging you."

Eugene's mind raced.

He had known of the forthcoming trip but had not been told when.

Trying to say nothing, he sputtered out "By now they must have gone to Limerick" in the end.

His father looked at him.

"How did you know they were going to Limerick? You have been kept home except when someone can go with you except when you go to church."

Eugene's mind began to spin.

"No, no, Father," he said. "I heard about it a few months ago. Other than the occasional note from Richard, I have not heard from any of them. I guessed Limerick since it is a short ride by railway from

Newport."

Eugene went back to his room after breakfast. Better to avoid any more conversation since as it was a holiday his father would be home.

Managing to slip money to the stableboy, he asked him to run down to the corner to buy copies of the noon papers.

Stuffing them under his shirt he took them upstairs to read. To his horror, he learned that his father had been wrong. The Suspension Act had gone into effect a day early.

Indeed, the Limerick reporter said that a warrant had been issued for Richard and that he and Smith-Brien had been forced to flee in hopes of evading the law.

That afternoon he stayed in his room, trying to digest what had happened. Too horrible to even take in because he had not thought they would want to arrest his friend.

No way to learn more either since all his messages had gone to Richard as the others were far above even him.

Guilt crept in when, knocking on the door, his mother came in to find her son lying on the bed.

With a feeling of relief that he had not been pacing, he told her "I have a bad headache. I shall be down for dinner."

His mother patted his hand.

"Oh, my poor dear," she said. "I shall have Polly bring up a handkerchief to wrap around your head and ease the pain."

She did not return and he was left alone except when Polly came down. His lunch came up on a tray, beef tea and toast.

Managing to compose himself by dinner time he went down and faced his father over the dinner table. Thankfully little more was said since his father economized by not getting the noon papers on Saturday.

Monday brought more excitement. His father made sure to send his clerk out to buy every paper available near his office.

As Eugene was coming in from his afternoon ride, his father appeared in the hall, hours early, wielding several papers like cricket bats.

Ducking as the papers swung through the air, Eugene asked what had happened.

"Come into the library and I'll tell you," his father said. "Your 'friends' have gone even further including your beloved Smith-Brien."

As Matthew O'Reilly had not paused to leave his umbrella in its stand they had reached the library door.

Eugene's father steered him towards a chair.

Handing his son one of the papers, Eugene's father said "Here, look at the headline. I don't know where your friend Richard has gotten himself to. But Smith-Brien is in even more of a tangle than he was before."

Taking the paper, his son read that Smith-Brien had become involved in a siege outside Ballingarry. His father heard a choking sound from across the room for Eugene knew that Smith-Brien could barely load a firearm let alone aim it.

Eugene put the paper down and composed himself.

Then he picked it up again and read further down, the words swimming before his eyes.

Looking up at his father, he said, "I know nothing of this. Doesn't make sense anyway. Smith-Brien is terrible with guns. I went hunting with him last fall and he couldn't hit anything."

His father shook his head and began shouting, saying:

"What! You've known him that long? If I'd known that I would have taken you out of your lodgings and let you live in your room so I could keep an eye on you. I wanted to, but your mother dissuaded me. If you had only gone to university in England, you never would have met any of this bunch."

His son as always tried to say little and let his father's wrath dissipate.

"Read on," Eugene's father said. "There is more about your great leader. But read it aloud. Maybe then it will sink in."

Doing as he was told Eugene read the rest of the story, flipping to page five to finish it. He learned that a new recruit had been killed just as Smith-Brien had been attempting to lead his group away before the authorities arrived.

His father said something about Smith-Brien that he managed to overlook.

When he was finished, his father told him that the other stories were much the same.

Eugene's father looked at his son.

"I hope you realize now that this is very serious," he said. "That you are not detained as of yet is a blessing. Were it not for me you no doubt would be."

Eugene shook his head.

"I didn't think anyone was going to get shot let alone killed."

"Naïve although not perhaps at your age. The British always have bullets, my boy. You can rest assured they shall not leave a stone unturned to search for them as someone shot at the police from inside the house. Ballingarry is a tiny place but part of their realm. I am watching you like a hawk for fear of what may befall you."

The tension in the house was so thick it could be cut with a knife. Eugene in his room by day, a strained peace that emerged at night when everyone was asleep.

The O'Reillys second son, emerging with the

noonday sun, crept down the back stairs in his stocking feet to preside over his meetings nearly every other evening. Something made easier for, his father having gone back to London on business, his mother was distracted by the final planning of James' wedding trip.

Eugene was often out more often than he was in since his mother was often downtown seeing various hotel and railway agents.

Living in fear that she would find out he feigned illness in the mornings.

Once she had gone out, he was free to leave at will. Entire afternoons were spent with plans for the Corstown rising before he had to head back uptown in time to let himself in just before his mother arrived.

One day at breakfast his mother took him to task.

"Eugene, you aren't up to anything are you?" she asked. "Either you are ill or you are doing something your father would not like."

"No, no, Mother, I am only resting," he said. "I leave to ride but with the stableman making his reports you know I am in the park. I'd have Richard over for billiards if I knew where he was but I know I cannot."

"Stay far from Richard, please. Maybe you can help me buy packet steamer tickets today at the pier. You are looking pale and it will get you out of the house."

When his father arrived home from dinner at his club on his second day back, there was a minor explosion.

Marching his son into the library Eugene's father told him what he had learned, adding "Be careful. You are one of only two or three that they are not searching for. One move and you shall be in a cell."

Eugene was so used to lectures that he let his father go on.

Sneaking out once his parents were asleep, he headed for his old neighborhood. Word had come that he should unite with Meagher's aide, Thomas Luby. The groundwork for the Corstown and Dublin risings needed finishing.

A man in the back whom he had not seen before raised his hand as the discussion began about acquiring the necessary items.

"Mr. O'Reilly," he asked. "How are we to pay for them and how are we to buy them without being noticed?"

Responding, Eugene said, "Smith-Brien sent money with his message. Mr. Luby here has donated some more. Perhaps you would like to contribute?"

"I cannot," the man said in a huffy voice as he sat down.

Eugene found his response odd but forgot about it all together as he and the others tried to figure out how to purchase everything.

One or two items per gunsmith so as not to arouse suspicion. The list being rather long, cartridges and pistols with caps and balls along with many other items.

As they were finishing up the man who had spoken came forward. Suggesting a gunsmith down near the docks, he collected his things and left.

Once they were gone, Luby turned to Eugene, murmuring "Very vague. Didn't offer more than the name of that shop. I'm not sure I've seen him before."

Eugene queried the members.

"The fellow must be new or else someone would recall him. I am sure the British haven't found us so he can't have infiltrated our group. They are only interested in Meagher and the other two anyway. But I shall make a mental note to look out for him next time."

Sorting out the lists and divvying everything up took another half hour. A long standing member having taken two shops, Eugene took the ones in town leaving Luby to cover the rest.

Eugene spent his days in an ever-widening circle for the downtown smiths asked too many questions.

In the end, Luby was forced to go up to Belfast to obtain the pike heads because Eugene had had to visit some of the shops on his list.

The end of July and the final item being acquired on what was the last possible day.

Heading down the street for a meeting at the tavern on the corner Eugene sat down on the back bench.

Straws drawn over a pint, Luby drew the wagon and Eugene the horses.

"Perhaps you should drive," Luby said. "Not one of the members we have found to go has the experience with horses that you do."

"I would, but my father will be home tonight so I cannot get in and out unnoticed," Eugene said.

"In any case, the fellow drives well enough. The cart horses will be the calmest I can find. Not enough time to find anyone else. O'Rorke shall do. The wagon is small and we need the other four to assist the locals with their guns. If my father was back in London, of course I would."

"All right," said Eugene's companion. "Not much better with horses so it makes no sense for me to go. Then too Smith-Brien wants me in Dublin for the rising around the Castle. The man you have chosen will do."

Purchasing the horses the next afternoon, Eugene went to a dealer on the other side of Dublin where he had never been.

At four, he led them to the agreed upon spot deep inside the Preserve where all the munitions were stashed. Once the horses had been hitched up and tethered and the pistols and other items loaded handshakes were exchanged and he headed for home.

Coming in, he beamed his best grin in the direction of the drawing room and headed up to his room.

Eugene crept back out once his parents had retired.

A squeaking stair tread was followed by a whinny from Mr. Moonlight, who had been left tethered to the hitching post.

Riding at a fast gallop he reached the Preserve, arriving just as the men were leaving for Corstown.

"Good luck," called Eugene. "No worries. I am sure they will rise when you arrive."

Chiming in, Luby said, "Just try to keep the horses quiet until you clear the Blanchardstown gate. Otherwise, the night watch may suspect something."

Eugene rode Mr. Moonlight at a trot instead of a gallop all the way home because it was quieter.

Tiptoeing back up the stairs one at a time instead of two Eugene managed to reach his room undetected. Still half-dressed he laid down on his bed. Insomnia haunted him instead of dreams. The anticipation of the morning kept him awake till dawn.

Meanwhile, the team of five had left the Preserve headed for County Meath.

Two hours having passed the men began to approach the Blanchardstown gate on the outskirts of the city. Clip clops and the occasional word reached their ears, but they assumed it was the night watch.

O'Rorke stopped just before they reached the tollgate.

"We need to stop and rest the horses," he said to his colleague who was sharing the box. "In fifteen minutes we can go on. In another two hours, we shall be in Corstown."

His colleague agreed for the horses did look tired.

As they sat, a jingle could be heard from behind. A farmer's cow lost in the woods, they whispered, thinking nothing of it since everything had been done just as it had been ordered.

The horses having rested they headed for the gate. To their surprise, they were challenged. Shouts came from out of the darkness telling them to stop so the wagon could be searched.

Putting the reins down, O'Rorke called out, asking, "Who are you? We are just some travelers headed for Dunshaughlin. With our own baggage, that is all."

The driver picked up his whip.

His colleague whispered, saying "No" just as a large man approached.

Brandishing his gun in their faces, he said, "We are the law. Stop and I won't have to shoot you."

The whip having been put back down, they drove through the gate. Once they had been ordered out O'Rorke and the others sat in a row on a nearby tree trunk.

To their horror, they were forced to watch as the police began their search. The munitions having been carried down they were stacked on the roadside. A younger constable counted it all up while another wrote it down.

As their boots sank into the mud, lights came up in the distance and even more constables appeared.

One, taller than the rest, walked over.

"I am John Hawston of the police detectives. You five are going with us to the local station house. You told my officer you have personal baggage. Quite interesting. You can't wear pike heads and have brought guns with you instead of boots."

They were marched to the station house and questioned at length, their only response being that they were headed for Dunshaughlin.

With a thin smile and nod, Detective Hawston said, "If you want to tell that story you can tell it to the magistrate. More likely you are with Mr. Meagher's little band. This afternoon we shall take you back into Dublin to see the magistrate and he will decide what to do with you. Till then you can think in the cell."

Into Dublin by three. Arriving all five were very surprised, for there was a large crowd. More journalists too than had awaited Prince Albert, the news of their arrest having spread across the city.

They were carried off to court where they were committed to Kilmainham. Just as they had suspected, the constables had friends on the bench. A feeling of numbness took over as the great gates of the jail swung shut because Mr. O'Reilly had said they had nothing to fear.

Matthew O'Reilly heard of the arrests in the morning, his clerk pulling his aside as he arrived for work. Gossip but important. A warrant being sought for the young master.

Turning, Eugene's father ran downstairs dragging James behind him. Once at the courthouse, they managed to run up the steps and into the main hallway, which was swarming with police.

The government's lead barrister appeared as they reached the stairwell, the police commissioner by his side.

Matthew began feeling queasy because he could hear snatches of their conversation.

"Perhaps a sizeable reward too," the commissioner said. "A warrant isn't enough. These Irish continue to be inclined to protect their own. It distresses me. I know Mr. O'Reilly's father but that cannot be helped."

The lead barrister turned.

"You are right," he said. "As there is a five hundred pound reward out for Mr. O'Gorman we should post the same for these two."

The commissioner cut in.

"That should be enough. Even in the good part of town. An announcement as we leave and another in the papers, the second edition as it is too late for the first."

The lead barrister spotted Matthew in the crowd as he and the commissioner were approaching the main doors. Both apologized, shaking Eugene's father's hand as the doors opened.

As everyone swept out, Matthew stood behind the barrister as he began to read the warrant. With all his powers of stoicism in use for he dared not weep, he listened as his friend read:

"We have secured warrants against both Eugene O'Reilly and Thomas Luby. We have information that they organized the fiasco of two days past. We are offering five hundred pounds for each for information leading to their whereabouts. With a reward they can be found faster."

James pulled his father down the steps after the lead barrister was done.

Once they were headed home, James spoke.

"I think Eugene must have done it," he said. "He had a strange look like the kitten that got the cream last week when I ran into him with Elizabeth after Mass."

His father glared at him, saying, "First stop smirking. Your infantile rivalry with your brother is terribly upsetting under the circumstances. You must stop thinking of yourself and think of your dear mother. She will be horribly upset.

"As for Eugene I am proud of what he has tried to do but it is terrifying. He will be in Kilmainham before nightfall. Hopefully, they will both be home so I can figure out what to do.

"I told him to quit, but it didn't work. Your dear mother is beside herself at the prospect of having a child transported or put to hard labor which would be the death of him. Who knows how he could have done such a thing. Not only did he not do as he was told but he went several steps further and helped organize the affair with Mr. O'Gorman or his ilk."

Continuing, Matthew O'Reilly said, "I shall get a good barrister for your brother this week. Doesn't sound like they have much evidence. Enough to detain him but not much more.

"That I shall think of later. More concerned about your mother. Hopefully, Eugene will not be there long. He has the strength of youth and your mother and Polly do not. Oh, what a mess. But what could I do? I couldn't tie him down to the bed."

James helped his father down when they arrived.

Walking up the steps, they went into the front hall. Wails could be heard as James opened the pocket doors.

James rushed in and ran to his mother, finding her in Polly's arms both of them hysterical.

Emily O'Reilly looked up and saw her husband.

"What will happen to my baby?" she asked.

Her husband sat down and took her hand.

"I am not sure, sweetheart. But where is Eugene? I thought he would be with you."

"Master Eugene is in the dining room eating breakfast for he just got up," said Polly. "All was fine until we saw the midmorning paper and a broadside about the young master. The stableman went to buy hay. On the way back the newspaperman said there was something about Eugene in it so he purchased it."

"Once the missus read it she burst into floods of tears," Polly added, "so they came upstairs for me and woke Master Eugene. When I reached his door, he was coming out so I told him to go down because something was very wrong.

”As I got to the drawing room door he was reading the article. The poor lamb turned white. He was too upset to see his mother’s arms being held open. I told him to go eat as he could not be of any use.”

Eugene’s father felt pale himself for he had never seen Eugene do anything of the kind.

Leaving James to do his best to console the ladies he proceeded into the dining room. There he found his youngest born, stylishly attired as ever, enjoying a late breakfast of tea, toast, and soft boiled eggs.

As his father approached, he could detect fear in Eugene’s eyes.

“Why aren’t you in the drawing room comforting your mother? She is more distressed than I have ever seen her. How could you have done this? I have begged you over and over to stop. Now the game is up. They have a reward out for you now.”

Replying, Eugene said, “I am sorry. I thought no one would find out. We were very careful to make sure our meetings weren’t infiltrated. The article says an informant told the police they would be headed for the gate. Someone was there who seemed a little odd, but then we forgot about him. I thought Limerick would be successful. We had checked everything. I can’t believe that it all went wrong. I feel terrible about Mother. I know I am her pet and I am as worried about her health as anyone. James is wrong if he thinks I don’t care.”

James came in.

Asking Eugene to go to their mother, he said, “You are the only one who can calm her.”

“Eugene is still too shocked to help,” their father said. “I need you to stay with him while I attend your mother.”

James sat down next to his brother, saying "Oh, little brother, what a mess you have gotten into now. Though how you crept in and out without waking anyone, I am not sure."

Eugene drank the last of his tea.

"Polly knew, but she didn't tell anyone. What else could I have done? I couldn't stand staying inside like a prisoner or living as a serf under that pudgy queen."

James reached out, taking his brother's hand. It was a gesture that meant much. Though they seldom did it now, as small children they had walked everywhere hand in hand.

Then he said, "First you know I agree with you about England although I lack your adventurousness and would not have done what you have.

"But why Corstown? They are so placid there. But we shall speak no more of it. The memories of swimming together and playing with Patrick in the attic run too deep. Oh, Eugene, what shall I do if they send you away? I cannot bear it. I need you to stand up for me at my wedding."

Tears formed in both their eyes.

Rising Eugene embraced his brother for James never wept. Saying that he was sorry for he had never thought it would come to this, he added that he would like to see the broadside. He had read the article in the paper but only glimpsed the other before it had been grabbed away.

James hugged him back.

"Oh. I thought you knew. It has all been very fast, too fast for me and I guess for you. This morning the Queen's barristers went in front of the magistrate at the main court and got warrants for you and Thomas Luby."

Looking even paler, Eugene said, "I thought they might obtain a warrant for the men who were at the gate but not that they would be interested in me."

The maid came in just then to clear the dishes in preparation for lunch.

Once she was gone, James added, "Look. I know what you think, but we have to deal with what the government says for now. They have posted a reward, five hundred for you and another five hundred for your friend.

"Father will know better what to do. Let me go see how Mother is and ask him. If you come, that will help. Your presence will comfort her. That and the new cloth has to be laid."

Rising, both brothers walked into the drawing room.

As the sight of Eugene only worsened his mother's tears and hysteria Matthew asked James to take his brother to the morning room.

"As soon as your mother is better I shall be in," he said.

Just as James began shuffling his mother's cards for perhaps a game would settle his brother's nerves, his father walked in.

"James, please go and attempt to console the ladies. Your aunt has come to assist us, but you shall still be a help."

Sitting back down Eugene's father could see that his son was a little calmer.

"Son, how are you doing?" he asked. "Much as I thought this would happen it appears you didn't. I do wish you had heeded me about avoiding the radicals at Trinity. But it is too late for that. We must deal with the circumstances that are here."

Eugene lifted his eyes to meet his father's.

Responding, he said "In some ways I wish I had but after what the English boys said at Mr. Hall's I could not. I thought that I could ride down to the docks and get the next packet steamer for France. No one knows what I look like. My picture is not in the paper so no one would know me."

Reaching out, Eugene's father took his son's hand.

"A bad idea," he said. "They will go harder on you if someone should recognize you and turn you in. For someone on the docks five hundred pounds is several years pay. It will be easier if you turn yourself in."

"I don't want to be in a cell with thievish sorts," his son said. "What can I do? I don't think they will let me stay home."

"They won't let you stay here. Kilmainham at least for now because it is the main jail. My son, you could have avoided this altogether had you stopped a few weeks ago. I shall find a barrister this week and am hoping that whoever I retain can get you bailed out or else moved to a less notorious prison. But for now there is nothing we can do. We shall need a bit of patience."

Eugene's father managed to calm his son down, telling him that whatever happened he would go with him.

Eugene's mother came in on James' arm, feeling calmer with fewer tears though still rather faint. Clutching Eugene so tightly to her bosom that he could barely breathe she covered his face with kisses.

Everyone sat down to a cold lunch. Meat from the evening before, the gentlemen not having been expected, but no one saying a word. Glad they were to get together no matter what the sandwiches were composed of.

Eugene's father looked round at everyone as the maid departed with the last tray.

Nodding, he said, "I know it sounds hard, but I have a plan. After lunch, I shall accompany Eugene to the police station to turn himself in."

"Matthew is there no other way?" his wife asked in a

distraught tone. "He is too fine to go there. I shall go with him. He needs me."

"Yes he is," said her husband, "but there is nothing we can do. It will be all right Emily. I have had a long talk with Eugene and explained everything."

As Eugene's mother turned to look at her younger son, Eugene said, "Yes Mother. Father is going with me. I am not sure you should go. I think it would be too upsetting so we should say goodbye here."

Emily O'Reilly sat still as both of her sons urged her to stay.

Finally, she agreed, saying that she could not bear to hear the magistrate send her baby to jail. Eugene winced for he was much too old to be called her baby, but he let it pass because she was so upset.

Once Matthew had finished the last crumb of cheese they went back to the drawing room, his wife helped up by Eugene with her sister in law in the rear.

Eugene and his father began getting ready to leave once Emily O'Reilly was seated.

As Polly had gone up to his room while they were eating his grip was ready. It held his Bible, writing portfolio and a clean nightshirt. She had not been sure what would be needed and so had taken the first items that came to hand.

Looking through it Eugene's mother said, "This should be enough until someone can come and visit. He could use a clean shirt, but we can't wait any longer for I can't bear it."

Her husband began to cross the room towards Eugene.

"Son, you need to say goodbye for now you have at least a few things. I can bring more. The longer this is drawn out, the harder it will be. In any case, you shall be able to see everyone again. I am sure of it."

Eugene rose to his feet with the same pale look, still

not any too sure his father was right. A nightmare for they should have risen in Limerick. Perhaps they were right and the farmers were more concerned with their crops than their freedom. With any luck, Smith-Brien might work a miracle yet.

His father coughed.

Turning Eugene saw his mother's face. There were hugs all round, one from Polly and a very long one from his mother.

Walking over to his father he went into the hall and towards the front door for the carriage had been brought round. He waved to his mother and she waved back as they went around the corner.

5 DUBLIN & BELFAST

Eugene's father gave him a squeeze as they stepped through the station doors.

Nodding when he saw them, the constable said, "Mr. O'Reilly we have a warrant for your boy. Thank you for accompanying him."

To Eugene's surprise, his father shook the man's hand.

"I would not have let my son come alone," Matthew O'Reilly said. "He has been persuaded that he would be better off turning himself in so here we are."

As Eugene stood in back trembling with fear, his father added, "I would like to accompany him to court. I shall be retaining a barrister, but it will take a few days to accomplish. It would mean a lot to his mother and me if I can go with him."

"Of course," said the constable. "I know you are a man of your word. I am sorry to have to arrest him."

Another constable emerged from the back, a copy of Eugene's warrant in hand for his father to read over.

Sitting down together, they waited till the carriage was brought round. They headed downtown once it had come, walking up two flights at the courthouse.

Eugene was almost in a dream state.

Even after the bailiff ordered him to his feet he had to be pulled up. Once he was vertical, the magistrate began.

"Mr. O'Reilly, you are now in the Crown's custody. I order you detained at Kilmainham under the Habeas Corpus Suspension Act."

Saying nothing Eugene stared straight ahead. His father was allowed to embrace him one more time before the manacles were fastened and his son led out.

Down in the courtyard, Eugene climbed into a closed carriage filled with the latest batch of common prisoners.

He tried to chat with them as they rolled along. Granted they were meanly dressed and obviously not gentlemen. Still it might help to ease his mind.

Turning to the young lad next to him, he felt relieved as a smile beamed back once he had explained.

"That's why they caught me," the young fellow said. "Suspicion of picking a gentleman's pocket by the railway hotel. There was a huge crowd there waiting for the mail train with the five chaps."

"Oh," said Eugene, saying no more as the hotel in his mind was for tea, not wallet taking.

He stared straight ahead instead.

The man opposite spoke. Something about being picked up for assault by the docks in a bar fight. A look of disappointment too for the man added that he had just left Kilmainham and was now being returned.

Each one slumped into a corner as they bounced along. Finally, the older fellow said that he could tell from the noises that they were getting close.

Eugene was still in shock when the gates slammed shut and the guards came running up.

Asking "What are they going to do?" as the others stuck out their hands and feet he sat very still. Maybe they were to be chopped off though he was not sure.

No one spoke as the steps swung down and the

guards climbed in.

Watching, he saw them unlock the manacles first on one side and then the other. Simple really, wrists and ankles held out to assist the guards.

As they were being pushed out Eugene looked around.

A sea of granite and barred windows, the serpents wrapped in chains straight ahead and gates behind.

A guard tower in the corner with armed men who faced both ways, two towards the court, the others towards Inchicore Road in case of any escape.

Odd.

Only two days ago he had seen the guard towers from the other side when he had brought the horses. A touch of queasiness too. Now he was on the other side with guns aimed to kill if he decided to flee.

Guards and soldiers came pouring out of the entrance like mice out of a moldy cheese.

Eugene's hands went straight up when he saw their fixed bayonets, only to be put back down like the others. Part of the drill of a world he had never imagined.

As soon as they were formed up the prisoners were marched inside. Eugene walked in the middle clutching his grip with the few things Polly had packed, some peppermints from James and a miniature of Elizabeth.

The guard marched him down towards a pinpoint of light at the very end.

Rubbing his wrists since the manacles had been very tight he was blinded by the sunlight as the hall ended. Glass and iron girders overhead like a railway station with three tiers of cells like a layer cake. Yellow brick for granite but otherwise much like the outside.

Entering the cell Eugene could barely see as the light was very dim. One small window and no light from the walkway because the cell door was covered with clothing.

Four cellmates emerged from the murk, two boys of nine and twelve and two adult men. Tiny for so many he thought introducing himself round, the same size as both nurseries put together.

Iron cots, a table too small to lay his portfolio flat and a broken down chair by the window. A bucket of uncertain water by the door rags in a heap opposite but nothing else.

Eugene stood in the middle of the cell.

He was afraid to speak. Indeed, he had met more of the meaner sort in one day than he ever had before. He had not even known that that class of Dubliner looked upon him as a hawk would look upon a bird.

Rising one of the men showed him his cot. Eugene decided to use his jacket for a blanket since the sheet looked filthy.

"Thank you. I would like to sit and read my Bible," he said.

Once he had sat down to read, he could barely make out any letters because his cot was the furthest from the window.

Swallowing hard, he asked if he could sit on the chair since then he would block the light.

To his relief the same man who had shown him his cot answered.

"I am the only one who can read," the man said. "You can sit there as you like. Nothing to do but play cards and talk so it doesn't matter."

As Eugene sat down, he looked around, hardly able to believe his eyes and nose for it all looked very mean.

Even worse, he realized, than the abandoned crofter's cottage in Corstown that James had thought of using for a fort. Horrid smells, water to drink but not bathe and straw tickings no doubt filled with bugs. Trapped and locked inside too, unable to go out when he wished.

He stared at the others as they stared back. The oldest one even asked if he was British.

To his horror after he had explained that he had been born in the city the chap said, "That makes no difference. You are one of them."

Reading his Bible verse, he asked the Lord for help and then opened up his ticking to rearrange the straw. A groom at Mr. Hall's had done that to help get rid of bugs, he remembered.

Someone went over to the window frame and nodded. Supper time, one of the lads murmured.

Eugene became curious about how they knew.

Asking the man who had shown him his cot, he said, "I am curious. Without timepieces, how do you know it is time for supper?"

The boy who had been asleep earlier spoke up instead, saying "Partly by the noise on the catwalk. We know the routine of the guards as they change shifts and walk to and fro. But also from the quality of light coming through the window as it is strongest at noon."

"Come here, let me show you something," he added as he crossed to the window.

Eugene joined him. To his surprise, there was a series of scratches on the frame like a primitive sundial.

"Did you make that?"

"No," the lad said. "My father told me about it when he was here before. But I made the scratches deeper and easier to read. In summer, it works very well. In winter, we mostly just listen. Fortunately, we are on the northern side of the building and get enough sun. On the other side, they can only tell by the guards."

Eugene was quite impressed. Even though the lad could not read at least he understood how it worked.

Thanking the young man, he said, "You shall have to give me a lesson tomorrow if you don't mind. Very clever."

Forming everyone into a long crocodile, the guards marched them off to the dining hall.

Eugene took a surreptitious swipe with his handkerchief over everything at his place. The napkin was so grease stained he put his handkerchief to the left of his bowl to use instead.

He stared straight ahead as the food emerged on trays heaped just as high as the eating club platters.

One trusty after the other, smocks and aprons instead of gay uniforms. Food that smelled rather more pungent than Mr. Hall's punishment rations in large cooking pots for tureens.

Eugene looked at his soup before taking a sip. Very thin, mostly warm grease with a faint taste of chicken as though the cook had dipped a drumstick in the pot and removed it without any of the meat falling in.

As he was finishing his broth, two large pieces of bread appeared on his plate. Eugene called the man back as he went back for more.

"Sir," he asked, "is there butter or jam for the bread?"

To his humiliation laughs could be heard all round as the trusty bent his head back and replied.

"No. You must have come today. We have no butter or jam."

Eugene blushed beet red. It had never occurred to him that bread could appear without butter.

Smiling his neighbor said, "Don't worry, I thought that too. The only place in Ireland where there is no butter with the bread. Your slices don't look very hard but what we do is dip them in the soup."

The man introduced himself, saying, "Happens every

time someone new arrives. Up in Belfast, they are supposed to have butter. Maybe one day they will get it here too."

Thanking him Eugene shook his hand. He choked his bread down with tea for the broth was gone.

A final man with small bowls of tapioca pudding which he had always detested came round at the end. He managed to choke down a few bites since it was a long way to breakfast.

Noticing, his new friend said, "You have to eat what they have or you will starve. Your family can bring things, but you have to eat them fast so they don't get eaten for you. Chocolate since it can be consumed on the spot. I know. I had some tea taken only last week."

Eugene looked around to see if he could spot Mr. Luby but could not find him though the hall was so large it was impossible to be sure.

Asking a tablemate for advice, a response came from three seats down that there were several wings and numerous dining halls.

"How else can I find out then?" Eugene said.

"I can't ask the guards," he added as laughter erupted up and down the table.

Finally, his seatmate suggested it would be best to look in the exercise yard since inmates from different wings were allowed out at the same time.

There was a clanging bell followed by the trusty with his tray, this time to collect everything.

Eugene watched the others wolfing down their pudding as the man approached.

As half of his went back, he realized that peasant manners would be needed, hopefully to be forgotten once he was back home. His mother would be horrified if he did not put his fork down between bites.

Eugene shared a desultory round of euchre once they were locked back in till it got too dark. Made all his Gaelic lessons come in handy, he realized, for he could pick out most of the words.

As darkness fell and no one moved near the candle, Eugene went over to the cell door. Banging on it with his boot, he asked the guard for a lamp.

Much to his shock, the guard peered in around the shirts and laughed.

"Prisoners are not allowed to have lamps," said the guard. "You should have asked your fellows. They would have told you. You can light the candle but since it has to last for two weeks, you'd better not waste it."

Eugene glared back.

"How shall I read?" he asked.

The guard stared back, saying, "Did you not understand me? One candle every two weeks. If your father brings more, we shall take them. You can sit and think instead unless they let you light it," he said as he turned and walked away.

The man he had been playing with picked up the candle. "Two inches at least until Saturday next. Six more days."

Eugene said nothing.

Sitting down on his cot he tried not to think. Only that morning he had been in his own room in his own house. Sheets, three pillows and a wool mattress that was turned every few weeks.

He laid face down on his cot, his thoughts racing like squirrels running up and down.

A poke in the side, too, from Elizabeth's miniature that he had stuffed in his pocket. Tears welled up making his jacket wet as Elizabeth's sweet face swam before his eyes.

He wondered what her father would say. After the news of the presidential visit had broken Mr. Sullivan had forbidden her to write and his mother had had to make multiple visits to get him to change his mind.

But Kilmainham. The old man might never allow it no matter how many visits were made.

He fell into a fitful sleep, awakening towards dawn as he was not used to being in a sea of snores.

When he first lifted his head, he was sure it was a nightmare. As he remembered his head sank back down.

He got up as the sun pierced his eyelids.

Once his teeth were brushed, he splashed his face with water using a corner of his nightshirt for a towel. His hair brushed he did his best to pat it down, checking to see how it looked with Polly's small mirror.

Putting on a clean shirt and stockings, he pushed yesterday's laundry to the bottom of his grip. Then he made up his cot, not as tight as the maid's but the best he could manage.

His cellmates started to stir as he sat down to read his Bible.

Just as he had begun a third verse the eldest, who was the toughest looking of the four, growled, saying, "That's the light for all of us. You have to move. You can stand if you like in the corner nearer to the window if you insist but not the chair. Or you can stand by the door."

Eugene stood and then sat down on his cot. As they were all common men, it was safer not to argue. Straining his eyes, he was able to make out a few lines.

He watched as the fellow sat down to clean his teeth with a wisp of filthy straw, pulled a long clay pipe from his inner pocket and began to smoke. Something fit for a dim corner surely.

Watching the minute hand of his watch crawl he waited for seven o'clock and breakfast. Noticing the pipe smoker's envious gaze, he jammed his watch back into his pocket.

Another crocodile.

There was oatmeal with a little milk and two mugs of tea. Eugene wanted a little sugar for his porridge. Managing to curb himself, he did not ask since the trusty was the same one that had commented on his attire the day before.

Best to blend in.

As he looked around the hall very few even looked like they had attended Trinity. Mostly they looked like peasants or the longshoremen that hoisted trunks.

A new bucket of water to replace the old arrived as they were locked back in.

Eugene stood staring out the window. He had found that if he stood on the tips of his toes he could get a glimpse of the city.

Just as the shadow reached the second scratch, the cell door was unlocked making everyone jump and turn as the guard said "Come on men, time to exercise in the yard."

Two flights down and a left by the dining hall entrance instead of a right. And into another passageway that was like the first with its ever growing blink of light.

Out into bright sunlight and a sea of stone with not a single blade of grass.

Standing by the door, he gazed up until one of the guards prodded him with a gun, saying, "O'Reilly, walk forward. Can you not see they are going in a circle?"

Startled Eugene started following the others.

Round and round a few times he went before he looked up. To his surprise, there were a good hundred men walking with him. Chatter rose up all round for it was the one time to talk to friends from other wings.

As he went round, he spotted Mr. Luby just as Mr. Luby spotted him. Rushing towards each other, they embraced and then resumed their circle.

As Luby struggled to catch his breath, he said, "I was looking for you. I thought you might be here. I didn't think we would be. A true shock to learn from the papers that they caught them at the gate. Not sure whether it is better or worse that you were not there."

Eugene nodded.

"Maybe," he said. "At least this way my family had a little time before I ended up in front of the magistrate. I wanted to flee for France, but my father thought I should turn myself in because of the size of the reward. He went with me, first to the police station and then the courthouse. Is that how it was with you?"

His compatriot glanced around to see who was listening. All the chatter being in Gaelic, he responded.

"I thought of the Continent or perhaps America. I might have done the latter but what with the reward and the fact that the only vessel taking on passengers in Queenstown was headed for Canada I stayed."

"My father said the same thing about the reward," Eugene said. "Had I waited in Queenstown for the next New York ship I would have had my presence reported to the local constabulary."

"I had thought about Kilmainham," said Mr. Luby. "But I thought our meetings were secure. The odd man at the last one must have been an infiltrator. You remember him, Eugene, the one in the back asking questions."

Eugene nodded.

"Yes, I remember. Left just as we began on the list. He must have been planted. How else could we have been linked to the wagon?"

As another bell rang, they made their farewells.

"An odd way to converse," Luby said as he walked to the door, "but the only one here outside of Sunday Mass. I shall look for you there since I am sure our keepers will not lighten up.

"Afraid of a break I learned yesterday. The number of prisoners and detainees is much larger than that of the guards. Peasants made desperate by the famine in the city leading a life of crime to keep themselves."

Reentering his cell Eugene, was in a happier state of mind.

Despair crept back. One of the boys was seated on his cot going through his things. He walked over to take his grip but said nothing.

One of the men came up from behind all the same, shouting:

"Leave him alone. Rich people like you have too much anyway. Plenty to eat. Not a care in the world in Dublin while out in Galway we are starving."

Eugene nearly bit his tongue in two as there was nothing to say that would help. A certain street urchin pugnaciousness that he lacked as it could not be learned at Mr. Hall's or Trinity.

Better to keep everything on his person to protect them. If the boy was that desperate, the others must be too.

A note written to Elizabeth in an attempt to explain for his father to mail when he came. A glare earned from the others as he reached for the candle to melt the sealing wax.

He began counting off the days as they blurred together, each one much the same though Mr. Luby did not appear again.

On Saturday afternoon, he got ready as his cellmate who was expecting his wife put on his cleanest smock.

Taking his last clean shirt, Eugene did his best with his hair. Two guards appeared just as he finished washing his face, the first for his cellmate, the second to let him know that his father and brother had arrived.

He went down the catwalk. Going through a series of corridors so mazelike they reminded him of a labyrinth he entered a large sun drenched room with his father and James at the other end.

Eugene left the guard in the doorway, running past the other visitors into his family's arms.

He did his best to ignore his brother's shocked look for even unbathed he was glad to see them. He was ashamed to have to let them see. Surely they would know there was nothing he could do.

Embracing again, all three stood silent for a few minutes overcome with emotion. The two brothers managed to sit down on a nearby bench.

"Oh Eugene, it is good to see you," were the first words out of James' mouth, followed by "Make a list of what we should have Mother and Polly get together to bring besides shirts and stockings. Oh no, forgive me since I did not mean to say that. It is just that I have been worried about you."

His brother did his best to be reassuring.

"I know I look terrible," Eugene said. "You do not know how bad it is. Nowhere to bathe and not even a shaving mirror."

James knew that these issues bothered his fastidious brother more than anyone else.

"We know that you can't help it," he said. "Let us talk of other things for this is upsetting. But let's sit down with Father since he looks so sad at seeing you in this place."

Both O'Reillys sat down with their father and talked, mostly about their mother for it was her little attentions that her youngest pined for.

His father said, "She wanted to come and even had her bonnet and parasol in hand. But she is still so distraught I was afraid for her heart and persuaded her to stay home, promising to make a full report."

Panic rose in his younger son's eyes as Matthew continued, saying:

"Son, don't worry so. She is better than she was. Not as distressed as when I came home from the magistrate's court.

"Then she was lying on our bed weeping, unable to rise without collapsing into the arms of your old nurse. We were worried and thought of summoning the doctor. After a few days, she felt well enough to come down to dinner. An emotional upset yes but her heart is fine.

"By now she has progressed to sitting in the morning room with her missal. As a token of her love, she has begun embroidering some handkerchiefs with your initials. As I left, she was waiting for your aunt to appear. When we return, they are headed down to the bookseller to buy you some books to help pass the time."

Eugene smiled and nodded.

"That will be much appreciated," Eugene said, "since I have only my Bible. No books here. In my cell, only one other can read. Hard to even imagine."

Going on, he said, "Has anything come from Elizabeth? Surely she has heard the news."

His older brother laughed.

"Little brother," James said, "everyone in Dublin has heard, and possibly the entire city of London. A letter just came from Uncle Andrew for they sent a pigeon to Paris. We forgot the letter, but he said to tell you to keep your chin up and try to read to pass the time."

James and Eugene spoke about their uncle for a few

minutes until James, looking in his father's direction, saw that he was upset.

Neither son said more as their father burst out, saying:

"Please, boys, I remember visiting him. Much worse than this. I never thought I would return. Let us speak no more of Andrew.

"Tell me, Eugene, how are you faring and what else we might bring you. Your mother can buy it and pack it up. I am interviewing the last possible barrister on Monday and then he will come out to visit you. My time has been taken up with that, leaving your mother to find the things."

"I am surrounded by the meanest sort, but I am doing my best," Eugene said. "Highwaymen who call us English because they are mostly from Antrim where the potatoes have rotted. My valuables kept on my person since I caught a boy going through my grip since we are all kept together not apart."

Eugene tried to stop since James looked to be on the verge of tears.

Their father spoke in a low voice.

"Like Andrew's stories," he said. "Belfast would be better. State prisoners are kept apart. A little far for your mother but Maureen could come instead.

"Everyone thrown together here. Lucky you are it is July since the candles are the only heat. My mother took Andrew eiderdowns, but they are no longer allowed. But try not to worry. They have no more evidence though you need to bear this for now."

Matthew took Eugene's hand, feeling rather pained because his independent son had turned into a needy child.

"It shall be all right, my boy," he said. "As I said there is one barrister left to meet. But unless he is excellent I intend to retain a Timothy Johnston whom I have known for years.

"Highly regarded for his work in criminal law and has worked with state detainees such as you. If I choose him, he will be out midweek to meet with you and discuss possible strategies."

"But Father they won't let me see him. We can have visitors only on Saturday," Eugene said as James broke in.

"No, no," said James. "He can see you during the week since he will be representing you. Don't worry someone was confused. Barristers attend court in the morning and don't visit clients on Saturdays so weekday afternoons are the only time."

There was a startling tap on Matthew's shoulder as their hour was up. All three exchanged hugs while Matthew reassured his son, saying:

"Don't worry. I shall tell your mother no more than she needs to know about conditions here. She knows nothing of such things as Andrew never shared it in his letters. About Polly, I don't know for she grew up a crofter's daughter on the Isle of Skye. But I don't think she'd share anything with your mother."

Eugene attended Mass the next day in a chapel so large he could barely hear the priest.

Taking his portfolio out after the others lay down to nap he started in. By supper time, all his letters were done and tucked into his portfolio for the barrister to mail.

Tuesday inching around.

The guard banged on the door as he was attempting to polish his boots.

"Your barrister has appeared," he said.

Going through the same set of passages as Saturday, Eugene took a turn to the right into the depths of the main building.

The guard led him into the barrister's room which

looked out on a court instead of the gates. It had several sets of tables and chairs, he noticed, instead of benches like the family waiting room.

There were two barristers when Eugene came in, one his own height, the other rather shorter and sandy-haired.

Rising as Eugene approached, the shorter fellow held out his hand in greeting, introducing himself as Timothy Johnston.

"I am very glad to meet one of Matthew O'Reilly's boys," said the barrister. "We have attended many business functions together but always when his family was not present."

Eugene noticed a surprised look in the barrister's eye but no words which was the best that could be hoped for. The guard retreated into the far corner of the room once the pleasantries were completed.

Mr. Johnston began.

"First I am sure you want to know about your friends. The five from Blanchardstown are all here with you and the honorable Mr. Luby. The others still being at large. Whenever they are caught, they shall be here or the new jail in Belfast, depending on where they are seized."

His new client shook his head.

"Luby I have seen," Eugene said. "About the others at the moment I don't much care. I need to go home. I cannot bear it here. My cellmates are a very mean sort and have already tried to take my watch."

Eugene's new barrister did his best to explain.

"Mr. O'Reilly that is impossible. They have only begun their investigation. Until they are done, you shall have to stay. The Crown is taking what happened in Limerick and the siege at the widow's house very seriously.

"These are very serious charges, young Mr. O'Reilly. You are in major legal trouble that could end with hard labor or half a decade in Tasmania."

Mr. Johnston continued.

"That is the technicality," he said. "Maybe it has not been explained plainly enough. Your case is weaker than the others. Because of your youth, I should be able to prove you were taking orders from Smith-Brien and his ilk.

"They have said in closed court that they managed to infiltrate the club you and Thomas Luby chaired. That is how they came to know of the wagon and its route. But against you, there is nothing else. Not enough to convict I don't believe or continue to detain you once the Suspension has expired."

The next sentence died on the barrister's lips. His new client had been rendered so distraught he had begun shaking. Several sips of Irish whiskey from Mr. Johnston's flask when the guard was looking the other way and they sat down again to continue.

"I learned today," said Mr. Johnston, "that O'Rorke is being shifted to Belfast within a fortnight since he has kin there. A precedent in your favor.

"I shall argue for you to be allowed to accompany him. Better since there is a separate unit for state detainees. As it has just opened, it has half the population. There will be only you in a cell built for one instead of five in a cell built for two."

Concluding, the barrister said, "Crumlin Road, as it is formally known, shall be better. Far more secure and from what your father told me there is family nearby. Lonelier, yes. On the other hand, no one can take anything. Unlike here, you shall be provided with a lamp and as much fuel as you need."

Eugene mulled it over.

Nodding, he said, "To be safe to read my Bible and write is far more important. My cousin Maureen is in Belfast and can visit with her son. When my mother comes up to visit, she can stay with them."

Mr. Johnston nodded his head.

"That will be well then. Try not to worry. I think it shall be allowed. I have to leave now and head back to my office. Hopefully, I have answered all your questions. When your father comes, give him my best and tell him I will be back to see you in a week. I should know more by then."

The rest of the week passed more smoothly for he was becoming more accustomed to the rhythms of the place.

On Saturday, his father came to visit though no James since he had gone to Liverpool on business. Two initialed handkerchiefs, a copy of Thackeray's *Vanity Fair* to read and with a final embrace Matthew was gone.

Eugene spent all of Monday fretting since so much depended on what the court had said.

His dreariness over his knavish cellmates was made worse because he had not spotted Luby in the yard for a week.

At two the next day Mr. Johnston reappeared with a smile as Eugene came in, lifting his client's mood considerably.

He began explaining as Eugene sat down.

"The magistrate decided as I asked," he said. "You must not tell anyone except for Mr. Luby. The others might steal your possessions to sell to their fellows once you are gone.

"Pack up when they aren't looking by next Monday since they will come early to fetch you and O'Rorke. Different closed carriages when you leave and in Belfast but together for the ride up. Do you have any questions? I am not sure what your father has told you."

"Not really. Looking forward to reading as I like."

"Then the lamp will be a big comfort. You will be able to read in the evenings and that will help to pass the time. I doubt they have hip baths, but there are two or three buckets of water provided daily so you should be able to bathe. Shaving mirrors are fine. That I asked about."

Returning to his cell, he began to pack little by little. Since he had pushed his cot into the far corner, his actions were somewhat concealed.

By suppertime, he had packed two clean shirts and a dirty pair of stockings in his grip. Enough, he realized, for no more could be done until later when the others would be paying more attention to the corn whiskey they had smuggled in.

Melancholy like a black cloud inched back over the next few days as Eugene began to wonder if Mr. Johnston had been wrong.

But no. Towards mid-afternoon two guards banged on the door calling his name.

"Mr. O'Reilly, you are being moved," they said. "We will be back in the morning so you need to gather up your things."

Gathering up what he had hidden under the old rags and straw, Eugene fell asleep as darkness fell. He used his grip for a pillow, putting his writing portfolio inside his shirt.

Eugene got up early to finish.

Three guards came instead of two. Standing stock still in the yard, Eugene blinked his eyes. The contrast between pitch black and dazzling sun was intense.

Two closed carriages stood before the gates, surrounded on all sides by soldiers with fixed bayonets.

Passing by on his way to the first carriage, O'Rorke gave a nod of recognition and Eugene inclined his head in return. Both were afraid to do more as there was no way to know what evidence the Crown possessed.

The captain prodded them forward.

"No time to waste. We must make the Belfast train," said the captain, a point he emphasized with a brandishing of his bayonet.

Eugene climbed in, saying, "Yes, sir" while wondering what had come over him that having a bayonet aimed straight at his heart had not even phased him.

The gates swung open with the same loud shriek that Eugene remembered from when he had arrived. An eternity ago it seemed, though counted out by days it had been far less than that. A right onto Inchicore Road and one Trinity friend spotted but no more.

He felt a little seasick as the carriage rocked back and forth on its ancient springs.

Before he knew it, he was riding by the hotel where he had seen Elizabeth.

The carriages drove in through a back entrance into the roundhouse as they did not want to risk coming through the main gate.

There was a little time to chat since the soldiers had turned to watch the crowd. Being escorted on they were led into a middle compartment closer to the rear with soldiers between cars and two more in their compartment.

Staying glued to the window Eugene gazed out.

After Kilmainham, the normalcy of passengers boarding the train for the north was fascinating.

A few comments were exchanged about the countryside as it flew by but no more for who knew what the soldiers would do. Small villages the size of Corstown, Belfast's linen mills and more soldiers and carriages as they pulled in.

Whispering, Eugene said, "It must be because Belfast is quite sympathetic. Twice as many subscribers to the paper here as in all of Dublin."

Eugene looked round for Maureen, his father having mentioned that she intended to be there. Relief replaced his concern as they arrived at the prison for he noticed her by the gate holding Little Matt up and waving his hand.

Eugene waved at Maureen as Little Matt waved again, his spirits lifted higher than they had been since he had gone home that fateful night in the Preserve.

There was the same drill as before inside the gates with hands and feet out over even more bayonets.

Whispering as they were taken inside, O'Rorke said, "It terrified me the first time and now barely at all. We must be getting used to it."

Agreeing, Eugene said, "I think so. When I was with the Guards, they showed me how to fix them. Never thought they'd be aimed in my direction. Hopefully, it will not have to be endured too many more times."

Another crocodile down another hall to something called the circle. Funny, he thought as he marched along, like being inside a four-legged spider with the warden in its belly.

Reaching the warden's office, he sat down to wait with O'Rorke on what looked to be the same bench. Then they were led to their new cells which were at opposite ends of the wing.

Eugene sat down once the door locked behind him. Feeling tired from his journey, he looked around.

Like Kilmainham but cleaner with a cot that looked nearly new as did the blue blanket draped across it. A desk which he had not expected. Even the promised lamp. All of it exciting in a sad way. But good for reading would help pass the time even though it was not as much fun as riding.

Standing up, he carefully unpacked with books in

one corner of the desk and his writing portfolio opposite.

He put Elizabeth's miniature by his pillow. Clothes folded and put at the end of the bed. Better that than the floor or the shelf as the shaving mirror would knock them down.

He sat down at the desk.

First a letter to his mother as he had promised and then another chapter. Hearing the cell doors slam open he pulled himself back, kept his place with his silver bookmark and took out his watch. To his surprise, it was five and time for supper.

Supper was much the same but with the promised butter. O'Rorke being nowhere to be seen, Eugene joined a fellow from the Munster club that he had met in Richard's suite.

Eugene introduced himself.

"Yes," said his seatmate. "Good to see you again. You must be the new transfer from Kilmainham that we heard about."

Eugene finished his gruel.

"There are two of us, myself, and Mr. O'Rorke," he said. "You are lucky you weren't sent to Kilmainham. I was barely able to shave.

"You are spoiled here. Locked in with the meanest sort in Dublin. Watch poking me every night since I had to keep it on my person. One bucket of uncertain water for five people. That's why my barrister got me moved here."

Once the crocodile had been reformed, they headed back.

Upon reaching his cell, Eugene waved to his associate. To his surprise, the guard yanked his arm down, saying contact of that sort was forbidden. Eugene apologized because he had not known he could not wave.

Much to Eugene's regret, there was oatmeal for breakfast. Somehow he had convinced himself that the food would be different, not bacon and kippers but perhaps eggs.

Feeling relieved as there were mugs of hot chocolate from large pitchers instead of Kilmainham's eternal tea he drank two mugs.

Forcing the oatmeal down, he decided he would never have porridge again for the rest of his life as it had appeared twice a day without fail. Something the peasants did not mind, but he was used to higher things.

New routines to learn. Early morning exercise with his block instead of mid-afternoon. The same tramping in rows in an endless circle with only the circle's shape changing as the yard was shaped like a wedge of pie instead of a square. O'Rorke passed him once or twice but said nothing lest the guards become angry.

Another crocodile after but to the chapel, not back to his block.

Briefly, Eugene thought it was Sunday.

No, his neighbor whispered. This jail had chapel every day.

Another man overheard.

"This is how they hope to reform us," he said. "Not even our own priest. An Anglican instead."

"They won't reform me," Eugene whispered back as he looked round.

Ugliest chapel he had ever been in with communion ware in pewter instead of silver. Only a piano for there were no organ pipes.

Better not to think about it. At least, he was out of his cell.

He managed to do what he had always done when his father lectured him, daydreaming while appearing to pay rapt attention. A skill finely honed at Mr. Hall's that had been useful ever since.

A most pleasant dream it was, stone skipping at Corstown while the sermon droned on, something about the evils of crime.

Each day he became more accustomed to the new bells and shouts. Even with his watch left out on the table sorting it all out was useful.

His sense of time gradually passed into a dreamscape, with letter writing that took hours and naps that took minutes.

On the third day, there were stomping sounds in the yard. His curiosity woke him up, an outbreak seeming rather doubtful because of the number of guards.

Standing on his tiptoes, he gazed out, only to see what looked to be an army of his fellow inmates. They were all headed across the yard to a large building he had not noticed earlier.

He felt puzzled until he recalled that Mr. Johnston had said something about hard labor. Oakum picking whatever that was. Must be the convicted men headed off to work.

At dinner, he asked another detainee about it.

"How long do they work? In Kilmainham no one did. They look exhausted just walking over, even hunched."

"Lucky we are not to be of their number," the chap said.

"If they convict us we may be. Oakum picking or else working in a quarry as they are talking about building another jail near one. At any rate, they work from dawn to dusk."

"But why here and not Kilmainham?"

One of the others answered from the next table, saying:

"Because Kilmainham was built first. They have a new idea that if you have a solitary cell, chapel every day and work, you shall be redeemed."

Everyone's laughter attracted the attention of the guard in the corner so Eugene said no more.

Quietly finishing his hated tapioca, he realized that the hours alone reading and writing made him the envy of the others.

Truly an odd thing to be grateful for. In school, he had also read for hours but no one had envied him for it.

Maureen came to visit on Sunday, a blessing because Eugene had begun to feel entirely closed away in the world.

After thanking her for having been at the gate, he gave her an embrace.

"Of course, cousin," she said. "I shall do my best to come every week except when Uncle Matthew and Aunt Emily can come up. If Little Matt did not have a cold, I would have brought him too."

"Are you sure Oscar doesn't mind? I am in a mean kind of place," asked Eugene.

Maureen shook her head.

"No, since you were merely trying to shake off our overlords. He just wishes you hadn't been detained," she said, reaching into the sack she had brought.

As she took out two towels and what looked to be a pillowcase she said "Auntie asked me to bring these since she was unable to come before you were moved."

Taking the things, he held them all to his chest.

"I had forgotten," he said. "I have something for you. A letter for Mama. I have folded and sealed it but don't trust the guards to send it."

As tears began welling in his cousin's eyes, Eugene

continued, saying, "Don't cry as that will not help. Pray that the barrister can get bail instead."

Maureen dabbed her eyes.

"I already am," she said. "It is that you called Auntie Mama. So upset you must be despite trying to act brave."

Eugene turned beet red with embarrassment.

"It slipped out. Until I got to Kilmainham, I felt like a full grown man and now more like a little boy who needs his mother."

"Makes sense," Maureen said. "Don't worry. All will be well. I shall come when I can and the others too. Uncle Andrew sends good wishes. Maybe you will end up in Paris with him."

Eugene started to respond. But as the guard had started to beckon since his hour was almost up he kissed Maureen instead, watching with a sad face as she vanished out of sight.

He waited for Timothy Johnston to come up since the court had been put on hiatus due to the heat in the capitol.

One book ended he began another, doing his best to mend his shirt though that did not go well as sewing had always been a ladies' thing.

In early August Matthew wrote, saying he would be up for a visit, adding that Eugene's mother would try to come but that should not be counted on. His birthday passed by as he tried not to remember cakes and such.

The third Saturday in August arrived.

When he walked into the visiting room tears came into his eyes. His mother had come after all.

Running, he stood in her embrace and sobbed with her, Emily from relief combined with distress and Eugene from her having to see him there.

The other visitors having begun to stare, Matthew

looked away.

Saying nothing since Eugene's behavior was no doubt due to his terrible circumstances he turned and did his best to stare at the opposite wall.

Eugene's mother sat down with her son and pulled out a bag, giving him more books and a letter from Elizabeth that had just come.

Thanking her Eugene put the books aside and the letter in his pocket since much as he wanted to rip it open on the spot it would be rude.

Then too if it was bad news he didn't want his visit tainted by it. Plenty of time for that in his cell he knew. Way too much time and not much to fill it.

Once his wife had given everything to their son, Matthew O'Reilly began to relay what the barrister had said, explaining as he went along.

"Son," he said, "Timothy Johnston has been hard at work on your case back in Dublin. He wanted to come up himself, but I told him no. I can explain it all. It will save a little money besides which we need for your brother's wedding trip.

"We met over dinner at my club last week. He has learned that the Crown has no solid evidence against you other than the word of the informant."

Eugene's father continued, saying, "It seems that they do not know whether you were behind the Blanchardstown incident or another man was as the informant thinks two were mentioned. Very favorable. Unless the Crown can find something further, the word of the informant alone is probably not enough to convict you as it cannot be substantiated.

"That is all he knew since the court is going back into session tomorrow. He will come up to speak with you about it in the next few weeks as he will know more by then. This place is not as bad as the other and you will probably not have to bear it much longer. You are lucky to be an attorney's son. It has helped in finding such a good man to help."

"I know," Eugene said. "I thank you, Father, especially for explaining it as I don't understand it all. Yes, it is a better place. My watch is safe and I have my lamp. But lonelier. The priest is an Anglican too, inflicted upon us for we are all Romans."

At that last, Emily O'Reilly looked even more distressed.

Sobbing, she said, "They are even trying to take your faith away."

Giving his wife his handkerchief to dry her tears, Matthew O'Reilly said, "Tell him about the wedding, my dear. We only have an hour and half of it is gone."

With a weak smile instead of a tear Eugene's mother began.

"First the date has been fixed," she said. "Cushendall on the tenth of November with a reception at Susan's home. Last week James ordered your new outfit from the tailor, the latest fashion whatever that is and some new pumps. Early, but the tailor needed the orders in before his rush commences.

"We are hoping that you can attend. I have written the MacDonnells about a delay until you are back home, but they have refused, saying that no one knows how long you will be here. Then too Susan's mother had already made some of the arrangements before you were put into Kilmainham."

Finishing, she said, "James explained that it meant everything to have you stand up for him but they refuse to wait. They even threatened to send the ring back so there is nothing we can do."

Eugene's mother dabbed her eyes again.

Eugene patted his mother's hand as he thanked her for trying.

"I understand," he said. "James' happiness is the

important thing. If I can't attend, you can describe it. Hopefully, I shall be able to go. I wish they would wait but if they can't, it cannot be helped."

Just as Eugene managed to calm his mother down, he had to go back. He stood in the doorway to see them leave, his mother turning with a small wave as the visitor's door closed.

Dabbing his own eyes as the guard barked it was time to go back Eugene turned. He recovered himself, returning to his cell with Elizabeth's letter stuffed in his pocket.

Once all was put away, he rearranged his books and straightened his blanket as he wanted to delay opening the letter as long as possible.

Washing his hands with a sense of foreboding he sat down, crossed himself for luck and broke the seal he knew so well. He read:

10 August, '48

My dear Eugene,

First I would like to extend birthday wishes to you. May the New Year treat you well and see you in a better place than jail.

I have not written because it has been hard to decide what to say. You had promised to turn from your radical friends and I trusted you. The lack of trust I cannot bear despite my fondness for you.

I love you but we need to end our correspondence for now you have been detained.

Even though it is for Ireland, it is proof of a lack of trust which cannot be regained even if you are acquitted which I hope you are.

Just the fact you were associated with Thomas Luby and took orders from Smith-Brien and Meagher means that you have been too much of for lack of a better word a scamp for me to consider marrying.

I do not hold your friendship with Richard O'Gorman against you as he is your old Trinity friend. But even that causes upset as Mr. O'Gorman had presented himself to me as conservative and it has not turned out to be true.

Indeed, it is nearly as problematical as your having done so.

I know this is a hard letter and I have tarried in writing it for that reason.

But now my father has forbidden any more correspondence forcing me to pen this note. Otherwise, I would have waited until you left Belfast for Dublin whenever that might be.

In closing, I wish you luck and ask you to destroy my letters as I have destroyed yours,

Yours ever,
Elizabeth

His chest tightening up, he finished reading.

Lying down on his cot he sobbed. He had hoped she would remain loyal for she had been his girl for so long. Certainly he had suspected bad news since the old man didn't really approve but still to see it in black and white was very hard.

Managing to sit up, he opened his portfolio, extracting a sheet of notepaper.

Dipping his pen in the inkpot, Eugene did his best to respond but no words came, just scribblings to be hatched out.

A puzzlement it was since he had thought Elizabeth would love him anyway even if her father hated republicans.

After being awakened for dinner, he splashed water on his face so no one would know as he took his place in the crocodile.

Noting his distress his dinner companion said, "I got one myself last time. Don't worry. When I got home, she changed her mind. At least, you can hope for that."

He played a game of patience afterward in an

attempt to settle his nerves and then sat down for another try. There were fewer crosshatches than the first so he slipped it into the stack of mail for Maureen to take.

New routines stretching out over the next few weeks. Exercise, chapel, and a visit from Maureen and Little Matt.

An hour's time spent chatting by the window, Little Matt in Eugene's lap since he liked to jump up but his mother's dress was ill-suited for use as a trampoline.

Bringing a bag each time, Maureen left with it filled with letters to be sent and dirty linens to be washed.

Once Patrick came which was a great treat. Otherwise, as it was far from Dublin nothing seemed capable of penetrating the prison's gray walls.

Mr. Johnston wrote that Smith-Brien had not been found.

Eugene wanted to ask more questions, but it seemed better to wait. The barrister seemed very busy and far more interested in his case than Smith-Brien, which made sense. Indeed, the man kept writing that when he knew more he would come up and explain in person.

Eugene wondered how much longer it might be but avoided asking as it seemed it would not help.

Week by week he felt himself becoming more accustomed to life in Crumlin Road and that did not seem good.

Just as the leaves began to turn at the end of September Timothy Johnston appeared.

Entering the room Eugene saw that his barrister was smiling which could only be a good sign.

As he sat down, Eugene said, "It must be good news."

"Yes, Mr. O'Reilly I believe it is," the barrister said. "The special magistrate made an announcement

Monday. As the informant's word cannot be substantiated and because of your extreme and impressionable youth he will allow you to be set free on bail once you are in Dublin.

"That is unless they unearth more evidence which is unlikely since they have searched high and low without success."

His client's hands shaking less with each sentence the barrister continued.

"The second hurdle, the first having been when you were transferred. My hope is that you will be given a sentence of time served and released though you must not count on it. Just being in your parents' home will be an improvement. After we can worry about the rest."

Eugene inclined his head.

"Thank you," he said. "What my father had hoped for. Yes, to be at home will be better than this. Perhaps my lady and her father will change their minds too."

"About your lady I don't know," said Mr. Johnston. "Women are hard to understand. But yes better your father's house will be than this. Though this is better than Kilmainham. I visited a client there last week and it was as overcrowded as ever.

"In any case, our time is nearly up. But yes I foresee no trouble. At your age, they know that Smith-Brien had no trouble influencing you. They feel the cart must have been his idea."

"That's true," said Eugene. "He wanted to have risings in Meath and Limerick at the same time."

Mr. Johnston's eyes rolled around in his head as Eugene watched.

"I am as republican as anyone," he told his client. "But with the peasantry worried about starving risings are not likely to occur. At your age though I would not have thought that. However, what you are telling me can only help you.

"But we must wind up. The guard is headed this way.

Here is a letter from your mother and one from your brother which I was entrusted to bring."

Eugene skipped all the way back to his cell. Certainly the barrister's news had been more optimistic than what he had heard earlier.

Better to keep his spirits up and try to plot out how to get Elizabeth back than measure days. Hopefully, they would find nothing more and he could be set free.

Life on a seesaw more or less, deepest depression over Elizabeth alternating with hopeful optimism that he would be allowed bail. The tension being unbearable since there was so little to do.

Just as his nerve ends could bear no more on the evening of October seventh, the guard banged on his door.

"You need to pack up," the guard said. "Word has come that you are being moved back to Dublin tomorrow."

Eugene managed not to jump up and down.

"Do I get to go to court when I get there," he asked, "or straight to the jail?"

"I am not sure. As the train doesn't leave until two, I would assume Kilmainham since court closes at four. You shall be going down with Mr. O'Rorke. That is all. Just be ready by dinner time as I don't know when the soldiers will be here to escort you."

Turning Eugene pulled his grip out from under the cot. He began packing, a process which took longer than it had at Kilmainham because of the things his family had brought.

He was done by ten, needing only to stuff in his dirty shirts for he didn't want to anger the guards by asking for a sack to put them in.

Eugene awoke, first in sorrow and then, remembering he was headed south, with a smile. Hopefully straight home from the court but he could bear anything for one night. Surely if they were sending him back, they must be intending to do what Mr. Johnston had said.

At one as had been promised the guards came back. More endless corridors, out the main gate and then south.

At breakfast, he could not find O'Rorke, which seemed a bad sign for he must not have been kept in a temporary cell.

Eugene tried hard not to think about it. The harder he thought about it the guiltier he felt. Had his father been away he would have been the one on the box instead.

Concentrating on dressing and shaving as well as possible, he barely heard the guards when they came.

"Follow us with your grip," they said.

"They are ready to take everyone over to the court. We are running late. You must hurry or his honor may be upset."

Eugene answered, saying that he was ready for he had been for hours.

Walking out of the cell for what he hoped was the last time he followed the guards out under the frieze.

Joining several others, he entered the first carriage and rolled out the gate.

To his surprise, O'Rorke was already seated by the opposite window.

"They told me to come with you. Must be the same magistrate. My father will be there along with my barrister."

"This way we can support each other," said Eugene. "I am very nervous. I shall be glad to see my family, but the magistrate and his huge wig scared me last time."

O'Rorke nodded, saying "Me too. At least, we are together. But I wish you had known about the man in the back. Otherwise, I would not be here. My father is very angry. He is not as republican minded as yours."

Looking at him, Eugene said, "I wish I had known. Had my father not been away I would have been driving. Please, what more can I do? Anyway, it is Smith-Brien they want, not us."

"I know. Still I don't know if they will let me go home and I think you will get to."

After that, there wasn't much to say so Eugene said nothing.

He looked out the window in wonderment instead. Somehow after a summer spent in jail every shop seemed exotic.

Fifteen minutes that seemed like thirty. The thought that something could yet go wrong was terrifying.

Another set of clanging gates as they rolled into the entrance to the court and yet another crocodile.

Eugene headed up the stairs and then down to the right, O'Rorke on his heels. Entering the courtroom, it was even more splendid than he recalled with the special magistrate on the bench looking as intimidating as he had before.

Looking round, Eugene spotted Timothy Johnston and sat down. To his joy, all the male members of his family were just behind, even Patrick, who must have traveled south to get there.

He did his best to keep his hands unclenched, but they crept into his pockets seemingly by themselves.

O'Rorke's case was taken first, ending in a ride back to Kilmainham, which put fear into Eugene's heart. Fortunately, before he had time to think he was instructed to stand.

To his relief instead of being returned his honor

merely proclaimed "Mr. O'Reilly you are being granted bail. Once your family posts it, you shall be free to go to your father's house. You must return in three weeks to be sentenced. That is all."

Sinking back down for he had been so anxious he had barely been able to stand Eugene was pulled upright by the combined efforts of Patrick and James.

They went out into the hall where another guard ordered Eugene to sit.

"Why?" Eugene asked. "I am with my family. They won't let me leave."

"You have to stay here and wait for them to return from the office," said the guard. "Since they knew the amount yesterday they should be back shortly."

Not wanting to hear more from the guard Eugene sat in silence. James and Patrick kept him company until the other three returned.

Once they come back with a receipt for the guard to his delight Eugene was free to go for the first time in what seemed like forever.

He was so happy he wanted to dance down the stairs. As his legs were a little weak, he walked between James and Uncle Jarleth instead.

Breaking into a loud cheer as they walked out the front door he made them all smile.

An embrace from Tom and then they were off. Eugene's mother was on the front steps as they pulled up ready to cover his face with kisses, followed by Polly with more of the same.

Eugene having been properly congratulated, the O'Reillys proceeded into the dining room for a grand luncheon with all of his favorites. Roast chicken, potatoes and a large trifle which he consumed large amounts of for he had not had any since he left home.

He headed upstairs for a very long bath. Dressing

from the skin out in clean clothes he felt like his old self, or rather a new person whose sartorial deprivations had been left behind.

Descending the stairs, he handed the maid a message for Elizabeth which had been written in Belfast but not sent as it had seemed better to wait until his arrival.

Once the note had gone, he went back up for his riding boots. As he took her letters out of their cubbyhole, he thought about taking them along to feed the ducks in the pond. But no. It would be far better to wait and decide.

Running downstairs, he went out to the stables. Tom and Mr. Moonlight were happy to see him. Tom because he had had to exercise all the horses in Eugene's absence and Mr. Moonlight because he had missed his master.

Once Mr. Moonlight had been saddled up, he swung his leg over and rode out the gate. It was something he had looked forward to the entire time he had been behind bars. Truly he felt freer riding than anywhere else.

The maid handed him Elizabeth's response as he came in covered with mud, heading upstairs to change. To his dismay it read:

10 October, '48

Dear Mr. O'Reilly,

Thank you for your note. I am glad you are home but am still forbidden to correspond. Please do not contact me again.

Sincerely,

Elizabeth

Once he had read her note, he tossed it into the fireplace. Even though he had rather expected her response, he had hoped for a different one.

Sitting down on the bed, he stared at her letters and then thrust them back into where they had been.

He freshened up before heading downstairs, a huge smile on his face. He was so happy to be home nothing could mar his joy.

The next few days resembled a continuous fete. First a theater party with James and Susan, followed by a visit to Navan with Patrick for the remainder of the week.

With hugs and kisses all round for Maureen had come down with Oscar and Little Matt he headed south because he needed to see Timothy Johnston.

He attended Mass on Sunday with his parents, followed by an afternoon spent listening to his mother talk about James' wedding plans.

His grateful father, having managed to escape to the library with his cigars, smiled. He was glad Eugene was there to listen for he now knew more about the Lake Country than he had ever wanted to know.

Eugene felt disoriented when the maid came knocking on the door about his bath.

So accustomed had he become to his cell in Belfast he barely knew where he was. In a second he breathed a sigh of relief as it sunk in that he was home with the early light pouring through his lace curtains.

Appearing two hours later, he descended frockcoat in hand to the dining room and took his place. He ate large portions of everything, so much so that there was no toast left for his father.

"Why are you eating everything?" asked his father. "You shall become very stout. You just consumed four pieces of toast and who knows how much bacon."

Eugene responded, saying, "I am sorry. I didn't mean to eat all the toast. All they gave us was porridge and tea for breakfast. Bread with dinner but never toast. I don't think I've had an egg the entire time as everything was watery. Tomorrow I shall eat less.

Already I feel stuffed and a little ill."

"That makes sense," his father said. "Terrible food in the jails though after Mr. Hall's grisly mutton it probably bothered you less than some of the others. I remember you eating like that when you would come home. Just leave me some toast tomorrow.

"Lunch out today I think. First we must see Mr. Johnston. Afterward, we can cab it and lunch with James at my club since the ladies are visiting today. So try to stop eating so you can avoid having to waddle."

Eugene laughed for he didn't mind being teased by his father.

"The jail food was worse than Mr. Hall's though I do believe the tapioca was better. But cook's efforts are better by far. Another cup and I shall be ready. I brought my coat down so we can leave directly."

Eugene sat in the dining room luxuriating. What had seemed ordinary now felt like a palace.

Just as he was finishing his tea, his father came back in and said, "We are running very late."

Handing his son a large parcel he continued, saying "Here, carry this. Some of the documents connected with your case. Timothy didn't have space for everything but he needs these today. Come on now, don't tarry. The traffic will get worse soon.

"While your mother has been shopping I have been helping Timothy. Much time taken from my own work, but James has made much of it up. Very tiring but in a few days it should be over."

Eugene looked down at the carpet.

"I know and I thank all of you. I am not sorry for what I did for I hate England, but I am very worried about being sent back."

Matthew O'Reilly looked his younger son in the eye.

"As I told you getting bail was the first step," he said. "We are going downtown to discuss the other. Try not to worry about it for now. Remember that you will be there to listen. If you don't understand something, I shall explain afterward."

They stood on the front step till the carriage was brought round. Once downtown Tom had to hold the door since Eugene needed both arms to hold onto the papers.

As they entered the office, Mr. Johnston emerged from the back. Having his clerk take the parcel he escorted both O'Reillys into his office, seating them by the windows overlooking the street.

Once he had looked through everything the barrister rose and sat down again before starting in.

"I have been thinking about what to tell the special magistrate who I am sure will be sympathetic since he already issued your bail," the barrister said. "What we are trying for is a sentence limited to time served. This means, Mr. O'Reilly, that the time you have been in Kilmainham and Crumlin Road would be considered sufficient."

Eugene pulled his fists out of his pockets.

"That sounds very good. I don't want to go back."

"We are hoping you don't have to," his father said. "Tell us Timothy of the meeting that has been scheduled since it shall decide the issue."

"All right, Matthew," said Mr. Johnston.

"A meeting has been arranged," he added, turning towards Eugene. "In two days' time in the magistrate's chambers with the Crown and a man from the Special Commission. I am hoping they and I can come to a final decision.

"From my meetings with the Crown's attorney yesterday I have learned that they are leaning towards time served because of your youth and your minor role in the summer's fiasco."

Nodding, Eugene's father managed to respond.

"Good news," he said. "The best we can hope for. I am sure Eugene does not quite understand all of this since James and I handle all the legal matters. However, I am sure he understands about not going back to jail."

At that, his son chimed in.

"Yes I do," Eugene said. "I know you and Mr. Johnston are doing a good job for me."

Timothy Johnston looked at his client.

"I gather you are comfortable with having your father make explanations," he said. "But yes the main thing is that they are leaning towards not asking for you to be sent back. What else they want I do not know but that would be the crux of the matter."

"My second boy is very bright but impulsive," said Eugene's father. "This is the best outcome we can hope for as he insisted on continuing. I shall not go into it further. What is done is done. He would pay any more lecturing no mind anyway. He is already daydreaming and looking out the window."

Turning Eugene said that he was paying rapt attention which neither attorney believed. Like all young people, Eugene ignored what seemed boring.

Rising, Timothy Johnston said, "I shall send a message after the meeting. Meanwhile, as you leave the clerk will set up a time for next week so I can report back."

Breaking in as he wanted to make sure he understood, Eugene asked, "Shall I be here or just my father and brother?"

Both attorneys laughed though not unkindly before Timothy Johnston answered.

"No," he said. "Maybe James but definitely you. You will find out what happened and then go back to court once more to be sentenced. Then you will be done."

Smiling he continued. "What is second nature to us is not to you," he said. "But yes that will be the end."

Once the time was set, they met James for lunch. Heading home afterward, Eugene managed to sneak past the ladies and take a long nap.

The next week passed in a blur. Eugene did his best to avoid thinking about what might happen.

Returning downtown with his father they were greeted with the good news that the barrister had hoped for.

Eugene's anxiety disappeared. At least, he wouldn't have to go back.

He was so elated and filled with relief that he barely heard the rest of the sentence, but then he heard the last word, "exile."

"What!" he cried. "I thought I was done and could go home and back to the Guards."

Barrister Johnston looked very startled.

Shaking his head, he asked, "Don't you remember what I told you last week? In return for a plea and lesser sentence, the Crown was likely to insist on you're leaving Great Britain. Surely you considered the possibility as it is what befell your uncle."

Eugene shook his head no.

"We did tell you," said his father. "Timothy, I think he was so relieved to avoid Kilmainham that he paid it no mind."

Mr. Johnston looked at Eugene, saying, "That must have been it. In your excitement, you did not hear but it is part of the arrangement. The magistrate will tell you so from the bench.

"The Crown shall not budge on this. Unless you are willing to leave, they shall withdraw our arrangement. You will be sent back to Crumlin Road with a five-year sentence of hard labor. Even for one as young and healthy as you, it would be very hard and might take your life. You would be better off just to accept the conditions."

As the two attorneys sat talking, Eugene sat between them looking stunned. His father wondered if he even understood until Eugene suddenly burst out, shouting:

"I don't want to leave. I need my family. But the men looked terrible crossing the yard to pick oakum. I don't think I could bear it."

Taking his son's hand, Matthew said, "Son it is a very good sentence and you must accept it. The alternative is not tolerable either for your mother or I for you. Do not look so afraid. Perhaps Palmerston can help us. In the meantime, you can go back to Paris. Andrew shall be happy to have you.

"Between your riding and the Guards surely an overseas commission will turn up. Hopefully, you can return in a few years but don't count on it. The Crown is laxer on this than in '96 but it may be quite a while."

Eugene turned to his father.

Fighting back tears he said, "I know it is a good sentence, the best I could hope for. It is not that I mind having to go overseas it is that I have to stay there. But perhaps I can leave after November. James very much wants me to stand up for him."

His father nodded.

"Yes," he said. "Your mother and I do too so we can be together. I don't know if they will allow it but can you ask Timothy as it will mean a lot to Emily and James."

"Matthew," said Timothy Johnston, "you know I shall ask, but it seems unlikely as the Crown generally allows only a week. So prepare for that though we can hope that as it is an important family occasion, it might be permitted."

Concluding, he said, "Now that your son has accepted what has been worked out I shall speak to the Crown and ask whether he might remain until then. But have your wife start packing his things in case they say no."

"No surprise to myself or James. A blow to Emily and Eugene as they have no knowledge of legal affairs. But I thank you for trying."

Home and then a frantic push to have everything packed. Another trunk needing to be acquired in the end since Eugene's boot collection had grown since his departure from Mr. Hall's.

A week and then back downtown. Twitching because he felt terrified Eugene stood in front of the magistrate. He accepted his sentence as Uncle Jarleth offered encouragement from the bench behind.

6 PARIS, NICE, PALERMO, STAMBOUL & NOVI SAD

One more breakfast and down to the pier.

Matthew and his sons stood in silence with Eugene in the middle. Reaching out for Eugene's hand, James squeezed it tightly. He was so upset he couldn't speak.

Eugene did his best not to weep. Knowing that he might never see Dublin again was painful. Having to make a new life elsewhere was terrifying.

As Eugene tried to form words his father said that they were proud of what he had done. It had been right even though so much had been lost.

Concluding, he said, "You like adventure and new fields to conquer. More of that in Europe I hear than in Dublin. Andrew shall look after you. He loves you as his own. A comfort. You will be near family."

The whistle blew.

Embracing his youngest for the last time, Matthew gave him fifty pounds to start with.

Walking to the gate, Eugene boarded the steamer. He ducked inside, and then, reappearing, waved his handkerchief as the packet steamer headed for the sea.

A much nicer cabin than the old ones, two carpets instead of one and a brass berth instead of wood.

Putting his grip down, Eugene sat down to write his mother. She had always been a closer friend than the others and had always understood.

Walking to the gate, Eugene boarded the steamer. He ducked inside, and then, reappearing, waved his handkerchief as the packet steamer headed for the sea.

Better too to sit writing than stay out on the deck and watch Ireland slip away.

The next morning, he was awakened by loud shouts and noises as the sailors tied up in Gravesend. For a brief moment, he thought he was back in Crumlin Road. Heading up on deck after breakfast he watched as the passengers boarded until they were off again.

The next afternoon Eugene arrived in Paris.

Embracing him, his uncle said, "I am happy to have you back though I am sorry for the reason. Terrible it was to hear about your detainment. It brought back bitter memories. Your mother has asked me to keep an eye on you and I shall. I am sure you will be able to manage. You are as feisty as me."

For the next fortnight, he lived suspended between two worlds, Dublin and wherever he might end up.

He went to the ballet twice. Otherwise, he sat in the cafes, spending endless hours fretting. If Lord Palmerston could not help and the Sardinians declined, he could think of nothing else to do.

On the second Saturday, Uncle Andrew brought it all up over dinner.

"You need to think about what to do if Nice declines," he said. "You can't sit in the cafes drinking absinthe forever."

His nephew sighed for they all talked like that.

"I know uncle. I am quite anxious. If they say no, I don't think I could bear a normal occupation. James likes boring but not me. Can I please wait a little longer? Waking up every morning and finding that I am not in

Crumlin Road is a gift. Having to leave was a shock."

Eugene's distress was so evident that his uncle softened.

"I can remember it all too well," said Uncle Andrew. "We shan't speak of it again. If the letter is negative, we can think of something else."

Towards the middle of the third week, a letter arrived from Dublin.

29 October, '48

My dear son,

First your mother and I send greetings.

We hope you are well and enjoying your Parisian visit. Mr. Moonlight misses you, but the stablemen wish me to let you know that someone rides him every day.

A note has arrived from London. It states that a commission in the Sardinian army has been secured for you as a junior cavalryman.

Also, a letter has come from Lord Palmerston. He writes that he would like you to make reports every few weeks about the strength of the various forces. They are very interested in obtaining information of a more factual nature than their consulate can supply.

You are to report to Nice in three weeks which should not be a problem as there is a direct train.

Upon your arrival, you are to report to the cavalry commander who has been advised of your coming.

Also included is a list of items that you will need which I have been sent. Andrew can help you purchase them before you head south. I have arranged to reimburse him so you need not worry.

Take care my boy.

Love,

Father

When his uncle came home, Eugene showed him the note. A look of relief crossed Andrew's face. The sense of anxiety draining was palpable.

On Saturday, Eugene's uncle took him shopping. On their return, Eugene apologized because he had bought a few extras.

Uncle Andrew shook his head.

"You have forgotten that there is an arrangement with your father," he said. "The rest can be a gift. However, I do not intend to tell him about the absinthe I have purchased and you must not tell him either."

Laughing, Eugene pushed his chair back.

Uncle Andrew laughed even harder. He understood his brother all too well.

Tears running down his face, he added, "I think it's the green color. You can take it along. It shall make you think of Paris which may or may not be a good thing. It should fit into your trunk if the maid rearranges it. Fortunately, your mother got a large one. But run along now so I can finish my article and then we can eat."

Each day Eugene grew more anxious to start. Much as he loved his uncle sitting around all day was becoming a bore. At least, in Nice there would be something to do.

The great day having arrived he headed south.

As the train pulled in he could see palm trees and a blazing sun filled with warmth. The barracks were much like the ones at Aldershot, the same yellowish brick but an arched veranda and tile roof instead of slate. Voices in a strangely accented French, better than the Italian he had expected for that he did not know.

Reaching the main entrance, he was introduced round, first a Dane and then a chap named Johann, who said he was from Hesse-Darmstadt. Men from all over, Johann said, but only a few Sardinians, all of them conscripts living closer to the town.

Once inside, the captain approached.

"I am in charge of you along with most of the others," the captain said. "Eager we are to see you mounted. Your reputation for horsemanship has proceeded you. We have needed someone. Many of the conscripts can barely stay seated on the parade ground let alone rough country."

Eugene replied, saying "Yes sir. I have won quite a few blue ribbons. I also taught my brother who hates horses. Very eager to begin."

"A few days more. Some of the saddles have yet to arrive. You must be exhausted so I will let you rest. I shall see you at dinner."

Eugene began unpacking. After dinner, he sat down with a game of dominoes. All the talk was of the latest rumor that they would be off to seek out Austria in the spring.

Towards the end of the week, Eugene met the conscripts he was to help train. Studying Savoyard in the evenings, he kept his lamp lit way into the night. Necessary it was. Without the language, the drill would be impossible.

His new routines began taking hold. Bells like Mr. Hall's, two mornings with the infantry followed by afternoons out riding with the new cavalrymen.

A mixed collection they were, he found. Some very talented but quite a few others who could barely manage to keep their seats. Must be in it for the glamour and the girls.

Within a week, the head instructor noticed that Eugene was the most talented of them all. A few more days and even the captain noticed.

To Eugene's surprise since he had not expected a new assignment for months the captain took him aside.

Smiling, the captain said, "Might you be willing to be in charge of training, Officer O'Reilly?

"You have the patience for it along with the skill the others lack. A lot to do, I know, but as you are a born cavalryman, you can skip the infantry drill which shall give you time."

Having learned enough of the dialect to have something to tell London, he sent off his first report. Better something short than wait as something was needed every few weeks.

He wrote it up page by page between rides, keeping everything in the back of his portfolio. Blotting it up, he enclosed it in a letter to Uncle Andrew. It could not be sent directly because the commanders checked the mail.

Late February 1849.

Word swept the barracks that they would be off to Turin soon.

Eugene discounted it as there were many rumors, all of them different. But the commander called a meeting, confirming it.

"We are leaving in ten days," said the commander. "Just battle gear and an extra pair of boots. Everything else can stay. We shall be back soon. No room for it anyway."

Johann said that he was not sure the men were ready.

"Lieutenant they are ready or as ready as they'll be," said the commander with a shake of his head.

"We have been ordered to take the field. Officer O'Reilly has done a decent job with them. Hopefully, they'll perform. Austria awaits us and we cannot tarry."

Surprised that the commander had mentioned him, Eugene sat very quietly, saying nothing for none would listen. At any rate, they would soon find out.

On Monday, he headed up the coast with the rest, doing his best to think about strategy. Somehow the views of little harbors and waves scudding as they reached shore pushed it into the back of his mind.

March twentieth, 1849.

Spotting suspicious silhouettes on the horizon on the second day he borrowed glasses. As the silhouettes turned into enemy riders, he put the glasses down, taking out notepaper to send a message off.

Just as he began his second line, a messenger appeared from the captain with a note that read:

Officer O'Reilly,

Austria has been spotted off to the right. A village I am told is called Novara. Make camp as they have seen us. We shall fight in the morning. It is too late to fight today.

Between nerves and a dreadful headache that not even absinthe would have helped Eugene barely slept.

Managing to drop off before dawn, he was instantly awake when his horse began to whinny.

Once the tether was retied, he laid out his new battle jacket. No point in trying to sleep again since the sun had begun to rise.

Eugene buttoned his last button, listening as the band struck up time to assemble.

He peered through the fog, the enemy campfires reminding him somehow of the fairy lights in the park at Christmas.

He ducked as an Austrian shell screamed overhead with a loud whooshing as it sailed towards the rear.

Picking up his reins, he put them back down when the captain shook his head. Better to just do one's best to avoid being hit until it was time to charge, he said. No glory in it otherwise.

The sun rose higher in the sky.

The cannon began along with a cold rain that was as

bad as fox hunting in the drizzle had ever been. Damp, cold, and then a sense of sartorial distress as the blues and reds of his battle jacket slowly bled into his white breeches.

A message came towards noon that the right flank cavalry needed to ride up into position and prepare.

Collecting his wits, Eugene touched the Saint Christopher's medal his mother had had blessed.

Once the men were ready, he picked up the glasses again.

To his dismay, there were great clouds of dust and smoke but no falling Austrians. Turning to the captain, he asked what to do.

"Another runner," the captain said. "They need to correct. Still we may have to charge. Their line needs to be softened."

There were more shells as the artillerymen checked their coordinates.

Eugene and his men headed down the hill, traveling a hundred yards in what seemed like only a minute.

Eugene pulled out his sabre. As the opposing shells began to worsen, the conscripts fell on either side.

The bugler sounded retreat.

Thoughts crowding into his mind, he gathered up the men who were scattered up and down the slope. Only a few men lost at least. A shell it must have been for they were all in a heap.

At dusk, word came that the battle had been lost. Eugene sat by the fire watching as another messenger approached. To his surprise, the general wanted to see him.

As the general looked Eugene up and down the heat warmed him up.

What a grand thing to be a general with a charcoal brazier. Indeed, the general's tent was almost as warm as the nursery had been.

"Eugene O'Reilly," said the general, "we must flee north which I am sure you know. But it was the artillery so I cannot fault your charge.

"Your bravery and leadership have not gone unnoticed. I have summoned you here to make you a lieutenant from this point onward. If I had lieutenant's bars, I would give them to you. But your pay is effective today. Congratulations."

Heading back to his unit Eugene was so excited he nearly tripped over a rifle abandoned in the mud. There was barely time to think once he reached his men for the camp had been broken.

As he headed into the Alps, he thought of what to write. Everyone would be proud, even his father.

When they stopped, he composed a note, writing of his promotion but not the cold because that would worry his mother.

Once they had gone into camp, he did his best to stay calm for there was nothing to do besides stare into the fire.

Taking Elizabeth's miniature out of his pocket, he kissed it when no one was looking.

Only a year and knee deep in snow, reduced to searching for kindling instead of waiting for coal scuttles to appear.

If only he had gone to Oxford. No doubt Meagher and the rest were nice and warm in Spain while he sat in ice.

A friend's shared flask of whiskey helped make his spirits rise.

Drinking it down, he said, "Thank you. Better now even though my toes are frozen."

Feeling better in the morning for the main thing was that he was free Eugene tried not to think about Elizabeth since it would not help. Surely the Austrians would tire of it all and they could head back to Nice and its girls on the beach to admire.

As the snow began to melt, the captain called them over.

"They have surrendered. A ceasefire so we can leave. Out through the Austrian ranks which is pretty bad. Humiliating."

Johann sat staring into the fire.

Eugene listened as his friend said "Good that we can leave this cursed place. Otherwise, you shouldn't look so happy. They must be worried about money for another season. We shall be dismissed and need new posts.

"Maybe they'll keep us on in Nice until they go out again. I would have gone with the Austrians, but they weren't hiring. We shall have to see."

In the morning, they headed southward. Eugene agreed with the captain that walking through the Austrian lines at the station was almost worse than the snow and ice.

Once they were back at the barracks, the captain sent the conscripts home.

Like Paris, Eugene thought, as he waited for something to happen and the other shoe to drop. Cards, cognac and rides through the countryside with the lances but not much else to do but sit.

Another fortnight and then word that the king had signed agreeing not to fight for a few more years.

Eugene sent the news along to London in a special report, feeling pleased to have something to say since it was hard to learn anything with the men gone.

He wrote a note up for his father for perhaps he had an idea. Soldiering suiting him, another commission would be best, he wrote.

Eugene's father wrote back in a few weeks. His son felt relieved just seeing his father's seal.

19 June, '49
My dear son,
Greetings to you from Dublin.

I was so pleased with your news. We are so very proud of your promotion. The Sardinians did not acquit themselves well, but you did which is what matters here.

The wedding I shall spare you the details of other than to say they both are very happy.

I can write London and ask, but your brother tells me one of his friends has joined the Hungarians. Perhaps that would work.

I would suggest Hungary, at least for the time being. I shall send you a round trip ticket and have James write that you are en route.

Love from your mother and me,
Father

Eugene sat down to think. Hungary sounded like a good idea. Ladies that were no prettier no doubt but a good fight and more promotions. Better than banking at any rate.

Sailing east when his ticket arrived he went ashore in Palermo to send a report and then headed to a café for some wine. He told an old veteran at the next table about Hungary.

To his surprise, the old man made a face, saying, "Young fellow, you'd best turn around and go back to Nice. They surrendered a week ago. No point in journeying on."

"Nothing but drill in Nice. I am glad to know not to go on, but the only other place offering is Vienna and I already fought them."

"About that they don't care," said his new friend.

"They probably would have taken you. They will fight again soon somewhere. They always do."

Another day's wait for the westbound steamer.

Crossing his fingers, he arrived back in Nice hoping they would take him back. To his relief, the captain agreed.

Afterward, there was more drill but in the new fashion. A new sort of lance, the latest thing the others said and useful to learn for more opportunities would come in his direction.

Easier in a way since they were lighter, more colorful too with red pennons fastened to their tips that made it easier to hit the target.

To his distress, everything else was a bore. Reports, euchre and entire afternoons spent on the beach watching the girls in their gauze dresses but nothing else to do but wait.

Another meeting once word came with words that were expected but still a shock.

Eugene clutched his handkerchief with sweaty palms as the commander rose to his feet, saying "Bad news I'm afraid. No funds until next year, not even for drill. You may remain until Christmas. Perhaps we shall fight again, I don't know."

Eugene headed back to the café. Wine was in order and a few bottles at that. Steeling himself, he wrote home.

A note from Dublin arrived by return post and he sat down by the window to read it.

14 August, '49

Dear son,

I am sorry your commission has run out.

A bit of bad luck with the Hungarians. Even James' friend is back by now.

I have written London. Palmerston's clerk having praised your reports, they should be willing to help. I am glad your hated English classes are bearing fruit as is your French.

Patrick and Maureen send their love. Enclosed is a drawing of Little Matt so you can see how big he is. Your mother detects a resemblance. A merry little fellow with your blue eyes.

Uncle Jarleth also sends greetings, he is sending you a separate letter as are Susan and your mother.

Once we have learned where you will be assigned your mother will send you the things she has accumulated. Books, magazines and some warm gloves. She has stopped weeping but still misses you as much as you miss her.

Love,

Father

Eugene waited to hear. Quite nerve-wracking it was. Once most of the others were gone the captain and his strange looks were difficult to avoid.

A letter finally arrived that said:

5 September, '49

My dear son,

First I enclose a shamrock which James has sent along for good luck as some has found us.

To my great surprise, a note came from Lord Palmerston with a dinner invitation for myself and your mother.

Very pleasant and great company. That your mother shall tell.

After dinner, he mentioned your promotion and the unfortunate end of your commission. As they would like your reports to continue, he has spoken with the Ottoman ambassador inquiring about a post.

The Turks are seeking young western officers we were told to train their forces for their next conflict with the Russians.

The ambassador has written Constantinople and is waiting to hear back. Quite encouraging but we must wait.

Perhaps you could return to Paris for now. Andrew will not mind having you.

Meanwhile, be well and know that we are thinking of you.

Love,

Father

Doing his best to avoid the commander for there were only five men left waiting, Eugene did his best to stay calm. An interesting notion, further away it was true but all right.

A fortnight and then another reply.

15 September, '49

My dear son,

Good news. The Porte offers you a commission as bimbashi which is equivalent to major in the queen's forces.

A lancer squadron attached to a garrison near Novi Sad up on the Danube. Just south of Hungary where you wished to be.

Further from your uncle but that can't be helped. The Prussians do not need fighters which is a pity as Berlin would be closer.

I must go as I am at my office. Your mother shall write with our news.

Remember to let me know. The charge d'affaires, a Colonel Rose, needs to notify the Porte. Their lead general, an Omar Pasha, wants to engage as many officers as possible and has a short list of others.

Love,

Father

Taking out his portfolio after dinner Eugene picked up his pen. A letter to Dublin to let them know he would accept, another for Paris. In the morning, a finished report and then the entire stack to the post.

Another fortnight followed by a note in a different hand.

This time from Colonel Rose himself stating that he should report in thirty days, adding that a Michael Jones of the consular staff would be at the pier. A long postscript too, saying that there would be a few days of briefings before he headed north, information about foreign troops being invaluable.

Eugene told the captain who looked relieved.

"Good," the captain said.

"They want the barracks closed. The Turks have great riders. Kurds, the best horsemen in the world after Cossacks, not like the sorry conscripts we get."

Packing up, Eugene caught the next eastbound steamer. The stormy season but that could not be helped.

Sailing eastward, the steamer passed through the Dardanelles headed towards the Golden Horn as the captain had said Constantinople's port was called.

The city looked lovely. Hills covered with houses giving way to forests, the strait headed east and a huge harbor larger than Cherbourg though it looked rather more like Palermo.

A sailor stood next to Eugene, pointing out the different areas. A central part on the right and a foreign quarter that was known as the Pera on the opposite bank.

Hagia Sophia with its minarets by the water's edge behind the sultan's marble palace too. Something to write his mother about. Having belonged to the Byzantines, she would be interested.

Feeling nervous since it was his second commission he managed to collect his things before heading off to the customs shed with his papers.

As he came out, Eugene looked round for Mr. Jones.

To his relief, a man who looked British came up and addressed him.

"Major O'Reilly?"

For a second Eugene said nothing. Certainly the chap didn't mean him for he wasn't a major.

But the man repeated himself. "It must be you," he said. "At any rate, I am Michael Jones, come to meet you."

Extending his hand, Eugene said, "Yes, that is I. I am sorry. I don't think of myself as a major yet."

Michael Jones tried not to laugh.

Smiling, he said, "It must be new. I am the colonel's assistant as they must have told you. We need only get your trunks to the caiques and we shall be off. But you must have questions having never seen the Levant before."

"The cavalry is not a concern," Eugene replied, "but what are the ladies wearing on their heads?"

"They are veiled," said Michael Jones. "They have those and cloaks. Part of their faith so strange men cannot see anything besides their eyes and hands. If you should meet one, just smile. The ones in oxcarts it is better to ignore. They are part of a rich man's harem."

With a frown, Mr. Jones whispered. "Sshh," he said. "Ask later. Not here."

Eugene apologized, saying "All right. No one told me. I didn't know. But where are the bridges so we can get across?"

"There are no bridges here."

"What! How can that be? Dublin has bridges."

"Yes, I know. But not here. The Prussians are helping with one now. Not ready yet. Part of living here to get used to. There are caiques to get back and forth in, like water taxis in London. Two today, I think, because of the trunks."

It took fifteen minutes to cross to the opposite side as there was a decent breeze.

Once the trunks were lashed to the back of the waiting carriage, they headed up the hill. The driver's complaints echoed as they went for both trunks were filled to the brim.

Stopping off at the baths, they freshened up. Almost like the ones in Paris near Uncle Andrew's but different days for ladies and gentlemen instead of separate rooms. The same sort of wooden clogs that pinched his feet but dates and coffee at the end instead of wine.

They walked up as the driver had gone ahead. Eugene's legs were still so rubbery from the sea voyage they made the four blocks seem like eight.

They headed up the drive. To Eugene's surprise, the consulate looked more like a big house than a mansion. There was a walled garden with stables off to the side, but it was much smaller than the embassy in Paris.

Colonel Rose came out, shaking hands as Eugene came up the steps. He was rather tall and looked a little like Tom of all people with the same shock of brown hair.

Smiling, the colonel added that the trunks were in the guest room to be gone through before heading up the coast as not much would be needed.

"I thought I would be given my own space since they made me a major," Eugene said.

Colonel Rose explained, saying, "They are. But you won't need much. Just personal items. It is way up on the border, too far from Belgrade to socialize. You can live in the uniforms. Then too Turks have no dressers and shelves. Just chests and the occasional wall niche. Better to leave it here."

Michael said something about a sherbet house later as they turned to go in.

Eugene nodded, following the colonel into his library. Time to be briefed he thought as the door closed once he sat down.

Tea having been ordered, the colonel started in.

"First, welcome to Constantinople. I am sure you shall be calling it Stamboul like a local in no time. You will do well with the Turks I am sure. The reports are vital these days. London is very concerned about Russian movements in Wallachia and the behavior of Omar Pasha."

Biting his tongue at the thought of helping London, Eugene managed to choke out "It will take me a while to learn anything. I shall be busy with the men."

"We know," Colonel Rose said. "Whatever you can glean from them. The secretary has written about the quality of what you send. Very impressive. Glad I am that you are here. A great addition. Odd, though. Most young men aren't interested in the Levant."

Eugene tried to think of what to say.

Not the truth though perhaps they didn't know. They must take the Times but maybe not all the editions. A common name too. Perhaps there had been no mention in the various dispatches since Stamboul was a long way from Trinity.

The colonel seemed to forget as he droned on, muttering something about Saint Petersburg as he rose to his feet.

Another appointment, he said, with time to meet again after dinner.

Eugene headed upstairs for a nap, stubbing his toe on his trunk on his way to the bed. At six, he raced to get ready for dinner for he had not intended to sleep the afternoon away.

He headed downstairs in his Parisian frockcoat. A little dowdy but Stamboul seemed behind anyway so perhaps it would not be noticed.

After dinner, he stood waiting in the hall with his coat. Michael emerged from the back with two paper lanterns. Apparently there were no lights along with the lack of bridges.

Outside it was pitch black with only a few stars.

Holding his lantern high, Michael explained that otherwise you would be thought a criminal sneaking in the dark.

Heading down the hill, Eugene asked about the sherbet house but Michael was in too much of a hurry to explain. Not a baby thing he muttered as they arrived.

Eugene felt relieved once they went in. It looked more like a tavern than anything else with sherbet instead of whiskey and hookahs for pipes.

Once he had been introduced to Michael's friend the talk turned to beach cafes, girls in lawn dresses and a western store called Stampa's that sold whiskey and books.

Hoping for dates the next morning he got kippers and eggs. Odd to have traveled so far for Mr. Hall's kippers but he said nothing because it was better not to offend.

Going back upstairs afterward, he sat down to read.

Strange how he liked some things but not all. The veils were strange but not the hookah. No Elizabeth to complain about the smoke either. Good and bad everywhere it seemed.

The afternoon spent unpacking with everything put into two piles, one to take, and the other to leave.

All the boots along with the breeches and crops. Traveling clothes and a few sweaters but the rest could stay.

He put the satchel on the bed and began filling it. A red scarf from Elizabeth, the pictures, and his mother's pillowcase. Books, the portfolio and the rest of his writing things under the brushes and soap. Perhaps another bottle of ink. There would be lots of time to write.

Too much rest if such a thing was possible, but an outing on Friday to Stampa's as promised.

Ink, stout and a few bottles of Irish whiskey, followed by a large steak and rice lunch at the table in the back.

Eugene got a bad case of dyspepsia from eating too fast but managed to go down for dinner as his absence would be noted. The fish course made him feel rather queasy, but the custard was quite good. Cardamom, a local spice, the colonel said.

As he was heading upstairs, the colonel beckoned to him in the hall.

"Something to take along," his host said, handing Eugene a large parcel.

"Foolscap, red wax and more ink. You can have it all. Turkish ink is terrible. An expense with all your reports. You would have to return to get more. A gift from Lord Palmerston, one might say."

Eugene said nothing. If only he had known, he could have bought more whiskey instead of spending it all on sealing wax.

He managed a weak smile as the colonel continued, saying:

"It shall all prove useful. But you need to go back up and finish. Michael shall fetch you at nine as the coach leaves the depot at nine thirty to head north. If you have any notes to send, write them tonight so they can go out in the pouch. Much faster that way."

Eugene was up early because he was too excited to sleep. Not just the new post but the riding too, it having proved impossible to borrow a mount.

Finishing a note for his mother, he watched as the servants carried everything down. With Elizabeth's miniature in his pocket for safekeeping, he made his farewells and went out into the hall to wait.

Michael apologized for the delay as they were heading down, saying "We are rather late but as I have your ticket you should be fine."

When they arrived at the coaching depot, the tickets were being collected. There was only time to shake hands before Eugene took his place in line.

Tripping on the first step because it was rather steep, he tripped again at the top as he went in.

Once seated he looked round at the others. There were four gentlemen, one in each corner, three speaking Turkish and the fourth perhaps French judging by his clothes.

The Frenchman nodded in his direction. A fellow officer from a different post probably but someone to talk to at any rate.

Waving to Michael as the coach went round the corner, Eugene sat back as they headed north.

The coach skirted the hill, driving along the shore with the sea on the left and tiny people on each side of the road. Minarets rose from the Turkish quarter until they reached the outskirts of the city and its fruit trees.

A week's run up the coast, much the same as Corstown with what looked to be the same peasants by the road. Men in smocks and women in shawls who could be in Galway but with apples instead of wheat.

Once he had tired of looking he sat back. Trying to pick out a few words, he listened to the Turks and spent time chatting with the Frenchman about Paris.

Odd it was. Somehow he had thought everything would be different.

But no. The coaching inns were nearly the same but for their window frames carved like dragons. Identical lumpy mattresses and innkeepers' daughters had it not been for their veils. Yogurt for porridge and fruit for bread along with the occasional lamb.

The Frenchman was deposited at his depot on the sixth day out.

Riding in the next morning, Eugene strained to see. Flowers instead of dragons on the eaves he noticed as he descended. Must be a different group.

Two men in uniform approached.

Eugene tried not to cringe as the older fellow embraced him because Michael had warned him that it was the custom.

Shaking his hand instead, the younger chap said in English "We are here to meet you, Bimbashi O'Reilly. And nearly on time. A wonder as the coach runs late. I am Stephen Bruce, the other European here. With the infantry and shall interpret until you know enough Turkish. It will be good to have you here."

"Glad I am to see you," said Eugene. "A friend is always welcome. Hopefully, I will not need your help long. I managed to learn Savoyard rapidly and hope to do the same here."

The commander introduced himself in an oddly accented French, saying, "I am Armagan Buruk. We are glad you are here and happy that you had a timely run."

The satchels having been put in, they entered the carriage. Eugene stretched his cold toes towards a brazier set into the floor, chatting in French as they drove along since that the commander could understand.

Twenty minutes later they headed up the drive into the yard. The barracks looked more like Mr. Hall's than the ones in Nice. Must be the snow. No need for arched porches to catch a breeze.

Servants ran by with his bags as they walked in, heading for the officer's lounge so Eugene could meet Osman Senturk, the squadron leader.

Bracing himself for more embraces he listened as the officer said "We are glad you have arrived for the men do not know the lances. My friend in Varna tells me you are a good leader and one of the best on horseback. That the men shall respect."

Eugene thanked him before sitting down to chat. First about the snow and then about the man in Varna who seemed to be a friend of the Spanish chap back in Nice.

Asking about the men and their horses, he learned that the men were at rest elsewhere but that the horses were available for visits.

One of the aides who spoke French took him upstairs. Handy Eugene thought. The Turkish boys must study it too.

The aide opened a door that was halfway down the hall and on the left.

His own suite, Eugene saw. Smallish rooms but two of them as had been promised.

A toasty sitting room with a big hooded fireplace and roaring fire. Wall niches, divans like the sherbet house but the same sort of carpet over instead of on the floor. No chair but a small table to pull over to the divan for a desk.

He asked the aide about the chairs. No, the chap said, or at least not until the river froze because they sold such things in Novi Sad on the other side.

Following the aide, he went into the bedroom. A camp bed by the window that they must have troubled themselves to get, a few chests, hooks in the corner for jackets but no armoires. Ah well, he thought, at least he could lay the breeches flat to keep the wrinkles at bay.

He waited for the aide to leave, took off his boots and began unpacking.

Once all his boots were in a row in a corner and his breeches into a chest with his sweaters on top he sat down on the bed to admire the uniform.

Going back to the sitting room he glanced around and sat down on the divan to think. After a week in motion, it felt terrific.

Small but a step up. Somehow acquiring a divan of one's own seemed rather unsettling though it was nearly as comfortable as a sofa with all its carpets and cushions.

He sat cross-legged upon it which seemed to be the habitual thing. A new skill like hookah smoking though rather more painful.

Odd somehow without furniture. No wonder the colonel had warned against bringing everything up. It would have had to stay in trunks.

Standing up, he went back to his rearranging. Enough space for all the books in one wall niche, portfolio and ink bottles in the other by the window.

His pictures put out by the bed he looked round. Bright yellow walls in the sitting room instead of his mother's maroon and black wallpaper. Orange curtains, the sun streaming in and light everywhere. Not quite home but it would be soon.

The servant knocked on the door with more wood. Eugene smiled to himself once the man was gone for he had managed to pick up enough Turkish to thank him.

Once he had warmed up again, he went back to the bedroom to finish.

Pushing his satchels under the bed since there was nowhere else to put them he rearranged the pictures.

Going back to the sitting room, he pulled the table over to start in on his writing.

Having started a new report for London he began composing a note for his mother which said:

1 October, '49

Dearest Mother,

I hope my last letter has reached you. I hope you are well and have finished the Thackeray book. I wish we had been able to read it together.

My suite is very pleasant with a fire and divan as these Turks call a sofa. Wall niches for books with bright walls and curtains. No wallpaper but lovely carpets to sit on which are all dark red and blue.

My room has a camp bed, not a divan, which is one of their indulgences to make me happy.

Odd to have no armoire but the coats and jackets are on the hooks and all else in chests with my breeches flat against wrinkles and sweaters on top.

Hopefully, I can have a chair and small table to write. But that I shall have to ask.

When you write, please send everyone's news.

A paper would be nice. This is good country for riding but very isolated. Tomorrow a long ride along the Danube, which shall be fun.

If Elizabeth has sent something, perhaps you could send it along. She must have gotten the letter I wrote before leaving Nice.

My best to Polly.

Your loving son,

Eugene

He sealed the letter, putting everything back in his portfolio.

As he sat down, he remembered that the colonel had reminded him to hide the reports. Even though only Stephen could read English, Stamboul had been most emphatic.

Just as he finished putting his draft in the bottom of the chest, a gong went off followed by the aide's return.

Dinner, the fellow said, though with his Breton accent it was hard to tell just what the gong was for.

Eugene went downstairs and through the archway on the right into the mess.

Standing in the doorway, he glanced round. Divans rang all four sides with low tables in front rather like the sherbet house, each set with coffee glasses, spoons, and napkins.

Osman patted a spot by him.

As the waiter came round, the commander picked up his spoon.

Bread and yogurt soup like the inn, like warm clabber and just as tasteless. Eugene choked it down, watching everyone else take two portions.

Taking out his knife when the others did, he watched as the stew emerged from the kitchen.

He copied the commander again for the Turks in the coach had eaten in varying fashions, some with spoons and some with bread.

Once Commander Buruk had picked up his bread, Eugene followed suit, managing to consume a fair amount though a spoon would have been easier.

The stew tasted odd. Fish and dried fruit, dessert and meat together. With a smile, he realized that Grandmama would have been most upset since she would have thought it dangerous.

Eugene finished the rest of his bread since it tasted all right.

Chatting as the waiters came round with coffee, he asked about learning Turkish.

"That would be well," said Osman. "We know French, but none of the men do. Even then it's a different dialect. But you shall catch on. Perhaps Stephen can help you. Or one of the aides."

Afterward, the commander went back to his quarters

while everyone else went into the lounge.

Nice almost had it not been for the divans and the backgammon boards. Something new to learn since the sherbet house had had them too.

Reappearing the commander announced something in Turkish. Eugene caught the words Omar Pasha but understood little else.

Once the commander had left the room, everyone began speaking.

Stephen came over, saying "You look confused, but then why wouldn't you. They always announce things in Turkish, not French. A pride thing.

"Anyway, he said that Omar Pasha is coming to make an inspection with one of the sultan's sons in tow. In winter quarters in Vidin off to the east but will be here as soon as the mud dries or perhaps earlier. Here last summer but without a princeling. I am not surprised as he is in charge of the Danubian sector."

Eugene smiled.

Now the excitement made sense. It had been much the same when Prince Albert visited Mr. Hall's.

Stephen spoke again in a louder tone as the others were shouting.

"Of course, we want to make a good impression. He can make someone's career. He might want to meet you. I would not be surprised. They take who they want not the other way round. You they must have wanted badly. They took very few from Nice."

Eugene chatted with Stephen for a while before heading off to bed. His boots off and nightshirt and cap on, he burrowed under the covers. He drifted off thinking about the great man's visit. At least, the Kurds could ride which would save a lot of time.

Eugene barely had enough time to wash and dress

the next morning before Osman appeared. With Stephen behind they went off to visit the stable together.

As they were crossing the yard, Osman explained that it was a standard squadron with a hundred fifty men and two bimbashis.

Eugene replied, saying, "That was the size in Nice. I am used to working with fifty men, but this shall be much the same. I gather they are born riders. Back in Nice, they could barely keep their seats."

Osman laughed and laughed.

"No wonder the Austrians beat them," the squadron commander said.

"Ours are all Kurds. Nearly born on horseback. Fine in any terrain and I am sure will adapt to the lances. Discipline is the question. They gallop as they please. But you shall see."

They reached the stable doors.

Embracing the head stableman, Eugene walked down past the rows of stalls with the others. The horses were half a hand smaller than the Savoyard ones had been. Very sturdy steppe ponies bred for the southern mountains no doubt.

There was a mare in the last stall with her colt, but the rest were stallions or geldings.

A few cows and their calves on the other side. Milk and yogurt, Stephen said. They ate so much of it that it made sense to keep them.

Eugene asked about the water. It seemed odd that there was no well.

"It's all right," replied Osman. "The winters aren't bad enough to justify the expense. The creek is behind us. If it freezes, there is the river."

"Ah," said Eugene. "Sounds more secure the other way somehow. No time to look at the creek today, though. I would like to see the saddles instead. To figure out where to put the lances."

Osman having left for a meeting, Stephen and Eugene went into the tack room with one of the grooms.

Eugene took out his pencil and poked the pommel.

Explaining, he said, "I'm trying different spots to see where to brace the lances. At home, there would be rings but here I must improvise. I am almost done. Then we can leave as I have to go up and write it all down."

Once he had finished Eugene headed back to his suite.

He began to draw up new diagrams and lists, using the old ones from Nice.

Fewer lessons as they all could ride but a different drill with and without pennons, the lances upright and horizontal.

He added sabres but with a question mark. Those they probably knew. No point in retraining from the tactics book. It would take too long and get to the same place.

In the afternoon, he rode out with Stephen in tow, following the men across the meadows to the river and then down into the shallows.

As they splashed along, an Austrian waved from the opposite bank. No wonder the colonel wasn't worried about them. They appeared completely harmless.

Galloping back into the woods after the men there were some big jumps. Stephen wanted to go back because he was nervous. Good that he was infantry, thought Eugene, for he rode no better than James.

They headed across the meadows and back. It was dusk with the moon beginning to rise.

In the evening, Stephen came to visit with a bottle of Scotch whiskey to share. Rinsing the dust off his glasses, Eugene broke them out. As it was a pure malt, it was a good time to christen them.

Eugene's feet felt warm as he held them up before the fire, suddenly feeling ice cold as Stephen asked why he had come.

Eugene's mind raced as he figured out what to say.

Stephen asked again.

"I had trouble with the Crown," Eugene said. "Then too I didn't want to be a lawyer like my brother. At Aldershot for a while but overseas looked more interesting. With the Sardinians after that ended. My father's friends in London helped me find this."

To his relief, Stephen said little, just that he had been bored in Torquay but had hoped for Stamboul, not a backwater.

Continuing, he said, "This does make more sense. The Turks need help where the Russians will be."

Feeling very relieved Eugene replied.

"It does seem more like Corstown where my Grandmama was than Dublin. But eventually we may be sent elsewhere, Armenia or perhaps Iran. At least, the post should last for a good while. The main thing since I have already had to move once."

Stephen sat quietly as he was intent on finishing his glass. They had a second round after the first but no more because it had to last.

The next day's drill went better than Eugene had expected.

Omar Pasha having grown up in the west, there was no need to start at the beginning. Then too since the Kurds hunted with spears they would not have much trouble switching from spearing boar to charging Russians.

He managed without Stephen's help. The other bimbashi knew a little French and his Turkish was coming along.

Then what seemed like a week of days spent over backgammon and stout as storms made their way through.

Helping to shovel out afterward he attracted some odd looks but still it was better than sitting.

Somehow the cold made him miss James though maybe it was the snow since it was part of Christmas. He tried not to think about it, but it all came welling up anyway. So far from home, no church let alone any angel chimes.

Running upstairs to collect his letters, Eugene rode off to the coaching inn since the southbound coach would arrive the next day.

He purchased apples and dates next door. Heading back through the darkening woods, he put the fruit in a bowl in his sitting room for the apples reminded him of games with Patrick and the others.

In the evening, he sat in the lounge practicing his backgammon. A useful game to learn since they all played and an even better way to practice the officers' Turkish.

Stephen argued back, saying one form of Turkish was enough along with the French.

Replying with a shake of his head, Eugene said, "I know four already if you count my rusty German. One or two more won't be very difficult. It should help later. Fortunately, for me, languages come easily."

When the commander came out to inspect, he didn't mind the men's eerie shriek when they charged. Better ignored, he said, as to train the men out of it would be very difficult.

The day after the inspection Eugene was called over after dinner.

Feeling anxious, he made his way across the room but it turned out Commander Buruk only wanted to chat.

"Bimbashi O'Reilly," the commander said, "I commend you. They are doing better with their lances than I would have thought. Their charge was much better than last week. You need only continue as you are."

The next week Eugene began drill for the shock and melee. It did not go as well as he had hoped. Though the men were quite good at charging the second group did not want to wait.

Sitting up late, he rewrote his lesson plans which took up much of his correspondence time but it could not be helped. To his relief, even the commander said the shrieking wouldn't bother the general.

Living from post to post everything blended with his letters. Rides into the village timed to the coach runs, London posts on alternate Tuesdays and the rest around them. The commander's clerk asked him to pick up the post's mail, a sensible thing as he sent so many letters off.

He rode off to the post at a gallop, a letter from Dublin on the top of the stack.

Better to open it in his room since something was inside. The letter burning a hole in his pocket, he sat through the weekly lecture.

Pulling out his letter knife, he sank into his divan. A dried rose and note in Elizabeth's hand fell out of the envelope.

Pouring himself a glass of whiskey Eugene opened Elizabeth's letter.

No kinder than her last, he thought, hurling it into the fireplace followed by the dried rose she had enclosed.

As tears began to form for surely she was dancing

with someone else he retrieved the whiskey bottle for another glass.

Waking up with a bad headache, he spent the day in his suite in tears. Meantime everyone had gone off to the mosque since it was one of their holidays so it was quiet. When it got dark, he had a glass of stout and an apple and went off to bed wishing he was home.

The sun came out for a treat the next morning after the rain that had matched his mood making his spirits lift.

At the commander's meeting down the hall, he heard the latest news from Vidin. Late February for the general's visit, Buruk said.

A sigh ran around the room, there being only nine weeks left to fix everything as everyone chimed in with talk of what needed repair.

Eugene said little as he was not well.

Mentioning the stable doors, Osman suggested a ladder for the hayloft along with the parade ground fence and gate.

Shaking his head, the commander said that there was enough money to repair the baths but not everything though the village carpenters could make ladders and such.

Stephen asked about Christmas once they were in the hall, saying:

"Last year the other fellow and I celebrated together. An Anglican but that didn't matter since even the Christians here have their own customs. The commander will let us have two days. Boxing Day being another of their holidays we shall have three."

Eugene smiled because he had been about to ask.

"A wonderful idea," Eugene said. "Maybe we can find some boughs. No mistletoe but then no ladies either. Dates and apples from the village store."

Stephen sighed. Prayers together and the Christmas story, he said, far better than being alone.

Eugene collected boughs from the trees along the river, wrapping them around the windows. Pretty, not quite as nice as Polly's garlands but the same Christmas smell.

A quiet holiday on the twenty-fifth but very peaceful.

Turns taken with the Christmas story on the twenty-fourth and more of the same the next two days until it was time for backgammon downstairs.

January and not enough hours to go round as the pace of things picked up.

A blessing that he had learned enough to make himself understood in the men's Turkish, Stephen being much too busy to help.

Work in the morning, drill, and patrol after dinner.

Gradually everything was repaired.

As February began inching by even the horses seemed nervous but a strange calm set in as the great day drew near.

A few days before the general came there was a grand rehearsal with the entire squadron.

Lining them all up, Osman rode past as Eugene played Omar Pasha's part. A few mounts were skittish, but otherwise, everything went well.

The next day Eugene spent the morning in the tack room. Checking all the harnesses for they needed to be in good repair, he watched while the grooms polished the saddles to a high gleam. The general was sure to check.

One last inspection the day before since the commander was very anxious. Fortunately, everything was in order.

The barn whitewashed, copper kettles polished, gate hinges replaced and another mock review that ran like clockwork.

The new red silk pennons even matched the sashes of the new uniforms that had come up from Stamboul with their dark green over tan. Something the prince was sure to notice, Eugene thought.

Eugene headed back to his suite to relax for the men had done well with their turns and hit nearly all their targets.

Taking out his new uniform, he tried it on. The sleeves were a little short, but the cuffs could be yanked down. More stylish than Nice's red and blue, gold braid instead of black. The boots were tight, but they had a nice sheen.

When the gong rang, he changed before going down because he might spill.

There was complaint upon complaint in the lounge after, something about yellow boots.

Stephen explained, saying that they had had yellow boots and robes until the grand vizier had switched to western uniforms.

Whispering back, Eugene said that he was glad. To have had to wear colored boots and dressing gowns would have been too much.

The next morning everyone was awakened early. Eugene's new boots pinched his toes as everyone lined up to salute.

The dignitaries came up the drive as everyone tried not to stare. Omar Pasha with all his medals, the prince wrapped in furs surrounded by aides on Arabian mounts.

Standing still Eugene and his men watched as the prince emerged from his carriage. To Eugene's delight when the general returned their salute, he seemed to be looking straight at him.

Heading inside, Eugene came back out. He headed for the stables to meet the aides and their horses. Both were too fine for cavalry but glorious.

Reluctantly he went back inside when the gong rang, changing his mind once he was in the mess. It had been transformed with even the commander's carpet brought down.

A procession of flute players exited the kitchen, leading the kitchen staff with their huge platters of shish kebab and pilaf. The music continued in a circle around the mess and up the center.

Kneeling before the visitors, the cooks offered everything. Like Buckingham Palace, it must be, just with different food.

Once the food was done, the speeches began. The commander first, followed by Omar Pasha and the prince.

Eugene tried to understand since the prince spoke very fast and with a strong Stamboul accent. Something about the sultan sending greetings, but he could not catch the rest.

There were cheers all around as the prince sat down. Omar Pasha rose to his feet followed by the prince. Both pleading exhaustion they swept out headed for their suite.

Eugene followed them back upstairs, settling in once he reached his sitting room because there was time to read another chapter.

He had only finished five pages when there was a knock on the door.

To his surprise, it was not the firewood man but rather one of the aides saying that the general wished to meet him.

Putting his jacket back on Eugene went down the hall. He felt nervous for who knew what they wanted. Taking his place on the divan behind the hookah, a million thoughts ran through his mind.

He said nothing but smoked and waited.

The general turned in his direction.

"You must wonder why I have summoned you," the general said. "Don't worry. Nothing is awry. I merely wanted to meet as you came so well recommended by your Novara commanders. Doing well here, I am told. Even learning common Turkish, they tell me."

One of the aides spoke once the general was done, something about better field glasses having been ordered from Paris.

Managing to speak because he wanted a pair Eugene smiled when the general responded.

"Then I shall give you a pair. Very useful for detecting troop movements and on patrol. Only one per squadron though as they are an experiment. If they work out, the Porte shall order more."

Eugene had one more cup of coffee and then was dismissed.

Crossing to his room, he was nearly in a dream state. Something more exciting than apples and dates to write home about too. Surely his mother would be thrilled that the general had wanted to chat.

In the evening, he went down into the lounge.

Laughter was ringing off the walls because all the aides were there. There were two backgammon tournaments instead of one along with gossip about the latest tidbits.

The Russians still not ready to fight though it must still be coming. With more wheat being shipped their old worry about the Dardanelles must be back. Like a volcano awakening for they wanted to control the strait.

Eugene listened, taking mental notes because it was

something new for London.

Drifting over to the backgammon boards, he played a round with one of the general's aides as the man could prove useful. He fared badly, but it was worth losing to be able to speak of things military.

He played one game and then another.

Rising, the aide introduced himself.

"This I should have done earlier," he said. "I am Ibrahim Acer of Stamboul, chief aide as they told you."

Continuing, the aide said "Pleased I am to be chatting with you. So few at the posts on our tour are interested in such matters. Not even the Russians excite them. A true backwater but important, the Austrians being so close. They speak of the lancer squadrons day and night in Vidin so it's good to speak with the bimbashi of a squadron."

Eugene smiled as he introduced himself.

"I learned the lances with the Sardinians at my last posting. Glad I am that you are here. The officers' interests being limited to Belgrade since it is closest and not the enemy. I wish the Russians were closer. They are more critical than Austria."

His new friend looked up as he set up the board again.

"Varna tells us that the enemy looks for the lances," the aide said. "They are easy to pick out on hilltops as they are carried upright. Rifles can't reach that far, but the new Krupps can. The Porte is still deciding. They take forever. But the general thinks the best course is to carry the lances in battle position at all times. End against the saddle horn. Then they don't stand out."

Yawning, Officer Acer said it was time to retire. Walking him upstairs Eugene fell into bed because he was too tired to work on his draft.

Time for that in the morning, a paragraph or two about the Krupp guns. Perhaps London should put in an order.

A most useful chat. Enough information for two reports if not three.

Pacing the next morning to calm the butterflies in his stomach, he hoped the weather would cooperate.

Eugene ran downstairs to eat, back up for his sabre and then out to the parade ground, arriving just before the notables arrived. The men and their horses did well with the targets being hit each time. Applauding the Kurdish exhibition at the end, the prince went back to rest.

Eugene worried about the last gap in the fence as the great man made his way down the line with Osman. To his relief, the general said nothing.

Once Omar Pasha had finished his review, he rode back up the line waving as a great huzzah rang out. A very good sign the other bimbashi whispered.

Back upstairs Eugene changed his boots. They were so new all his toes tingled.

He went back to his report as there were, at least, four pages to add, hoping that no one would knock until he was done and the report back in its spot inside the window frame.

Dinner was nearly as good as the day before. Everyone ate until they were stuffed. It would be back to yogurt soup once the visit was over.

Afterward, several of the aides sat smoking in the lounge but not Officer Acer.

Feeling disappointed as he had hoped to learn more, Eugene waited until the chief aide reappeared around ten.

They played backgammon until the servant banked the fire before heading upstairs. Eugene was not sure what to do. Somehow it looked awkward to ask to correspond.

Just as they reached Eugene's door, Ibrahim asked if he could visit for a few minutes, asking if they might write as their shared military interests would make for a lively exchange.

"We are occasionally in Stamboul. Should you be there at the same time, perhaps we could see each other."

Eugene nodded his yes.

Smiling, Ibrahim continued.

"That will be great. It'll be when they have another big meeting at the Porte. Perhaps my friends can come along. But first the addresses."

Eugene sat fascinated watching his new friend sit cross-legged. That he had tried but it made his knees ache. Must be all the practice he thought as he wrote his address down.

Standing in formation the next morning, his leg starting to numb up, he waited for the dignitaries to appear followed by Ibrahim and the aides. There was one last huzzah and then they were down the drive and headed south.

Eugene stood still already missing them. Once the men had been seen to he headed upstairs.

He sat penning page after page since he had letter after letter to write. Sending a letter each week to Dublin, he wrote several more for Paris each month because the reports were enclosed in them.

He memorized the mail schedule. Two weeks it took for a letter to reach Nice and then another few days for Dublin or a day for Paris.

His Christmas package arrived. Putting it in his saddlebag with the fruit, he rode straight back. The fewer questions about how long he was gone, the better.

He ripped off the brown paper, smiling as red wrap covered with angels emerged. Like Grandmama's, surely something his mother had combed Dublin to find.

He laid everything out in a row on the table. Several books, black kid gloves from Maureen and a scarf from Patrick in one corner. Ten pounds from James and Susan and a shamrock for good luck from Uncle Jarleth at the other end.

At the very bottom, there was a packet wrapped in paper with holly from his mother.

Fetching his pocket knife, he cut the string to find a tin of cocoa and a small cone of sugar in its indigo paper. A surprise. Maureen must have told them.

He stared into the fire and mixed a cup of cocoa. So many memories, all telescoped after two years but still. Dublin and its pantomimes. Nice and now with three hundred Turks in the mountains. Only the warm cocoa was the same, that and the horses for they never failed him.

Wrapping his shawl around his legs against the cold he read all the letters. Tears welling up in his eyes, he opened Maureen's because she had enclosed a small watercolor of Little Matt.

There was a thick letter near the bottom of the stack in his father's hand. Numerous clippings about his fellow detainees fell out after it had been unsealed as two had been found.

Funny how long ago it seemed somehow. Meagher captured but not tried and Smith-Brien still missing. Something about Richard being spared a longer sentence but still Crumlin Road. Just the reading of it was painful. A month had nearly killed him but who could endure a year.

His mother's letter was at the very bottom. Just the sight of her handwriting made him sigh.

Two paragraphs about the Season and word that riding boots now had yellow cuffs. All the rage she said.

Useful for a Stamboul leave though he did not think he would be there long enough to attend anything let alone meet any young ladies.

Smiling, he read that she had purchased a subscription to Dickens's new magazine as a gift. It would come late, but then the border was much too far away for the story to be spoilt.

As winter began to wane, the old patterns resumed. Not as much drill since that the men had learned. Daily patrols instead for those the general had requested.

Eugene led the men out through the shallows and over the ice, copying the Austrians as they did the same on the opposite bank.

Spring came. There was mud everywhere that rose to the horses' knees.

A true surprise, Eugene thought.

He had never seen so much mud. Worse than Mr. Hall's even. But at least there the servant had cleaned all the boots. Another reason to stay long enough to become a colonel. Then a servant would have to do his boots.

Fall following summer followed by another visit from Omar Pasha, this time with Ibrahim and the rest of his suite but no prince.

Then Christmas and a month's leave in June.

There was a happy feeling in his heart as the coach trundled south because Ibrahim would be there. Not enough time to find a girl but still a few weeks with no drill and sherbet houses.

Michael met him at the southern depot but with the carriage as the bridge was finished.

As they rode across Michael apologized.

"I have too much to do to stop on the way up," he said. "If only there were young people. It would be better for you. I know you must be anxious to get out.

The colonel's nieces are back in London having been here for Christmas."

Eugene frowned as he had hoped to stop off at Stampa's.

"That's all right. No need to disrupt everything. If only the nieces were here. I miss having ladies about."

Continuing, Eugene said, "My Ottoman friend Ibrahim Acer is in town for meetings with the Porte. A messenger should appear tomorrow. We have plans on the baths or the sherbet house in their district. No need for you to waste time amusing me. Ibrahim and I shall be happy together."

Michael looked very surprised so Eugene went on, saying:

"I suppose it's because he's Ottoman. Here westerners can be friends with each other. Up on the Danube, there are only a few of us. One finds friends where one can. He is a good man. I need contacts in Stamboul to rise higher which he can help with. In any case, he can distract me. Having missed the Season there shall be little to do but read and rest."

Things improved on the third day when Ibrahim came to collect him for an evening out with some of his friends.

They visited a more elaborate sherbet house in one of the Ottoman quarters that featured dancing ladies with finger bells and musicians.

By the end of the evening, Eugene had managed to nearly win the backgammon tournament instead of coming in almost dead last which made him smile.

A few outings to the baths but otherwise days filled with sleep and books.

On Sunday, he headed down the hill to Saint Matthew's.

Otherwise, he slept in. It was nearly as boring as his post.

Arriving for dinner on Friday the French consul brought his niece, a Marie-Genevieve Gibson, who stood as hostess since the consul was a bachelor. Not exactly pretty Eugene thought but very chic.

They walked outside in the garden. Eugene found it fun speaking with a lady in French though when she called him Major O'Reilly it felt strange as he was not used to it.

As they were passing by the arbor, the lady asked when he would be gone.

Admitting that it would be the next week, Eugene said, "I wish it was later. I need to get back. My commander will not let me linger."

"Oh Major O'Reilly that's too bad," said Marie-Genevieve. "I wish we could have met earlier. There is a little dinner at the Spanish embassy next week. I would have gotten you an invitation. More's the pity you cannot join us from the border for one night."

Eugene swallowed hard. If there was anything worse than no dinners, it was hearing about ones he could not attend.

He muttered that it was a disappointment, adding "On my next leave, whenever that is allowed. Maybe I shall see you at Mass. I should like to meet whoever attends though I am sure they shall forget about me before my next visit."

His last Sunday came all too soon. Thanking God for Ibrahim he took his seat in the pew. Otherwise, he would barely have gotten out.

Chatting with Marie-Genevieve, he said his goodbyes to the priest. The latter a good connection for he had known Cousin Eugene but a worrisome one for perhaps he read the papers too. Although as Cousin Eugene had been as republican as they came it was probably all right.

Borrowing a few Walter Scott novels once he was back at the consulate he headed back upstairs to pack.

In the end, he had to borrow Michael's satchel, what looked to be an entire ream of foolscap proving impossible to jam in on top of the whiskey and stout.

A special dinner on his last night, roast beef with a large trifle and a few glasses of sherry.

Eugene followed the colonel to his library for a last briefing before heading north. Much the same as his first he realized. Even Lord Russell had liked his last report.

"Especially the part about the Krupp guns," the colonel said. "A rather large order having gone in on the strength of what you wrote. Otherwise, they ask me to remind you to keep them hidden until they can head for Paris. No leaving them around for curious eyes.

"Whatever else you can glean. Anything about the Austrians. I know that there is no contact, but still the Hungarians keep coming. Perhaps their troops are still present."

Eugene nodded, saying:

"My friends tell me it is a mere trickle now. Their rebellion is done. Many soldiers a year ago but not now."

Colonel Rose glanced down at his watch.

"That I shall tell them. Busier than before so I shall write it down. That's why the French were here. Under orders to cultivate them. The niece is a nice girl. Perhaps you can become friends. I know you have lacked for excitement and she organizes things for the young people."

The next day Eugene headed back. The sun shone as he headed for the depot with Michael

There were even more ships than when he had first arrived. Made sense, the colonel having mentioned that the Golden Horn was larger than Gravesend and Cherbourg together.

As they were riding over the new bridge, Michael pointed them all out. Russian grain boats heading east and European steamers going west, next to Ottoman shore craft that sailed in both directions. Algeria to Sochi, a very long way.

North inside a cocoon being transported from one place to the other.

Everything was just as it had been when he arrived. More drills and grain boats that were very low in the water with the wheat harvest heading east to the Black Sea.

He dined with Stephen at the sherbet house on his birthday. Not as good as western food but a nice break from the mess even though it was too small to have dancers.

Picking up the mail on their way back out, Eugene noticed that there was a fat letter in his father's hand on top of the pile. More clippings fell out when Eugene broke its seals as dusk fell.

Smith-Brien captured after managing to escape his jailers in Tasmania. Picked up by both the *London Times* and the *Illustrated News* he saw. Made sense, Smith-Brien having been the leader.

If only he had never met the chap. He had brought only bad luck. Even panning for gold in the Antipodes was not too bad. At least it was warmer than Serbia.

Things began to run together again. Two years with everyone having to stay put in case the Austrians did more.

Another leave with even less to do because everyone was even busier.

Eugene managed to see Ibrahim who was in meetings at the Porte but otherwise it was one long boring briefing. Still he felt cheered at the sight of a note of thanks for his troop estimates from Lord Palmerston in his own hand.

Managing to get away for Mass, he was called back to the library upon his return.

Doing his best to stay awake and not yawn as he had been out late the night before, Eugene sat and listened.

Complimenting him on having learned both forms of Turkish the colonel said "Very useful it is. If you intend to stay the languages are invaluable along with your friendship with the Acer young man."

Continuing, the colonel said, "I know you are bored there, but your wonderful work should bear fruit once war begins. Another promotion I expect, perhaps in Silestra."

His eyelids drooping shut Eugene bit his cheeks. He explained that he was good at languages, that and it was necessary since officers knew French but not the men.

He added that Ibrahim was a good friend, a correspondent and someone to see on leaves. Useful too, the family being influential.

"The father is very important at the Porte," the colonel said.

"That is why his son is chief aide. Very talented. I have been there a few times, but your friend was away. Elaborate inside as their houses always are. A younger brother who rides. Must be from a junior wife."

Eugene looked started as the colonel continued, saying:

"Don't ask. It shall make trouble. It makes sense to them as does having mothers raise their own babies. No nurses, just the occasional slave girl to help. Odd yes but we are in their country, not the other way round. Good people and, of course, he is a good friend.

"But I digress. The reports are the main thing. Glad

you bought more foolscap. You shall need it. I will send more up if necessary and see you in a year or two."

Osman was at the depot when Eugene arrived with a grin that stretched from ear to ear. He did not complain about the weight of each satchel and grip as he always did.

Very odd since Osman loved to tease about the size of his correspondence as it was far greater than everyone else's. That and Osman's refusal to explain though it was obviously good news, saying only that Eugene needed to see the commander.

Upon their arrival, Eugene ran upstairs. Tossing his things on the divan, the bottles chinked.

The aide admitted him.

Sitting down, his smile grew broader once Commander Buruk had explained that Osman was being transferred.

He added that the general had requested that Bimbashi O'Reilly take the squadron over. An immediate pay increase though the same rank. The Porte being against rank increases though that would change once hostilities commenced.

Continuing once the hookah was relit, the commander said, "Ozgur shall replace you. The bigger suite you can have once Osman is gone. One more room, a tiny study which I am sure you will appreciate. Useful for both your own correspondence and the drafts of my reports for the general. The last would be helpful if you can manage it."

Eugene smiled back. Good news all round, more space and more money.

He sipped his coffee.

Taking a turn at the hookah, Eugene said, "I can do the reports. Glad I am that Omar Pasha has remembered me. And thank you. A good chance for

Osman too. The study shall be nice. I can organize my notes for your reports. Though my written Turkish may have to be gone over."

The commander stood up, saying:

"I can have them gone over so that is not a problem. It will be a busy few weeks what with training the new fellow, but I am glad you are willing. Though for now you must go unpack and rest. You must be tired."

Eugene waltzed his way back down the hall since there was no one to see. It was great news and far more interesting than Marie-Genevieve's gossip about the Russian ambassador's wife.

A study, too, useful for things would be easier to find. The Turkish drafts did not sound too difficult, something to paraphrase from Palmerston's. Good practice too. The secretary would find his mistakes. They must be there not matter what Ibrahim said.

New routines settling in once his birthday had come and gone and Osman had left.

Eugene had more trouble translating the reports than he had expected. Still it was a good thing for it kept his name before the Porte.

As he began corresponding with Osman at his new command near Varna, everything began to blend. Two patrols each day instead or one along different parts of the river, headquarters being worried about Vienna.

Indeed, it was not in the least surprising to hear it was much the same in the east as the sleeping giant had begun to stir again.

Struggling to find out more to report back since the Petersburg pouches were being held up, he managed to fill in with news from Osman about the Pruth.

More artillery and a major review for the sentry had seen the tsar's personal standard from his tower.

He still spent his Sundays lost in talk with Stephen

since there was not much to do until there was a war. Way too much to do after and more promotions too. Even London saw no point in paying more in peacetime, something even the generals could not change.

Eugene's melancholia began creeping back as the February cold arrived for word came that Stephen would be moved. Part of the shifting to the east and closer to Silestra.

Just the other side of Belgrade, fortunately not until after Easter so that they could at least share. A holiday leave at Christmas perhaps though it was hard to know.

Out of the blue, he was granted another leave. Buruk explained that with the war coming there would be no more until the Russians were defeated.

Eugene was not sure he wanted to go.

Finally, he caught the coach south.

Marie-Genevieve had written of a new stationer, a place called Simpson's, and it would make sense to stock up.

Stamboul was as crazy busy as he had thought. Even poor Michael looked gray.

Funny how the veiled ladies looked normal and the western ones exposed as they rushed up the hill since the dispatches awaited.

The staff was all atwitter about the ambassador, a Lord Stratford Canning, who would be coming from Madrid. Michael would be staying he said, but the colonel's private secretary would be going with the colonel since the new man would bring his own.

Sitting in the drawing room, Eugene told Michael "At least you shall still be here so we can visit. My last leave until the war is over. Once it starts, I won't be granted another. Palmerston is hoping I can meet the new chap but it may have to wait."

"Yes, the war controls it all," Michael said. "I think you are right and it will be soon. The Russians look more and more distressed."

Eugene looked at the gardens before going off to the baths. He headed upstairs to dress for dinner. Marie-Genevieve and her uncle were coming.

He put on his best frockcoat and Maureen's silver cufflinks. His uniform jacket would have looked better, but he had forgotten to bring it along.

Once downstairs he sat chatting for it was good to see his French friends.

He managed to remember to use his fork but nearly scooped up the squash with his bread. Hard it was to concentrate on table manners while paying attention.

The ladies having left for the drawing room the colonel fetched his brandy decanter and cigars.

Turning to Eugene, Francois Gibson asked if he was acquainted with an Adolphus Slade down at the Porte.

Replying, Eugene said, "The name sounds familiar though I am not sure from where. I have heard that the Porte was out looking for sailors. My Acer friend told me so."

Looking rather startled, the ambassador nodded his head.

"I have heard that you know the son. I had a meeting with the father only last week. Dinner at his house once or twice. An important family to cultivate. Big at the Porte. Very pleasant."

The decanter came round again.

"He is very pleasant," said Eugene.

"A good contact. I count him as a friend mostly through correspondence as we are seldom in the city at the same time. He has helped me a great deal with my Turkish as only the officers speak French. They are in Silestra now. Hopefully, they will be in Belgrade next and we can see each other. Supposedly a railway is going in."

The ambassador said no more as they went back to the drawing room to listen to the ladies sing duets. Eugene did his best to look appreciative for Elizabeth could outsing them both.

The next evening, he met Ibrahim's friend Koray at a new sherbet house that was not as much fun as Ibrahim's but much better than sitting in his room. The dancing was not as good as the other place, but the baklava was better. Towards the end of the evening, he managed to take a first in the backgammon tournament which brought a grin to his face and another round.

The next afternoon Eugene set off for Simpson's, his eyes shining with anticipation. It would be much more fun than even the tailor as it could all be taken north instead of being left behind in a trunk.

Ignoring Michael's teasing about buying too much, he doubled his list just before setting out.

What with the war, he might not be back for years. Better some extra India ink over what Silestra might have and cheaper too. Combined with the embassy order there would be a discount.

There was lots of traffic. The ladies were all out and about in their arabas en route to somewhere.

When they arrived, Eugene gazed around looking like the Cheshire cat, almost purring with delight.

Everyone had been correct. It looked just like London. All manner of letter paper perfumed and mourning, card stocks with lots of fonts and oceans of blotting paper.

The salesman approached, taking Michael's master list while Eugene looked around and began to go down his list.

A few books from the corner bookcase once he had crossed everything off. Some extra blotting paper to go with the rest. A combined pile in the end so huge it would all have to be brought up since there was way too much to carry.

Once back up the hill Eugene returned to his packing because he would be off on Monday.

At four, he went downstairs. Sitting by the drawing room fire, he read another chapter of Scott's *The Lady of the Lake* for as Simpson's had had it too, he would not have to wait to read the rest.

Michael sat teasing him after dinner. To Eugene's relief, he was hushed by the colonel who said that Michael should stop since he could always get more, but Major O'Reilly couldn't for even Belgrade had no India ink.

Awakening early Eugene finished his packing.

In mid-morning, he headed down to Stampa's for another satchel as his Simpson's order would not fit. Odd since he had skipped the new seal and its wax but still everything needed cramming in.

He went downstairs for a final briefing.

To his relief, Colonel Rose spoke of the Stratford Cannings as he returned from the dining room with snifters of brandy.

Looking rather worried, the colonel said, "I do hope you shall visit when you come. I have grown quite fond of you."

Eugene smiled, saying that he intended to.

"That I would like," he said. "I had hesitated to inquire, but it will make things easier. I am afraid Lord Canning will be an adjustment. They tell me that he speaks only French and will never go to the Porte."

"It is true that he would rather head for Paris," said the colonel. "Still he is a good man. Her ladyship can be a little difficult, but there are two daughters who are a little younger than you. As we speak, they are embarking on the eastern steamer. Glad I am to be staying on in the city under the Queen though in what capacity they haven't decided yet.

"Lord Canning has decided to reappear. Otherwise, I would remain. But all should go well when you return. Michael shall still be here. His lordship's secretary and a lady's maid but otherwise the staff will be more or less the same."

Concluding, the colonel said, "For you it shall not change. The reports are to go to Paris as they do now. Canning will get the gist of them as I do. A good arrangement. The Porte suspects nothing.

"He has been briefed about you and sent documents to read while he is en route. When he arrives, I shall explain further. You need not be concerned. It would be better if you could return before the Russians start but that will not be possible. After shall have to do."

In the morning, everything was brought down. There was twice as much as he had brought, but Michael managed to bit his tongue.

A true kindness. Surely he would be teased for it up north.

Down to the depot and out over the Golden Horn for another run. To his delight, Eugene managed to make a new friend, a Scotsman, William MacDonald, who had already been seated when he climbed in.

An engineer, MacDonald said by way of introduction, heading north to build the new railway.

7 NOVI SAD, BELGRADE, KALAFAT & VIDIN

Eugene arrived back, feeling as though he had barely been away. Ozgur had an even more frantic air than Michael when Eugene introduced him to William MacDonald.

Once they were on their way back to the post, he added that they were late for an important meeting. Something had come from headquarters, he said.

It took three servants to get everything upstairs. Changing out of his traveling clothes, Eugene walked down the hall to the commander's suite. He took his seat and waited as the coffee came round again.

Buruk started in, saying:

"As you have heard, orders have come from Vidin that all is in readiness. A good thing. Menshikov will attack along the river even though it is doubtful they will get help from Vienna."

Continuing, the commander said, "Better to get everyone where they will be needed and away from this end of the line. If there are more maneuvers, the lancers shall remain here under Ozgur with Eugene heading east. Belgrade but probably Vidin. The next report shall say.

"I can take a few questions, but there shall be even fewer answers. We must all wait and see."

The meeting having ended Eugene headed back down the hall.

He unpacked the Simpson's parcels first. Foolscap in towers next to his desk, blotting paper and wax in the drawer. The books in the wall niche with the others as there would be nowhere to sit otherwise.

Sitting down, he started in on his correspondence.

To his joy a note from James announcing he would be a father in May was on top of the pile. Must have been the surprise his mother had mentioned in her last letter he thought as he penned a reply.

Once the stack of letters to be sent was high enough he rose. Going into his bedroom, he rearranged his boots by color instead of height.

Like a miracle almost for they were all cleaned and polished. The servant and his magic brush what with the local mud that aged the leather so fast.

Dining every few weeks with William MacDonald, he spent the rest of his time at his post because there was much to be done.

Three patrols each day instead of two, no matter what the weather. Orders from Silestra, Buruk said, the generals being worried all along the front. Hard to know more, what with the gossip rarely spreading past Belgrade.

Evenings filled with backgammon interspersed with evenings spent writing for there was no one to share a whiskey with anyway.

The Turkish reports took the longest. They needed copying over, once for the general and again for the

Porte. Their composition went quickly since they could be copied from Palmerston's, but somehow the amount of foolscap consumed was immense.

Oh to be a lieutenant colonel and have a clerk. More and more reports, less and less time to do them in.

The riding was glorious. The best part for the Danube was beautiful, far better than the drill though the correspondence was the worst of it.

Better to ride while he still could. In Vidin, it would be more like being a commander, stuck inside and all meetings.

Better than Kilmainham too. A winter spent there would have been dank as a tomb.

As winter began to lift, Eugene started feeling better.

Spending an extra afternoon in his study, he managed to get caught up. It took two hours each day just to stay abreast of his correspondence and he did not want to get further behind.

There was a knock on the door. Stuffing his report behind the cushions, Eugene went to open it only to find one of the men in need of advice about a personal matter.

Dusk having begun its descent as the door closed behind the chap he lit another lamp. Staying up late, he finished a hurried note for Dublin since the coach would come through on Tuesday.

The new orders came through.

Eugene took his seat at the meeting, crossing his fingers he was headed for Vidin.

"News has come from both Stamboul and the general," said Commander Buruk. "The enemy has mobilized, along the Pruth to the north of Silestra. A meeting has been called for Vidin in two weeks. Another in Kars.

"I need an aide and have chosen Bimbashi O'Reilly. Many here are qualified. But since he is headed for Vidin it would benefit him. He can familiarize himself with the citadel and meet those he is likely to serve with. No room for one more as the compartment must be shared. If I go again, I shall choose someone else."

There was a question from the back of the room about who else might be moved.

"I don't think so, at least not for now," the commander said. "They are still not worried about Vienna. The post having been built to protect the peasants and their wheat perhaps some shall leave for Belgrade. It being more defensible as they have an actual fort."

Eugene headed down the hall as the others congratulated him. Thanking them all, he asked if anyone had been stationed east.

The lieutenant on his right nodded, saying he had been in Vidin. A large citadel, he said. Bigger now and very impressive, the stronghold for the western sector as it was south of the major Moldavian towns.

Eugene thanked the commander at dinner.

"You are good at detail," Buruk said. "Perhaps you can see your friend Acer. Enough time to write and ask though not enough for a reply. To Belgrade with the carriage and then east on the railway. Should save a day. They say it is faster."

Eugene did his best not to smile because the commander was very excited about taking the train.

Maybe once they had one they would build another to the capitol. What a true improvement that would be.

On Sunday morning, he wrote and wrote. Ibrahim in Vidin and then everyone back in Dublin. After patrol, he started in on a clothing list.

Ozgur came up to help figure out the sabre that went with the dress uniform. A clip on the belt he had somehow missed which made him blush.

Eugene practiced walking back and forth. The sabre still hit the back of his leg but by suppertime not quite as much. Fortunately, there was a week to practice. By then he might be able to not hit anyone.

He organized the piles and began packing them up. His tightest boots since there would be help to get them off. Otherwise, he'd have to sleep in them.

Extra writing supplies too and a borrowed portable inkwell for his could not be found. Must be back in Stamboul. It had been on his list for Simpson's.

Leaving in the morning, they headed for Belgrade in the post carriage.

A run that felt much like the southbound one, green seats instead of battered red and what looked to be the same innkeeper's daughter though surely it could not be.

They arrived in Belgrade, the citadel looming before them like Kilmainham over the Preserve. Feeling exhausted, for a minute Eugene thought they were the same. But no he realized as the sentries were offering plum brandy instead of gruel.

Watching the others walk up and down the platform at the depot the next morning, Eugene tried hard not to smile. An ordinary train, like the one on the Belfast run.

He held his handkerchief over his face as the steam built up. The pressure of trying not to laugh was horrendous.

Eugene shared a compartment with the Belgrade fellow with the two commanders just ahead.

He watched the countryside slip by, feigning sleep as the afternoon wore on with his jacket for a pillow for the chap was a most talkative sort. Just as excited about the train as the others. Apparently none of the Belgrade garrison had been on it.

Towards evening, he awoke as the moon rose over the trees.

Plucking up his courage when they reached Vidin, Eugene inquired about Ibrahim.

"He is here," the chap who had met them said. "Getting ready for tomorrow no doubt or he would have come out.

"We have been on the move so he probably didn't get the note. I can come up for a minute when we get to the inn. Otherwise, it shall have to wait since I must get everyone situated before I head back."

Eugene thanked him.

"Much appreciated," he said. "We had hoped to connect in Belgrade but with the Russians that may not happen."

He felt relieved when he saw the inn. Much nicer it was than the coaching inns with a large wooden balcony in the great hall, but with animals, not flowers.

Heading upstairs, the aide on his heels, Eugene looked round as he sat down to write. A decent suite with a balcony with the same florid woodwork as downstairs.

The aide started tapping his foot.

Eugene picked up his pen and began.

My dear Ibrahim,

By great good luck, I was chosen by my commander to serve as his aide for the meeting here in Vidin and have just arrived.

I did write, but there may not have been enough time for you to have gotten my letter.

The fellow who met us has offered to bring you this note. You need not respond as I shall see you shortly rather more splendidly attired than you have seen me before.

Your friend,

Eugene O'Reilly

Once it was folded and sealed, he handed it to the aide who said "You have my word that Ibrahim will have this within an hour. I am happy to have met one of his friends. I think he has mentioned you, are you the lancers commander near Novi Sad?"

"That would be me. We are the only post south of there."

"Then all this is terribly exciting. He has mentioned you many times. As my colleague is at the door, I must go. I look forward to seeing you at the dinner if not before."

Heading back upstairs the next day after the morning sessions Eugene pulled some purloined bread out of his pocket. There had been barely enough time to eat what with all the introductions.

After taking a nap, Eugene began dressing for dinner, laying everything out across the back of the divan like the tailor in his shop.

White stockings, tan cashmere breeches stiff as boards and a white linen shirt to match. Dark green jacket with all its braid and gold buttons at the far end by the window along with the cummerbund and cap. The sabre too with an extra clip to keep it from sliding around.

Once he was dressed, he walked about in the boots to soften them up.

As he was making his way back to the doorway from the balcony, Buruk emerged. He had an Order of Valor pinned to his jacket something Eugene had not known of for the commander was not one to brag.

The manservant having checked the clips on Eugene's sabre they headed down.

Worrying about tripping over his sabre, Eugene made it into the mess intact just as everyone headed in to look for their seats.

He stood by the door in all his glory.

Suddenly there was a tap on his shoulder and then an embrace as Ibrahim said "It is our lucky year. I thought I wouldn't see you for months. The commanders are eating together so we can visit."

Eugene replied, saying, "I would like that. It will be much more fun. I promise to do my best not to hit you with the sabre."

"I shall sit on the other side. You can poke the others instead."

It was a grand dinner even by Ibrahim's standards. Like his cousin's wedding with the same wagon wheel platters, he commented, with dancers nearly as good as Stamboul's.

Eugene sat listening to speech after speech as the general droned on, the medals that covered his chest glinting in the light.

He was so stuffed he could barely move once everything was cleared away.

Making his way to the carriage, he managed to climb the stairs to his suite even though his feet had gone entirely numb.

Sessions all week that were all much the same. Questions that went round and round for much was still unknown.

If Vienna attacked, it might be Belgrade for Silestra as the British wanted the railway protected.

Much the same the generals said about reserves. Probably Algeria but a decision for the Porte so it might be Morocco men instead.

Very confusing Eugene thought as he sat writing everything down. Hopefully, London could straighten it out. Too many places with odd names.

Finally, there was a free afternoon to visit with Ibrahim since the commanders were meeting in private.

Walking around the walls as they could not leave the grounds they spoke of things personal as well as military.

Eugene asked about Ibrahim's father as he had been ill and of little Mustafa and his riding for on his last leave he had taken Mustafa up along the strait.

"Quite an impression you made," Ibrahim said. "He is still writing about it. Wants to have his own squadron now. A mite tedious at times. Already he is asking to go again. Hopefully, you can because none of us can outride him."

Eugene replied, saying, "It was fun. He is a bright little chap."

Glancing down at his watch he continued.

"We need to get going," he said. "I need my ride back. Hopefully, we can get an evening off for the sherbet house or the baths. Not as grand as Stamboul, but a break from all of this."

An evening spent on Friday at the sherbet house with Ibrahim and his friend from Silestra. Smaller than Stamboul's but larger than the one in the village. Plum brandy because they were too far east for sherbet.

In the morning, he had a terrible headache. Worthwhile he thought as it had been fun. Then too, the Silestra connection might prove useful as there was talk of another meeting there.

Running out in the afternoon, he bought more paper from the bookseller. To his surprise nearly all his foolscap was used up with only eight sheets left even though he had bought fifty. Very dear and rough in feel but the best that could be found.

The smallest Turkish ink in its round bottle too. Very watery but there was no India ink to be had. A gift for Buruk's clerk, the man being used to it.

On Wednesday, he headed back with the commander. The trip seemed to take forever. Somehow going was always quicker than heading home.

Daydreaming of Vidin as they rode along, Eugene tried hard not to think of the reports.

Enough time for a round of backgammon downstairs once the notes were copied over with any luck.

But no.

Breaking into his reverie, the commander said, "Can you write it all up by tomorrow? Short notice but it's urgent for the others need to know. Just the notes. You need not write it all out. That way it will save time. Then too you won't have to write the general."

Forcing a smile Eugene agreed. He stayed up late copying everything over.

In the morning, he rose at dawn to start in on his draft wishing he had known for he would have made two copies. Before he went downstairs, he hid the pages in their window frame.

Better to be careful than to chance it. If he was caught sending notes from the general's conference he'd be sacked before being shipped off in disgrace with no commission in sight.

January 1853 coming in more or less as December.

Endless chatting and drills with Ozgur against the day he would be moved to Vidin whenever that might be. Home missed a little less with each passing month or so he thought until a note arrived from James.

Reading that they would like to name the baby after him if it was a boy Eugene smiled. A little namesake, quite exciting but hard because Stephen was not there to help raise a toast.

The next afternoon he noticed a letter from Lord

Stratford Canning that had ended up at the bottom of the pile. There were two notes inside the envelope. The first was in a clerk's boilerplate that said:

13 January, '53
Stamboul
My Dear Major O'Reilly,

This letter is to inform you that I have returned and resumed my duties.

I look forward to meeting you on your next leave unless hostilities should have begun by then keeping you up on the border. Her ladyship and I look forward to sharing the embassy with you.

You shall be pleased I am sure to find that Michael Jones is still on staff. He has stayed on to assist me in my work.

Yours sincerely,
Stratford Canning
Viscount Stratford de Redcliffe

Picking up the second note, Eugene saw that it was in the viscount's own hand and spoke to his reports and Colonel Rose's recommendations. He sighed in relief having feared their loss in the changeover in the capitol.

Pen and paper fetched, he sat down by the fire to write back. Two or three crosshatches for he barely knew the man but a note which said:

30 January, '53
near Novi Sad
Dear Lord Canning,

Thank you for your kind letter. Hopefully, I will not need your help but I know you stand ready to assist should something befall me.

As Colonel Rose told you, I am progressing in my career with the Porte's forces.

I was chosen to attend Omar Pasha's meeting in Vidin and should be transferred there in short order. A posting that shall assist me in learning useful information as only mere rumors penetrate this far west.

I look forward to meeting you and her ladyship. I feel as if I know you already from the kind stories I have heard.

As you say, I will be pleased to see Michael Jones. We have become close friends over the course of my various leaves.

Sincerely,

Eugene O'Reilly

Once it was blotted he reread it twice to check the language, sealing it up after for a prompt response would be the most proper.

More and more snow fell as Eugene wondered about Vidin. The post was so northwest it was as much a cocoon as the coaches were.

Falling upon a letter from Colonel Rose that arrived in the next mail he read:

25 *February, '53 3 PM*

Stamboul

My dear Eugene,

A quick note. I know Lord Canning has sent off an official letter announcing his arrival to all the British citizens in the country.

However, I wanted to write you myself as I have come to regard you as a friend.

I have moved to the house I had secured while you were in the city now that the Cannings have arrived.

I am not sure of my new position yet. That shall have to wait for Lord Aberdeen to decide once hostilities have commenced.

The rest of this is for your eyes only. The Prince Consort himself has just been informed.

Last week Menshikov reappeared from Sevastopol on one of the Russians' newer warships. As he is a fighter, not a diplomat, I doubt he shall meet with much success. I am told he appeared improperly dressed which upset the sultan.

Not sure what they want but I am sure the mission shall not succeed. But as of now he is still in the city as the grand vizier has yet to decide.

Best wishes,

Hugh Rose

Eugene sat back, wondering what would happen. If Menshikov failed, it could only be a help.

He managed not to say anything, not even to Paris though the suspense and temptation grew worse each day.

Finally, another note came from the colonel.

Encouraging news, Menshikov having departed eastward for the grand vizier and sultan had said no. A small step but at least it was in the right direction.

The winter continued on, a horse falling through the ice as its only excitement.

As the ballet between Tsar Nicholas and the Porte continued, Eugene worked on his lists. No point in doing more. It might be spring before anything began to happen.

Just as the ice began breaking up Commander Buruk pulled him aside, saying:

"The men from Algeria have been authorized so the officers must go to command them. If you can start packing as you need to meet the eastbound coach in four days. Had I known earlier I would have mentioned it.

"A new assignment too which shall please you I am sure. A larger squadron to command for its commander is being sent to Silestra as soon as you arrive. Omar Pasha's man writes that if you manage to do well in the first few skirmishes, you will be raised to lieutenant colonel, for the Porte will approve it then."

Concluding the commander said, "One more piece of news. Stephen Bruce is being shifted to a fort closer to Vidin. You may be able to see him since the railway runs there. Lastly do not worry about your correspondence. Anything that arrives before you are settled I can hold until you have time to send your new address. The innkeeper shall miss you I am sure for half of the letters go to you."

Eugene smiled.

"My only concern. It would distress my mother if her letters were returned. Tomorrow I will take the men out for one last run by the river. I enjoy it and it keeps the Austrians on their toes. Not enough notice to do more but I shall miss all of you."

"No worries about the mail," said the commander. "I am glad to have had you under me. You have the makings of a great cavalry leader and a wonderful way with horses. But now I shall dismiss you. It will take a day just for your foolscap and blotting paper. Better to start now so all will be ready."

On Wednesday, he rode out with the men for a final run. When they stopped to water the horses by the bank, he spoke to them about Ozgur taking command.

He thanked them all. Commanding a group of such horsemen had been wonderful. There was a lump in his throat as a huzzah rang out, loud enough to stir the Austrians on the opposite bank.

A final round having been played in the backgammon tournament he headed upstairs to finish packing.

Once that was done, he composed a note for his mother since she would be worried. Necessary even though Uncle Jarleth had written, mentioning that he had explained that being a squadron leader was safer. Surely she would fret otherwise.

The next morning, he shaved and then finished his packing, the ink bottle tossed into his satchel last along with the whiskey the servant had not wanted to pack.

Heading down the drive Eugene wiped tears away once they could not see. It was harder to leave than he had thought.

By the time he reached the inn, his distress had been replaced by excitement.

Feeling surprised, he mulled over why there were three satchels of riding things and only two of everything else. Waiting for the coach he finished his last bottle of whiskey since it could not fit.

Once in Vidin, he was shown round the citadel with everyone else since only a few had been at the meeting. Not many new rooms the aide said for they had spent more on fortifications.

Eugene yawned into his sleeve when the man was not looking for he had seen much of it with Ibrahim. The redoubts were unusual, though, more like the ones in Lombardy than those in Belgrade.

To Eugene's relief, the next stop was the tower where the officers' quarters was located. Another aide jumped out, offering to show him to his room.

Granite walls, smallish windows, and a very bright eiderdown along with a big fireplace so it would be nice and toasty.

"The Egyptians shall be in town," said the aide.

"Granted you have one room and they have two, but eventually someone will be in the sitting room. This you won't have to share. But if you don't mind I must leave to show someone else around. If you need a larger table, they shall try to find one. By the time you return from dinner, they should have brought up your things."

With a bow, the man was gone. Eugene almost bowed back as it sank in that he had moved up. At the post, no one would have bowed.

Putting on a dry jacket, he headed to the mess. Much the same as before, he saw. More hookahs scattered about, but the food being far closer to the post's than the general's. The same yogurt soup and bread but with a touch of cardamom that left it much improved.

Once dinner was done, he headed back.

Doing his best to put Crumlin Road out of his mind for even the ceiling had the same downward angle, he began to arrange his things.

Ink closest to the fire so it would not freeze, pens on the left and sealing wax opposite as they had been before.

Taking his pictures out of his inside pocket he lined them up on the chest by his pillow.

He was introduced the next morning to his new junior officer, the old commander having already left.

After a brief embrace, the chap began as they headed to the stable, saying "We ride out every few days alternating with the other lancers. You are scheduled to meet their squadron leader Erdem Pekkan later today. He would like to plan out some joint patrols for the practice will be helpful."

"We can chat later," said Eugene. "But as we are near the stable I would like to collect my mount and go meet the men."

He made a brief speech at the riding ring to introduce himself before heading out the gate to lead the patrol. A beautiful mount, he thought, better than his last.

Five more minutes and they were there, a quick gallop following later when they returned at dusk with a crescent moon to light their way.

A late evening with Officer Pekkan spent in discussion of tactics and the occasional smoke. Days and weeks that turned into months following, taken up with patrols and practices though it was unclear how many Egyptians would be sent.

Difficult as it was impossible to tell how many men would be in the command. Still a good thing for the horses and something for the men to do.

Eugene spent nearly every evening writing. Fewer reports he found but more Dublin letters because Susan had had her baby. A little girl named Jane Emily after her grandmothers, something pleasing to both ladies.

He tacked the pen and ink of the baby that his mother had sent up by the fireplace so everyone could see.

As he got to the bottom of the stack, he found another letter from his mother that was filled with news about the baby.

Skimming to the last page, shock came over him. She had left the worst news for the end. He read:

Your father had a bad fall from his horse last week. She was spooked by a carriage downtown.

He is better and you are not to worry. He should be back to work on Monday and will be fine.

All my love,
Mother

He had had barely enough time to digest it all when word came from Silestra to head for Kalafat. Opposite the ford and a quick crossing, someone said at dinner, though much needed arranging first.

Extra drills, a round of letters for everyone and a new report for London. Eugene sat up so late on the last evening sealing everything that he forgot to pack before falling into bed.

There was little time in the morning so he took only a few things besides his uniforms. Two bottles of whiskey, the portfolio and Elizabeth's miniature with an extra stick of wax jammed in at the end.

October 27, 1853. Chatting for hours with Erdem Eugene waited at the ford as everyone else had to cross over first.

He sat by the fire, listening as the other officers spoke of campaigns near and far. Hungary, the Syrian rebellion with its sand and camels and tales of Black Sea raids since Erdem had heard the stories at his last post.

Rather more chatter of Syria, several having been there.

Interesting at any rate, a new commission perhaps after the war.

There was a final meeting over coffee the next morning in the commander's tent.

Riding off on the left flank with the men, Eugene and Erdem heard a horn in the distance followed by what looked to be a group of Cossacks.

As the group drew closer under their white flag Eugene could tell they were not Russians for they wore the smocks of Galway not the coats of the steppe.

Eugene pulled back on his reins.

The leader came closer, shouting, "We wish to join you. They have taken our villages and stolen our grain."

Agreeing, Erdem and Eugene let them stay because they could prove useful.

A few minutes later the peasants began riding up a winding path that led through the woods. Both squadrons followed. It was far better than riding into the guns.

The battle seemed very far away until the Cossacks came on with shouts louder than Kurdish shrieks.

Eugene sat for a moment watching them ride forward. They were wonderful riders just as everyone had said and a joy to see.

Poking him in the ribs, Erdem said "Stop dreaming and start fighting my man. They are almost upon us," as fifty riders approached at a gallop.

Continuing on for it was impossible not to Eugene

led with his men.

Men went down as more and more Cossacks came through the fog and smoke. Both squadrons were nearly overwhelmed. Suddenly the Cossacks seemed to be retreating though it was hard to tell with so many riding to and fro.

A Russian bugler sounded retreat followed by a Turk.

Smiling, Erdem said "Over, at least for now. Hopefully, the commander will understand. He will know a charge was not possible. Let's go check on the men. Lucky today. Only a few were wounded. Would have been worse had the peasants not come."

They pulled up for a second as they rode back to camp.

"I know," said Eugene. "I think one has a leg wound and the other an arm. Sabres as Cossack riders carry no guns. Had we charged the center it would have been very different.

"Once I have seen the men I shall write to the family of the man I lost. I forgot my mourning paper. Foolscap shall have to suffice. Maybe you could read it over and make sure it is correct."

Erdem nodded.

"That's fine. Don't worry. The paper doesn't matter, just the sentiments. But it must wait until after I see my lancer."

Eugene headed off to the medical tent and then went back to the fire. He gazed into the flames trying to think of what to write.

Thoughts of charging the Cossack leader took over his mind for he had not known how things would go. Only his second time, he realized, that and Novara.

He dipped his pen in the ink and managed a few pages, sealing them up with a few prayers before Erdem took the letter off to be sent.

The smell of wood smoke hung in the air as they made coffee. Too late for the field ovens, yogurt soup and dried cherries for supper instead.

The commander's aide came to fetch him in the morning.

Rising to his feet Eugene's hands shook. They had not followed the bugler's charge and the commander was supposed to be very strict.

Entering the commander's tent, Eugene felt relieved as the commander was very kind.

"I wish to commend your performance of yesterday," said the commander. "Even with the peasants' help I do believe it was your training that carried the day. If the Cossacks had turned our flank, it could have meant disaster.

"Therefore, I am writing Omar Pasha this day to let him know you have risen to the rank of lieutenant colonel because you have earned it. Greatly deserved I might add. Once we have returned, a clerk will be supplied as well. There is no one suitable here."

Doing his best not to dance because he had not been sure what would happen Eugene walked away. But no, he thought with a grin, for it had and with a fancier uniform too he was sure along with some new boots.

Eugene sat down once he reached his tent and began writing his father. Matthew O'Reilly would be thrilled. Not only had his son been promoted but he was the first westerner to achieve such a rank in the sultan's forces.

The next day Eugene went back to work. He spent two days patrolling around Kalafat so it could not be retaken.

Riding towards its inn afterward, he wished he had known there would be a lengthy stay as he would have brought the rest of the whiskey along.

He asked for permission to go back for his things, but it was denied. Not even an afternoon the commander said for the enemy might reappear.

Another fortnight.

The quartermaster was sent back along with several aides to retrieve the mail and its messages from Stamboul.

Pacing around the room as he waited Eugene hoped there would be better news of his father's health along with new pictures of the baby.

The quartermaster reappeared towards dusk, making piles of letters on the chest downstairs.

Chagrin covered Eugene's face as he came down. Only the commander had a bigger stack.

Walking back up, fear gripped his heart because the one from Dublin had a black border. Perhaps a friend. Surely his father was fine.

Crossing himself he sat down and read:

14 November, '53

Dublin

My dear son,

First the good and then the bad. The letter came about your promotion. I am so proud of you. You are faring well under the Turks and make us proud even though you are far away.

But then the bad. First I pray you are seated. I have hard news, my beloved son. We have lost your father. Oh, if only there was an easier way to put it.

He never quite recovered from his fall. Yesterday he had an apoplectic fit in his library and was gone. James found him when he went to fetch him for lunch.

Oh, it was terrible. I loved him so and he loved the two of you to distraction, but, at least, he is no longer suffering as he was.

I wish we could be together. It breaks my heart you cannot be with me. It makes our present circumstance harder to bear, but we shall do our best.

Much love,

Mother

P.S. James or I will write after the service to describe it. Also, Susan has more news of the baby who looks more like you every day.

Eugene's hands began to shake from the shock as he sat staring into the fire. His father should have recovered. He was not that old really.

Falling back against the divan, pain began to grip his heart and tears rose up in his eyes. Impossible it was to return even though they needed him.

Barely eating he sat upstairs for two days in floods of tears. On the third day, Erdem fetched a priest.

A blessing to be in Kalafat for at least there was a church. Odd it felt praying in Turkish, but a comfort all the same. A glow began warming his heart as the father chanted that helped him feel calmer. He managed to go down for supper once the priest was gone, sitting afterward with Erdem by his side.

Once he reached his room, he felt better. The glow's echo was still there.

He poked the fire and then sat back down, spotting a letter from Osman wedged between the hearthstone and the table. Must have been under the one from his mother since he had dropped everything when he collapsed.

Breaking the seal, he read:

10 December, '53

Varna

Dear Eugene,

Greetings from Varna.

We hear Omar Pasha has gone into Wallachia so I hope this letter reaches you without much delay. May Allah protect both you and your men.

Here there is not much to report. Since the Russians sank nearly every vessel when they attacked Sinope, the navy has barely ventured out since.

That it remains at all must be the work of your countryman Adolphus Slade. He has spent much time training our sailors as you have the lancers.

It is very quiet here. They are thinking of sending us to Silestra. If they do, I shall write and let you know.

Yours,

Osman

Pulling out his portfolio Eugene put it back down. Somehow it seemed better to wait to reply until he felt a little less low. Hard enough just to chat downstairs let alone write.

Perhaps after the priest came again as the respond in need of a reply stack had inched up to a terrifying height.

He felt better the next morning after the priest's visit.

Taking his portfolio back out, he wrote James, explaining about the father as very special it was to have a Muslim friend fetch him.

Adding several pages about their father he included a final postscript about Jane Emily's picture along with a description of how it was proudly displayed.

As he was finishing up a burst of energy washed over him. Once the servant had come in to bank the fire, he headed off to bed, the stack of responses left on the table ready to be sent out.

The next few weeks were much quieter, patrols to be lead around the walls but not much more since the Russians had gone into their winter camp.

Riding back to Vidin with the quartermaster to fetch the mail, Eugene managed to bring back a few more of his things. The baby's pen and ink and another bottle of whiskey but nothing else, there being no room in his saddlebags.

The priest having made it a point to invite him he spent Christmas morning at the church. The Orthodox hymns sounded odd, but at least it was Christmas surrounded by Christians which he had not expected.

His melancholy beginning to seep back, Eugene asked for a short leave. Belgrade for a few days to see Stephen for that should help.

But no for Omar Pasha was ordering everyone north. Nine miles instead of five, not too long a march. Cetate because that was where the enemy was encamped.

All the old Vidin routines inching back. Days with the men and nights spent in frenzied writing since who knew when anything could be sent again.

He ran out for more foolscap. Packing everything up on the morning of December thirty-first he ran down with his letters before collecting the men.

They neared Cetate by noon as it was only a half day's march. Chaos ensued for what seemed like a month but was only five days as they were sent forward and then back again for the Russians seemed to be slipping south to Kalafat.

At noon on the sixth day, Erdem called out as the messenger left, saying:

"Very hard to shift positions with the lances out. Hopefully, we need not shift again. Who knows where the enemy is or where they are headed."

Eugene shouted over the din.

"I know," he said. "Their Cossacks can turn up anywhere. I don't see any. Perhaps they are elsewhere. But let me borrow your glasses for perhaps I can."

Eugene looked northward, raising the glasses to his eyes. A dust cloud on the horizon turned into a band of riders as he watched, complete to the steppe ponies.

Turning back, he remarked, "No, there they are. I was dead wrong. Trouble too. They appear to have sabres not lances."

Erdem checked for himself.

They began getting ready for the riders were much closer. Must have gotten past the lancers ahead Eugene thought as he lined the men up to accept the charge.

They fought hand to hand up and down the road for the Russians were determined to drive them back. As the next wave of riders began making their approach, the snow showers turned into a squall.

Eugene shouted, saying, "They shall have to stop. I can barely make out the next man. I think I managed to slash his thigh, but it might have been his mount."

A Russian horn off in the distance blowing retreat followed by a Turk since even the commanders could not see.

Lining up the men waited as the supply train came forward to put the tents back up until the weather lifted.

Snow and ice crunching under his boots Eugene made his way to the fire. He sat in a field chair, watching the servant heat water for coffee. Better than a log but otherwise much the same, Russians for Austrians but the same snowy landscape.

The next morning, he got the men into their ranks, ready to follow the enemy.

Another bugle cry, two messengers, and orders to turn south again as they needed to reach Kalafat before the enemy did.

"That must be it," said Erdem. "A message must have reached them from the scouts. Better for us anyway. Cetate is tiny. No inn and only a few mean houses."

With Eugene in the lead, the Russians gave chase as they came racing down the road.

The horses were lathered as they rode in the gates. Better to be under siege than a winter with no sherbet houses.

Heading upstairs to his old suite, Eugene saw that there was a new maroon coverlet with different embroidery. Everything else was much the same. Even his copy of *All the Year Round* was still under the divan where he had pushed it by mistake, his page helpfully dog-eared to let him know where to start.

As he sat down and began reading, the commander's aide knocked on the door. Something about a meeting in the morning at ten.

Eugene looked up and did his best to smile, wondering what was wanted for the commander's grumpy look had not changed.

He leapt to his feet since a clean uniform was in order. He laid everything out flat for days of rumpling in a saddle bag had done no good. Brushing his jacket with his hairbrush only seemed to make the lint worse.

Falling into bed, he made sure to put the hairbrush on the washstand. His hair he could affect. The water would dampen his curls.

Eugene spent the morning flattening his curls and shaving because there was no barber.

His feet squeezed into his newest boots he made his way down the hall. As his watch reached ten, he stood before the commander's door, still feeling rather anxious.

As the sentry announced him, he walked in.

Rising the commander embraced him.

"Why do you look as anxious as you did the last time?" the commander said. "I have good things to say, not bad though first I must thank you for the excellent work of your squadron. Near impossible staying ahead of the Russians. We weren't the only ones wanting to winter here.

"But that is not why I have asked you to come. Rather it is because the certificate confirming your rank has come from the Porte."

There were congratulations all round as he sat gazing at the proclamation. All covered in ribbons and drawings, like the Book of Kells Uncle Jarleth had taken him to see but signed by the grand vizier and not a monk.

Most of it was about his new rank but at the bottom, there was something about being given a new name, "Hassan Bey".

Feeling rather confused, Eugene asked, "Who is Hassan Bey? It says it is my new name. Is it part of my new rank?"

The commander responded, saying, "It is a title as well as a new name. Bey, as you know, means lord. There is always a Hassan Bey amongst the officers.

"An honorary title held last by a fellow who was killed on the Black Sea so it has been assigned to you. A great compliment, never given to a westerner before. They must be very fond of you in Stamboul. At any rate, it will be easier for the men to say. You deserve it. Your work with the men is exemplary. They are as good with the lances as the Cossacks.

"Which reminds me of the third item. Very impressed I am with your work so I have put in for an Order of Merit. I am not sure Omar Pasha will approve, but I think he shall. Comes with a second squadron whose leader was lost."

Concluding, the commander said "For now a respite and time to regroup and rest. You with your letters, the others with their backgammon.

"Tomorrow I shall arrange for you to meet your new squadron. You can do some patrolling around the walls on warm days. Not too often for we must conserve hay, just enough to keep them exercised. Perhaps a bit of drill. The aide will ask the mayor about space for it this week."

Eugene began to ask a question. As the words began forming on his lips, the commander rose for he had other things to attend to.

Eugene managed not to dance as he made his way back to his suite, his heart pounding once the door closed and everything began to sink in.

Twelve months back to the post and all its tedium but now luxurious winter quarters complete with a private balcony. A higher rank and decoration along with the second squadron.

Too much to absorb at once, he thought as he collapsed onto the divan with his feet held out to the fire, a grin spreading from ear to ear. Nothing much to do until spring, a chance to rest his feet if not his hands.

Picking up his pen since his mother would want to know he wrote a long letter because she would be very proud.

The servant having come in to light the lamp, he started in on his new report for London. Before heading down, he hid the draft inside the balcony threshold.

Even more to lose, he realized, should they happen upon it.

As the winter wore on everyone's nerves began to fray. Rides around the perimeter a lance length from the walls but nothing else.

Afternoons over backgammon and a weekly outing to the sherbet house to keep his spirits up.

The writing much the same as always, like a hungry caterpillar. It was always growing and never shrank.

In April, he was nearly hit by a Russian shell that rained down while he was visiting the men. Still the war somehow seemed very far away.

There were rumors of fighting to the east, but it was impossible to learn much more.

The commander rarely mentioned Varna. He only spoke of Omar Pasha's reports, never about Vienna or anything closer.

Odd, William Macdonald having written of troops near Belgrade. Surely they must be concerned but no.

He did his best to concentrate on his writing, his upset over the shell having gotten him behind schedule. Too many hours in idleness by the fire with thoughts that were hard to shake off of his mother getting a black-bordered letter from the commander.

Making a start for the stack was way too high Eugene fetched a glass of whiskey and then uncapped the ink.

Near impossible just staying even, but his mother would worry if she did not hear.

Once the draft was retrieved from its hiding place, he finished it up. The last two pages, blotted and enclosed in a note for his uncle. Messy with too many blots since there was not enough time to copy it over. Hopefully, they would understand.

The sun reached its zenith, beginning its descent as the stack of letters grew higher.

Uncle Jarleth's he saved for last. Eugene told him what had happened, begging his uncle not to let his mother find out because she would be so distressed.

The siege ground on and on.

As Silestra was in the same position, no reserves could be sent.

Eugene got used to his new name. A little hard to pronounce. Easier for the men. The old one they had always massacred.

Scratching lines on the window frame like the lad had done in Kilmainham, he counted the days. There was not much else to do. He had read every book twice and his last bottle of whiskey was empty.

Late May 1854. Going down to the wall each morning Eugene walked on top with Erdem's glasses.

Better to watch the Russians looking like ants in an anthill than sit inside. Too utterly claustrophobic. Even at Mr. Hall's they had managed to get away.

As he looked along the Cetate road one morning, the Russian ants were not acting as they had the day before. They seemed to be packing up. The tents were coming down and even the guns were silent.

Going back to the turret, he fetched the captain of the guard.

"Could you come look?" he asked. "They seem to be striking their tents and heading east."

The captain agreed, sending a man for the commander's aide.

"I think you are right," the man said. "There is no smoke coming from the hills. Perhaps they have been made nervous. Once the aide agrees, we can go back with the news."

The aide appeared and yanked Eugene behind the tower for he had been standing in full view of the enemy.

Surveying in each direction, he agreed.

"You are right. They are pulling out. Silestra I would expect for there are a few skirmishers who look to be headed that way. Menshikov must have sent orders. Follow me. The commander needs to be told."

Rumors had already begun spreading as they reached the ground, the southern guards having confirmed that the enemy was headed east.

Eugene rode out the next day with one squadron, an eye kept out for sharpshooters. The next day he led all the men out for the mounts needed exercising. All the Russians were gone.

A state of grace, just having enough room to ride

after so many cooped up weeks.

The commander sent messages east to the general and south to the Porte followed by what seemed a very long wait. They might be done or headed for Silestra.

Another meeting was held the day after the messages were returned.

Taking his seat, Eugene tried not to fidget as a few more straggled in and the hookah made its rounds.

Rising the senior aide made an announcement.

"As you know the orders have come. Some will be heading for Silestra. A few shall remain here or head south. Much to be sorted out but Erdem is headed east and Hassan Bey south, perhaps to go elsewhere later."

Eugene said nothing for it had all been decided. Better to have been chosen to head east to help Ibrahim but there was no point in asking. Erdem's lancers would do as well.

Heading south two days later, he rode into the Vidin forecourt to a mighty cheer. The garrison must have been following their successes closely, he realized.

In a few days, it felt as though he had never left.

Much back correspondence that needed catching up on, a huge pile of mail having been on the table when he walked back into his room. To his joy, several copies of *All the Year Round* and another literary magazine were at the bottom of the heap.

Slipping back into his old pattern of patrols and meetings Eugene felt suspended in time. Much like when he had sat awaiting orders for Vidin at his old post, he thought.

He read his way through all the Dickens installments.

Much to his relief the promised clerk materialized, making it possible to get caught up on the mail. A true blessing for the fellow did not mind copying over all the

Turkish reports.

The English ones still needing to be written out, but it was faster as he need only translate from the Turkish. Impossible for Palmerston to ever learn, more time to ride out too.

Word of the Silestra siege having been lifted arrived in a letter from Ibrahim that read:

24 June, '54
Silestra
My dear Eugene,

A quick letter just to let you know I am fine as you must be concerned. We heard that the enemy traveled here from Kalafat. I presume you are back in Vidin as you are not here.

More importantly, I congratulate you on your new command. The squadron leader who was with you has told us.

Then too I have welcome news. You need not worry about the Russians. With the larger Austrian presence near your old post, I know they were a concern.

Omar Pasha has learned that Vienna has given them an ultimatum that they would attack if the Russians failed to depart.

As you can imagine the joy here was great. Living under siege has been very difficult.

I must stop. I need to seal and post before the staff meeting. Hoping to see you soon perhaps in Stamboul.

Your friend,
Ibrahim

Eugene smiled. The note was a great comfort. No more Kalafat ice and snow at any rate.

Funny, though, Osman having mentioned that all the Union Jacks in the harbor had headed east but the quiet so thick in Vidin it could be cut with a knife.

Eugene's old melancholy began inching in. He

managed to beat it back by reading for he had managed to borrow a few books from the other officers.

Rumors began to seep in, this time of the Crimea.

He asked again about a short leave to visit Stephen.

The commander refused.

"You may not leave," the commander said. "Word has come that you are wanted in Giurgevo where the Russians are not leaving fast enough. Maybe the enemy will be gone by the time you appear. Otherwise, you can encourage their departure. They need cavalry because it is surrounded by mudflats. Too much for the infantry or I'd send them."

Sleeping under the stars as he headed east, Eugene gazed up at the moon with a smile. More like sleeping in the fields around Corstown with James than being in a war with the same blackness and shadows.

The followed the river eastward past Ruse, hunting for the ford as Giurgevo would be directly across.

Chatting with the other officers as the men crossed over, Eugene said, "I hope this is it. If they do not go, we may have to winter over. Somehow winter camping has lost its charm. Hopefully, Vienna has persuaded them to depart. If not, Bucharest is only another day's ride. That should encourage them even more."

Taking out the glasses after they crossed the mudflats, Eugene managed to make out the town in the distance just before they stopped for the night. Rather noisy with the horses hobbled in the meadow but still the pickets would give an alarm.

In the morning they rode forward, engaging the enemy.

Both wings attacked. The Russians dispersed, fleeing east rather more quickly than Eugene had thought, there having been far fewer at Cetate.

Resting for two days, they headed northwest towards Bucharest. Staring straight ahead Eugene said nothing as they went which concerned the others since his melancholia was never far from their minds.

Appearing at the house where Eugene was quartered, his junior officer asked, "What is wrong? You are so quiet."

Eugene looked up.

"Such magnificent country," he said. "I could keep riding forever, all the way to Bessarabia if it was allowed."

"That Omar Pasha will not allow. But you are right. It is magnificent. After the war, we can come back and hunt. From the last report, it seems they have left Bucharest. Back to Vidin to wait and see what they want next."

Heading back, they resumed life as pawns on a chessboard. Eugene did his best not to worry. Surely there would be new orders about where to go next.

Another fortnight. The Porte having approved his Order of Valor, the commander called him in. Not as useful as the name, Eugene thought, but still something.

Agreeing, the commander said, "Well yes, the name is more useful at present. By now you have added to your successes and it is even more fitting. The orders you can wear in the victory parade when we are done.

"We are finished and our objectives achieved as the Russians are gone from here. Whether you get drawn to the eastern sector, I cannot tell. You might. You can ride nearly as well as a Cossack."

Another embrace and he was dismissed, rather more happily than before, the commander having offered a few days leave as the aide ushered him out.

Dispatching a note off to Stephen Eugene headed off to Belgrade.

They visited not one but two sherbet houses

followed by a performance by a traveling dance troupe the evening before Eugene caught the railway back.

The waiting started up again as fall began settling in. In mid-October word came.

Calling everyone in again, the commander announced:

"Word has come that they are all in Bessarabia. A small garrison the size of the earlier one will man Vidin. As for the rest of you, there are two choices. Either back to your old posts or south to Stamboul with the Tunisian recruits."

Going back to his room Eugene thought it all over. Stamboul, all winter if they would have him that long. A new commission would be more likely to come knocking there too.

A good word from the general along with the new name and decoration should help. Surely they would want to keep him on.

Somewhere warmer would be nice, but anything would be better than being a banker in Paris.

He pulled out his inkpot, writing two paragraphs to explain his situation and another about making amends for his long overdue visit. Crossing his fingers that her ladyship would approve he sealed it up.

Colonel Rose otherwise, he supposed. Though with the colonel off in Varna the house might be closed up.

To his relief, a reply arrived from his lordship in rather short order. The entire winter, the ambassador wrote, as the guest room was not in use.

A postscript that took up its own page too. The Misses Canning hoping a few distractions could be arranged with Miss Gilbert of the French embassy, their father wrote. For she was said to dance well.

Feeling cheered for he had forgotten all about the Misses Canning Eugene accepted. Rather young Michael had said, but certainly there would at least be dancing.

Once everything had been packed the railway beckoned as he headed back to the capitol eager for a new assignment.

8 BEIRUT, DAMASCUS, RASHAIYA, BELFAST & STAMBOUL

Dining that evening in Belgrade with Stephen, he headed straight south into Michael's arms. A few more gray hairs Eugene noticed but otherwise much the same.

Michael smiled.

"The fighting must suit you. You look even younger."

He continued, saying "A helper now. Still with all the financiers in the city, it never ends."

"The wages of moving up I'm afraid," replied Eugene.

"Being an embassy, you must mean. A fancier name, longer guest lists for her ladyship but the same work. Which reminds me. The Pera has acquired a new look. More shops, a western restaurant and even a new chapel."

"I shall get used to it I am sure. Hopefully, I can economize at the tailor since I intend to go back in the spring. A few pairs of trousers and short boots. I can wear my dress uniform to dances. I shall watch you shop instead."

Michael laughed though not unkindly.

"At least, you'll have fun at the new jeweler. They have studs and cufflinks along with flatware. A Turkish fad as it were. Though they still eat with their hands in that disgusting way."

Saying nothing as his companion ran on Eugene managed to change the subject.

They headed over the bridge and up the hill. There were even more shops than Michael had said, two or three on every block.

Pulling up the drive Eugene barely recognized anything. The façade looked different with what looked to be an enormous tongue sticking out into the garden.

Lord Canning heard them come in. He introduced himself, asking Eugene to come down for a chat after he freshened up.

Encouraging but more formal too. Otherwise, the ambassador would have been out on the steps.

Having changed Eugene found himself before the old familiar door.

A different chair to sit in, larger desk and drapes that looked to be the same. The bigger desk seemingly even larger than it was for his lordship was far more portly than the colonel and lacked his height.

Eugene's host shook his hand.

"Welcome to Stamboul," his lordship said.

"I have been keeping up with your reports. Very glad to meet you. Indeed, you have a following so large even the London papers keep up with you. Her ladyship very much hopes that you will attend her New Year's ball as it is a hallmark of the Season."

"That is why I brought my dress uniform along," said Eugene. "It shall suffice for formal wear as I have no other. Not much use in the field I'm afraid."

Concluding, Eugene said, "I am glad they find the reports useful. Much of what they contain comes from my friends amongst the Turks and cannot be found elsewhere. Nothing much to report now, the action being in Sevastopol, but that you will know more about."

His lordship looked up and agreed about Sevastopol. Then he asked Eugene whether he intended to return or stay.

Balling up his fists, Eugene tried to figure out what to say. Surely the *London Times* had been sent on to Madrid but maybe not.

Words ran through his mind as he began to explain, saying:

"Stamboul seemed a better choice. A new commission is more likely to find me here. In any case, they did not need me back as my rank is that of my old commander.

"Hopefully something with a southern garrison. I am tired of snow and cold. I thank you for your hospitality and hope not to have to impose for long. In the meantime, I look forward to the embassy ball and the other dances for I was never here to enjoy them."

His lordship chuckled.

"Be careful what you want," he said. "Syria is nothing but sand. They don't call it an inland sea for nothing.

"You are welcome here. Omar Pasha having promoted you twice the Porte must be fond of you. Quite a few garrisons in need of commanders too. You must wish to remain. I am told that you have mastered Turkish and made many friends."

Concluding, the ambassador said, "I must leave you as I must meet with the Spanish chap. More gentlemen being needed, her ladyship shall be glad of your ball acceptance. Early for lunch but my daughter Catherine shall be pleased to show you the ballroom. It has just been finished. So many receptions that it was needed."

Catherine Canning was in the hallway when Eugene left the library with her father. Portly too but with a pretty face he thought.

The ballroom to his surprise was the equal of the ones in Dublin. Band alcove, very tall windows and a gleaming parquet floor. He gazed into the garden from the terrace for there was no time to walk out as they were overdue for lunch.

Following Miss Canning into the dining room, he half expected to see no one at the foot of the table. Somehow it was the same house but then not the same.

Her ladyship stared as they began the second course. Looking down, Eugene saw that he had begun to scoop up the chutney with his bread.

Turning he spoke to Miss Canning's younger sister Mary. Pleasant enough, though as she was still in the schoolroom, her giggling was hard to bear.

The next day Eugene visited the tailor with Michael. He tried to keep his order small. Somehow a plaid frockcoat kept sneaking in.

No point in ordering more. With any luck, he'd be in the field by June. Better to buy stationery and whiskey instead.

Retreating upstairs after tea, he made a new Simpson's list for his last sheet of blotting paper was only usable on the edges. New cards too from the new stationer her ladyship had mentioned. Simpson's minimum being a thousand it would be impossible to use them up.

Friday and dinner with Marie-Genevieve and her uncle.

Wrapped in Michael's cloak Eugene rode down the hill, narrowly avoiding being crushed to death upon his arrival as his hostess's skirts appeared to be iron lined.

Managing not to faint, Eugene said, "I have missed you too. Very glad I am to be back and to find you both here."

As dessert came round the chatter was of the Season and her ladyship's ball.

Eugene smiled for the ball sounded like fun.

"I should be here for a while," he said. "Not needed on the Danube or in the Crimea. I am hoping for something with one of the garrisons, perhaps Damascus or Sidon."

Marie-Genevieve nodded in response, saying:

"Colonel Rose was consul general in Beirut before he came here. A lovely place he said. I don't remember if it had a garrison. That I did not think to inquire."

Feeling startled for he had not known Eugene replied.

"There is one in Aleppo and another in Beirut to protect the port. Damascus too because of the pilgrimage. Trying not to worry about it for Omar Pasha is looking out for me. Better to enjoy the Season and dance with my dear friend at the foot of the table."

Christmas with friends and then a week spent getting all in readiness for the ball. Well brushed uniform, decoration pinned to his jacket and boots polished with brandy dregs.

Eugene waltzed several times with Marie-Genevieve as the chiffon of her gown swirled around his ankles.

Escorting Miss Canning into supper, he managed to partner Marie-Genevieve in the de Coverley at the end. Fun but bittersweet, he thought, having last danced it with Elizabeth in what seemed a lifetime ago.

The rest of the winter passed in the same fashion, dances alternating with dinners and then back again.

Eugene paid several visits to the new bookstore. It had all the latest offerings, even Dickens' *Bleak House* which was in all the reviews. Trying not to buy too much since more would be needed before he went back out, he started a new list for the field instead.

He sat in his room reading. Like Kalafat, but better than being downstairs with her ladyship's questions for no word had come from the general.

Paris again. Anything would be better than her ladyship and her domineering ways.

As the sleet began to end a fat envelope arrived from Dublin stuffed with numerous clippings. Eugene looked at them. All about Smith-Brien. His gold panning days were over and he had returned.

Something about being allowed to come back, his mother said. Part of his plea bargain but still James was making inquiries as perhaps it would be allowed. The Queen's service instead of the sultan's and closer to home.

Putting everything in his pocket as he had opened it in the hall, Eugene went upstairs to think.

Made sense to write James even though his remarks about Kilmainham were humiliating.

Odd it was. His stint with the Guards should mollify anyone. But even if they said yes it might not work. Indeed, the magistrate had said he could not fight for the queen. No occupation and having to start over again for even Palmerston would be unable to help.

Paris to join their foreign legion, but no for the beginning would be much the same. Better to stay. Surely the Acers would help.

His anxiety began lifting like a storm cloud the next week. A note came from Ibrahim that said:

28 February, '55
Belgrade
My dear Eugene,
I am writing for two reasons.
First because I shall be back in Stamboul in ten days' time.

Omar Pasha must attend more meetings at the Porte. We can go to the sherbet house again or else the baths.

Also, my father would like to invite you to dinner. The governor of the Syrian province, Namiq Pasha would like to meet you. He is in need of commanders or aghas as they are called. The Porte has suggested that he see you.

The governor and one or two others shall be there, plus the two of us and Mustafa, who is eager to see you again.

Please write back and let me know.

If you can come, I shall let Father know and he will make the arrangements. The sherbet house we can plan for ourselves.

Yours,

Ibrahim

Shouting so loudly that the maid knocked, Eugene reached for his portfolio. He settled down once the maid had gone, composing a note for James that was way overdue before he laid down for a nap.

Noticing Eugene's excitement across the dinner table, his lordship asked if he was all right.

Nodding, Eugene explained. The note from Orhan Acer's son and the Syrian governor, important as he had never been inside the house let alone invited to dine.

As the maid handed the consommé round, Lord Canning said "Very encouraging. Only this afternoon I heard that they are out to improve standards in Damascus and Jerusalem. After Kalafat, they must be interested in you. If there is time I can learn more."

Eugene replied, saying, "Ibrahim said he would be here in ten days' time. So soon after that. Nerve-wracking but optimistic at the same time."

Smiling her ladyship listened as her husband replied.

"If they are going to all that trouble, they must be seriously considering you. But now for the joint. I am starved."

Another week. Several afternoons spent cufflink sorting, the gold diamonds in the end. If only the colonel was in town to advise. Somehow his nerves were growing worse and worse.

The Acers' messenger appeared with a note from Ibrahim that read:

9 March, '55
Stamboul
Greetings my friend,
We have just arrived. Just a quick note as I am at Father's heading off to join everyone at the Porte. He wishes me to tell you that the dinner is scheduled for Thursday at seven.
Hopefully, this is agreeable. It is the only time Namiq Pasha can come before he leaves for Beirut.
Ibrahim
I very much hope you can appear. Mustafa is badgering me to take him riding and you know how that will end.

Racing upstairs Eugene ran back down with his acceptance.

In the morning, he pulled everything out again as he was not sure. A different jacket for the governor might not like all the braid. Repolished boots since a good appearance couldn't hurt. He refilled his flask in case a little dutch courage proved necessary.

Thursday arrived. Nearly taking a spill because he was so nervous, Eugene made his way down the hill.

To his delight, the hazy sky made the lights on the sultan's minarets look like Saint Paul's. A good sign, he thought, as he rode over the bridge and back up.

The house was just as he remembered, a porch over the door like Vidin but with less carving.

Knocking on the door, he waited for a servant to emerge.

Following the voices down the hall, Eugene found the sitting room where the other guests were awaiting his arrival.

Much like those in Serbia. Furs on the divans, a step down as one entered the room.

After embracing Ibrahim, he was introduced around, first to Ibrahim's father, Orhan Acer, and then Namiq Pasha followed by a member of his suite.

Thanking Eugene for coming, Ibrahim's father said, "Pleased I am to meet you, Hassan Bey. My son has spoken of you so often.

"I must beg your indulgence. Our small one Mustafa shall be here in a minute. I can hear him running down from the haremlik. He is hoping you can take him riding again. We hope you will as he remembers your stories."

Ibrahim walked over.

Whispering he mentioned a tour of the courtyard, something for Mustafa to do.

Eugene followed Mustafa towards the arches at the end of the hall. A large courtyard, haremlik stairs running up on the right and what looked to be rose trellises and a fountain. Must be lovely in the summer with the rose scent, like Grandmama's garden but with the ladies upstairs instead of on benches around the edge.

Following Mustafa, he passed under the archway on the left into the dining room.

Like the mess, better carpets of course and three windows instead of four, two into the courtyard, the other high up on the wall opposite over the alley. The priest's house in Kalafat nearly. The casements looked identical.

Being seated next to the governor in the place of honor which he had not expected.

Turning towards Namiq Pasha, Eugene looked back towards the door.

He watched as platter upon platter of food was carried in. Duck with chestnuts, something wrapped in grape leaves and pilaf platters that went on and on, more like a wedding reception than a dinner it seemed.

Eugene used the knife and fork that had been put by his place. It seemed better not to offend.

Rinsing his fingers at the end, he sat back to listen.

Ibrahim's father looked in his direction. "Hassan Bey," he said, "you must be wondering why I have done all of this. Partly it is because my son and I are rarely in the city the same time. Then too, the governor needed to meet you before he goes back."

Namiq Pasha put down his coffee, saying, "I am hoping you can be of assistance.

"I was appointed provincial governor last year. Upon reaching Damascus, I learned that the garrison commander is incompetent. Cousin to the last fellow but a terrible agha quite unfit to work with the men. Not as important as Aleppo or Gaza but as the northern pilgrimage leaves from there it needs a strong garrison."

The pasha continued, saying, "I have made inquiries as I need a suitable man to take back. As you have been recommended by Omar Pasha and the Acers, I would like to offer you the post. I very much hope you will accept. I need someone in place by mid-spring. There is another candidate. But he is in Sevastopol and not able to return."

Eugene did his best not to smile as it would not do to appear too eager.

"I had been hoping for such an assignment," he said. "I would prefer sand to snow. Then too I have longed to see Damascus since childhood. It sounds challenging. But having taken command of two squadrons at Cetate, I am sure I can handle it for they needed much training to act cohesively."

Namiq Pasha looked quite relieved as he said:

"First there is snow but way up in the mountains. Only a dusting in Damascus every few years. Hopefully, that is all right as the other fellow lacks empathy with the men. That I need. The last commander wasn't very approachable which affected morale. They are not all cavalry, but other than the artillery all are mounted. Ten field guns, not too many."

Eugene replied.

"The hardest part is the riding and that they know," he said. "But yes I would like to accept for it should prove quite interesting. But when do you plan to head back?"

The pasha responded, saying:

"A week from today. I am sorry it is so soon. I have purchased a block of tickets on the westbound steamer. Much faster by water, one week instead of two. Once on board a private cabin. Though on the ocean side if the others are taken. Should you need anything, it will be reimbursed. Just save the receipts. You may get the money in Damascus, but it will come."

Conversation ceased as pistachios and sweetmeats were brought round, resuming in the sitting room once coffee had been served. Everyone chatted away, Mustafa about his pony, his elders about past campaigns and the Porte. By nine thirty all the guests had flown out the door for the wind was picking up.

March seventeenth, 1855.

Eugene stood on the front steps remembering the celebrations back home as he watched the Porte's carriage came up the drive.

Arriving at the dock he found the governor and his family surrounded by mountains of baggage, the ladies no doubt accounting for most of it.

There was a new paddle steamer behind them,

hopefully better than the one he had come over in as it had been rather crowded.

Entering his cabin, he felt disappointed. No nicer, a little larger yes but on the ocean side. Better to say nothing since he had been warned. More time to work at least with only waves to admire.

Putting his grip down, Eugene went back up on deck. The engines throbbing under his feet he stood by the rail watching as Stamboul grew ever smaller and further away.

A week later they steamed into Beirut. A pleasant looking place, surely a French presence. Looking far more like Nice than Stamboul.

A greeting committee assembled on the quay as the sailors began mooring the ship. Whispering, one of the aides said that they were the local governor and his suite.

Spotting what looked to be several consuls for they were all in western attire, Eugene realized that it must be much like Vidin. Few visitors they must have and those far and few between.

Smiling he disembarked.

The Frenchman, who had been waving from the back, introduced himself and offered an invitation to his reception, saying "I hope you shall come and enjoy a glass of our wine."

Two days of meetings and then off to the reception.

Eugene's mood lightened as a glass of wine appeared following on the heels of a cigar. A far more amusing group than the Stratford Cannings he thought as he sat down on the porch with the consul.

"How long have the French been here?" he asked. "From the sea it resembles Nice. I had expected to see wood like Belgrade and Stamboul, but it is all stone."

"True. Beirut is a different case," the consul said. "We have been in Mount Lebanon for years as this is where the Afghani caravan routes reach the sea. Another port to the north in Homs for the same reason. Here for centuries, not mere decades like the capitol.

"Not like Stamboul. A foreign quarter but no westerners elsewhere. Perhaps if the Russians lose there will be more. They tell me you fought them. This is such a tiny place we know who is coming."

The consul concluded, saying, "Damascus is different. It has the various quarters. But you shall see. I gather you are headed in country in the morning."

Heading off in the morning Namiq Pasha set out for Damascus with a long cavalcade. The governor rode in front with the ladies' araba directly behind. Eugene followed with the Beirut garrison riding with its agha, the supply train in the rear.

Eugene looked back and forth and then ahead. He could see for miles, the orchards turning into foothills and then into the mountains behind with their snowcaps. Odd to be warm but be able to see somewhere cold at the same time.

The sun having reached its zenith, they passed through to a wheat filled valley that the aide had said was called Bekaa. Like the country past Corstown but no creeks which seemed rather strange.

He asked in a low voice.

"A lot of rain on account of the mountains being on either side," said the agha. "By the time we ford the Litani it shall be dark. No doubt to you it shall be a little creek after your years on the Danube. We should reach Damascus by noon. Another set of passes, across the Barada and then along its banks until the al-Ghouta appears with Damascus in its midst."

In the morning, they moved on until green appeared amidst the sand.

Borrowing the agha's glasses, Eugene looked again. A brown mound with a few turrets surrounded by palm trees came into focus just as the agha had said.

"That must be it," Eugene said. "Are the towers the citadel or part of the walls?"

"Some belong to the citadel. Goes back to Roman times but not to worry as they have fixed it up. The palms are part of the oasis. To the east, the desert starts. To you, it shall all be new I know. Different here even from Beirut. Hot and dry much of the time. Cooler in the winter. Some rain but nothing like the coast."

Eugene rode in through the main gate, the roar of the crowd in his ears. Drawing closer to the main square the crowd grew and grew. Someone waved and he waved back.

Having followed the others in, he looked up. Every flag and regimental banner was snapping in the breeze.

His new garrison was lined up on the left, the imams and consuls on the other side. Once the final words of the last speech had died away, the departing agha handed over the keys.

The dignitaries having retired, Eugene headed for the citadel.

Riding in he looked around. The citadel was much larger than it had looked to be with three gates instead of Vidin's two.

The second in command, having introduced himself, gave Eugene a tour of his new quarters. Not as grand as the Vidin commander's but larger than Buruk's he saw with a smile.

A good sized dining room, a small study in the back and charcoal braziers scattered about instead of fireplaces. Stone walls a foot thick against the heat and odd metal grilles over the windows for glass.

Sitting down Eugene reflected once the man was gone. Two more rooms than at Trinity along with two manservants who would be by later.

A new clerk too if one could be found to help with the Arabic. French of course as all the officers seemed to know it. No wonder they had made him study it in school. Funny how much more useful it had turned out to be than the rest of it.

Eugene stood up and began unpacking his grip.

Unwrapping Elizabeth's miniature and his pictures of the two babies, he set them down by his pillow, putting his copy of *The Newsomes* by the lamp as he was not quite finished.

The rest of the books he managed to squeeze into the wall niches since there was no room left by his divan.

Once all had been put away, he took his portfolio into the study. The books instead, he thought, for the table was very small with only one lamp. Better to write in the dining room. Unless someone came, he could eat in the mess. It could easily be put back if anyone appeared.

Lining everything up on the dining table, he placed his inkpot and pens in their usual spots.

As memories of home ran through his mind, he sat down to compose a note for his mother. Proud she would be though perhaps he should have pressed James to try.

He wrote a few paragraphs, adding a few sketches because she had spoken of Damascus since he was small. The drawings were not as elegant as Maureen's but still one could see.

Once the note was sealed, he went back to his bedroom. Fetching James' Christmas present, a large framed ambrotype of their mother holding Jane Emily, he set it out on the sitting room table for all to see.

Towards three, the steward came round with the manservants.

All three having bowed Eugene questioned the steward as the others only knew Arabic.

"The first one cleans," the steward said. "The second fellow brings coffee and meals for when you dine here instead of with us. Either way, everything is supplied. You need only buy tobacco in the bazaar."

Responding, Eugene said, "For now I am using the dining room for a study. He can bring my yogurt up along with the coffee. I shall leave enough room."

At six, he headed downstairs to the mess. A bit of companionship and more fun than eating alone though the food was much the same as the village sherbet house. Yogurt, eggplant and bread but with an extra handful of mint. A Damascene touch he guessed.

Coffee appearing and laundry gone as if by magic the next morning.

The coffee trays made their rounds as the meeting got underway at ten.

Eugene tried not to be nervous. Somehow his hands kept finding his pockets.

Standing up, he sat down again and began.

"I am glad to meet all of you as I have much to learn. The governor tells me drill is needed should the unrest worsen. That I have done up on the Danube but until I learn the language, I shall need a translator. From what they tell me this is a quiet spot other than when the pilgrims depart and then when they return."

One of the officers nodded.

"That's right," the officer said. "Then and in summer when the Bedouin come out of the desert because they argue about their grazing rights. The caravans are the main thing, though. Much too important to rely on one of the agrawals as the nobles are referred to here."

Eugene interjected as the chap had begun to run on, saying:

"The pilgrims are the main concern. Summer is months away. The caravans will soon commence. Hopefully, we shall have a more cohesive force by then. I am relying on you since you know them well. Namiq Pasha has described some of the problems with the last fellow. Hopefully, they can be rectified. Morale being the most important thing."

He reviewed the men at three. When he returned to his suite, the servants had begun emptying his chest.

Fetching his book, he read a little more until they had finished. Once they were gone, he found a loose panel in one of the wall niches that was large enough for his drafts.

Then sitting down with one of his tactics books he began to make notes.

Starting in full force with the men the new rhythms of his life began to take shape.

Drill much like Vidin and visits to the governor's mansion with its courtyard. Much like the Acers' it was. Sun-dried brick for wood though and whitewashed walls that reminded him of Ireland.

Even with the clerk's help the piles of correspondence never shrank. Somehow they kept growing until the table disappeared under a sea of paper.

Eugene sat writing late into the night. A weekly note for Uncle Andrew, three pages each afternoon to his mother because she felt poorly and was in need of his support.

Impossible. Somehow they had begun to grow old though it seemed he had left for the Levant only yesterday.

Whether she should keep the house or move in with James and Susan, hard decisions made harder by the pain of widowhood. Being able to see the baby more would be a blessing she wrote but to give up her home seemed impossible.

Hard, Eugene thought, wishing it could be kept though that could not be said to matter as the main thing was what was best for her. If only he could be there though at least the letters must be a comfort.

So much time spent writing there was no time to read.

If only he was in Stamboul, he could at least see Marie-Genevieve but then he'd have to stay with her ladyship. Better to be out in the desert with an inkwell than the embassy surrounded by giggling girls.

The pilgrims began to trickle in, jamming the city as everyone had said with every nook and cranny taken even in the Jewish quarter.

Eugene rode down to the river several times to visit the camels but did not take a seat since he had gotten seasick riding one in Beirut. Then too, their humps and bells were most fascinating but their spitting was not.

The caravans formed up for Mecca.

Going down to the gate he watched them go. An entire afternoon which he had not expected. Camel after camel for what seemed like miles, pilgrims wrapped in white nodding atop each one.

He felt the sleepiness come creeping back once they were gone. Boat rides on the river, dinners with the new French consul and mint sherbet at the sherbet house now and again.

In April, a surprise reception at the governor's just before the pilgrims returned for his Medjidie had arrived in all its glory.

Everyone breaking out into a loud cheer, the governor pinned it on.

Eugene sat watching as the servants brought everything out.

As many trays of sweetmeats as there had been for the prince. So much tobacco he could barely make the dancers out as they wove around the room.

Sitting down that evening, he made a pen and ink as his mother would be pleased. He wrote a note for the next post, enclosing the drawing for encouragement was needed since she had decided to join James and Susan.

Painful, he realized, for much of what he had left behind would be gone. Susan had promised to save his riding awards but nothing else.

He capped his inkpot as the clock struck eleven.

Smiling he struck the last addressee's names off his list. The done stack under his paperweight was as high as the paperweight itself.

No list might be better, he thought, counting the number of names that were left.

His new Damascene routines began superseding the old.

Pilgrims that came and went, drill and Bedouin pastures to be sorted out in June.

Months running together from one sleepiness to the next. Must be because with less unrest on the coast there were fewer bandits to deal with.

Early 1857.

A letter in Colonel Rose's hand atop the mail stack, arriving just as the pilgrims began to depart. Something about a new commission. India, the colonel wrote, to take command of the Poona division.

Another note from Stamboul in May, this time from Francois Gilbert letting him know that the Stratford Cannings had departed the capitol.

The pilgrims came and gone as the year turned again. An official missive arrived, this time in his lordship's hand. It read:

15 January, '58

London

My dear Colonel O'Reilly,

A brief note to let you know that I have resigned as ambassador to the Porte.

As my resignation has been accepted, I can advise that Henry Bulwer has been appointed to take my place and shall be arriving shortly.

Should you need assistance, he can be reached through our man in Beirut.

It has been wonderful to work with you and I wish you all future success.

Her ladyship sends her greetings as well.

Sincerely,

Lord Stratford Canning

Odd hearing now, his lordship having been gone for months.

Hopefully, the new chap had already been installed. What with the colonel being gone finding out what Stamboul was thinking seemed impossible.

The end of April approaching the pilgrims returned. A messenger arrived as the officers' meeting ended. A meeting at the governor's mansion in two days.

Taking a seat by the door, Eugene clenched his fists as Namiq Pasha began.

"First," announced the governor, "I thank you all for coming. Orders have come from Stamboul. I am to be replaced by Ali Pasha.

"I would prefer to stay, but someone more experienced is needed in Tripoli. And right away I am afraid. I sail for Libya in a month. A few aides shall remain to assist. The others shall accompany me, other than Hassan Bey, who will be returning to Stamboul. The fellow is staying on in Tripoli and Ali Pasha is bringing his own man out."

Eugene sat with his mouth wide open, his chest tightening for he had not seen it coming.

The governor tapped his shoulder.

"I know it's hard," Namiq Pasha said. "I'd take you along if I could. You have done a wonderful job here. A grave error since you have had great success with the various tribes.

"But do not worry. I am in communication with my old schoolmate at the Porte, who with the general is arranging a position there. In the meantime, you can cross over with us and catch the steamer east."

Eugene tried to smile. At least, there would be a position. A desk at the Porte no doubt but something to be thankful for.

"Perhaps the city would be better," he said.

Namiq Pasha laughed, saying:

"Maybe, but you are a good fit with the garrison. Here they come with more dates. We can talk before we head for the sea."

Afterward days that moved all too quickly. It was harder to leave than he had thought. Somehow Damascus had come to feel like home. Three years but somehow it had seemed like weeks.

Packing his correspondence into boxes Eugene stacked them in the little study. He held his last review the day before Ali Pasha's arrival, followed by a small dinner for the French consul and the garrison officers in his suite.

The next morning, he sorted out the servants' money gifts before riding out of the citadel towards the central square with the keys. To his surprise, his replacement was a good fifteen years older which he had not expected.

He rode out the main gate in Namiq Pasha's train in the same order as before, the garrison in some semblance of square as that they had not practiced.

Arriving in Beirut two days later surrounded by the governor's aides he looked round for the British consul.

A Frenchman approached, his hand extended in greeting.

"I am Count Bentivoglio, the new consul general," the Frenchman said.

"Here because our chap in Damascus wrote that you were coming. You can stay with us as the Queen's man has not yet arrived. Better than the inn. Glad I am to meet you. Very few visitors at the moment. Then too we have heard so much about you."

Eugene breathed a sigh of relief. A place to stay and even with wine.

"I had not heard, about the consul I mean," he said. "I have been buried with my garrison. I would love to stay. We can share tales of Paris though I have not sat in her cafes in many years."

To his surprise at the consul's reception on his second evening, there was a long line of people all wanting to chat.

Funny. Somehow he had not realized he had become a minor celebrity. Whether it was due to his decorations or a lack of new faces was hard to divine.

His mood lightening for the wine was as delicious as the company his melancholia drifted away. Somehow sitting on a long porch surrounded by pretty ladies was a far better distraction than even a new Dickens.

Eugene managed to stagger aboard when the steamer arrived as he had had rather too much wine the night before. He slept nearly all the way to the Dardanelles, the count's address added in a firm hand to his long list of friends.

Standing in the bow, he could see that there were more ships than ever.

Michael was standing where he always stood. His hair was grayer and his middle rounder but otherwise he was just as he had been back in '49.

Eugene collected his baggage and embraced his friend.

"I thank you for taking the trouble to come down," said Eugene. "How are you faring under Bulwer?"

"The ambassador is all right. His assistant, Ted Jordan, is a bit much, but there is enough work for two so I say nothing. But enough of me. You have grown quite dark. It must be all the sun."

Ambassador Bulwer was on the doorstep as they came up the drive. Better than last time. His reputation must have proceeded him.

Chatting over dinner about the Balkans and Syria his host said, "I am sure you will be back in the field soon, no doubt very soon. The grand vizier is very impressed with your work."

Eugene smiled.

He replied, saying "Glad to hear that. Quite a shock it was with no warning. Granted I can make more contacts here but I shall miss the quiet of it all. I am not sure about where to send my reports after, though. My Parisian uncle is quite frail. Another arrangement is needed."

The ambassador coughed, saying:

"I had forgotten. Just send them along to me. So

many of our countrymen here now that they won't notice."

Eugene nodded his thanks. A simple solution really. An insurmountable problem it had seemed, too important for the Syrian chap and far too private to write.

Starting in at the Porte next day, a position that seemed ideal since it involved translating documents from Iraqi Arabic into Turkish.

Having to report to Ibrahim's father seemed rather tiresome. Must have been like that for James.

Another cocoon of work and writing interspersed with the occasional hand of euchre with Ted over a whiskey, Michael seeming a little old for such things.

All of it rather boring as having a garrison was far more amusing.

Granted the city was easier in terms of writing. Far simpler it was to visit in person than pen paragraphs late into the night.

Eugene enjoyed Ibrahim's wedding which to his surprise consisted of parties every night for a week. No imam either because they fed each other bread upstairs after instead of visiting the mosque.

A house to share with Stephen Bruce's cousin Thomas and, a month later, a dinner invitation from Adolphus Slade after an embassy reception.

Odd since he had heard about him for years. What with being the only westerners with Ottoman names they were always lumped together but they had never been properly introduced.

An acceptance. A fruitful connection even if the man did hate the Turks as he had made clear after several sherries.

Still Eugene felt rather bored. Wedding after wedding with their weeks of parties but no invitations after.

Even the baths were not very amusing since Koray's little son needed watching because Koray refused to leave him home with the ladies where he belonged.

Perhaps he should take a bride. Surely a colonel's suit would be accepted but no. Not one lady interested in leaving Stamboul.

Months slipping away, a summer and then another one. Eugene made friends with the fellow who read the Syrian dispatches. Very useful because the chap would let him look.

Smiling one afternoon as Ibrahim's father headed down the hall, the fellow held out a dispatch.

"Here, look at this," the chap said. "Getting bad there again. Last week, it was only Aleppo, but now the Druze have killed a Christian abbot."

Eugene thanked him, saying:

"Old man, I am grateful. Let me know what else comes. If it gets worse, they will probably say something but I am not sure."

As fall began creeping by the man showed him more dispatches. Trouble near Damascus, not just the coast the dispatches said.

Ted having been persuaded to arrange a dinner invitation, Eugene put on his best frockcoat and rode up the hill.

He asked for help once the port had been poured.

"I think in the end they shall ask you," the ambassador said. "We are pressuring them to do more. The Beirut governor has failed. Fuad Pasha instead, but with power over the entire province to be in charge of security and all else once the uprising is crushed. A gendarmerie and garrisons instead of relying on the agrawals and their warrior bands."

The ambassador concluded, saying, "You just need a little patience. Easier for me since it is a hallmark of my profession but with your reputation for working with diverse groups you should be fine. You should not take another year's lease. You will be gone by then."

Responding, Eugene said, "That I won't do. No more civilian clothes. They are a waste out in the field. Better Simpson's. I can always use more foolscap."

Ted laughed.

"Makes sense for you to buy clothes and me more paper," Eugene said, glaring back. "With any luck I won't be around long enough for them to be ready but my correspondence is never ending."

Laughing so hard he began to cry Michael said "The two of you are like peas in a pod. We have been long acquainted so it all makes sense. A decade, an eternity in the diplomatic corps for we move more often than the troops."

The dispatches began blending together, horror upon horror, but Orhan still said nothing.

Eugene paid a brief visit to the Acer house to see Ibrahim's little son since he had not been allowed downstairs earlier.

He took a bright green blanket for a gift. A pastel would be much too pale.

The baby looked a little like his grandfather, but even more like the first pen and ink of Jane Emily. Surely little babies must all look like each other instead of their grownups.

There was a beaded necklace around the little one's neck that seemed odd.

But no. Koray's son had had one when he was littler. Against the evil eye, he recalled. All the Damascene babies had them too.

Late May and a message arriving from the minister of war. A meeting with Fuad Pasha.

Everything having been fetched out in advance, Eugene managed to arrive early. The great man rose with an embrace before sitting down as the servant lit the hookah.

Eugene listened as Fuad Pasha began, saying:

"I thank you for joining us. I have very much wanted to meet. We are set to sail in July. I am in need of an Arabic speaking aide de camp because the province shall need to be remade. That language being rare here, you have been recommended."

Eugene sat up a little straighter.

He replied, saying, "I shall accept. Partly because I enjoy field assignments but also because I love Syria. My Arabic is not perfect but should do well enough with the tribes."

Fuad Pasha smoked as the minister began nodding his head.

"I am glad you have accepted, Hassan Bey," the minister said. "Few are up to the challenge what with the French influence. There is a meeting here next week that you must attend. The first secretary and attaches shall be in attendance."

Eugene sipped his coffee.

Responding, he said, "That shall be fine. Some I must know personally and the rest as you say by reputation. The French consul in Beirut is halfway to a friend. I could speak to him about the French."

Fuad Pasha grinned from ear to ear.

"That shall no doubt prove useful. But for now we shall let you go. We have kept you overlong."

Riding back home Eugene crossed all his fingers. Even with his lucky boots, the minister might have changed his mind.

To his relief things went smoothly. The messenger

appeared as promised.

The next week he rode back down the hill still in his lucky boots. Drinking his coffee, he listened as Fuad Pasha began.

The twelfth and Beirut on the seventeenth, that and a question about Bentivoglio. Encouraging for they had remembered. Doubtful the count could have the expedition held, but at least the connection had been recalled.

Everything proceeding apace as the twelfth approached, dinner on the seventh with the Gilberts, a long briefing with his host and a note for his mother into the diplomatic pouch.

Riding down to the harbor with Michael, Eugene thought that the twelfth had come entirely too soon.

He stood in the bow, waving until Michael was out of sight. The expedition's flotilla headed down the strait for Syria, its senior aide de camp hoping it would end better than the last because he wanted no more of the Porte.

July seventeenth, 1860.

Eugene's spirits began to soar as they came into Beirut. Its French mansions and blue shaded mountains felt like home.

There were no troops on shore which seemed a good sign. He had not heard back from Count Bentivoglio, which seemed rather a bad one. Perhaps they canceled each other out.

Softly scented sea air filled his lungs when he rose in the morning. Setting off to see the count, he hoped to be received as there had been no time for a message.

The door opened after one knock.

Finding himself crushed in a bear hug with a snifter of cognac nearly poured down his back, Eugene smiled as the count said:

"Oh, am I glad to see you. I got your letter but was afraid you would not come. But here, come on in. You can have cognac or coffee. Either goes well with cigars."

Eugene drank two cognacs for courage lest the count get angry.

Asking about the expedition, he felt relieved when his friend merely said:

"I would end it if I could. But my emperor has ordered it and they are en route from Nice. But let us talk of the local ladies as not all wear veils. A more interesting topic. If you are here long, I can introduce you. Though I suppose you will be in country shortly. Not sure what you see in it. Fellow in Damascus understands, though."

Two days to regroup. Fuad Pasha asked Eugene to head for Damascus instead of Rashaiya. The Bedouin had begun rising.

The French having managed to start a road the trip went faster than Eugene had expected, a day and a half instead of two.

Following the dirt paths that led down to the desert, Eugene stopped and picked up his glasses. Damascus appeared in the distance like a mirage with sun rays that bounced off its minarets.

He rode closer, holding his handkerchief to his face. The stench of death and ruin was atrocious.

Becoming more and more upset he rode through the front gate. He rode on through the Christian quarter towards the citadel in shock. To his horror, nearly all of the houses had been destroyed.

Odd being back in his rooms he thought as he sat listening to the new agha speak of the destruction and massacres.

"Terrible," said the agha.

"The entire quarter was destroyed. Some Christians were killed, but we were able to shelter many here. They were terrified as they came swarming in. The mob was on their heels. But now the tribes have begun to rise. Impossible to control since the city needs to be watched."

A new summons appeared just as he begun settling into his old haunts.

Sidon, the Druze halfway to an upper hand, their governor like a beetle on its back unable to do anything. No wonder they had sent in Fuad Pasha. These people were hopeless.

A flying visit back to the coast for another set of meetings. A bore what with all the complaints about the French but a visit with the count which made up for it.

In country again, all that traveling just to go back. Ah well, at least there had been time for the new race track and some flirting as Damascus had little of either.

Two fortnights and another request that he speak to the count which made him feel rather like a billiard ball moving around the table.

Fuad Pasha appeared at the consulate once Eugene had arrived.

Finding his aide seated on the front porch, thc governor said, "I thought you would be at the citadel, but I am sure this is better. You can get further with the count than I."

Fuad Pasha continued, saying, "I have a favor to ask. A tribunal is needed for Sidon and I would like you to be on it. Like the one in Damascus but easier because you won't know anyone in the dock. Thought it could be avoided but the Porte is insisting."

"A great honor and I shall accept," Eugene replied. "But when is it to begin? Rashaiya may need my attentions soon."

The coffee tray came around again.

"It is set to begin hearing evidence next week. You can go in country to stay once the hearings are finished."

The tribunal started. An interesting change and a most pleasing one. Far better it was to be on the bench than in the dock. But in the end an eternity running straight into fall that seemed to take forever.

Eugene settled in, dreaming of Christmas on the coast as November slid into December. But no. The day the last session ended he was sent off to Rashaiya. No Midnight Mass or parties, only a Bible and sand.

Riding into Damascus on Boxing Day, Eugene dined with Abdel Kader and the agha. The next day he asked about Kader as the man had seemed unique with many fascinating stories.

Explaining, the agha said, "Been here a few months. His past makes the governor nervous, but he can't be asked to depart because of the French. A good friend of Lady Ellenborough. Your countrywoman but married to one of the sheiks. In the desert now but here in the summer. They are thick as thieves."

Eugene felt startled for her name was familiar.

"She's here?" he asked. "They used to gossip about her when I was at school. Her I would love to meet. On my next trip if not this one. I should be here when the pilgrims leave."

1861, a spring that began slipping into summer as he rode back to the coast.

Du'ad Pasha to be swapped out for Fuad, who had been reassigned back to Stamboul.

To Eugene's relief a new position as of that he had not been sure. Head of security, he learned at the interview, and all on horseback. Almost cavalry but with bandits instead of Russians. A blessing for he could stay.

He began. The recruitment going rather better than he had hoped, for even in Gaza and Amman they had heard of Damascus. His old battalion reappeared as they were eager to serve under him followed by the agrawals complaining mightily since they were used to their old ways.

Managing to sneak away twice before the New Year returned he went out into the desert to meet Lady Ellenborough and then into Damascus to stay at the citadel.

The agha cautioned him over sweetmeats and coffee, saying that Abdel Kader was best avoided. It would make the Porte nervous, the chap added, for they feared a new insurrection on the heels of Algeria.

Doing his best to be polite, Eugene said nothing. The next day he met with the man at the sherbet house. Surely the Porte would never know.

The second year to his distress did not go as well. The Porte having decided to cut their funding it was difficult keeping the men paid and the tribes bribed.

As the caravans began preparing to head south, Eugene wrote Beirut.

The message that came back did not help to ease his nerves. It said little other than that he should do his best for the gold had not yet come.

Another missive arriving from Beirut on the heels of the first. Something about the Porte being anxious about the loyalty of the gendarmerie and the grand vizier needing to be coaxed.

Rather disheartening, he thought, though the small bag of gold that accompanied it seemed a plus.

His old melancholy started setting in. Pulling himself

together he managed to make it pass. Better to write politely in any case. Rudeness would do no good.

The tribes hard to tell apart he wrote. The occasional name easy to misread yes but on the sultan's side. Complicated all round, he wrote the ambassador, mostly because there was not enough gold.

Eugene sent a note off to Ibrahim asking him to inquire since that should help. Painful it was, fifteen years in the country and post after post but still not being trusted.

The pilgrims besieged amid complaints from al-Yusuf and the other agrawals. The tribes quieted but then starting up again.

Beirut to explain. But no, for everyone was so touchy. Better to try and cope than chance being recalled.

Eugene bit his fingernails down to the quick because there was nothing left for bribes. So sensitive nowadays the Porte seemed to be, a puzzlement without a solution at least from Rashaiya.

Late fall brought a letter on embassy letterhead. Tearing it open since Sir Bulwer must know something Eugene read:

1 November, '63
The Embassy
Pera, Stamboul
My dear Colonel O'Reilly,
Greetings from Stamboul.

I am writing in an attempt to explain the thinking at the Porte. Since your departure, a new man has been appointed to deal with concerns about risings in the various provinces and Syria in particular.

It is not merely directed towards you and your mounted gendarmerie of whom I have heard great things. For some unknown reason, he is particularly worried about the Jerusalem viceroy.

Then too Fuad Pasha has fallen into a state of disgrace as a new grand vizier has come in. All of his appointments are therefore being questioned which always follows such circumstances.

Francois and I have been at the Porte in an attempt to dissuade them from distrusting every appointee. We are meeting with some success.

Hopefully, you shall be able to remain. I shall keep you updated on any developments as they occur.

Sincerely,

Henry Bulwer

The news not being terribly reassuring Eugene tried to think of how to proceed.

Spending hours sitting inside he barely rode. Being tarred with the same brush as the viceroy seemed impossibly hard. Doing his best to stay calm he spent Christmas with Lady Ellenborough.

Du'ad Pasha having arrived from the coast he rode back into the city to attend the meetings about the season as New Year's Day approached.

Dinner the first night was more convivial than he had been expecting.

The opening session the next morning was rather worse. Du'ad Pasha was in a vile mood. Rising to his feet, he said:

"I think it would be best to rework the gendarmerie, having the militia leaders signed on as captains. The minister feels that the gendarmerie often takes the field against itself as it can be hard to tell friend from foe. But I would like to hear you out. First Hassan Bey and then the rest of you."

Everyone speaking at once, a buzz worked its way around the room as the pasha sat down.

Al-Yusuf leaped to his feet shouting to be heard, saying "Then I shall resign. Unless I am in control, I cannot answer for the tribes."

Marching out of the reception room he glared at Eugene with what looked to be a rude gesture.

Better to ignore it. Who knew what was proper amongst the tribes.

The caravans departed and returned peacefully.

One of the tribes emerging months early which seemed rather strange. Al-Yusuf's doing perhaps, the others not having seemed very upset. More oddnesses after, the men needing to be funded from his own accounts and his best squadrons lost to a commander who could barely ride let alone command.

All Syria was against him it seemed as he wrote Beirut and then Bulwer. To his distress, nothing came back.

His mind spinning and a deep sense of foreboding with pockets as stretched out as they had been after Blanchardstown. He could not recall being in such a state since.

Praying, he did his best to police everything, hard though it was since his best men were gone.

Another letter came from the embassy, as fat as the last with page after page. Orhan with an appointment to see the grand vizier Bulwer said.

Sinking onto his knees Eugene prayed, hope against hope.

Another fortnight and another messenger, this one with papers from the Porte covered with as many ribbons and seals as the Danube commander's had been during the war. A letter of support he thought as he opened it up. To his shock, it was a summons.

Reading it through, he could see that Orhan's visit must not have helped. Charges of aiding a conspiracy amongst the Damascus tribes to oust the sultan.

Eugene sank down as his knees gave way, thoughts running through his mind. He had expected to be called back to the coast but not the Porte.

He rode into Damascus the next morning to see the agha and the governor.

Better to show them than vanish for then they would think he had deserted. Both men were shocked. They had known of the Porte's concerns but had not expected what had come.

The governor said, "If I had known I would have told you. Must be the work of the new officials. Abdel Kader, you should have avoided. Him they are in fear of."

Eugene replied, saying, "I shall head back to Beirut to await the steamer. I am sure the count will have me or else the British chap will. In such a hurry, I did not even say goodbye to my men. My junior officer can take care of that."

Sleeping in his old sitting room, he laid down as his mind spun around. Impossibly hard. With his father gone, he would have to save himself.

A letter for London though surely it would arrive too late since the steamer would arrive at the Golden Horn long before it reached Cherbourg.

Something at least though perhaps it would not help, Michael having written that the grand vizier was very concerned about western influences.

On Friday, he headed for the coast surrounded by the garrison in square much like the British in Kilmainham. Odd leaving Damascus surrounded so he could not flee as it seemed more home than anywhere.

Mount Hermon's snowcap gleaming in the sun, they crossed the Bekaa.

Gazing out at the sea as they came through the last

pass Eugene stopped to look at the town with its apple orchards. It looked like paradise after the desert as it always did. Riding down to the harbor he fixed it all in his mind for he might never return.

To his relief a reasonably happy week in the end as he waited for the steamer. His old room at the count's with all its comforts instead of a cell which he had feared since the Jerusalem chap had been put in the Gaza jail and forced to wait.

Everything blurred together.

Days spent back and forth amassing letters of support and reassurance from the Queen's man that Palmerston would help.

Rides out along the beach on the count's gelding, large dinners and a final outing to the racetrack to watch the count's horse take a second.

Better to have fun instead of worry since it would do no good.

The steamer pulled into the Golden Horn a week later, docking beneath the Topkapi under the sultan's eye. As the ropes were being tossed out Eugene managed to spot Michael, which brought a smile to his face since he had expected no one.

Michael did his best to calm Eugene down because he was frantically pacing back and forth.

"Old man, you look white under your tan. Don't worry. Bulwer has already been to the Porte twice. It seems the worst of it will be the loss of your post. I know the charges are scary, but the Crown is behind you."

"Somehow I had thought they would understand," Eugene said in a small voice.

Eugene stared out as they drove through the central district. Much the same with quite a few of the Turkish ladies in western dress under their cloaks. Funny. There were only one or two in flounces in all of Beirut.

As they pulled onto the embassy drive, the servants came running to take his things.

Ted came out to greet him and swept him down the hall towards the library where the ambassador stood in the doorway ready to beckon him in.

Once Eugene had sat down Sir Bulwer started in, saying:

"My dear Colonel O'Reilly you need not look quite so distressed. I would have waited for you to freshen up, but it did not seem fair to make you wait any longer. First I don't think they are being fair. They are recalling nearly all of Fuad Pasha's men. But kindly explain why you dined with Abdel Kader so many times after I explained that he worries them."

Eugene fidgeted in his armchair. Near impossible it was to get comfortable after all the divans.

Responding, he said, "Because the man is harmless. He barely communicates with the tribes let alone the Druze."

His host laughed, saying, "Why I am behind this desk and not you. You should have steered clear. The appearance of it matters greatly. No point now in going over it as it can't be changed. We must look forward instead.

"I assume Michael has mentioned my visits to the Porte. Not so much your command of the gendarmerie in their eyes. Rather why it was not more effective. Much distressed they are by the attack on the pilgrims as they are the main concern. Not the tribes and their pasture requirements."

Doing his best to defend himself, Eugene handed over all the letters he had amassed.

"These should help. In any case had they sent the gold everyone could have been paid. I have had to use my own account. My best squadrons taken too. But I did my best. I think more was expected than could be done."

He felt surprised as the ambassador interrupted since he had thought the man would agree. But no for Bulwer was shaking his head like mad.

"None of that matters. They won't care. But here is pen and paper. Write that you have arrived and would like a meeting. The boy shall take it over."

Eugene arrived at the breakfast table the next morning barely able to breathe let alone eat. Somehow his jacket was much tighter than he had remembered.

Lady Bulwer said nothing but Ted remarked that he was overdressed. Eugene glared back, muttering that over was better than under.

The Porte sentry having let them in Bulwer dismissed the carriage. The ambassador did his best to calm Eugene down for he had begun to shake.

Walking into the minister's office, Eugene's heart pounded so hard that he felt giddy.

He felt relieved for the jail was not mentioned. The minister was very polite as he read down the list of charges, nearly all of them about the treaties with the Bedouin. Odd. Somehow they had liked his knowing them before.

Taking all the letters along with a note from the Damascus agha, the minister rose to his feet. Eugene was so weak at the knees the ambassador had to take his arm as they left.

A fortnight filled with meetings, followed by a cocoon of a different sort since the wait for a decision could take all winter.

Too many hours spent pacing followed by entire days spent rummaging in the attic as the days and weeks dragged on. Lady Canning's romances, as many as could be found since he had read everything in the shops.

Another summons to hear what had been decided arrived as the trees began leafing out.

Eugene put on his dress uniform again, pinning both decorations to his jacket. He wore the new gold and diamond cufflinks he had purchased the day before.

Teasing him, Ted said, "You look brighter than the sun."

Eugene retorted that it was better to gleam than fade and that dutch courage was better than none at all.

What looked to be the same sentry followed by an embrace from the minister, bringing a smile to Eugene's face for surely it was a good sign.

"All of your letters have carried the day," said the minister, "especially the one from Omar Pasha. The grand vizier is convinced of your innocence. Concerned enough to not send you back to Rashaiya but you are free to stay in Stamboul and look for other work."

Eugene wanted to ask about Syria but as the minister looked rather stern, it seemed better not to inquire. He asked the ambassador on the way out instead.

Sir Bulwer frowned.

"I don't think you can. Their decision was milder than I had originally expected. But asking to return no. They might change their minds and exile you instead. Better to wait and look at the agencies. Perhaps home for a while. Palmerston might know of something or else Colonel Rose. Try not to be upset. They were quite kind."

Eugene dashed off a note to James once he reached his room. Certainly he had more than enough for the ticket, there having been nothing to buy in Rashaiya.

He sat thinking of what to say. The truth was not an option.

Finally, he wrote that his assignment had ended,

adding that he would like to visit before seeking another. It sounded good and was partly true. Better half true than another missive about impulsivity with James' seal.

Crossing his fingers, Eugene watched as Ted slipped it into the pouch. Paris if James said no though somehow absinthe and cafes seemed a young fellow's thing.

Penning another note for London, he started in on the next romance.

A positive response came from Dublin with permission granted. James wrote that their mother would love to see him, adding that young Thomas would be thrilled. He had inherited his riding skills sideways, James said, and could ride bareback clinging to his pony's mane as his uncle had in Corstown.

Time sped by as his cocoon began lifting.

Racing downtown to the ticket agent as the next westbound steamer was in ten days, Eugene described it all to Ted over dinner.

"It shall be wonderful to see my mother," he said. "James I never got on with, but his little boy is supposed to love horses like me. Needing help, no doubt. James can barely keep his seat.

"London for a spell after. If I stay away for the winter, they will forget me here which will be well at the Porte but not in terms of finding something. One of the agencies or something diplomatic in Morocco since they are independent. Stamboul does not rule there."

Smiling his friend said nothing about Eugene's diplomatic hopes for which he seemed dreadfully unsuited.

"A change of scene," said Ted. "A good time to go as there aren't as many storms in the summer. More likely to be out on deck than sick below. But you should leave some things here against your return."

Nodding in agreement, Eugene fetched the port and

cigars from the sideboard. The Bulwers had gone out and no one would know.

Everything began to blur.

Dinners, receptions and farewells that were more painful than the last time for he might not return. One thing to have begun again in '49 but somehow he felt too old to do it anew.

Losing track of time Eugene found himself racing downtown the day before he sailed because he had forgotten to buy any gifts. Running from shop to shop he bought shawls for the ladies, cigars for the gentlemen and toys for the children.

Once the gifts were packed into the trunk, everything was so jammed in the servant had to sit on the lid to make it close.

Arriving at the pier, he watched the smoke begin to erupt from the smokestack.

To his relief, the passage west went smoothly with only one delay, an overnight in Southampton to wait for the packet.

Standing in the bow the next day he looked round as the packet steamed towards its pier. New buildings, a veritable sea of hound's tooth plaid and the ladies' skirts so wide they could barely fit through the gates.

All doubts of his welcome faded away once he reached James' house.

He was enveloped in hugs so tight he could barely breathe. First his mother and then the children who leaped into his arms climbing him like a tree.

Kneeling down once they grew too heavy Eugene deposited them on the carpet. He stood them side by side, gazing into their faces. He had come to see them as much as anything.

Both of them looked just like their pictures, Jane

Emily with her dark curls and her brother with James' brown hair. His own eyes danced back from little Thomas' face as Susan came running down with an embrace.

Susan sent a message downtown while Eugene went out to the stables with Thomas to be introduced to the new pony.

Coming back in through the back door he went straight into James' arms. Despite everything, it was hard to be apart.

They sat in the library, talking about everything and nothing. Summers in Corstown, Mr. Hall's, their mother and Damascus but not the veiled harem ladies. That Eugene was sure James would never understand.

A scone with homemade strawberry jam appeared. Eugene took a bite as James asked straight out why he had come, saying:

"We are happy to see you, but why now and not earlier? You didn't overstay your welcome with the infidels did you?"

Replying, Eugene said "Ah no. I was busy. First running the garrison, then at the Porte and back in Syria again. Between things and wanted to see everyone. I have changed you know. More cautious like you nowadays and doing my best to be careful."

James smirked.

"Maybe. Whatever it is I am glad to see you since there was always just us two. Thomas is already happier as I lack the stomach to visit the horses."

"I did nothing wrong. One thing ended and the next has yet to begin. A good time to come. I am happy to visit the horses. My unclehood has been remiss over the years being so far away. As patience is not still not my strong suit putting the pieces together to go back will be a challenge. Hopefully, I can line something up in London."

Eugene felt comforted being back. Everyone looked ancient like a backward time machine, but it was home in ways the Levant was not. Everything in English, no veiled ladies, and Mass when it suited him instead of having to wait till he was on leave.

He spent each afternoon with Thomas, visiting the horses as he had always done. Thomas having outgrown his pony he looked round for a small riding horse.

Saying nothing at tea, he smiled at Thomas. Somehow James had never had any sense about four-legged creatures of any sort.

Once the horse had been purchased Eugene headed downtown to the tailor with Thomas in tow. Ordering a new riding ensemble complete with red-topped boots he told Susan who complained, something about the expense.

Her brother in law ignored her. How was the boy to ride without the correct accoutrements?

Spending each morning upstairs with his niece he rode out every afternoon with Thomas for neither could bear to stay inside.

By the end of the winter, Thomas had progressed to being able to execute low jumps and Eugene had begun to long for children of his own.

As February began slipping into March word came of Uncle Andrew's passing. Eugene was devastated since he had visited so much.

Fighting back tears, he sat with his mother at the service as a wan smile crossed his face. Funny how it had all worked out. Had it not been for the fiasco and its aftermath he might never have gone. A blessing in disguise.

Not just a memory of cafes and absinthe he realized. On the heels of the service, a letter arrived with a copy of the will. Seven thousand pounds and all for Eugene, the entire estate.

James read the will over. As the family legal expert, he did everything of that kind.

Finishing, he put the papers down on his desk, saying:

"I wish I had gotten something for the children, I mean it's just you."

His brother gave him an odd look.

Responding, Eugene said, "First I am sure he made me heir because of my visits. I intend to give you five hundred pounds towards Thomas' education. Something to help with Mother and Jane Emily's hope chest too.

"The rest I need. It shall help carry me with what I have managed to amass as there was nothing much in Rashaiya to buy. When you live in uniform, you don't even need tailors."

James sat back, saying no more. Five hundred pounds would fund nearly three years at Eton.

"I don't mind paying Mother's expenses, but the help is appreciated. I understand why it was left to you. Just an outburst which I hope you can forgive. Then too you paid for Thomas' horse and riding outfit. We may be even but the help for Eton I thank you for. Just having you here is a treat. Dreading the day you leave for fear you will be gone as long."

Eugene reassured his brother, promising that he would not take as long to reappear.

Heading back upstairs, he mulled over what to do. The money would be a help. A backstop for what he had.

Surely a position would come along before he needed it. Still it was time to start looking around for one would not find him. Fun riding and visiting everyone but easier by far to stumble over something in the capitol.

Putting an order in with the tailor, he wrote Rex since staying at the Crottys' would be cheaper than renting rooms.

He wrote a note out to Palmerston as Colonel Rose was still en route from India. The colonel was the most likely to help he thought, but it made sense to at least inquire elsewhere.

Eugene felt much better, almost as he had before the Porte had written. London and Belfast seemed a fine plan.

Rex's return note arrived with an invitation, a response from Ten Downing Street following on its heels. Its seal impressed James, which was always a good thing.

As the lilac came into bloom, he headed for the harbor asking everyone to keep their fingers crossed. Something in the Levant he hoped, an agency or the diplomatic service, whichever would have him.

He left his trunk in the box room so Thomas would know he would be back. It was hard to leave but necessary. He could not sit forever as even his mother understood.

Eugene was warmly greeted at the station for his mischievous ways and kind heart had been legendary at Mr. Hall's. He found himself missing his niece and nephew which he had not expected though Rex's wife Alexandra and their son helped to take the sting away.

He slipped right back in.

After a few days, it was almost the same as everywhere else. Cigars and port that were just as Ted had brought them out the night before he sailed. Piano technique a tad better than Lady Bulwer's.

Claustrophobic though after so many years of divans

and wall niches. Gewgaws all over and even an embroidered thing on the wall for matches.

Too many velvet drapes too. The drawing room was even murkier than Damascus had been with the window grilles closed against a sandstorm.

Doing his best not to eat with his fingers, Eugene managed to cut up his green beans with his knife and fork. Surely Alexandra would be more horrified than her ladyship if he ate his meat with his bread and call him a crofter if not worse.

He paid a long visit to the stationers downtown, returning laden down just as tea was about to be served. Running up to change he dashed off a note to Lord Palmerston to let the prime minister know he had arrived.

He had just finished his last scone when much to his hostess's surprise a messenger appeared in the prime minister's livery with a dinner invitation for Tuesday next.

Mass on Sunday and then upstairs to lay out everything so he could choose something suitable. Rex came in with a horrified look as the loveseat and chairs were entirely encased.

Eugene explained.

"This must be everything," said his friend. "Reminds me of your boot sorting before the gymkhanas."

Eugene smiled for he had forgotten.

"Helps my nerves," he said. "Here. Come and help me judge. Hard to know which jacket looks better with my decorations. The navy or the one with all the braid."

Rex replied, saying, "Old man, it's rather out of my element, but I think they look a little better with the navy though I am not the tailor."

Eugene felt relieved once he arrived as things went

rather well. Having been announced, Lord Palmerston came forward to introduce him round.

To his surprise, everyone was more interested in Damascus and Beirut than the connection with his father. The Hassan Bey perhaps. Easy to remember but still it seemed odd.

It was rather startling so he asked them why. From his notices in the papers, someone said.

"Oh," he replied for he could not think of a better answer.

Explaining, he told the man next to him that he had not known as it was impossible to get the Times in Damascus let alone Rashaiya. He could recall being interviewed by a few correspondents in Beirut but had always been in country when the new issues arrived.

To his disappointment, his dinner companion was a rather plain lady.

Fortunately, he was seated across from a most interesting chap who had interests in Athens and was almost as knowledgeable about champagne as the count.

Port, cigars and a young woman singing arias with a pianist.

Standing in the doorway, Eugene wondered if the prime minister had forgotten him. His relief was palpable as the great man approached to ask if he could come back the following week to talk further.

Eugene went back the next Monday. Lord Palmerston told him that Stamboul had sent everything along.

Breathing a sigh of relief as it would have been hard to explain, Eugene asked for help.

A place with one of the consulates, Egypt or Morocco. Somewhere his background would be useful, far from the grand vizier and the agrawals.

"Colonel, I have read the reports," the prime

minister said. "Like Sir Bulwer, I agree that you should have avoided Abdel Kader. On the other hand, your career has been exceptional. That combined with my fondness for your late father means that I shall try though perhaps you would fare better with the business investors rather than the consuls.

"Hugh Rose knows more about the agencies, but I shall see what I can do. In the meantime, you can rest. Visit your old school which I remember your father mentioning. I shall send a message along when I know something."

The next few weeks passed rather swiftly. Eugene stayed with an old Trinity friend as his welcome seemed rather worn out at the Crottys'.

Better out in the field he realized than dining at clubs every day. Even if he had it to do differently, he would have ended up the same. Must not have been in the stars.

Another fortnight, a liveried messenger, and yet another appointment. Casablanca, perfect though the other fellow had to retire first. Just after the first of the year, only a little while longer.

His welcome having begun to run thin Eugene went back to Dublin.

A week later sitting down to his eggs and bacon he had a shock. A black framed announcement in the paper. Palmerston gone. Strange. He had looked fine Eugene thought as James sat staring.

Palmerston having been a family friend, they attended the memorial service at the cathedral together.

Eugene wrote London about the post since a month had gone by only to receive a boilerplate response mentioning other candidates. No one to take his part he realized so one of the others would get it. He tried the foreign minister, but it was no better.

Tedious, first waiting for Casablanca and now this for Lord John Russell had come in with his own people. Eugene did his best, trying to find a common connection, but it seemed impossible since the man wasn't Irish.

A note arrived saying he had not been chosen.

Eugene's melancholy began slipping back and he hid upstairs where not even Thomas could pull him out.

Stamboul might be best, a free place to stay at any rate, the rooming houses being so dear. James looked grumpier with each passing day and there was only one London friend left to ask.

Word came of Colonel Rose having reached Belfast.

Inviting himself for a week's stay, Eugene crossed his fingers. Far better it would be to arrive in Stamboul with something than not.

As the train rolled into Belfast a fortnight later, he did his best to ignore Crumlin Road. Better it was to forget all that.

He spent the week catching up with talk of old friends and then Syria since the colonel had been in Beirut for years.

Eugene managed not to ask for help as it would be far better to wait. Day after day passed until the last evening arrived.

In town for dinner at the club, he felt relieved when the colonel asked him about posts.

He crossed his fingers under his napkin, waiting for his steak and wine.

"I know you don't want to ask," Colonel Rose said, "but must be hoping for assistance looking for a post. I did not want to embarrass you by mentioning it earlier."

Eugene uncrossed his fingers.

"Yes, although I have come to visit as you are an old friend."

"No, that's all right," the colonel said. "I would ask if I was in your boots. First I have seen the reports. Being summoned back will not help you. Though certainly there is enough doubt to want to be of assistance.

"An Ottoman commission is off the table. It shall not be allowed. But of course, I have my friends. Not many here as I have only just taken over but quite a few there. Did you try the diplomatic service?"

Eugene sipped his wine, saying:

"Yes. Palmerston had mentioned something in Morocco. But after he died Lord Russell chose his own man. Palmerson had suggested trying the investors, but I was waiting to hear about Casablanca first. But I really don't know. Staying here near my mother would be nice if it can be arranged. So far I have had no luck."

Colonel Rose put down his fork.

"Hmm, might make sense to try London again. I'd offer you something but after that little excitement in '48, I can't."

Looking over at Eugene, who looked thoroughly shocked, Colonel Rose said, "Calm down boy. I knew about it when you came out but said nothing since it did not matter to the Turks. Even now it does not bother me. If I was Irish, I might have done the same.

"A youthful error but you pled guilty to sedition and are not allowed in the Queen's service. Otherwise, you would make a marvelous aide de camp. But I can do nothing as the Crown won't budge on that."

Eugene managed to calm down. His racing heart slowed as he stared into his rose.

"All this time I have wondered," he said. "No one said a thing. I thought perhaps all the Times issues had not reached Stamboul. Indeed, Crumlin Road gave me a fright as we rode by."

Nodding, the colonel said, "Half-forgotten and very long ago. I would not have mentioned it were it not for the fact that you can't be offered anything because of it."

Eugene took two bites of his steak.

"I wish I had not been involved," he said. "Difficult just talking about it. Bitter I am. They deceived me about how I'd pay and pay."

The colonel gazed up at the ceiling, saying:

"Well, it's done. I must say you have done well and made the best of it. Certainly you have risen higher than you would have under the Queen. Thomas Bruce may be your best bet since you have spent so much time there. By now Richard Lyons has replaced Bulwer. A decent chap who shall help you."

Eugene watched the waiter pour more wine.

"That I knew," he said. "Michael wrote and told me. He and Ted are staying on so it shall not all be new. Now that I think about it I have more built up over time than many do. I have kept Simpson's alive at times, but it is helping me now."

"Yes, they must applaud when you come through the door," Colonel Rose said.

"You should stay in Dublin while you can since you may not be back for a while. About the diplomatic efforts, I cannot advise. I think your best hope lies with the business interests because of the new cabinet. But do ask Mr. Bruce about Clarkson as he already knows you. Though I shall do what I can."

Eugene felt calmer the next morning as he headed back. All those years and it had never been mentioned. Surely he could never have managed it.

Steamer tickets he thought as he did his best to divine through the tea leaves. But no. Better to wait for Thomas Bruce's response.

A letter arrived from Uncle Andrew's attorney in Paris, saying that the check would be ready in a few months. Mulling everything over Eugene decided to wait. Better to pick the check up between trains. It would take longer if it was sent along.

As the leaves began turning in late September an offer arrived from Clarkson.

A man needed to cover the Danubian provinces for two years. Perhaps longer it said but at least it was a start.

Traveling back to London, he encamped in Rex's guest room. He felt relieved because all the interviews seemed to go well. The pay a little less than he had hoped for but still enough to take a small house on the edge of the quarter.

Ten days later an official envelope with an offer appeared. Eugene made haste to accept. Not as good as heading the gendarmerie but Stamboul at least.

Rushing to get ready as he needed to report by early November he raced back to Dublin to make his goodbyes. Everything was on a tight schedule with each connection needing to be made.

Eugene had to spend two days in Paris instead of one for he had to wait on the bank. Heading south for Nice he caught the eastbound steamer without even an afternoon to rest on the beach, there being fewer easterly runs in October.

Michael was on the dock when he arrived.

Heading for the bridge, Eugene noticed veiled ladies in what looked vaguely like crinolines all over downtown. Custom for all the western stores they must be as there was one or two more in every block.

He described his new position as they rode along.

"Not quite as interesting," he said, "but in Stamboul, which is why I took it. London was fun, but nearly all my friends are here. Thomas Bruce helped me along with Colonel Rose. They both put in a good word for me. Oh, I am talking too much. But I am so glad to be back.

"How are you getting on with Lord Lyons? I was told he is all right though the colonel knew little more. In any case, I shall be glad to get to the embassy. It has become a home of sorts as much as these other places have."

Michael closed the window to keep out the noise.

Nodding, he said, "Lord Lyons is all right. He likes adventure. More in common with you than Bulwer I should think. Your friend Ted has become even more tedious. I am still doing half his work. But you shall see that it is much the same."

Lord Lyons appeared in the library doorway as the front door shut, murmuring something about articles.

Strange how they had all heard of him for he had done nothing unusual really. Surely the papers could find someone more interesting to write about. But no. Somehow Lord Lyons was even more interested than Palmerston's investors.

Eugene took a cigar.

Lighting it, his lordship said, "I know what happened but agree with Bulwer. You could easily have been thrown out. Instead, you are back with what sounds like an interesting position. Lots of travel up to the border where you were stationed. Now you can visit in peacetime and see the difference.

"You may stay as long as you like. I shall enjoy the company. An honored guest. We are glad to have you here."

Concluding, Lord Lyons said, "Tomorrow I need to see the Prussian fellow but Nicolas Bouree, the new Frenchman, shall be here for dinner. I am hoping you can join us as he is eager to hear your stories. They tell me the Gibsons were good friends, but Francois was recalled last year."

Eugene frowned.

He replied, saying, "I know. I had tea with Marie-Genevieve when I was laid over in Paris. Looking forward to meeting their new man. His expertise may be helpful if I manage to go back."

Eugene slept until eleven the next day as it had been an exhausting trip. Dressing hastily, he went down to eat.

The dining room looked much the same. A new sideboard, Lady Lyons where her ladyship had sat, but the same place in the same spot at his hostess's right that he had always had.

He started downtown the next morning. A big office that was larger than the ambassador's library, two windows overlooking the harbor instead of the alley like Ted's.

He learned more as the week wore on about his new post. Somehow it had gone right by him in London.

A new rhythm to get used to for surely that was the main thing. Three months in the capitol being surrounded by reports followed by one up on the border.

Travels east to Varna and then backward to Novi Sad. The investors being interested in grain or textiles, whichever might prove more viable and easier to ship.

Eugene toured Silestra where Ibrahim had been several times. A great treat he thought to see where everyone had been after all the letters.

Evenings spent over hands of twenty-one and brandy with Thomas and Ted followed by Saturdays spent house hunting. Nothing suitable. Everything was too big or too expensive.

One of the agents finally found something that would suit.

On the edge of the Pera, a smaller version of the Acer house. Courtyard in the middle with a few benches strewn about and a three stall stable, one for his new mare Mirabelle and two spares. Two manservants were included, one outside and the other in.

Eugene moved in as the year drew to a close.

The quiet seemed awful, but the house was all right. Smaller than the one he had shared with Thomas but still only needing half the rooms upstairs. He slept in the largest room, took two more for trunks and out of season garb and locked off the rest.

Heading up north the next week, he caught the train east for Varna once the investors' embroidery orders had been placed. He had dinner with Osman at the sherbet house, but only one plum brandy for their days of three or four were gone.

He sat back in his compartment for the run back to the capitol. A real treat after all those coaching inns. Somehow he missed the veiled waitresses and yogurt soup.

9 STAMBOUL, HOMS, GAZA & BEIRUT

1867 and an ice storm to welcome the New Year. His trip having gone well Eugene decided to hold two dinner parties to celebrate. First the Turks, then the Europeans for Michael and Ted could not stomach Ottoman food.

Eugene felt relieved when the replies began coming in. Only Koray had declined.

He hired an extra servant because there were so many special dishes. Lamb, yogurt soup since it was Ibrahim's favorite and pistachio sweetmeats for dessert.

A rose scent perfumed the air as the manservant began handing the finger bowls round once everyone had eaten.

Sitting back after he dipped his fingers, Ibrahim asked his father "Isn't the yellow house we passed Derya Solomassy's? It seems to me that it is. I don't know him personally, but his brother Alihan was pasha up in Vidin when I was in Silestra."

"I think you are right," Orhan Acer said. "Yes, now I remember. Someone told me he had taken it. Odd as everyone seems to prefer Therapia these days. Hassan Bey, perhaps you met the brother. Though I am unsure as to which years he was in Vidin."

Putting the hookah down, their host did his best to recall.

"Offhand no. But then I was a bimbashi so the commander would have met with the pasha but not taken me along. Still the connection is interesting. Few here from Vidin. They all tend to head for Belgrade. I assume you mean the house two doors down. Saw it last Sunday as I went off to Mass."

"Yes, that's it. An ordinary sort of house but pretty."

The conversation having shifted Eugene remembered that there had been several young ladies in their drapings when he had ridden by the day before. Impossible to ask. Turkish gentlemen never discussed their ladies.

He held the dinner for his European friends two days later. The same furniture but a western helper swapped out for the Turk. Fish for lamb, parsley potatoes, and madeira after.

Pausing across from the yellow house on his way home from church, Eugene watched the shadows move behind the lattice. He wondered whether it was the young girls or the older ladies.

Impossible to tell for in Stamboul all the houses had glass instead of Damascene shutters and grilles.

The same oddness on the streets as there was every Sunday since he was on the line where the two quarters met. Uphill streets filled with westerners heading for church, carriages going downtown in the other direction as the Muslim Sabbath was on Friday.

Sitting in his library, he spent the afternoon on his correspondence. Dublin first and then a new note for Rex.

By dusk, his finished stack was higher as he had been writing for hours, but he was still not caught up. A correspondence of a good twenty-five that had grown in an amoeba-like fashion since Nice, all of it essential.

Hard but necessary he kept reminding himself as he snuck in the occasional ride. He kept his writing area in the same order as it had been in Rashaiya. He would be lost if the inkpot was not in the same spot.

Getting up late on Saturday, he rushed because he was late for his fitting.

He smiled as he reached the curb because the Solomassy ladies were heading out for a bit of shopping. One looked older than the other, a sister or cousin perhaps.

The older girl who looked to be around twenty had dark hair, squinty eyes, and the standard yellow boots.

The younger one was much prettier. Huge blue eyes, red-gold hair and a flounced blue dress with French boots peeping out from below her skirts.

Eugene managed to inch closer, so close he might have crashed into her had he not stepped back.

The lady having smiled he smiled back. Catching a brief glimpse of her trim ankles he turned because her great lady was looking his way.

He stood watching as the araba headed up the hill and hoped that her great lady had not seen.

He had his measurements taken for a new frockcoat, heading for the embassy to lunch with Lord Lyons afterward. To his joy as he stood on the curb the ladies reappeared, their araba filled with shopping bags and parcels.

His pretty neighbor glanced in his direction, first with a start but then a smile.

Smiling, he bowed back. Another smile and then she was gone.

He had a pleasant meal and two glasses of a most decent claret before heading down the hall in search of Michael and Ted. They sat around the fire over a glass of stout since it had begun to rain.

Eugene told them about the girl.

Smiling, Michael said:

"She sounds lovely. Must be a good sign that you saw her twice. Let me offer a hope that you shall see her again soon. Ramadan keeps the ladies in. Hopefully, she shall emerge before the month is out."

Ted poured another glass, muttering something about the Ottoman ladies looking like fat penguins under their cloaks.

Trying not to respond as Ted seemed to have had a bad week, Eugene shook his head.

"They aren't all alike. Hard to tell apart yes. Still many are very pretty and not fat."

Ted slouched in the corner, saying, "They cannot hold a candle to the ladies in Madrid, but this one has caught your fancy."

"Eugene, Ted is right," added Michael. "I haven't heard you speak of anyone much since you came out. Granted I am a bachelor but you don't have to be."

"Whoa, I don't know as I'd go that far having only seen her smile twice."

Ted laughed and laughed, saying "You'd be better off at a ball in Dublin, but we shall see."

Riding back down in the late afternoon he held his paper lantern up. More torches these days, but it was still awfully dark.

Once Mirabelle had been put to bed, he stood by the stables looking up. He could just make out a roof terrace up against the sky where the yellow house should be.

Clarkson stayed open as Ramadan commenced upending the city's rhythm. It was quiet during the day and loud late into the night as everyone feasted till dawn.

Eugene stayed home on weekends, getting caught up on his Dickens as he sat by the fire.

Spending his evenings feasting in the Ottoman

quarter, he stood by the stable each night when he arrived home. He stood by the wall listening to the feminine laughter from down the hill. Impossible to tell which terrace the ladies were on but he hoped it was hers.

Lingering outside on Monday since it was ladies' day at the baths, he managed to catch a glimpse of her. She smiled again though whether it was for him or the children on her lap was hard to tell.

Ramadan having ended, Eid began. Eugene went up on the roof to see all the minarets lit up. Lovely, he thought, an entire sea instead of Rashaiya's two or three.

He managed to catch another glimpse as she went by, no doubt for a picnic along the strait where Marie-Genevieve's fetes had always been. All those pavilions, enough for all the Ottoman ladies to rest.

He started in on his new Dickens, waiting for the new *Punch* to come. A blessing being in the capitol at least with the mails. Two at a time like Dublin instead of those vast heaps four times a year.

More distractions, though. Somehow it took twice as long to finish anything, whether it was in Turkish for work or Dickens.

Another buying trip in late May, Vidin and Belgrade with an overnight in Novi Sad.

Two embroidery houses, a Serbian tapestry firm and a ride on his last day out along the Danube near his old post.

He dined with Koray on his first day back.

On Saturday, he stood transfixed by the curb. She was standing right in front of him with no chaperones behind her. Peacock blue under her cloak, French boots and hair like a halo in the sun under her veil.

Plucking up his courage for she had smiled again he said "Hello" in Turkish as he was not sure which languages the young ladies were taught.

To his surprise the girl replied.

"Good morning," she said but in French.

Eugene tried to figure out how to respond, the language not the words since it was impossible to tell which she would be comfortable in. French, he thought, as it was more of a compliment.

"I speak that too miss," he said, "but was not sure which language you prefer."

"French is fine. I have had lessons for years. Here with my governess and before at home in Vidin. Then there's Hungarian if that would be easier."

"Then French it shall be. You are from Vidin? I was there in the Asiatic war. Very pretty and lovely this time of year. But I came here after you."

Extending her hand, the lady said, "Yes you did. But first my name is Mathilda."

Eugene draped Mirabelle's reins over the front railing.

Taking the lady's hand, he said, "I am Hassan Bey or Eugene O'Reilly, formerly of Dublin and Syria. Here working for a company that does investing between Novi Sad and Varna."

He wondered what to do next. An embrace was fine for a gentleman but not a lady. No one was looking their way so he kissed her hand as back home that would do.

"You have a complicated name," she said.

"In any case, we came from Vidin two years ago. My hometown but once my father was gone we came here to live with my uncle. I miss Vidin but with no male kin there we could not stay. But then here they have western dresses. We had dressmakers there, but they had no western patterns or styles from Paris."

"How long were you there?" she asked. "My father was pasha there and attended many receptions at the citadel. Perhaps you met."

"No," Eugene said. "At the time, I was a junior officer and would have been back in my room. Mostly I remember my quarters in the inn. Every inch was covered with animal designs. That was the first time I went out. After I was in the fortress itself and then north with my men. A few days last year going back and forth too but not since."

"A very pretty place," said his new friend. "Still the clothes are nicer here. Even a new dressmaker just up the street by the tailor."

She smiled again, saying:

"I saw you when we went there to shop. What I should be doing now. Off to the bazaar for some wheat and then the dressmaker. My friend told me that they got some new silk in. I must be delaying you. I am sorry."

Eugene beamed back in relief. She was a delight, a vision, and only a foot away.

"Well yes," he said, "but that's all right. In a minute, I must head down, though."

She replied, saying, "Then I shall let you go. I must hurry before the peacock green is gone. A jacket to go with my dress. Hopefully, we can chat again. I often go out at this time or on Mondays after we bathe."

Leaning down, Eugene kissed her hand through her glove. Even a butterfly kiss would upset the neighbors.

"I shall take care to be here then. Few here are from Vidin and wear peacock blue. I bid you adieu."

Eugene watched as she made her way down up the hill, wishing she would turn and wave.

He got next to nothing done downtown on Monday. Dreams of her kept running through his mind.

On the way home he paused across the street. He watched the shadows play, hoping they were hers.

Rising ninety minutes early on Saturday, he chose his outfit. He drank his coffee and then waited for what seemed like half the morning by the front door. Just as he finished ribbon braiding Mirabelle's tail she emerged.

Sitting down together on the step, he asked about her Hungarian. A sad look crept over her face as Mathilda explained that she had learned it from her mother whose family had fled the Austrians.

Asking what was wrong since he had not intended to pry Eugene patted her hand.

"It's all right," Mathilda said. "I lost her a year after we came to Stamboul. Sad because of that. Proud I am to know the language."

Eugene apologized though she didn't seem angry. Must be the child of an odalisque as the great lady was always Ottoman. Strange for him but not for her. Plenty of such ladies even in Damascus. Namiq Pasha had had two.

Mathilda looked up. Deep blue eyes, bedroom eyes Maureen would have said.

"That's all right," she said. "You couldn't have known. Anyway, I have my great lady, my sister, and the two babies. Much work to look after but a lot of fun."

Responding, Eugene said, "I know. I have a nephew of my own back home who loves riding like me. Probably begging my brother to take him out right now. A niece, too, but she is older."

Eugene wracked his brain as Mathilda rose to pat Mirabelle. An outing yes but just where.

A Sunday ride perhaps, the big park atop the Pera near the Prussian embassy. Better to be discreet and stay away from the Bosporus.

Gathering up his courage, he asked.

To his delight she accepted, saying she would love to go but that she had no riding horse as hers had been left behind in Vidin.

Breathing a sigh of relief Eugene smiled although he was not sure where to borrow a lady's mount. He told her he would find one, describing the park and its views since she had not been there.

"I shall look forward to it," Mathilda said. "That and the enjoyment of your company."

He turned his head and she was gone, heading off down the hill to the bazaar for they would wonder where she was. She turned to wave and he waved back, feeling as if he was on air.

Once he was inside, he sat down to eat, spilling Russian tea down his shirt for he had forgotten to go up and change.

He thought about Sunday once he had found a clean shirt. The livery stable having nothing calm enough the horse was the main problem.

Maybe one from the embassy. They always used the carriage on Sundays.

Having sent a message up on Tuesday Eugene headed for the embassy Saturday after Confession. His pick, Lord Lyons had written, since he knew horseflesh better than the grooms.

He chose her ladyship's mount because she was the calmest of all.

Once the mare had been put to bed in the second stall, he began figuring out his clothes. The boots alone were complicated. Some were too formal and others much too scarred.

Putting every divan on the second floor in use in the end, he picked through his jackets and breeches.

The following morning, he raced home. Getting dressed, he chose a peacock blue tie like her dress and his second newish boots because his black patent leathers had yet to be broken in.

He led both mares out to the street, their reins looped over his arm.

Mathilda appeared five minutes later, looking lovelier than she had the last time with a red skirt and jacket. Jane Emily's new habit almost but for the blonde hair piled up under all the veils.

Eugene walked down and offered his arm, hoping she did not notice the goose bumps that popped up when her hand touched his sleeve.

The block being too low, he helped her mount.

Riding off towards the park, they chatted about the Vidin countryside and her visit to the dressmaker as they had had just the right green.

Apologizing Mathilda said, "That I shouldn't mention. More of a ladies' topic."

Eugene laughed back.

"No. I love clothes just as much. Hearing about your dressmaker is fine. I visit my tailor just as often."

Chatting as they rode through the gates, Eugene showed her the different bridle paths since there was one on each side. They headed for the southern overlook with its glorious view of the harbor and the strait.

Mathilda pointed places out, the Sweet Waters first where he had been with Marie-Genevieve and another meadow opposite.

Eugene nodded, saying "I have been to picnics on the Asian side but not the other."

"Ah," she said. "Then you know it. The European one is further down. Closer to the Topkapi but nearly opposite."

Riding down another path, they dismounted and sat down on a bench.

The horses trailed them as they sat chatting the rest of the afternoon away. Eugene of his job, Kalafat and his Corstown summers, Mathilda of her sister and her mare back in Vidin.

Eugene asked about her riding since he had thought Stamboul girls never rode.

Tossing her head back, Mathilda laughed. Vidin had been different she said. There she had ridden out every day.

"Then I must ask you again."

She smiled, saying, "I shall accept though I mustn't ask you to borrow my mount. It is too much trouble."

"My house came with a three stall stable," Eugene said.

"I can lease another mare. She could live next to Mirabelle."

Mathilda looked worried. Must be the expense since they had barely met.

"Not to worry. I shall look around. If there is a suitable one, we can come up here more often. That I would like."

They talked on and on. As the sun began its transit into dusk, they mounted up to ride back down. Cook would be firing up the stoves.

Pausing at the steps, they rode down the alley. She insisted on seeing the stable which touched his heart since ladies were seldom interested.

A last pat for the mare once she was watered and then down the alley to the street.

Kissing her on the cheek, he said goodbye as they came abreast of the steps.

He asked her again.

"There is a concert Friday at the theater," he said, a blush deepening under his tan. "Perhaps you could join me?"

Mathilda agreed. He held her in a gingerly embrace for it was hard to know what was right.

Giving him a butterfly kiss back she walked up her steps.

As she opened the door, she turned, saying, "Till Friday, have a good week and I thank you for the riding."

Eugene felt very fluttery as he went back in. Something special there, not just the riding but a fondness for both grandmothers as she had spoken of hers along with the sweet kisses.

Friday came in a flash, the week having flown by in an instant. Leaving work early, Eugene fetched the carriage and went home to change. His new black trousers since they had the best crease, patent boots and a peacock tie in the new teal shade.

Waiting out front with the carriage behind him, he held a large nosegay. Mathilda emerged in a new gray silk that made her eyes even bluer under her green cloak.

Spotting the carriage, she looked surprised.

"We need the carriage so you won't rumple your dress. That and the flowers. Easier this way," he said as she sniffed her flowers, getting in as he handed her up.

"Oh," she said.

"It is better anyway. My sister can't see me and tell uncle's great lady."

Eugene did not respond as he was not sure what to say.

"I forgot to explain. My first aunt who is in charge of all of us. Me she doesn't like because Mama was an odalisque. She likes my sister better. Easier if she doesn't see me. She wouldn't like my going out."

Her beau gazed out the window. Just like Elizabeth's mama. All the mothers were like that.

Reassurance but what to say.

"I am a colonel. That should help," he said in the end.

The lady looking impressed he continued.

"I am glad you are here," he said, "even if your great lady would not approve. It should be a good concert too. I have been to many but not at this theater. They have not had enough musicians for a decent orchestra until now."

Escorting her into the theater they sat in the second box, the first having been taken.

Schubert, a champagne flute during the interval and then a Chopin mazurka. Mathilda's eyes began to dance and her feet to tap. Like the songs they had played when she was young, she murmured.

Mathilda thanked him as they rode home, her small hand reaching over to take his which made Eugene feel warm inside again. Love perhaps, though it was hard to tell after all these years. So long ago, all the way back to Elizabeth.

Passing by Saint Matthew's he pointed it out since she had asked him to.

Unexpected though her answer had made sense. Her mother having been outwardly Muslim but Catholic in her heart for she had been christened before the rebellion began.

Eugene was not sure what to say but asked if she would like to go with him on Sunday.

On Sunday, he escorted her to Mass, feeling relieved once he had taken his place in the pew.

One or two odd looks and stares as they sat down but not more since many amongst the agency staffs had married Ottoman ladies. Fortunately, Mathilda had turned to look at the stained glass and did not see.

A glare from Father McClure as they were heading down the aisle for the porch door.

The side door the next time till he came round Eugene thought.

He went back alone the next week, the Solomassy

ladies having gone visiting.

The priest asked about Mathilda in a frosty voice.

Eugene glared back, doing his best to be respectful.

"There are not enough western ladies," he said. "Her mother was Catholic and she is most delightful."

The priest responded.

"I know. It is not the lady's fault that her parents were not married in the Church."

August.

Mathilda being greatly admired at the consular picnic which he had been anxious about since she had barely met Michael and the rest. Raised eyebrows from Ted over her veils though the music seemed to help.

Everyone stood watching as they danced all three mazurkas. Eugene could still out dance everyone and his partner's footwork was as exquisite as his own.

Eugene sat thinking once he was home. She had put a glow in his heart and a lift to his steps. Perhaps she was it. Only a few months' acquaintance yes but still much in common.

His birthday and another fortnight as September came round.

Living from one Sunday to the next with its sweet kisses and deep embraces, Eugene made up his mind. He took money out of the bank for a diamond solitaire from the jeweler.

During the interval at the ballet, he rubbed the ring box in his pocket. Perhaps Sunday would be better he thought as the curtain rose again.

They rode back to the park on Sunday. Helping her sit he knelt down, both knees in the mud, and proposed.

Mathilda looked shocked.

Asking again, Eugene shifted his weight. Must be that she did not know what to do since they were all trained up for arranged marriages.

Mathilda took his hand, murmuring something about not having known him long enough, that and with his rank he must need someone grander.

Looking up into her eyes Eugene said, "Please, I can't live without you sweetheart" as he pulled the ring box out for her to open.

Mathilda opened the box. Hugging him she clutched the ring in her fist.

Gazing into his eyes, she saw his love reflected in them.

"I love you," she said.

"Give me half an hour so we can sit and talk. But it is probably yes."

He waited until an hour had passed.

Asking again, to his relief she said "Yes."

He pulled her closer for a longer embrace, the ring still in her hand.

Handing it back, she asked, "Which finger does it go on my love?"

Her new fiancé kissed her once again, slipping the diamond onto her left ring finger. Sitting down by her side on the bench they talked and kissed with more kisses than talk.

They stood clinging by the stable for a last kiss once the horses were abed.

Eugene wished he could ask her in. Impossible without a lady to chaperone he realized, walking her back to her door.

Mathilda's fiancé felt that he was walking on clouds as he tried to do everything and that all at once.

Long hours spent downtown since there was a London visit to prepare for. Evenings filled with letters home, first to his mother with his wonderful news and then everyone else.

Coming downstairs at eleven on Saturday as he had

been up late the house looked shabbier somehow. Nicer carpets for the divans, a few more courtyard plants and perhaps new paint as the sitting room looked rather dark.

Starting in on a list he put his pen down as he remembered that Susan had made her own. Better to leave it for her. A lady's thing everywhere it must be.

A loving reply from his mother on top of the stack. Thrilled, she wrote two paragraphs about wishing she could meet his fiancée and a request for a tintype.

Packing a copy of the latest in cardboard and tissue paper Eugene sent it off the next day. Mathilda in her gray dress and no veils, her face wreathed in smiles.

A note filled with meanness arrived from James the next week. Eugene wished he had not opened it for James had written that he was ashamed of his little brother marrying a heathen.

Sitting down, Eugene stared at the wall before he picked up his pen. He wrote two pages, saying that she was a Christian and that there were not enough European ladies to go round.

He sealed it up, hiding it in the middle of the stack. Just thinking about James' words was distressful.

Doing his best to stay cheerful Eugene stacked the replies under his paperweight. Two inches' worth, in the end, all of them wonderful except for James'.

He mailed Maureen a copy of Mathilda's picture, sitting down after to write his mother again. A kind word from his brother would mean a lot, but he could not bear to ask James himself.

As he sealed the envelope, there was a knock on the door, an invitation from Derya Solomassy for coffee in two weeks.

Spending each evening consumed in an endless rehearsal of what to say Eugene tried to remember what his father had done. He smiled. Obviously, the old man had come round in the end.

His anxiety grew day by day. Ibrahim mentioned that Mathilda's uncle had written his father.

Encouraging, Eugene thought. Surely Orhan would say pleasant things.

A message arrived from the Acers the evening before that said all had gone well. Eugene went back to sorting through his cufflinks. Having his boots repolished he felt a little better.

Rising early in Saturday Eugene had yogurt and bread with his coffee since he felt a little queasy. Tying his ascot, he walked two doors down and knocked.

The servant announced him as Mathilda's uncle rose in greeting. He looked like a stouter version of Commander Buruk. Clean shaven with dark hair, a loose jacket and lots of rings.

His knees having begun to grow weak, Eugene sat down after the embrace and looked around the room.

Same size as his sitting room but nicer looking. A low table but in a brilliant yellow instead of brown. Flowers in all the wall niches instead of books. Less tired looking too, must be all the bachelors who had taken his before.

Putting his coffee down, Mathilda's uncle began, saying:

"Thank you for accepting my invitation, Hassan Bey. I hear that you wish to marry my niece. Very excited she is of course. Since her father is gone, it has fallen to me to speak with you. To make sure of a suitable connection.

"As is the custom the bride's family investigates to make sure her young man is suitable. We have learned that your reputation is fine other than that unfortunate incident in Rashaiya. Fuad Pasha and I have discussed it as he is an old acquaintance. He has been quite reassuring and feels that you did nothing wrong.

"The grand vizier having been quite distrustful of my cousin who was entirely innocent we are willing to accept his explanation."

Eugene's knees felt nearly normal.

Nibbling a pastry, he replied.

"I enjoyed my time in Syria," he said. "Before that, I served on the Danubian front under Omar Pasha. There I was raised to my present rank. The Rashaiya incident was unfortunate, yes but quite difficult to explain. Glad I am that Fuad Pasha went into it with you as I shouldn't have been recalled."

Derya Solomassy nodded.

"Lord Lyons has said much the same thing. He told us that your father was a prominent attorney in Dublin and that your family has a good reputation in that city."

The servant came in with another tray. Eugene had another cup. Better up all night than rude.

Mathilda's uncle finished his cup.

Nodding again, he said, "I hope you are not feeling insulted. She was my brother's favorite and needs protecting. Many have volunteered favorable opinions including Orhan Acer. He tells me you have known Ibrahim since his days in the general's suite.

"We have met before, but I am sure you don't recall. A good hundred in attendance when Ibrahim wed, far too many to recall each introduction."

Eugene shook his head in apology.

"You are right," he said. "So many there that I am afraid I can't remember. But no I am not insulted. Back home they do the same. I feel you are taking my love for your niece seriously by asking everyone. I shall make a splendid husband for her. That I can promise with all my heart."

Mathilda's uncle looked relieved.

"I am sure you will. By all reports, you are a fine man and shall be good to my niece. You need worry no longer. I am giving my approval. A big wedding may not be possible depending on the length of your engagement. That being the only difficult part."

Breathing a sigh of relief, Eugene said, "We would rather have a small ceremony in any case. I have friends here, but it is too far for my family to come out. My mother would love to. But her health is poor. Perhaps at my church. Or at the embassy. We have not decided yet."

"It can be worked out," Mathilda's uncle said. "My great lady shall have a dress made up. Then there's the trousseau and its parade.

"For the ladies to attend to. Better to stay home. They are so much better at it anyway. Of course, most of it came down from Vidin so it won't take them long. A few more coverlets to embroider perhaps. She is handy with a needle, like her mother."

The man came in to collect the tray. Mathilda's uncle rose to his feet with a congratulatory embrace, offering to go upstairs and let the ladies know.

Eugene did his best to walk home slowly, relaxation replacing tension in his mind as he went. He had gotten the feeling that they rather liked him.

About the larger wedding, he was not sure because there was no room to entertain for a week. One party instead of nine perhaps. At least in Damascus only great lady brides got more.

But a trousseau parade. Too bad they didn't have them in Dublin. Susan would have loved it.

Everything looking even seedier as he came back in.

Sitting down, he mulled it over. Maybe a few vases and the andirons polished. A start as it were.

The next morning, he walked very slowly on his way to Mass, rehearsing what to say. Granted the timing was a little complicated, before the end of the year but after his next buying trip. Something the ladies could not help, Muslim weddings being so different.

Requesting an appointment once everyone was gone, the priest said that he had a few minutes.

Once they reached the rectory, Father McClure rang for tea.

"How can I help you?" he asked.

Replying, Eugene said, "As you may have heard, I and Miss Solomassy are engaged. Her family has approved. I need to arrange the ceremony, a small one as we would like to wed by the end of the year. Having attended for years, I think of Saint Matthew's as my home parish."

"I shall think about it," the priest said. "A very pleasant young lady whom I have chatted with several times.

"There is a difficulty. Her parents were not wed in the Church. She may not have been baptized despite her mother being a member of the faith. The second can be remedied of course but not the first."

"Please," said Eugene. "I hope you will change your mind. There are no Catholic churches in Vidin. She is from a fine family, a pasha's daughter. Her uncle in business here in the city."

Shaking his head, the priest replied, saying:

"The problem is not the Solomassys themselves. It is rather not having been married in the Church. It is more that the bishop would have to approve, not that I don't wish to officiate. If he declines, I must say no. I must answer to him and him to Rome. If I can help, I shall. I am glad you have met such a wonderful girl.

"I shall write today and explain everything. A reply should take only a few weeks, not more than three. He does understand that we are in the Levant, not Rome as there have been quite a few marriages between Europeans and Ottoman ladies recently. But none solemnized here."

Feeling dejected, Eugene headed home. Surely they had to be careful but one would have thought they would understand in a place where there were so few churches.

He brainstormed once he had finished his dinner, trying to think of another way as the ladies needed some sort of date.

Perhaps Lord Lyons. Her ladyship being very much against Europeans marrying native ladies maybe or maybe not.

Eugene tried to think of something else, but nothing came to mind.

Not the Methodists or the imams. The first would say no and the latter didn't even celebrate weddings. Lord Lyons in the end since he could think of nothing else. He penned Michael a note as a direct approach would not help.

Michael came down to the baths on Friday with an upset look.

Explaining that he had inquired after her ladyship had had her sherry, he added that it had done no good.

No luck, he said, Lady Lyons having turned red as a beet as she ran on through dessert. Lady Ellenborough and her sheik husband while her husband sat mute letting her go on.

Eugene pulled his towel tighter.

"He lets her decide way too much," he said. "Do you think a personal appeal would help? Here all these years. Sent all those reports back. They have done me very few favors. Bulwer did in '63 when I was summoned back. I have stayed at the embassy on various leaves and kept trunks there but the last time it was just for a few weeks."

"You have been a great help," said his friend.

"Assisting you and your off and on visits are part of the job, not favors. Still with her ladyship so against it, I am not sure the answer will be positive.

"Personally, I am glad you have found her. She shall make a wonderful wife. But I don't think the Lyonses will agree. That and they are off to Madrid soon. Not to return until the end of the year for the ball. After they may be sent to Paris leaving a small window to arrange everything."

"If you wait they may leave it to the next man who may not help," Michael added. "Likely to be Sir Elliot I hear. Very conservative he must be since he is at the Vatican now. They never choose a liberal for that posting. I wish I could do more. I am letting you down terribly."

Eugene did his best to smile.

"That's all right. I know you can't change their minds. Some are more amenable and others less. Colonel Rose would have approved, but he is back in Belfast. I shall think of something else. No point in asking his lordship."

Eugene sat staring into the fire whiskey in hand once he got home and tried to untangle it all.

All Saints Anglican but no because they were worse than Rome. Crete perhaps. An Orthodox or maybe the rabbi. Perhaps a yes in Damascus but in Stamboul a definite no, the city being far too big for that sort of favor.

Pouring another whiskey, he thought again. Someone to pretend to be Lyons. The Solomassys would never know the difference. Ted, not Michael, for Michael was much too good. Not much of an idea but something.

Having slept on it, Eugene sent a messenger up to Ted with an invitation to the baths for Friday next. Somewhere so deep into the Ottoman quarter that no one could understand English.

Ted arrived a little late on the appointed day.

Sitting in the back corner once the attendants had finished their scrubbing, Eugene did his best to explain.

Ted nodded in agreement, saying, "I think Michael is right. Lyons will say no as her ladyship will have one of her melts. Have you thought of Crete?"

Eugene sat staring. It had all been explained one time too many.

"Crete I am not sure of, but it is far too dangerous, like Damascus with bodies lying around. Not fit for a lady's eyes. All I can think of is you. I know you shouldn't, but I am desperate."

Shaking his head, Ted said, "Not that I won't help, but won't the fellow at your parish marry you?"

With an exasperated sigh, Eugene explained that he could not help. The bishop having declined for her parents had not been married in the Church. The priest having appealed. Rome not expected to overturn the bishop's decision.

Ted shook his head again, saying:

"Not sure about it but then you are in a major bind. If they do not bend, it cannot be helped. But only as long as you promise not to tell anyone. If London finds out, I'll be shipped back home instead of Paris. That I don't want. I need somewhere more civilized than here or Newcastle."

Ted glared as Eugene laughed.

"Not laughing at you. Funny how you hate it and I love it. Different careers, though. Mine can't move. Certainly I won't tell. We do need to figure out a day in November. One when Michael and the others won't be around."

"The date I shall have to check," Ted said. "Towards the end of November for sure. The ballroom. With the Lyonses away no one goes near it as the corridor is quite drafty. A chance we might be seen from the main house but, of course, the gardeners will not be out and about. That should work."

"All right. That shall give the ladies enough time. It being the tenth today late November would be best. Maybe the twenty-second as it is my mother's birthday. Since they won't be back until late December, that should be all right. I owe you a huge favor. I would do the same for you as you know."

Eugene did his best to ignore Mathilda's chatter about her coverlets. Somehow it seemed worse than all those afternoons filled with talk of the Lake Country back when James had been engaged.

Funny how the trousseau and the parties were the most important and not the dress for Susan had been the other way. An Ottoman thing, the Acers having been the same.

Explaining, Eugene told Mathilda that everything in the house was for her to decide. All to be done to her liking, downstairs and up. The courtyard too. Five rose bushes, but it needed more.

"Mums or wisteria," she said. "We had them in Vidin. The rest I shall have to wait and see. Blue I think since it is your favorite. But it depends on how the rooms are. Is it like our house? For that will help me see in it in my mind."

Her fiancé squeezed her hand.

"Identical," he said, "but in need of a woman's touch which it has lacked for some time. Trunks in two of the bedrooms as they are not needed. I am not sure which should be the nursery. James and I lived at the top of the stairs with Polly not down the hall from our parents."

Mathilda gazed at him with a shocked expression.

"All alone with a slave? No. The baby shall be by our

bed and then in the next room."

She did her best to explain because Eugene looked very surprised, saying "I am sorry, I thought you understood. Children with their mothers and aunties upstairs. Boys downstairs with the men once they are big enough. But the baby shall be with us in his cradle."

Eugene did his best to calm her down.

"Shhh, I know that," he whispered. "I just didn't know which room you would want to use. It sounds like lots of fun to have all those children to play with not just one. More like my summers in Corstown with Patrick."

Smiling a weak smile, Mathilda calmed down. "Of course, it will be fine. We shall figure it out, my love."

Eugene took her hand.

"Of course, we shall. It would have been lovely to be with my mother all day. Lucky you were."

Another northern run. Sofia for three nights and then home.

Eugene headed up the hill to see Ted and lay everything out.

Walking out to the gate they walked back again twice and found a place for the carriages to wait that could not be seen.

Eugene was so anxious afterward that Ted had to help him mount. He could barely throw his leg over Mirabelle.

Three days left. Mathilda went off to the baths in a grand araba with all the ladies, Solomassy and Acer. A lady's thing like a bridal tea with musicians and dancers someone said. Each lady groomed and hennaed and platters of sweets.

Eugene felt very grateful what with all the Acers' help. His oldest friends in the country but still he had not expected them to be so kind.

Not just one reception but two with music echoing up and down the stairs as the children ran back and forth.

The Acer ladies visited the Solomassys the following evening. Standing by the door, he listened to the music as it filtered its way up and down the street.

Eugene felt terrible in the midst of all the excitement. Two notes sent up to Michael, but the hurt was the same for he had been excluded. Not good enough really, his oldest friend in the country not allowed to stand up by his side to share his joy.

Truly a quandary as he could not be asked. Funny how the Ottomans thought the parties were the wedding but not Michael of course.

Better this way otherwise as everyone thought he had found his own priest. A comfort. At least, no one would know.

The twenty-first dawning cold but with some sun for Mathilda's procession day.

Everything heaped in baskets, musicians in front and at least ten servants to carry it all. Walking around the block, they marched in Eugene's front door and up to the second floor as the neighbors watched.

Eugene headed upstairs once they were gone and spent the afternoon choosing his outfit. Three hours instead of his usual two with his studs and cufflinks and another over boots.

The next day he left at one to unlock the garden gate.

The Solomassy ladies and Mathilda's little cousins arrived at two. Eugene handed Mathilda's great lady down first.

Taking Mathilda's hand, he smiled.

She looked glorious. A red velvet gown covered with silver embroidery, fur lined jacket that made her waist look tiny and a small veil. No bouquet but that must be part of their way.

Ted having waved that nothing could be seen from the house, Eugene walked up through the garden and into the ballroom.

Spotting his friend Eugene felt relieved because Ted was wonderfully garbed. Best frockcoat and trousers, one of his lordship's ascots and Eugene's oldest pair of cufflinks for those Mathilda would not know.

Ted walked over, introducing himself as Lord Lyons. The ladies all bowed as he was finishing and Ted bowed back with a smile for Eugene that was not his usual smirk.

Standing on the hearthstone, Ted opened his prayer book as Eugene and Mathilda stood before him hand in hand. He managed to read it all off as well as a clergyman.

Biting his cheeks hard Eugene did his best to look solemn. By a great effort, he managed not to laugh, not even during the vows for that would have been deadly.

Once Ted had pronounced them wed everyone turned round, heading back to the terrace. The children skipping through the leaves, the Solomassys walked down the path and climbed back into their araba.

Eugene breathed a sigh of relief. Even the great lady had not asked about witnesses. Must be their first western wedding. Otherwise, they would have known.

Riding down the hill, Eugene held Mathilda close. She took his hand as he reached for hers.

Hard that it was not a real wedding though certainly he had tried. Fine in Stamboul of course, special coffee, bread upstairs and it would be done. No wedding trip either but at least a ring.

Reaching the house, Mathilda was swallowed up in hugs, first the ladies and then her little cousins. She looked rather surprised as she was being carried in. Eugene did his best to explain. A British custom for good luck.

Mathilda followed the new maid upstairs to change. Her groom waited in the sitting room with a roaring fire and the special bread that the Acers had sent.

Reappearing, his bride was dressed in a bright green tunic with yellow embroidery and trousers. Funny how they all loved bright colors instead of Dublin's muted tones.

Looking around, Mathilda frowned.

"I know," her husband said. "Your house looks much nicer. I did think of having it redone, but it seemed better to wait since my choices might not be to your taste. I did get some glasses and a new set of cup holders as they were very pretty. Back home, at least, all that is a lady's thing to decide."

Mathilda looked up and took his hand.

"I am sorry for my look," she said. "It shall look much prettier tomorrow. They are coming over to help. That and the colors will be different and not white."

"It shall all be as you like. Peacock blue divans perhaps. Your dress of it is lovely."

"Hmm. I think the walls instead with a pretty green for the divans. Though my favorite is blue."

Eugene listened as she prattled on. First the paint colors and then the floor.

Indeed, they had barely been alone together unless the boxes at the theater counted. Susan must have been like this though of course James would never say.

Pulling her close, two kisses and then another as she sat close gazing up into his eyes. As the servants evaporated Eugene lifted her up, heading up the stairs lips on hers as he went.

The next morning as the ladies arrived Eugene headed into the library. Surely six hours of writing would trump the same span of paint color chatter and complaints about the divans.

Reemerging in the late afternoon, he found a new looking house. Cushions, new carpets, and the scent of a good scrubbing everywhere with fires laid and flowers in every niche.

Venturing upstairs he looked in the bedroom. Prettier, embroidered curtains along with a new set of pillows.

He went into the next room. It was different there too. His old trunks replaced by a baby's cradle and chests filled with baby clothes and blankets.

He headed back downstairs, following the noise towards the kitchen. Mathilda was standing by the door with her hair in her face, watching the servants hang up copper cookware.

Kissing her for he could not resist, Eugene said, "My dear it all looks so bright. New curtains too. Thank you. It looks as wonderful as I thought it would."

Mathilda replied, saying, "I am glad you like it. It does not look as dark now. The curtains I cannot take credit for since auntie brought them. I hope the green is all right. A dash of color in the corner. Yellow instead perhaps when the flowers start to bloom."

"If you want yellow then it shall be yellow," he said.

"I thank all of you. It looks brand new. Perhaps after you are done, you could come look at the library curtains. They came with the house and look very tired. The rest is fine as I had it redone. Green walls, white woodwork and red divans like my grandfather's study."

Going back Eugene finished Richard's note. There was a knock on the door just as he was slipping it into his finished stack.

Looking at the curtains, Mathilda frowned.

"The green curtains will be better than these," she said. "Their lace is falling apart. My love, otherwise the room is wonderful like Father's when I would chase my brother through it. The curtains and perhaps a few cushions. Green or fuchsia you can have your pick."

He felt enraptured as the days continued, far more than he had been expecting. A kiss each morning before he left and another upon his return, something new to adapt to.

More difficult for her he realized as Clarkson was more or less the same. Two ladies instead of a haremful and little cousins to miss.

The rest of it being rather complicated, but the food not so much. Honey with clotted cream for bacon and olives and feta cheese for eggs, both eaten by her new husband without a whimper to Mathilda's delight. Must be all those years in Serbia and Damascus.

A small tree in the sitting room for their first Christmas covered with ornaments from the new shop.

Calling them aside after Christmas, Mass Father McClure insisted upon a special blessing. A comfort of sorts Eugene realized as the stole was wrapped round though the other would have been better.

Declining for the New Year's ball Eugene accepted for the French embassy as the Lyonses were in the midst of packing and could not appear.

Eugene went up for dinner before the Lyonses departed.

Arriving, he headed down the hall to Ted's office for Michael was upstairs. Asking if anything had been written down in the ledgers he breathed a sigh of relief as Ted shook his head. In his journal, Ted said but not anywhere official.

Taking a deep breath as his nervousness began to ease, Eugene asked Ted to write once he got to Paris. Another correspondent and a new address for his lists.

Three days later they were all gone. Ted, their lordships, and more baggage than Namiq Pasha's ladies had taken.

Michael was quite relieved, Ted's complaints having been hard to bear, and Eugene even more so since his secret was safe.

Looking beautiful in her blue velvet gown Mathilda shone at the opening reception for Ambassador Elliot once he turned up in late February.

The new man not being one for waltzing there was a smaller band.

Both O'Reillys had a marvelous time. Mathilda with a smile, Lady Elliot having been most kind. Her husband because the ambassador had told him he was the most prominent Britisher in the city, making him grin from ear to ear.

March into April. Another invitation arriving as the month ended, a small dinner at the home of Admiral Slade.

A decline for the man was so arrogant. An acceptance in the end. The man was useful even if he could barely be endured.

Mathilda much admired in her new crinoline as they swept in. A joy it was, just having her on his arm.

The brandy and cigars having made their rounds, the conversation turned to talk of politics back home.

Everyone rose.

Waiting until the last chap was gone their host took Eugene aside. A new proposition, he said, for Syria.

Eugene replied that he was not sure and the admiral asked again.

Eugene stood stock still.

"Willing to discuss it," he said. "But not today as my wife is waiting. As I already have Clarkson, I am not sure. I do miss being in the field and am willing to hear you out. Wednesday perhaps as Mathilda will be out. But here. We might be overheard if we meet elsewhere."

Arriving at the appointed hour, Eugene listened as the library clock chimed six.

Slade sat back behind his desk and began.

"You must be wondering what they have in mind."

Nodding, Eugene agreed. Indeed, he had thought of little else.

Slade continued, saying "A group of Harrow chaps from London, there and Glasgow. An Indo-European railway is what they have in mind. Homs, Kabul and then Karachi on the western coast. Something the Foreign Office finds fascinating. Counteract all that French influence as it were.

"The same fellows are interested in getting a survey of the roads with the railway route being the most important of the two. My friend has written to see if I know of anyone to lead such a project. Naturally I thought of you. All those years, first in Damascus and then Rashaiya."

Eugene sipped his malt.

"A railway would be most helpful," he said.

"Expensive sending everything along by caravan from Aleppo. More bandits nowadays too what with the silk trade having fallen off. But how big would their expedition be? As a married man, I must be careful. The last time I ran into problems getting the promised gold. That was impossible."

Slade replied, saying, "They are thinking of several hundred, mounted and armed. Under your sole command with the gold all coming in advance."

"Sounds sufficient," said Eugene, "but when is this to start and how long will it go on? Then too they can't start from here. It shall be noticed."

Slade responded, saying "So many questions. Better

answered in reverse, I think. First the men are to sail from Athens with you to travel separately. That they will not question. Somewhere remote. It shall take weeks for word to reach the grand vizier.

"Next question. It is to start towards the end of the year. Cooler with fewer sandstorms. An eighteen month run perhaps. The men to receive British pay rates appropriate to their grade. You, on the other hand, to get forty percent more than what a lieutenant colonel would expect."

Extending his hand, Eugene smiled.

"Very generous," he said. "I will let you know by the weekend at the latest. Although I think I shall accept."

"Hopefully, you shall agree," said Slade. "You are the most ideal candidate. All those connections, in country and on the coast."

"Offhand I can't think of anyone else. Most here refuse to take the time to learn common Turkish let alone Arabic. Vital. The Bedouin can't understand French."

Spinning his pen round and round on his blotter Eugene thought it over at Clarkson the next day.

Twice the money, a help as marriage was turning out to be a far more expensive state than could be imagined. Nothing saved, every dime spent for the house needed fixing and Mathilda new gowns for the Season.

But only if the ambassador approved. Better that than being sent back.

Over the ambassador's brandy, he inquired a few days later between questions on other matters. Sir Elliot's fingers steepled as an uncomfortable look began creeping into his eyes.

Saying that he had heard rumors, the ambassador said "Not my place to decide. But even with the Crown knowing it will not thrill the Porte. Very touchy about armed men reporting to other governments these days. A little risky. Lucrative if the railway can be made to work."

"I feel better for you know of it," said Eugene. "Certainly there is a role for the railway. I have yet to make up my mind as I am not sure. But as Clarkson may be switching their emphasis to Russia I may have no choice. Better a warm expedition than freezing in the Petersburg ice."

The ambassador responded, saying, "That I hadn't heard. Puts it in a very different light. Perhaps you should go then unless there is something else here. But no intriguing. Nothing will upset the Porte faster than rumors of another native rising."

Bad news arrived the next week. Clarkson to be gone by the end of June.

Making several inquiries, Eugene received no favorable replies. In the end, he sent a message off to the admiral that he would accept.

Eugene put off telling Mathilda because that would be the worst of it.

Syria while still a newlywed, hard to envision let alone do. All that love with no one to come home too. Nights alone on a camp bed with sand drifting in since they would be on the move.

London first perhaps, but no, too expensive for his days of camping out in back bedrooms was gone. Better to go. Something learned of in Dublin would be gone before he got back.

A letter arrived in the mail from Paris in response for he had wanted Ted to know. Weeks it had been, but then Ted had never been too prompt with his replies.

Beginning in a normal fashion, the letter turned quite odd. Rambling that went on and on, something about Cairo and the sultan. The Egyptian succession he must mean as it had been changed.

Even more words had been scratched out on the second page making the words harder to make out. Something about gold to be handed out. A pretend rising as it were so the sultan would be forced to concentrate his eyes elsewhere.

A postscript at the end that did not seem encouraging, something about a roulette wheel and Monte Carlo.

Eugene's palms began sweating as he tried to think of what to do. It all sounded rather risky even for Ted whose notions had always been strange.

Doing his best to make out the words, the meaning became clear after several tries. So much had been scratched off that it looked like nothing more than gibberish.

Something about going to Lord Lyons about the wedding.

Eugene rose to his feet, closing his office door as his colleagues would only knock if it was important. He paced back and forth jamming his hands into his pockets. If the truth came out, he was done for.

A summons for having wronged a pasha's daughter and then the Acers for many of the connections were the same. Even Fuad Pasha would change his mind.

Far easier than Crete it had seemed at the time but somehow it had all turned around and bit.

Easier to agree, a pretense at any rate. Should be all right. Even with the agha around most of the Bedouin would still be in the desert.

Waiting a few days, he accepted, hoping it was all a mirage as he lifted his pen. No choice. Better that than exposed.

He told Mathilda about the expedition when he got home.

Asking in a distressed tone as she clutched him tightly, she said "What? Is it your job?"

"Yes," Eugene said. "A new job since winter in Petersburg with Clarkson seems impossible. Only eighteen months or so. After I should be able to find something here."

He continued, saying "To be separated shall be the worst of it. Much travel through all of Syria, not just Aleppo or Beirut. Too much almost for me. I have asked in the city as I was hoping to avoid being anywhere without you, but there are no positions needing to be filled."

Mathilda wept as tears came into her husband's eyes.

Straightening himself up, Eugene did his best to explain.

"I even had Ibrahim ask Fuad Pasha, but he knew of nothing. Not leaving until the fall. After we can go to Ireland so they can meet you. My fondest wish."

Her tears soaked down his shirtfront as he held her close.

Gazing up, she finally said, "I know, it is just that I will be lonely here without you."

They rode up the hill to their old park on Sunday.

The same benches and reins trailing in the grass but somehow not the same. Too many memories, perhaps the harbor next time to watch the boats for tears had welled up in her eyes.

Riding home, they went out again to Thomas Bruce's for dinner. Much more amusing than Slade's. Stephen would be there.

Embracing his old friend, he followed him into a corner to visit. With Stephen up on the Black Sea and Eugene in Syria, there had been many letters back and forth but not much more.

As Mathilda came in Stephen rose to be introduced. Taking his arm for he was the guest of honor she proceeded into the dining room. Once the wine had been poured the chatter was of Vidin because they had all spent time in the north.

Over the decanters, Stephen took his old friend aside, asking about his new assignment. Feeling rather peeved, Eugene said little except that it was not decided yet.

He mentioned it during the carriage ride home because she must have said something. As Mathilda began apologizing Eugene bit his cheeks for he had asked her to be discreet. An accident yes but a fortunate one since she knew nothing of Ted as that he hadn't mentioned.

He did his best not to yell for he would soon be gone. Must be getting old. Once he would have been screaming by now.

Leading one more trip Eugene took a final holiday.

August in Therapia, one of the smaller villas on the water by the summer embassies. Rides out with the other young wives, dances and a small dinner on the twelfth as he turned forty-two.

September and letter upon letter pouring in from Ted and all the investors. Eugene kept them all downtown. Better that than at home where they would set off another round of tears.

Staying up late night after night he worked on his lists. More men to hire, another five hundred needing to be trained for all were to arrive outside Homs by All Saints Day.

Eugene sent a long letter to Ted, letting him know the route had been changed.

More northeasterly they wanted now. Much the best at least on paper since the railway would have to go through the gap. Southeast through the Druze and Bedouin bands though the better luck would run near the Damascus tribes of course.

Clarkson closed in late September with a final handshake from the business agent along with a letter of reference for they had liked his work.

Things began moving in an old familiar way, there being only four weeks left to get ready.

Lists of supplies and horses for all the men. Markets in Athens and Tirana, a few from Dubrovnik in the end. Far too many to purchase them all from two places, there being spies everywhere.

Summoning him up, Sir Elliot told him to do his best to be careful. Tacit approval from the foreign office the man said.

No more than that, though, the envoy having told London that the Porte wanted no more armed foreigners, the French being more than enough.

Simpson's for foolscap and Stampa's for whiskey.

The bookseller for there was no time to read in the city but all the time in the world in the field. Spending twice as much as he had planned Eugene bought five books instead of three. Every back issue of *Punch* too. The mails so slow on the high desert that to get new ones would be impossible.

The last week in October arrived.

Kissing Mathilda goodbye at the house because she was too distraught to see him off at the pier, he headed for the harbor with Michael. Old campaign chests new saddlebags and what looked to be the same steamer.

Standing in the bow, he gazed out as she headed west. Suspension in yet another air bubble, one with plenty of time to read and catch up for there were no meetings.

On the sixth day at midnight, the steamer dropped anchor at his drop off point.

Eugene was rowed ashore in a large Syrian dinghy that much resembled Stamboul's caiques. As a local chap began to creep out of the murk, the smell of frangipani rose in the air.

Starting inland at dusk he arrived just before breakfast at what looked to be a sea of tents. He walked amongst them coffee in hand.

A motley bunch, mostly in it for the adventure. Old military men with a few from the northern tribes for good measure.

Turning they headed towards the gap, cloths wrapped around the horses' bits so they would not chink. A pretty valley, almost like the country around Rashaiya.

Picking up his pen he began to write as the cooks set up their stoves.

He wrote four pages filled with love, adding a small pen and ink of the valley with its wheat fields below his signature. The trees were not too well drawn but still easier than writing about it all.

His second in command came up just as he finished, asking "Hassan Bey, how far northeast do you intend?"

Eugene replied, saying "Fifteen hundred miles for the rail route. Then southwest for Damascus and Jerusalem once it is all surveyed. Sinai if time allows. Perhaps not quite that far."

The officer nodded, saying:

"A good expedition then. Plenty to see. Hopefully, the bandits shall be elsewhere."

"With everyone armed they should let us be," said Eugene. "Way out in the desert now anyway. Giving us time. May or June at least. Perhaps July depending on the rains."

Once the fellow had been called away, Eugene sat quietly, Mathilda's letter in his hand. Missing her of course but still it felt as familiar as his own skin. Odd, only his third trip to Syria but a feeling of homecoming sweeping over. The desert working its charm it must be as camel bells rang in the distance and quiet descended everywhere.

Riding out in the morning he went in search of dried fruit since not enough had been sent out. If only they had asked for Syrians lived on apricots, that and plums.

His letters with the innkeeper he turned east, the cartographer with his charts while the others checked the wadis for the rail line.

The expedition having reached its easternmost point not far from Kabul, Eugene headed southwest because there was not enough time to press on.

There was almost no trouble with the tribes, odd for Bentivoglio had written that the gendarmerie was gone and the militias back.

Weeks turning into months. Eugene led the expedition down the eastern side, far enough into the sand to avoid all the villages, there being few amongst the dunes to raise an alarm.

Doing his best to hurry them along he waited while the cartographers drew every feature. Impossible it was to move rapidly they said since the investors wanted everything.

Each wadi taking two or three days to chart Eugene slipped off into the desert at each pause once the tents were arranged.

Late April.

Slipping out just north of the al-Ghouta Eugene headed eastward to see Lady Ellenborough in her winter encampment. Too many feasts and, in the end, a week instead of three days but to his relief no questions when he returned.

Riding in a southerly direction, they slipped past Damascus and into Palestine. Jerusalem, Gaza and then towards Amman for none of the routes had been mapped.

He spotted what looked to be thunder clouds on the horizon when they were two days out from Gaza. Perhaps a mirage, the rains having not yet come.

Picking up his glasses Eugene stared as they came closer.

Men on horses, hard to tell just who for their uniforms looked odd. Regular army perhaps though that made no sense. Too far south for the Damascus garrison and too far from the coast for Gaza. Jerusalem maybe though they should have been further south.

Pulling back on the reins he waited for their commander to ride up. Twenty minutes that seemed like forever.

"Hassan Bey, I am not surprised to find you here though we had not expected such a large force," said the other commander.

Trying to find a way to respond Eugene inquired. They were regulars and should be up in Crete not amongst the dunes.

The commander replied, saying, "We were in Belgrade. The Porte has become quite anxious. Word has come of much intriguing amongst the tribes here and down to Egypt. The Jerusalem viceroy was just ordered back for the same sort of thing so we were sent out."

Continuing, the commander said, "Then too one of the agrawals sent a message down a few weeks ago that he had seen you at one of the Bedouin camps. A friend of al-Yusuf, your nemesis from your gendarmerie days they tell me. He was worried and followed you back to your men. Ever since we have been looking. I am afraid you must go back with us to Damascus."

Eugene said little as a memory slipped into place. Must have been the man who had hung back from the fire a few oases before her ladyship.

A three-day ride north, the men being left behind to their own way. No chains at least but not optional either. That they had made very clear.

Being marched through the side gate Eugene felt humiliated. Better than the main gate and its bazaar but not by much.

Escorted to the governor's mansion, he was marched in, a guard on each side.

He sat down and looked round. Memories started drifting back as he stared at the eastern wall for Namiq Pasha had stood there to pin the Medjidie on his jacket. His hands inched into his pockets, his fists balling up by themselves.

Four sergeants came marching in, the governor hard on their heels.

Eugene rose. Better not to offend even though they were of the same rank.

The governor having taken his place, the coffee made its way round since that there always was.

"Hassan Bey," said the governor, "a living legend you are here but I never thought to meet you under these circumstances. Rather at the French consul for dinner or some such."

Sitting up a little straighter, Eugene rubbed his signet ring for good luck.

"I am glad to be back in Damascus," he said. "I am not sure why I was brought here as I had the Crown's permission to be here with my men. First to look for a railway route to Kabul and then to survey the roads. As far as I know the Porte had been informed. Else I would not have left Stamboul."

The governor nibbled a piece of baklava. "Not so much your men," he said, "but rather that you seem to be back to your old tricks from '63. Not Abdel Kader this time. The Egyptians instead.

"Somehow I doubt there shall be another reprieve. Your papers have been searched and evidence has been found. About that I know little because a courier has already left to take it to the coast. For now, you are to stay in the citadel and await your consul's visit."

Eugene said nothing as the governor did not appear to be in a compromising mood. Surely her ladyship's winter house would have been all right.

Rising to his feet he watched as the governor left the room without even a brief embrace.

The new agha invited him in for coffee. His old suite, newer divans than his last visit but what looked to be the same grilles.

Relief began to creep across his weary brain. At least, there would be a room upstairs to sleep in instead of the caged cell at the bottom of the tower as he had feared.

His hand extended in greeting the consul appeared the next morning on the heels of the priest.

Sitting down, he chatted for several minutes of his time on camelback amidst the tribes for he had been in the country almost as long.

Eugene felt more relaxed as the chatter continued. His distress began inching back as the consul's voice changed, growing more clipped. More like Sir Elliot than a friend it appeared as he said that the charges were very serious.

Eugene attempted to defend himself though it seemed almost pointless as no one wanted to listen.

The consul interrupted, saying:

"Colonel O'Reilly, the ambassador must have told you that the Porte doesn't want armed groups in their provinces, especially those of a foreign persuasion. I shall berate you no more about that for it is done.

"Their concern is more around the intriguing. Surely you knew to stay away from the Egyptians. You may be innocent this time. But the visits look suspicious. Very suspect. And more so to the Porte than here. They think differently now. Back in '49, they wanted foreign officers. Now they make them nervous since there are so many.

"Enough. You shall hear much more as you are to be taken back to the coast as a prisoner to await the steamer. Doing my best to help you of course. Beirut I have already written, both our consul and that Bentivoglio chap whom they tell me is one of your friends."

Concluding, the consul said, "Sir Elliot must already know. They would have informed him long before anything reached my desk. The Beirut fellow shall visit. You may be there for several days waiting on the steamer."

Eugene clutched his ring, trying not to sob. Too much bad news and that all at once.

Pulling himself together, he said, "I tried to explain earlier. I don't think it's all on my account. They must be over nervous. The commander spoke of the Jerusalem viceroy. Something about the Russian consul and a letter. Forged he said."

Shaking his head again, the consul explained, saying:

"Yes, only a few months ago. Why they sent the officer over with his men. A big mess ever since they got the Topkapi to change everything in Cairo. Better if it had been left alone. But not our call.

"Otherwise, the Porte might have let it all go. But after the other incidents, they are much more concerned. Any punishment shall be more severe.

Worse than last time."

Eugene's mind began to spin.

"Believe me, I know to be worried," he said. "Surely Fuad Pasha will help. He is far more liked than I amongst the ministers."

"No," said the consul. "He passed away after you were gone. In February. No way for you to hear. Too remote. Not something Lady Ellenborough would be inclined to mention."

Eugene's heart sank all the way down to his toes as his head began to drop.

Managing to meet the consul's eyes, he said, "No I hadn't heard. Painful it is. He was a good friend."

The consul murmured something as he rose to leave that was hard to hear what with everything spinning around.

"I am grateful for the help," Eugene said.

"Hopefully, Lord Russell will take an interest. That and I am hoping for a carriage to the coast so no one can see the chains. If you could ask them, please."

Sitting down Eugene stared at the opposite wall once the man was gone. Nothing to do but wait, that and go over it all. Somehow everything had gone wrong. Not as bad as locked up but close. If only Clarkson hadn't moved and Mathilda's dressmaker had not been so dear.

As a vision of Mathilda's face began creeping into the front of his mind, he wondered what they would all think.

Derya at least had liked him, but his great lady not so much. The lady had been much upset when he sailed and who knew what she would think now.

Two days later he headed back to the coast. A closed carriage at least for that the governor had approved, very hot but better than everyone being able to see.

Approaching the first pass Eugene strained for a last glimpse of the city.

Guards all round as they came over the last pass, like Kilmainham just in different uniforms. Rubbing his ankles for the last four miles as they had been chained too tightly the night before Eugene hoped for a reprieve, the consul's instead of a cell.

But no in the end and as bad as he had feared. Kilmainham almost, warmer of course but the same filthy straw reeking of damp and what looked to be the same cellmates even.

Lying down for a nap Eugene fell asleep only to be awakened for a visitor had come.

Walking into the courtyard he smiled. It was Count Bentivoglio in all his glory, riding crop and all. A joy as he need not have come. A true friend.

The count hugged him, saying:

"Well, my old friend I am glad to see you. Less Beau Brummel than usual but that we shall fix. Not sure what happened. Many rumors sweeping the city and much talk since you are so well known. Very sorry. Angering the sultan is never a good thing."

Eugene did his best to smile. He managed to mutter something in Arabic as his friend continued.

Responding, the count said, "The shirt bothers you more than it bothers me. In any case, I came as soon as I could. Wine and cards in my pocket for a round of euchre. Perhaps stories of the ladies should you be here long enough."

Eugene lifted his head.

"All much appreciated," he said. "No doubt I shall have time for the stories. They tell me the steamer won't arrive for a week."

"Perhaps a bit longer," said the count. "A boon as I am working on a letter for Bouree, the new chap in Stamboul. More time to hear about your bride too. She wrote thanking me for the tablecloth, but I would love to learn more."

"She is absolutely lovely. Blue eyes. Red-gold hair. The only good part to all of this is that I won't have to wait as long to see her."

Rising to his feet the count said, "A lady that lovely shouldn't be left to herself. If I could find one half as beautiful, perhaps I'd marry too."

Eugene poured the wine and his friend began shuffling the cards. They played one hand and then another until the wine was done as dusk fell.

In the morning the priest from the new chapel with his prayers and Bible verses. The cell door had barely begun to slam when the guard reappeared because the British consul was at the gates.

Eugene began trying to explain, but the consul interrupted like the chap in Damascus.

"You must not understand how upset they are," the consul said. "If they weren't you'd be at my house now. Sir Elliot shall try for house arrest, but you mustn't count on it. In any case, I doubt he can do anything until after you arrive. Their jail I have never seen, but it must be a larger version of this.

"Though perhaps you can explain how the papers they are upset about came to be amongst your possessions."

Doing his best to recall a memory began to rise up. Ted's, they must be. Stuffed into the back pocket of his portfolio and forgotten, Mathilda having come in just as he was putting them away.

Pulling himself together, he started in.

"From a friend. Not in my handwriting as anyone can see. Only here to lead my expedition. Visited a few friends yes but nothing more."

The count came back the next day. Stockings, fresh

linen, and even a barber to help him shave. Eugene felt like a new man as they sat talking of ladies and horses, the count's favorite topics.

The count rose with an embrace as the sun began to set.

"I am off to Damascus in the morning on business and can't be at the pier to wave you off. I wish you good luck. Perhaps we shall meet in Paris. If not this year than the next. I have written Bouree asking him to put in a good word. That will go with the captain to be hand delivered once you arrive."

Embracing Eugene again the count left, turning to wave goodbye just as he went through the gates.

Eugene listened for the steamer's whistle as it came into port the next morning. Clad in the count's best shirt and surrounded by troops he was marched down to the harbor.

The other passengers staring at his handcuffs he was marched onto the steamer and down to a cabin.

Must be wondering what he had done since half of the commander's guard had come along. Odd. Nowhere to stop till Homs. A straight shoot after that.

He took a long bath once they were underway changing into a clean pair of breeches afterward because his campaign chest had miraculously appeared. To his dismay, it appeared to have been rifled through. His writing portfolio was nearly destroyed with its calfskin stained.

He went up on deck and sat watching the coast slip away. A week to be happy he thought. A treat not being imprisoned, pathetic, but there it was. Syria slipping away he did his best not to think. It was home, just as much as the other places.

He stood in the bow gazing at the cliffs which were as familiar as the Liffey's.

As they came into the pier, the guards began swarming with their handcuffs and manacles. Shrinking down inside himself as everyone stared Eugene felt horrid as the locks snapped shut.

Glancing off to the right Eugene smiled for there they were, Thomas and Stephen with Mathilda on Michael's arm. He caught Michael's eye and waved, feeling cheered as the carriage pulled away for they had come.

He looked out as the carriage rode out towards the jail on its rocky outcropping on the western edge of the city.

A cell much like the one in Beirut, three others instead of four, a small window high up on the wall and a barred door.

Chillier and darker though he thought as he introduced himself round.

Sitting down in the corner Eugene jumped as he felt something run over his foot. A rat as big as a cat, bigger even than the river ones in Dublin.

He inched over and sat down a little heavily, saying nothing as melancholy washed over him for it was no better.

Rats instead of buggy divans and nothing jumping around him but otherwise just the same.

He did his best to settle in. Long chats with the others in common Turkish, everything hidden under his coat and dirt rubbed on his shirt. Better dirty so they would think he was one of them than robbed.

The rest of the day inching by.

The food no better, meals in the cell like Beirut, a disappointment for that he had hoped would be different. Finally, he fell asleep, awakening at dawn as the sun stabbed his eyes.

Eugene had just finished his bowl of yogurt when

the guard knocked on the door because the ambassador had come.

Finishing his toilette as best he could, he followed the man down the hall and upstairs. Like Kilmainham, another rabbit warren with passages that led everywhere.

Sir Elliot shook Eugene's hand as he entered the visiting room.

Thanking him for coming Eugene pulled out his letters.

"These are for you," he said, as the ambassador put them in his bag. "From the various consuls in Damascus and Beirut. Meant to be a help. The rest you must have already heard."

"Of course," said Sir Elliot. "A messenger brought a copy of the summons up since you are under my purview. I have already been to the Porte about it and another matter. Another meeting in a few days with the grand vizier to discuss your case. Perhaps a fortnight longer for them to decide, not a winter like the last time.

"Not here then of course but I have gone through Michael's files. The hope at the moment is to get you out of here. Not sure they will let you stay, here or in Syria. Not likely that they will, but I shall do what I can."

Concluding, the ambassador said, "Only yesterday Bouree mentioned a letter from that Bentivoglio chap. Very helpful. The French have far more influence here."

"The count is a good friend," Eugene said. "But for now, the main thing is to leave here. No better than Beirut. The same sorry types. That and please let Michael know that I was grateful he brought Mathilda down, the pier being no place for a lady to be alone."

The ambassador nodded his head. A favor for an old friend he said, not to be worried about.

But then he pulled himself to his full height, saying:

"Colonel O'Reilly, no more chit-chat. You have brought it all down on your own head. You knew better by now. The Egyptian princes are bad eggs, out to get rid of the sultan. Back in '63, there was no real proof but now there is. I know I didn't forbid you from going but still."

Looking around the room, Eugene figured out what to say. Better not to make anyone mad.

"I visited Lady Ellenborough because she is an old friend," he said. "The other visits I was talked into. That I am sorry for. The letter I can't figure out. It I didn't write."

His visitor glared.

Coughing, the ambassador asked, "Hmmm, was it Mr. Jordan?"

A startled look crept over Eugene's face and his mind began racing like a hamster wheel.

Eugene replied, saying "Yes. He wrote about it. Some of the letters I read. Others I stuffed in my portfolio. But I know no more. I didn't know about the Russian fellow in Jerusalem."

Sir Elliot looked very solemn. A puzzlement Eugene thought for he hadn't sounded that upset. Must be framing his thoughts about something because he kept licking his lips.

"All that is very bad," the ambassador said.

"That and I have sad news. Only last week a message arrived for Michael from Lord Lyons to let him know that Ted was killed. Riding accident at the Tuileries. Very sorry. He must have been a friend. Complicating matters now making it impossible to verify anything. Hard to see why anyone would be at Ted's beck and call though I must say."

Eugene said nothing for what was there to say. The truth wasn't possible. That would only make it all worse and there was more than enough trouble already.

"He was my friend," Eugene said in a very quiet voice. "Very odd it is. The Tuileries gardens are flat with no hillocks at all. The horse must have shied."

Sir Elliot rose to his feet, handing Eugene a stack of books. "Perhaps," he said. "Very sad and you have my condolences. But here. Reading material. A few copies of *Punch* and *Tomahawk* too.

"Lord Russell has cabled with his reply. He writes that that we must all do our best. Talks about all your wonderful reports over the years and service to the Crown. But now I must go. Don't worry. As soon as I know more I shall return."

Eugene ran into Mathilda's arms for kiss after kiss when she came the next day. Sitting by the window, they talked quietly.

She asked what had happened. Her husband did his best to explain. Deceived, and that more than once, he said, rambling on.

Mathilda's great lady rose to her feet as the afternoon drew down. Holding her cloak tighter, she asked the guard to call for her araba.

Promises to return and of sugar lumps for Mirabelle. Like a mirage in the desert, there and then gone.

Sir Elliot reappeared on the heels of his meeting at the Porte.

Feeling shaky and a little scared Eugene listened. The words washing over him he tried to catch them all.

"I told them of Lord Russell's concerns," said Sir Elliot.

"Unfortunately, the grand vizier is still quite upset. The letter is the worst of it. I had not known its exact contents before but he let me read it over. No name or date but asking where the guns should be landed before the insurrection starts. But pray tell which princeling does the 'Altesse' refer to? Of that, they are not sure.

"Hassan Bey this and Hassan Bey that. A strict inquiry for that they have ordered done. Cairo being partially to blame and the Russian fellow in Palestine too. All of that is to the good, but your admission to the Damascene governor about the tribes does not help."

The ambassador concluded saying, "On and on, troops sent over from Crete and the sultan worried it could happen again. An admittance that Fuad Pasha would have spoken up for you. Something that does not hurt. Mathilda's being a pasha's child which speaks in your favor."

Eugene picked at his nails.

"I don't know which prince," Eugene said, "but, at least, they took all the letters. What do you think they shall do in the end, please?"

"They may be inclined to compromise," said the ambassador.

"London is insisting on something being done so that you will not linger here. But it is all depending on the Porte. I should think you shall be allowed to go back to the Pera. But only for a few weeks. They are likely to exile you. From all of their domain, not just Stamboul. From Paris intriguing shall be impossible.

"I am afraid you shall have to bear it a while longer. If only there was no letter. Then they would have very little."

Another week ground by.

Following the guard upstairs on Monday Eugene was shocked. Adolphus Slade, leaning against the window frame instead of Michael, two bottles of whiskey in his pockets as a gift.

Eugene did his best to be polite. A great challenge indeed for had he not attended Slade's dinner he would be home.

Messages too from both Acers but no visits. Must be fear. Otherwise, they would appear.

The priest having just departed communion kit in hand on Monday the ambassador returned for the grand vizier had summoned him back.

"Very gracious they were," he said. "The Queen's offer has been accepted. You are to be released and allowed to be with your wife. But by September fifteenth, you must be gone."

A huge smile crept across Eugene's face. Going back to his cell to collect his things he ran back up the stairs and rode out the front gates a free man.

His nerves having gotten the best of him he compulsively thanked the ambassador as they headed towards the Pera.

Sir Elliot tapped his shoulder. One more thing, he said,a final condition for both Lord Russell and the French. A report to be written up describing what had been done. To be kept in the embassy files but not shared with the Porte.

Saying nothing Eugene gazed out the window and looked away. Better not to argue even if they were all wrong. Not a choice anyway it was clear.

The maid was on the doorstep as they came up the hill and ran inside for Mathilda. Rushing to her Eugene went inside.

Eugene did his best to explain over supper. Free to go yes but into exile in eight weeks. Tears began forming in Mathilda's eyes as he explained that it was permanent for otherwise he would have been kept.

He sat watching the emotions play across her face. Impossible to know whether she would want to leave or stay.

Worry, love and at last a smile as she said she would go. Partly love of course she added. Otherwise, divorce and a life frittered away in her aunt's harem.

A week's rest and the first draft sent up. Painful it was for he had only been trying to humor Ted. No point in writing it all out again as they did not care.

Eugene rode up to the embassy himself, asking the ambassador to try again as Mathilda would prefer to stay. He felt humiliated as Sir Elliot's eyes rolled round.

Managing to speak, the ambassador muttered something about what would happen on the sixteenth if he was not gone.

Arriving home, he told Mathilda so the ladies could pack and started in on a new set of notes.

Rex, Lord Lyons, and all the rest. A separate draft for James with the truth stretched for he was sure to go on and on. The others not so much for at least they would not be horrified.

Everything finished up, Mirabelle back to the embassy along with Mathilda's little mare. The trousseau, all the books and his campaign chests of course.

Hard to decide what to take. So many things with a memory attached to each and every one.

The last weeks filling up with goodbyes. Mathilda at her sister's night and day, her husband's evenings filled with dinners and a reception at the Acers, which he had not expected.

Rex wrote back with a long list of hotels and an invitation to stay. Another from Richard that came as a surprise. A large house with two guestrooms, he wrote, not a small flat. Room enough for Mathilda too.

Two tickets for the fifteenth sailing and gone. With Mathilda clutching his arm, they stood on deck. The steamer headed west as her childhood home began slipping away.

10 BAR, DUBLIN, BORDEAUX, GIBRALTAR & FEZ

Mathilda was nearly overcome as they sailed westward towards the strait. Her husband said nothing for he was too busy watching the headlands begin slipping away. She gripped his arm with a hand that shook, missing his head by inches as her parasol swung through the air.

Turning, Eugene held her tight.

"My love it shall be fine," he said. "I know it's hard, but you'll see. A lovely trip. A honeymoon. Then too they may change their minds."

Mathilda said nothing.

The wedding trip part would be grand. But no sister to go back to, she thought, as the tears began welling up.

Managing a smile, she took his hand.

"It should be fine but already I miss my sister," she said. "Though I could not have borne to stay behind."

Nodding, her husband agreed.

"To be together yes. A nice cruise. They shall stop everywhere as they head west. Lunch in some places. Enough time for a room in some of the others. A treat for me as well. I have only come this way twice. The last time heading straight towards Malta as it was a British steamer."

When the wind began to pick up, they headed below.

A huge suite, twice the size of anything on the other steamers. Something smaller might have suited, but it had been the only one that had not been booked.

The luncheon bell rang as Mathilda was setting out her last hairbrush. Heading upstairs Eugene started to say something about the forks but thought better of it since she had done well at the embassy dinners.

Two days west.

Enough time in Crete for lunch and a stroll before steaming northward. Samos with its beach and Bar with its mountains behind. Close to his old post but new since they had never come this way.

Mathilda wanting to go ashore, but no, too close to Novi Sad. More complicated than the others, the Porte having more reach in Montenegro.

Trieste and then on to Venice. Gondolas, the pigeons at Saint Marks and a lovely suite by the doge's palace. A joy for she was happier, better by far than Bar with its echoes of Stamboul.

The rest of the cruise a bit boring, there not being much to see until Marseilles. Together, though, the main thing really, wrapped in a silken cocoon in a world without opportunity hunting or great ladies.

Dinner seatings, deck chairs and cathedral tours. Far more fun if you didn't live there he thought as more and more gold slipped out of his wallet. Better spent now in case the Egyptians tried to get it back. Surely something would turn up in London. No need to hold onto it all.

Naples, Corsica and finally Marseilles which reminded Mathilda of Stamboul. Eugene began to say no for it was more like Malta, biting his tongue since he had forgotten she only knew Vidin and the city.

Perhaps that was better, two places instead of ten, too many in a way.

Once through the customs shed, they headed for the hotel. A smaller suite, not as nice as the steamer's but only till Wednesday and the Paris express in any case.

Coming down late for breakfast on the second day Mathilda surprised her husband.

"Darling I have wonderful news," she said. "If all goes well we shall be parents in June. I have felt queasy this past week but was not sure."

Eugene stared back with an open mouth.

A bad sign, odd for she had thought he would be thrilled.

Plucking up her nerves, she continued, asking:

"Are you not happy, my dear? You have spoken of Thomas and Jane Emily so much."

"Oh no, it is the best news possible. I hope that she looks like you and not me with your wonderful coloring. Barbara after your mother if that's all right. It is a lovely name."

Mathilda relaxed. All would be well.

"That she would have loved," she said. "Emily Barbara for both our mothers."

Her husband smiled again, this time with a broader grin.

He replied, saying, "No. My niece already carries her name. Eugenie instead. Henry for a boy like my Trinity friend or Matthew like my father."

Mathilda looked up.

"The names are fine," she said, "though I think we shall have a little daughter and not a son."

Eugene sat in thought, so long that the tears began coming back into her eyes. Worried she must be.

Doing his best to be reassuring, he helped her to her

feet and then into the writing room.

"Let me fetch your parasol. A walk or we can sit on the terrace."

Mathilda leaned back, trying to rest. She tried to stand, but there were no sturdy edges to grip. No point in explaining since he was so used to going back and forth.

One world and then the other. Divans to sofas, fingers to forks and even different ways to spear meat on a plate. Easier just to live on bread. That you could hold in your hand.

Paris the next evening. One of Uncle Andrew's friends met them at the station for he had invited them to stay. Going upstairs Mathilda laid down once they arrived.

Walking out with their host, Eugene looked around in hopes of spotting Richard's old haunt as they were only a block from his uncle's old flat.

The cafes looked nearly the same, but everyone looked young, almost too young. He felt very old. Somehow it had been more years than he had thought, decades even.

There was a dinner invitation from the embassy on the hall table when he returned. Drafting an acceptance, Eugene handed it to the butler to be sent.

A smile too for Lord Lyons was far more important than the chap in Stamboul. A bigger and more important embassy, and an ambassador able to decide for himself.

Hopefully, Mathilda would be too tired to go. Otherwise, dinner with one of Ted's friend's though that she might wish to attend.

He took Mathilda out to Versailles on Sunday. An entire day instead of an afternoon, the railway being much quicker than the coach had been.

Having toured the hall of mirrors they visited the gardens, Mathilda on his arm and their host in tow with a bored look. Too many visits and all recent no doubt.

Heading to the embassy the next evening he smiled for Mathilda in the end had wanted to rest.

Things went well. Wonderful food and a dining room that was most impressive as it was twice the size of Sir Elliot's.

As the dining room door closed behind the last lady, the ambassador's cigars came out. Cuban, a treat, Stamboul's having always come from Cairo.

Clasping his brandy, Eugene's knuckles turned pale. All very pleasant but surely his lordship must know.

He chatted with the gentleman on his left.

Peering through the smoke, Lord Lyons patted the chair next to him.

"Here," said his lordship.

"Sit by me colonel. I have not seen you these past few years. Very glad that you are in the city."

Eugene moved over.

Lord Lyons continued in a low voice, saying:

"You must be wondering what I heard. First it was her ladyship who knew you had arrived. London said nothing. But of course I knew. Ambassador Elliot has written and Lord Russell too, asking for my input about the province and its goings on."

Doing his best to dissemble, Eugene tried not to cringe. His hand beginning to shake he finished his brandy.

"I wish I hadn't done it. Now I can't return. En route to London. Hoping someone will know of something. An industrial mission to Algeria perhaps, similar to Clarkson but beyond the Porte's reach."

His lordship poured another round.

"Much interest in northern Africa these days. Your languages would be useful there or in Egypt. Difficult.

The Ottomans don't want us these days. Not like '49 when they came courting. Now they wish to repel it."

"I know. The consuls and Sir Elliot said the same thing. I had hoped to be kept on but it was not to be," Eugene said.

Continuing, he said, "One more question if you please. Back in Stamboul, they told me Ted was gone. Pains me since he was a good friend. His mother I have already written as he had given me the address. But he had some of my papers. Those I did not want to bother the Jordans about."

The ambassador shook his head, saying:

"It was terrible. He took a tumble and hit his head. Never could keep his seat. The papers I don't have. Only his journals were sent along to Newcastle and everything else burnt because his mother didn't want them. I am sorry, we didn't know they were yours."

"Not your fault. Mine for I said nothing. Never occurred to me that he would be gone so young. A good chap. Drove Michael crazy but I liked him."

The butler came in to begin sweeping the crumbs. Rising, they rejoined the ladies for the singer was about to start.

Mathilda repacked both grips before they caught the boat train at three. Reaching Gravesend the next afternoon, they traveled towards the capitol. At four, they met Rex and Alexandra Crotty at Victoria Station under the clock.

Descending for tea, Mathilda looked round the drawing room. A sea of beige, like being inside one of Eugene's deserts.

As she sat down, Eugene squeezed her hand. Not to worry, he whispered.

Four weeks and then six.

Knitting, dominoes and talk of the baby since

Alexandra had offered to help.

Smiling back, Mathilda did her best to explain. Part of her trousseau, though more things needed to be bought. That and advice for Stamboul seemed very far away.

The O'Reillys managed to get out a little. More dinner invitations it seemed than theater parties. For the best, Eugene realized, since Mathilda tired easily.

Two visits to the tailor for figured shirts, the dressmaker for a few new dresses but not much more as no new posts had emerged. The wrong season. Easier in the spring Rex said when the budgets were set.

Sighing in relief, Eugene sat down with his accounts for some things were cheaper anyway. Half as much to the stationer, his correspondence having shrunk. A lending library down the road with books to borrow instead of buy.

Good. The money would be needed when a house had been found. The staff would be very dear.

Eugene went round with rental agents more and more as the weeks began passing by. They needed to move, Rex having said a few weeks not a few months.

Just before Christmas, he heard of something at Rex's club. A small house on the edge of Mayfair, the rent a little lower because there were just two bedrooms.

Meeting the agent on the doorstep the next afternoon, he looked round. The décor rather old fashioned as the chap had said but a deep tub in the bathroom upstairs.

Walking around the house to see the stables Eugene headed back upstairs. The agent followed with an odd look murmuring something about most people wanting to see the inside first.

Eugene smiled. The fellow had a most worrisome expression. Must be in need of the fee.

"I would like to take over the lease," he said. "But

first my wife has to approve. Would tomorrow at two suit?"

Running headlong into the garden the next afternoon Mathilda surprised them both.

Even Eugene had a quizzical look as she turned, saying "You do not understand since you are not Ottoman. All those hours in our courtyards. Far more important than any of the sitting rooms."

Her husband nodded.

"No, very sensible," he said. "I went to see the stables first. Indeed, we have left the agent entirely perplexed."

Mathilda sat down to wait while Eugene went up to look at the third floor. Smiling the agent looked relieved as they said they would take it for it was on the small side and hard to let.

The next week they moved in. Alexandra having arrived to help unpack, Eugene left for his friend's. Better to leave the ladies to their unpacking in peace.

Easier on his back too. Two days flat it had been after he had helped Michael reshuffle Colonel Rose's trunks.

The house looked transformed upon his return. Like Stamboul, carpets and cushions everywhere and all the sofas pushed back like divans.

Mathilda sat resting on the drawing room sofa, somehow looking tired and happy at the same time.

Her eyes dancing, they sat together over tea.

"A lot of work yes but they all helped me. Glad to be with you of course but I miss the others," she said, putting her hand over her mouth for the words had somehow poured out.

"I know it must be hard," said Eugene. "Men and lads downstairs. Women and all the children over their heads. But apart here. Children in the top of the house. All in separate houses not together. Granted Mother is living with James, but that is because she is old.

"Glad I am that you are here sweetheart. Our own house now. Fingers, not forks and Stamboul food. Lovely at the Crottys since they are very pleasant, but this will be better."

Smiling more as the weeks passed Mathilda sometimes had a sad look. Must be her condition making her miss her family more.

Sticking closer to home, Eugene did his best to help. The theater, Mass every Sunday and hours spent reading aloud in the evenings while she put her feet up.

As Christmas approached, Mathilda went shopping downtown for ornaments. Exhausting, numerous shops in the end but worthwhile because it made her eyes dance again.

Better to say nothing, her Simpson's it seemed.

They went to Midnight Mass on Christmas Eve, having a late breakfast the next day. Eggs, bacon and even crumpets for she had remembered. A real Christmas with Mathilda to make the magic wherever they might be.

Opening their gifts Eugene opened the Dublin parcel last. A card from James was at the very bottom. An invitation but for only one, something about Susan not wanting to receive her. Mean-minded but odd for he had not written of Mathilda's presence in the city.

A visit to see his mother but in late summer after the baby was born.

But a posting first. Otherwise, the I told you so's would be too hard to bear.

All the club dinners paying off for one of the Young Irelanders heard of something. A group made up of Harrow men in need of a leader, the man said, someone who knew the languages. Not too long, out to Algeria in September and back in the spring.

Eugene checked the salary against expenses in his account books. A few pounds less than he had hoped for.

Not enough for London but sufficient for a villa and nurse on the Continent in one of the smaller places, not Brussels or Paris.

He put off telling her, blurting it all out over luncheon when the baby was almost due.

Mathilda began to cry, her husband doing his best to calm her down.

"Sweetheart I know," he said. "Not much to be done about it. Arabic is of great use there but not here. If they wanted me now I would decline of course. No way around it that I can see. That and London is so very expensive. In France, we can have a nurse to help. I thought of taking you back to Stamboul, but it's much too far."

Mathilda sat weeping with a napkin to her eyes for a handkerchief. Hard he knew as he sat watching her weep. A strange place, her sister, and the baby coming.

She dried her tears, putting her hand over his as she said that she understood.

She said little afterward, thoughts of the baby crowding everything else out. Spending long mornings in the garden she spent her afternoons in the park once the warm weather came. Easier for plants were the same everywhere. Different sorts of benches but the same roses.

June 1870.

The baby came while Eugene sat holding her hand. A girl.

Mathilda held her wrapped in a shawl.

Eugene's eyes twinkled when he saw the black curls peeping out from under her baby cap.

"Is she still our Eugenie Barbara or would you like a different name?" he asked.

"Eugenie Barbara it is," said his wife as he leaned over with a kiss for each since the nurse had gone down to the kitchen.

Mathilda asked for her jewelry box and Eugene retrieved it from the dresser. Holding the baby, he watched as she took out a beaded necklace. An evil eye charm it must be. Ibrahim's boy had had much the same.

Saying nothing, he watched her put it around Eugenie's neck. Too late to talk her out of it. All right anyway. The dresses would cover it up.

But no two weeks later when Mathilda wanted to have Eugenie's ears pierced since that everyone could see.

Otherwise, a home filled with happiness, long hours by the baby's cradle and afternoons in the garden with the pram.

Doing his best to fit it all in Eugene spent his mornings in meetings with the investors. Evenings he spent in correspondence with agents for the house had to be given up before he left.

The response from the chap in Boulogne sur Mer looked the most promising, he thought. On the channel with a station, decent stable, and large garden since it was on the edge of town.

Mathilda sobbed for a few minutes when he showed her the drawings. Not wanting to leave Alexandra he suspected. No choice, that and France would be better for her English was better but far from fluent.

The meetings with the Harrow chaps over, Eugene headed downtown.

Signing the lease, he collected the forms to register Eugenie.

He stuffed them in his satchel for Mathilda to fill out. No time to look them over but easy they must be, the baby's name and that of the doctor.

They went into the library after lunch. Mathilda sat pen in hand at the desk while Eugene started packing up his books.

Becoming lost in thought, he jumped at her voice behind him.

"They need names. Ours and then the baby's. I am putting Eugene O'Reilly first and then Mathilda O'Reilly. Leaving Solomassy out. Too hard for them to spell."

Eugene spun round, turning beet red as the words poured out.

"No," he shouted. "Put Solomassy. We are not really wed. One of my friends in that ballroom. The ambassador was away."

He made his way across the room because he had not meant to shout. Mathilda rested her head on her arms, her tears soaking the blotter.

Clutching the pen, she asked why.

Eugene stood behind her, working his arms round into an embrace as he tried to think. Impossible to explain he mumbled, Crete too dangerous and the bishop having refused.

Mathilda tried to collect her thoughts.

Hundreds of miles from home, the baby and not even a real husband.

Words tumbling out between her tears, she said, "Why didn't you think of me? Eugenie too because you spoke of children. We must marry for our daughter's sake. It will hurt her."

Eugene tried to pull her up, but Mathilda's hands clung to the chair.

Kneeling by her side, he gazed up.

"I am sorry. I was so desperate to marry you. No other way. Perhaps at the church down the street, the Crottys for witnesses."

A cramp began to come on in his left leg. Staying on his knees, he waited for her to calm as she rarely argued back.

No luck he realized as she rose to her feet glaring.

"I am very upset," she said in a firm voice. "You have lured me here. I shall take Eugenie and go home. Uncle thought you were wonderful. A colonel and everything else. I shall go home unless we marry. For Eugenie's sake if not for my own."

Gazing up at the ceiling Eugene bit his lips. Anything to stay calm he thought as he responded, saying:

"Please, not Eugenie. I love her so much. I am sorry. No one here knows so you need not worry on that score. Of course, we shall marry. Probably in France. August already. Not enough time left. But before I leave. I promise you."

Straightening up Mathilda looked down into his eyes with a tear stained face. She rose and headed upstairs.

Eugene sat at his desk listening to her footsteps overhead, down to the hall to the nursery and back. No point in going up. It would be better to wait.

He prayed that she would not come down with enough gold to go back. His hands shook as he toyed with the pen. He had not meant to tell her. Even the census taker had been told O'Reilly when he came round.

Pulling himself together Eugene went upstairs to beg her to stay. A wedding, he promised as he knelt, at the church so she could be sure.

Eugenie reached out to take his finger.

Taking a deep breath, Mathilda began.

"We are together," she said. "You have been good to me. If I went to the envoy, I am not even sure that he would listen. Eugenie loves you. We shall stay. But you have to promise. The new church. Before you leave."

Leaning over with a kiss for each, Eugene said, "The two of you mean everything. To lose you would be unbearable. It is to take care of you that I am off to North Africa."

Mathilda rose, Eugenie sound asleep on her shoulder.

"That you have done. A good provider as Alexandra would say. That is not the concern. Rather that this is not proper. Our baby needs a name."

Easier to stay she thought following him down for tea. Better for Eugenie. No one to turn to anywhere. Even the Acers having been taken in. Odd for he had pushed to wed not the other way round.

Mathilda did her best not to think about it. Not difficult in any case since no one knew. Not even the Crottys let alone the neighbors as they went strolling with Eugenie in her pram.

Coming back in mid-August Alexandra helped pack. Everything back in the trunks and a drab little house again, like a fan ready to be reopened in France.

Gravesend. As they were boarding the channel steamer Eugenie fussed a little for a tooth had started coming in.

She awoke just as they reached France.

A very pretty harbor and piers covered with fishing nets. White houses with red roofs marching up the hills with an old belfry towering above. A tourist thing Eugene recalled for the agent had sent brochures.

Making their way through the customs shed they hailed a cab just as the sun came out.

Twenty minutes and then up the drive with sighs of relief because it looked just like all the pictures. A spruced up house with stables behind for Eugene to fix. Everything freshly painted with a ceiling border of kittens chasing their tails in the nursery.

Going up to the nursery Mathilda fed Eugenie while

Eugene went off to see the stables.

He had just finished looking at the hayloft when Mathilda came in with the pram for Eugenie had not fallen asleep.

Her father took a turn, pushing her round the garden, first the back and then the front. Very tiring, he thought, as the baby's eyes closed.

Sitting down on the front steps, he rocked the pram with his foot. Mathilda sat down beside him, taking his hand.

"The garden is lovely," she said. "Nicer than the other since it extends around the house. Boring inside but the cushions will make it pretty. The unpacking will be harder with the baby. She has so many things. Easier when it was just me."

Eugene laughed, saying "Twice as much as us. So many clothes. Three times as many dresses as you! But yes, much more complicated. Easier back when my commands changed. Everything into saddlebags and a chest. Three saddlebags worth in Rashaiya but not much more. Two on the Danube.

"Hopefully, we can stay. A son perhaps. Eugenie starting school. In French of course. Hopefully, she will not lose her English."

Mass at the new church and a priest who was quite friendly.

Mathilda said little on the way home, everything sputtering out as they reached the drive. Eugenie's christening. Scary what with the surname but important as her mother had not been allowed.

She felt relieved as a smile appeared instead of a frown. Of course, Eugene said, for it was part of the faith. A new christening gown, though, the other having been left in Dublin.

Eugenie cooing in her arms, Mathilda smiled back.

"Yes. Plenty of time for me to work on it. April after

you return. But a bonnet too. It shall be cold still. Alexandra's lace shawl to wrap her in."

"That and the parish ladies seemed very nice so you can make friends there. I am sorry. Had I known about Algeria we would have come straight here. A hop skip and jump from here but not London. Marseilles train and the steamer across instead of the sea with all its storms. Much easier this way."

Filling the time with happiness they tried not to count the days till October. Mathilda bought purple velvet for a baby dress and Eugene set up a string of accounts.

Eight months instead of six in case there was a delay. The grocer and the coal man. A dressmaker too along with eight months' rent and the servants' pay.

Spending hours in his library, he did his best to prepare. Old lists and new with reams of foolscap over every surface.

Everything was settled, the last account touching her heart for it was with the florist. An arrangement each week, he said, to warm her heart until his return.

The manservant brought his campaign chest down to the hall.

Saying their last goodbyes, Mathilda stood on the doorstep for one last kiss. Waving her little hand, Eugenie watched as her father left for the station.

Mathilda's chest felt constricted watching him go round the corner. Much more painful it seemed than the last time for there was no sister for company.

Not enough time to have married either. A simple ceremony, perhaps after Eugenie's christening with the same guests.

Going upstairs, she put the baby down for a nap.

Sitting by the cot, she worked on Eugenie's little coat. Once the hem was done, she sat wondering where he was for he must be nearly all the way to Paris.

Eugene sat lost in thought as the train steamed out.

Pulling his pictures out of his pockets, he put them on his lap. Hopefully, the last mission for leaving had hurt more than he would have thought possible. Torture just being unable to turn around and go back.

Paris and then south for the desert, his spirits rising for Boulogne had seemed rather boring at times. Nothing else to be done anyway since they needed looking after.

Lunch in Bordeaux since there was a three-hour wait for the express south. Very pretty, a larger harbor of course but quiet. Might have been a better choice as it was more convenient than the other.

Gibraltar, and then, coming in, a glimpse of Oran. A sea of Arabic dialects and colonial buildings that lined the quay like Beirut.

Eugene led the mission out the next day. Carpets, wools, and spices though they were harder to find.

Weeks as long as months, market to oasis and then back again. Some wonderful berbers and a little nutmeg in the end as they began heading back to the coast.

Feeling homesick once they reached the hotel, Eugene sat and read. There was nothing to do until the shipping arrangements with the bey were complete.

Dining with the French consul, a nice chap who was one of the count's friends, he did his best to stay calm. Too much thinking would not help he was sure.

Mathilda's Christmas packet of photographs made him feel better. Having them all framed he put the first on the table to be admired and the second by his pillow. Eugenie on her mother's lap in green velvet and then on a little bench.

Word came that they were done. London first, three meetings with the main group, the board having insisted.

Not running back was near impossible but little could be done because he was needed to chair a few sessions.

Another week and Gravesend.

Everyone's arms at the pier, kisses all round despite Eugenie's suspicious look. Five minutes of squirming and then a scowl as she held her arms out to her mother.

Eugene handed her back.

"She has forgotten me," he said. "But glad I am to see that she still resembles my baby pictures. Her curls still look the same."

Mathilda responded, saying, "She has not seen you since October. In a few days, she will remember. For now, you can help chase her. She can crawl like a demon."

Coming round by the end of the week Eugenie began climbing up for a story and a kiss.

Her father tried to rest once he had put her down on the carpet, but no for she insisted on heading straight for the coal scuttle. Like Polly's stories though somehow they seemed less funny now.

Afternoons rocked away, upstairs and down. Bedouin and Hungarian songs along with Polly's lullabies as Eugenie tried to sing along in her little voice.

New clothes for the christening, there being no need to look dowdy. Eugenie's parents both laughed because she still had the best outfit, a christening gown in satin and lace that Mathilda had made.

Richard having offered to serve as escort Eugene sent the first invitation off to his mother.

But in the end Richard traveled alone, holding Eugenie at the font as Emily O'Reilly was too frail to make the trip.

Bundling her up the next week, Eugenie's proud

parents took her back to the photographer. Two versions, they had decided. The first in her christening gown and shawl. The second in her new dress and the yellow boots her father had brought home.

Riding down to the beach with Mathilda on sunny afternoons, Eugene held Eugenie before him on his saddle.

Her parents tried to sit on their blanket and chat.

Eugene had to keep jumping up instead since his daughter had found a new game. She crawled into the waves, heading back out every time he sat down.

Mathilda laughed as Eugenie crawled off.

"She has you trained my darling," she said. "A game for she knows you shall fetch her. Glad I am you are here to take a turn."

"She must be like me judging by Polly's stories," said Eugene. "I led them on a merry chase and that from morning till night."

Smiling with both of her teeth, Eugenie giggled as her father continued.

"Not in the ocean of course. Mud in the park, that and the coal scuttle. I swear I didn't teach her."

Traveling back to London in mid-May Eugene caught the Dublin packet after.

Staying with James because Richard was in Belfast he spent most of his time with his mother as James was still being James.

Less pleasant than the railway hotel but fun at least in the nursery. The new baby, Gertrude, looked like a smaller Eugenie. The same dark curls and dancing eyes. A twin-like resemblance to his old pictures making him miss Eugenie all the more.

Setting the new pictures out by his bed with the others, he sat down to read Mathilda's note. Something about the wedding.

What to say, he thought, chewing the end of his fountain pen. Too many trips to London and not enough time for the banns he wrote, that and his mother's pleurisy as it made it impossible to plan.

Eugene dined with Richard before heading for London as Richard had returned. To his delight, there was a framed print of Eugenie in her christening gown and another of Mathilda on the drawing room mantel.

Easier it would have been if Richard had been around earlier. He could have brought them both and had his mother over for tea instead.

Heading back to London he had another interview that did not go well. Five days off to knock about since he was not expected back till Monday.

Newcastle to fetch Ted's journal. But no. Made more sense to wait until a Jordan cousin could bring it down.

Back in Boulogne Eugene headed off again on a lightning trip to Paris to see Sir Bulwer. Upon his return, Mathilda had the cook prepare his favorite roast chicken before telling him her news. A new child, perhaps a son.

Bastille Day. Mathilda bought more blue wool from the shop for a new shawl.

Riding down to the beach Eugene watched Eugenie so her mother could rest. He watched as she sat munching seaweed and consuming sand by the handful. Funny how good it had once tasted only to look so disgusting now.

September slipping into October.

Traveling to Dublin, he saw his mother before heading to London and another interview.

A shorter trip and the pay a little short. Necessary, though, the money from Oran being almost gone.

A second interview followed by dinner at the lead investor's club. Seemingly positive even though they were not sure they would proceed.

Going out to Jane Emily's school the next day, Eugene brought her into town for dinner. An uncle thing because Uncle Jarleth had done the same.

He went back to Dublin to say goodbye before heading home for Christmas. He could not bear to miss another one.

Gifts spilling out of the cab he covered everyone with kisses. Five trips to get it all inside. A teasing too, the doll house being twice Eugenie's size.

Wrapping paper scattered across the carpet, their fifth Christmas but their first together with Eugenie.

Gifts were strewn around the room. She had moved too fast, getting into everything while her father had gone off to fetch a book.

Mathilda came downstairs, saying nothing. Nearly all toys anyway and not fragile enough to be destroyed.

Eugene spent much of the winter inside for there was storm after storm. Mathilda felt relieved when a letter arrived from London saying that they would know more in the spring.

Eugene did his best not to worry. Better in some ways. With the new baby coming his help was needed.

Spending entire days with Eugenie, he looked at pony listings in the paper because she loved to ride. June if she was tall enough since she could barely fit behind his pommel.

February 1872 and a fortnight more.

Henry arrived on the twentieth of February. A fine baby, a few ounces heavier than his sister with Mathilda's golden locks and green eyes that had come sideways from Jarleth somehow.

Picking Eugenie up, Eugene set her down on the bed

to meet her new brother.

A comical face with a scrunched up nose, glare and then a smile. Like James, Eugene imagined, something to be worked out between themselves.

A playmate, there being no small children at their end of the road. A little friend down the street yes. Impossible though for Mathilda to walk her every day.

Mathilda gradually recovered. The new baby was a joy, more cuddly than her first. His little body sank into hers as Eugene sat wreathed in smiles since he had been hoping for a son.

Her old worries began inching back, not the christening for that he would welcome but the other.

Henry's registration papers with their blank spaces needing to be filled out. Still not married despite his promise. Something about needing to wait for the baby to come and a fancier dress.

Ordering his favorite dinner, she waited until he was done.

Plunging in, she said "Dear, how are we to register Henry? The priest is insistent that it come before the baptism."

Mathilda gazed down the length of the table, watching him lower his hands towards his pockets as his jaw turned pale.

Swallowing hard, she continued, saying:

"Look, I am not trying to upset you. I have no choice. Otherwise, he cannot be christened."

She sat back and braced herself.

Eugene clenched his jaw, saying, "Of course he shall be christened my dear, and in Eugenie's gown and the blue shawl. Since we cannot avoid having him registered, it can be 'Henry Hassan' on the form. After me in a fashion. Here they shall think it a middle name. That should do."

Dropping her napkin Mathilda reached down to pick it up. Feeling rather faint, she managed to respond.

"That should be fine. But still they need our names too."

She waited, her heart in her throat, for his answer, hoping he would not stand. But no for he stayed seated.

With a voice that stayed level and in a low tone that brooked no arguments he replied, saying:

"Look, I told you we'll marry again. Surely we are wed with two babies. We'll put O'Reilly for us. Perhaps for him. That should suffice."

Mathilda watched him stand and take his hands out of his pockets.

Walking down the length of the table, he kissed her twice.

"I am still sorry you know," he said. "The outburst after Eugenie. Caught by surprise then. Please don't worry. I love you dear and am trying. Of course, he shall be registered as an O'Reilly. Here. Give me a kiss and we can finish our wine."

Trying to think, she watched him go out to bed down the horses. Difficult though he had been polite at least, that and he adored the children.

But still all could be arranged and that in short order, the church porch and two witnesses off the street. An ordinary married couple the neighbors must think.

Better to stay. Surely he would keep his word. A short wait, the christening needing to be arranged before he left.

Henry looking adorable in Eugenie's gown as Richard held him at the font. Enough time, too, for everyone to have acquired a new outfit. Eugenie in her striped frock, a bright blue day dress for her mother and Eugene in his new coat that had arrived the day before.

All three Crottys having appeared the house was nearly filled. Champagne all round, a pistachio blancmange, and a baked brie.

Heavenly smells wafted out of the kitchen as all the children exhausted themselves running in and out. So much excitement that Henry had to be tucked in upstairs before supper.

The next week a disappointment, the London group having changed their minds.

Eugene traveled to Paris for another interview. A group wanting Oran like the others but in a year instead of months.

He came back with tales of the city and news of the Bulwers. His lordship having asked for a new photograph while his wife wondered why everyone had not come along.

A letter on top of the stack as May began. Another London group, this time for Fez. No one able to make up their mind it seemed.

Better to stay while he could.

A joy it was just having someone to come home to. Funny. He could not envision not having had Polly for that had only happened in Corstown.

A June that was very warm.

A new stall put in, Eugenie's pony delivered and riding lessons commenced. Difficult, Mathilda having told him that once he was gone there would not be much time for riding. Still, in the end, she had agreed.

Managing to get everything set Eugene took Eugenie downtown on Saturday for a new habit.

Eugenie hugged the dressmaker, saying, "I need a habit and boots to ride Princess, my new pony. Mama is very busy. I have come to be measured so you can make it up."

"Ah, very good," said the dressmaker. "But what colors? Ladies' perhaps. Black, red or dark green."

Stamping her foot Eugenie shook her black curls.

"Scarlet for the jacket," she said. "Bright green or blue for the skirt. Black boots like Papa."

The dressmaker frowned as Eugenie's father stood lost in thought. What to say, all the bright colors of Stamboul but needing to be toned down a notch.

"Sweetheart," he asked, "why not a black skirt and red jacket like the lady we saw yesterday?"

Eugenie stamped her feet again as her eyes began to flash. Not a good sign the dressmaker thought as her small client replied.

"No! No boring colors," Eugenie shouted. "Only bright ones like Mama. I hate black except for boots."

Another customer opened the shop door as the dressmaker twisted her tape around her wrist. Surely the colonel would give in, that and another tantrum would not help.

"We need something she will wear Colonel O'Reilly," the dressmaker said. "She is wearing bright yellow with red boots. Perhaps if you allow a red jacket she will agree to a navy skirt."

Eugene agreed, giving Eugenie a horehound candy from the little bowl.

Sitting down while the dressmaker waited on the other lady, Eugenie looked through the swatches. The morning slipped away. Eugenie did not decide on red and blue until she was halfway through the tweeds.

Mathilda smiled when Eugenie showed her the ribbon samples. Not surprising considering whose child she was, she thought as Eugenie ran out of the room.

"A little indulged," she said as Eugene came in, "but then she adores horses so it makes sense. At any rate, it will look sweet. Indeed, I have no time for it. It shall be an exquisite fit. Tending Princess will be more complicated. I shall take care of it somehow."

Everything turned topsy-turvy the next day. A cable from James. Terrible news. Emily O'Reilly was dying.

Eugene rushed to kiss Mathilda.

Waving goodbye to Eugenie, he headed to the harbor for the noon steamer.

Gravesend, the Liffey roads and then a cab to the house.

Susan having become less welcoming with each visit he had hoped to stay with Richard. Not possible he realized, his mother being much too ill. A moan echoed down the stairs. Tossing his umbrella towards the coat rack, Eugene hurried up two steps at a time.

He knelt down next to the bed taking his mother's hand.

"Mother it is I, Eugene. Come from France. James let me know."

Her eyelids fluttering open, she held out her arms. Her second born had always been her pet.

When the monthly nurse had filled her basins, Eugene rose. He headed down the hall to unpack before going up to the nursery.

Eerie it was how much Gertrude resembled Eugenie. She looked more like a twin than ever. She laughed and laughed as he sat showing her his pictures for she thought they must be her.

Over the port, James said something of his own. A friend having seen all the photographs at the O'Gorman house.

Eugene bit his tongue as his brother ran on. More heathen garbage and mean-spirited to boot especially with their mother upstairs. Granted James had never approved but still.

Eugene sat day after day by his mother's bed. Letters written, books read aloud, dinners with Richard and rides with Thomas. In the end spending all his time upstairs for she would not touch her toast if he was not there.

Better too than downstairs with James' rambling on. Eugene tried not to respond, but the words came blurting out. Mathilda a pasha's child, the same as the solicitor general's son. None of them fit to be stable hands. Higher than all of the O'Reillys put together.

A few days in Belfast because James would not be there. But no. She was far too ill.

Ten days. A string of specialists and their medicines, none of them able to help for her pneumonia would not loosen its grip.

Coming upstairs, the grooms helped push her bed over to the window. Eugene sank down by her pillow so she could die in his arms. As the priest began to pray, tears ran down his face.

Eugene headed downstairs once she was gone for he could kneel no more. If only Mathilda was there. Somehow the others seemed like strangers.

Mass and the family plot in Glasnevin by her husband as she had wished. Eugene began packing the next morning and got ready to go back.

London first and then France. If only it was the other way round for he was crazy to see everyone. But no, the meeting needing to be kept since he had heard no more from Paris.

Climbing into the cab, an odd feeling crept in that he would not be back. It made no sense, but he got out and went down the line again with another hug and kiss for each.

In London, he was delayed for the chief investor's holiday had not quite ended. July finally arrived with Mathilda's warm embrace.

Mathilda being busy with Henry he rode out nearly every day, Eugenie in tow in her new habit. Like a living

Union Jack what with all the red and blue.

Eugene went back to London in late September to begin looking around again, perhaps something with fewer meetings.

If only Paris had worked out. Easier, just the train instead of the steamer. Hard to be gone so much. Even little Henry was far too used to it for he screamed whenever Mathilda went down to the pier.

Mathilda bit her tongue, doing her best not to complain as it made for a happier home. So many trips and nearly all wasted since they always changed their minds.

Hard too being left behind when he went to Dublin. It was almost as if he didn't want his family to know them. Very odd since he adored Eugenie.

"I am glad for the interviews," she said over tea. "It's just all the back and forth. Granted you had to go early for your mother. Difficult. Eugenie gets used to riding out and that I cannot do. At least not every day. Because of Henry."

"I told you I'm trying," said Eugene. "I'll ask Bulwer again. If only Palmerston was still here or even Fuad Pasha. But oh you do not know how hard it is to be away from you and the children. I could hardly bear it in Oran. Wanted to run home. Henry's screaming at the station cuts right through me. But I must, for all of you.

"With any luck after this no missions for a while. Twice as many pounds as the last. That and some money from my mother. Time to travel or stay home. Back to London or Stamboul if they can be persuaded to change their minds."

A smile inched across her face as visions of her great lady stuffing sweetmeats into Eugenie crossed her mind.

"Stamboul it shall be then. The babies shall love it. They can see the courtyard and our park. Hopefully, the grand vizier will relent. London otherwise but together. No more separations. The main thing."

He sat down on the sofa.

Pulling her closer, he said, "Sweetheart, I try so hard. Setting up all the accounts. Easier then leaving you to write out checks. The children are enough work as it is. That and I adore them. A long way from Stamboul so, of course, you are concerned. But nothing will happen. I shall always be with you."

Mathilda said no more for there was no more to say. A good father and a decent provider. Better if he was home more, though. Humiliating, the way it made Henry scream.

Spring and summer passing under a happy cloud. Everything was more fun because he was there.

Another trip to London towards the end of July but a happy surprise when he came back through the door. A signed contract and check for past expenses. Gibraltar, Casablanca and then on to Fez.

Heading down to the station they went on to Paris. A week's holiday to celebrate with both babies in tow.

Past all the cafes, this time en route to the park. The drinkers looking younger than ever he thought as he pushed the pram towards the Tuileries gardens.

They spent the next day with the Bulwers. Dinners out with one of Uncle Andrew's old friends and a new signet ring for Eugene. A peacock blue bonnet for his bride, toys, and more toys.

Eugenie bounced up and down on the seat all the way home.

They had tea in the garden.

Sitting on Eugene's knee under the grape vines, Henry shouted as Eugenie helped her mother cut flowers and prune the roses. A reshaping, perhaps a few more in the spring.

Eugene's words came tumbling out.

"Better not," he said. "We may have to head south. Something they mentioned in London. More missions. Might be better to get closer to Gibraltar. Save a day on the train. Not sure yet. One more meeting and then I'll know. Maybe Bordeaux. Nearly as pretty as Nice. A villa this size or a little larger."

He watched her face crumple.

"I wish to stay," Mathilda said. "Fine for you but not us. We have friends now and have joined the church. To start over just as you leave will not help. The baby is so small yet."

Eugene replied, saying "On my mind since the last trip. I wish we could stay. Of course, moving shall be hard. But we only came because London was too dear. Easy to get to Gravesend and Paris too.

"Now that I shall be heading for Morocco it makes sense to head south. Less snow. That will be easier even if the rest is not. I thought of Spain, but there is much unrest. I would fear for all of you. Bordeaux is very pretty. Lots of bridle trails for Eugenie and Princess."

Mathilda settled Henry down to nurse under her shawl.

"Less snow would be nice," she said. "A new parish of course. But hard for Eugenie and her little friend down the street. We shall have to be more particular. A neighborhood with more children. That and Princess. Eugenie's weeping will drive me insane once she is sold."

"That I didn't mean. We can bring Princess along in the special car. One of the riding horses too but not both. I'll be gone and you will be so busy."

December 1873. Another week.

Heading back to London Eugene met with the

investors' board. He returned with good news. A contract for two more missions. All the dialects being needed since few were able to speak Arabic let alone the rest.

He was gone so long she was afraid he would miss Christmas.

But no. He came up the drive on Christmas Eve in a cab overflowing with presents. More toys than ever before too, fifteen things just for Henry.

The children's happiness changed to distress as she had known it would once he left to find a house.

One letter, then another filled with pictures for he had found something. They cascaded onto the carpet as Henry waved, an approval of sorts, she thought. Easier if she could have gone. Dull colors no doubt but once everything was put out it would be fine.

Eugene having returned the children cheered up as they had missed him. Mathilda did her best to enjoy the rest of the winter and the lovely spring that followed. A new baby too, not due until December.

It took less time to finish packing than she had feared. Her trousseau, everyone's personal items and the children's cots.

Eugene fetched the trunks and campaign chests down from the attic. Three for the second floor, two for the first and a sixth for all the baby things. Retrieving his old uniforms and boots from the attic, he headed downstairs for his books.

Eugene offered to deal with Princess and all her gear. Something to do he thought, the melancholia having begun to creep back.

Mathilda did her best to stay calm and not upset him though some of it could not be helped. The baby on the way forcing it out somehow.

The wedding she said.

But no, he said, no time. Bordeaux. Easier once everything was set up.

Always willing to help with the children, she realized. The park and then the beach on a Saturday, Eugenie on Princess and Henry in a donkey basket with his father at the reins.

Late August. Two days to Bordeaux, the animals in the special car behind. Henry fussing with Eugenie racing up and down as they reached the station.

A beachside hotel in Arcachon when they arrived as the villa was not quite ready.

The rain making it impossible to go out, the other guests complained about the children's noise.

Going downstairs, Eugene spoke with the manager. Easier by far it would be in the villa with no one to complain.

The sun emerged. Taking both children down to the beach, he hired a rowboat and sailor and had the chap take them round the harbor twice. Eugenie nearly fell in, having to be pulled back by her sailor collar. Henry shouted for he had seen a kite.

Their father walked back, Henry on his shoulders and Eugenie by his side. He did his best to live in the moment. Surely they must be expecting him to go.

All four headed back the next day.

Sitting up on the promenade Mathilda watched as she was too unwell to hike up and down. A glorious day, azure blue skies with no clouds at all.

As they were starting towards the lighthouse, a burst of pride came over Eugene. A beautiful wife, Henry beside him and Eugenie just ahead.

Riding to the end of the beach they turned and looked back. Henry waved with a giggle for his mother looked so small. Mathilda waved back, first with her handkerchief and then her parasol.

Riding back, they went back up for lunch. She

opened the picnic basket. Spreading out the sandwiches and deviled eggs, she pulled out everyone's jacket because the sun had gone behind a cloud.

A slight breeze but still better than the dining room. The silverware posed a challenge. Not enough fork lessons. Even the gentlemen kept sending odd looks their way.

Family life picking up where it had stopped once they moved in. Eugene back to his letters, Henry with his blocks in the nursery. Eugenie found a sunny spot for Madeleine and her other dolls by the window.

Going out in the garden their mother looked round. Making her think of home, she realized with a smile. Better weeded and with even more roses than the last.

Walking down the road, Eugene found a new parish. Mass was the same everywhere and would help the children feel grounded.

Days of peace, ending all too soon as the campaign chest was brought back down to be filled. Harder this time. Tiny as he was, even Henry seemed to know that his father was going away.

Sitting in the cab as she headed downtown with her father, Eugenie cried and cried. Eugene picked her up, holding his handkerchief to her eyes.

Trying to soothe her he asked what was wrong.

His daughter told him.

"You must be going away," Eugenie said. "You always buy paper and talk to the stores for Mama."

Eugene brought her home for lunch, going back out afterward.

He left Eugenie home the next day.

So many errands and places. Nine months for the rent and six for the grocer, sufficient for he should be back by March.

A checking account he thought as he walked past a

bank.

No, he decided. No need for a local one and no time to show Mathilda how to write out the checks. Better to keep it all in London.

He brought Eugenie along to the dressmaker the next morning. The last account, twenty pounds and fabric for a new scarf.

As Eugene walked out the door, his daughter reached up for his hand.

Piping up, she said "Papa, must you go. We need you. Not just me. Henry and Mama too."

Her father picked her up, holding her tight.

"Sweetheart," he said, "I would stay if I could, but this is what I know to do."

Tears welling up in both their eyes, he continued on, saying:

"Don't worry. I shall be back soon. Velvets for Mama. Boots for you. Toys for Henry and the new baby. He shall have come by then."

They stopped at the confectioner's for candy before going home. Her eyes were dry by the time they arrived as he had hoped.

Everything gotten ready. While Mathilda finished packing his grip, Eugene rode out with the children.

Morning came all too soon. Kissing everyone goodbye at the villa, he waved till he was out of sight. Mathilda in red and white, Eugenie in green and little Henry in his sailor suit getting smaller till they could no longer be seen.

Two days to Gibraltar and one more for Casablanca.

Setting all his pictures out by his pillow, Eugene laid down to rest.

His melancholy started seeping in, far worse even than the last time. One more mission and then home, far better than London to search for another.

The schedule needing to be tweaked, everyone having arrived on the first.

Tangier for Berber carpets. The Tangieri tribes wove the best ones.

Four days taken in the end to rework it all. Painful it was for the children were in his heart. Better three more days in Bordeaux than Morocco.

He laid on his divan, remembering late into the night. Everyone dipping up their stew of all things, an odd vision but a comfort.

Eugenie's lessons with the governess down the road, English since she mostly knew French. Hard they must be as somehow languages and Mathilda did not agree. All right in the end it would be, but no more than four. Six were way too confusing.

The run taking forever once it got underway. The maps bad and the railway extended for a hundred miles, not two.

As they were waiting for a caravan to pass, the sandflies came out. Eugene covered up, but the flies were not deterred. A very determined swarm they must be, all zeroing in on one tiny spot left exposed.

A desert plague he explained as the investors began to fret. A nuisance but better than their Damascene cousins as those had an awful itch.

The expedition reached Fez on the ninth.

Eugene's spirits rose because a letter in Mathilda's hand was on top of the stack of mail. Sipping an orangeade, he cut the envelope open.

The children's drawings cascading onto the table, he read:

1 December, '74
My beloved,
We have a new son, Armand, born only yesterday. All having

gone well with the help of Francoise Le Notre, the nurse Father Bernard from our new parish had suggested.

Oh, how I wish you could have been here but you shall be soon. He takes after you like Eugenie. The same curls though of course that may change. Good lungs and feeding well.

Eugenie has held him twice. Henry being rather less fascinated. Must be the age.

Other than that I have started in with the Christmas shopping. Even with all the toys you bought, Armand still needs a blanket and Henry a sweater. Very hard waiting till the twenty-fifth to see what you chose.

That and, of course, we have your gifts. We shall have to celebrate a second time when you return.

I shall write again later. Armand needs to be fed.

I send all our love,

Mathilda

Tacking the drawings up, he hoped enough carpet sources had been found.

Near impossible it would be to have to miss another Christmas. Better than Rashaiya for the others would be there but still. No crackers or plum pudding, that and date brandy instead of Guinness.

Christmas Day spent with the investors he started up again on Boxing Day.

Visits to one merchant after the other, all needing to be seen before they left.

The first two visits went well. By the third, Eugene began feeling a little off. A trifle warm, perhaps a cold. Surely not the sandflies since his ankles had barely been bitten. Certainly not ague as Fez had few mosquitoes.

Two days later he felt much worse.

Trying to rise, he collapsed just as the lead investor came in. The investor sent the boy down to the front desk to ask for a nurse.

Eugene inched his way over to the table to write

Mathilda so she would know he was ill.

A shock it would be coming on the heels of his Christmas note, but it could not be helped. He blotted and sealed his note, enclosing the steamer schedule so she would know when to come out.

The lead investor took the note.

"Colonel," he said, "I shall send a message off to the coast in the morning. A few days and she will know. But the manservant tells me that he has had sand fly fever and recovered. So all should be fine. But don't worry. The note shall go with the rest."

Lying back down Eugene tried to stay still. He felt so hot that he turned over and over trying to find somewhere cool.

He thought of Mathilda's cool hand on his brow, that and Christmas. Eugenie's toys opened and Henry's new boots on his feet. Mathilda in her new shawl, Armand in her arms.

He remembered back. A long remembering, Uncle Andrew and his pigeons in '48. But no for the *London Times* lacked a man in Fez.

If only for she could start for Casablanca in the morning instead of another week. A cable from Gibraltar instead.

December twenty-eighth. A western doctor, a bad sign because they always used their own.

The doctor listened with his stethoscope.

Rising to his feet he looked down at his patient.

"Colonel, you appear to have a touch of dysentery along with the fever," he said. "I am leaving medicine with the nurse. You should write Bordeaux again to let them know."

Struggling, his patient managed to sit up.

"Perhaps I am dying and you are not saying. I need help. Someone to dictate to. Far too exhausted to sit at my desk. In French or Turkish. Maybe English. My wife is from Vidin and can't read Arabic."

"I can or else one of the investors," said the doctor. "French would be best. That she must know well. Alarming enough that it will come from a stranger."

The lead investor reappeared, writing everything down while the doctor sent for a priest. The nurse helped Eugene change into a clean nightshirt.

Sitting up, he sipped what tea he could manage.

Dozing off once the priest had gone, Eugene awakened with a start. The bank letters and address lists, for he had taken them out and left them in a heap.

Desk drawers filled with correspondence back in Bordeaux. All sorted out but none with envelopes since they took up too much room.

Probably nothing from the bank either unless it had come since November.

Struggling to stand and then to crawl he fell back onto the divan.

He did his best to explain to the nurse, but she did not understand. Better to wait for the priest. He could help when he returned.

Arriving at six the priest was filled with dismay for the colonel had slipped into a coma. Dusk sliding into night, candles all round, last rites given and rosaries said.

Eugene slipped away at sunrise as the priest sat holding his hand.

After the lead fellow did what he could. Two letters, the first for London. Another to be cabled to Bordeaux from Gibraltar so the consul could inform Mrs. O'Reilly. Better that than she learn of it from the papers since they would surely pick it up.

Everyone attended the graveside service in the English cemetery. The lead investor arranged for a man to come out and do a pen and ink. No one closer than

Casablanca with a camera.

The priest recommending a local mason for the stone, no drawings though of course as the carving would take weeks.

The lead man ordered everything packed up for there was no point in staying without a guide.

Reaching the port, he wrote out another note to be put into the colonel's chest where Mrs. O'Reilly would be sure to see it. A small comfort for sure but she would want to know of his last days and where he was.

Bordeaux. Nothing from Fez since Christmas.

Odd, she thought, must have been several storms. No longer than it had taken from Oran. Somehow it seemed more wearing now that the children were old enough to ask.

Leaving Henry and the baby in the nursery with Francoise, she took Eugenie out for a ride. A distraction though in the end not helpful for more questions came as they were riding along.

Mathilda did her best not to show her fear. Something should have come by now. Indeed, he had written of being back a few weeks early.

A shower having begun they headed back.

Reaching the foot of the drive Mathilda spotted two tiny figures in black at the door.

Odd, she thought, straining to make them out. Father Bernard on the left with his roman collar. The other figure the consul perhaps. Hard to be sure really, Eugene having only introduced him once.

Eugenie said nothing as they rode up. The horses' hooves clattering on the gravel a bubble filled with gloom descended from the heavens. Mathilda could think of no good news that that pair would bring.

The manservant came out, taking the reins. Mathilda began inching forward, her legs frozen to the ground and barely working. Father Bernard spoke, something about wanting to come in.

The front door opened and she saw Eugene's campaign chest behind Francoise. Mathilda sent Eugenie upstairs for it was better that she not hear. A sense of impending doom seizing her heart, she followed her visitors into the drawing room.

GLOSSARY

Abdel Kader (Abdelkader ibn Muhieddine): Algerian. 1808-1883. Led the resistance during the French invasion of Algeria, 1830-1837. A resident of Damascus 1855-1883.

Accounts and Papers of the House of Commons: British. August 16, 1860. Description of Eugene O'Reilly/Hassan Bey's activities in the province of Syria at the time of the Druze massacres.

Act of Union: British. Legislation passed by Parliament in 1800 in the wake of the United Irishmen rising. Limited Irish rights.

Ancestry.com: 1870 British census records confirming the residency in London of Eugene O'Reilly and Mathilda Solomassy, Mathilda being shown as Mathilda O'Reilly.

Antipodes: British. Australia and New Zealand.

Araba: Ottoman. An oxcart rode in by ladies.

Arcachon: French. A resort town near Bordeaux.

Belgrade: Ottoman. Now part of Serbia. At the confluence of the Sava & Danube rivers.

Beirut: Ottoman. Capitol of present day Lebanon. Before the breaking up of the Syrian province, it was the port city for Damascus. The province of Syria was governed from Beirut.

Agrawal: Ottoman/Syrian. Local warlords or aristocracy.

Bankhead, James Monroe Jr.: American. 1818-1856. Unpublished memoir. Can be found on buffalonet.org website. The boarding school pranks in Chapter 2 and physical descriptions of Mr. Hall's School are drawn from this document.

Bar: Ottoman.A coastal town that is now part of southern Montenegro.

Barada River: Ottoman. A river, rising in the Anti-Lebanon mountains and ending in the desert outside Damascus.

Belgrade: Ottoman. Present day capitol of Serbia, located at the confluence of the Sava and Danube Rivers.

Beqaa (Bekaa) Valley: Ottoman. Valley between the Lebanon and Anti-Lebanon mountains located between Beirut and Damascus. Part of today's Lebanon.

Bordeaux: French. Major seaport located on the Garonne River.

Boulogne sur Mer: French. A fishing port on the English Channel.

British Foreign Office Archives: British. Eugene O'Reilly/Hassan Bey's statement confessing his involvement and intriguing in 1869-70 is located here, enclosed (but not bound) in FO 195/806. Another copy is located in the archives of the French Foreign Office, Gay de Tunis, September 20, 1868, AEPol/10.

Bulwer, William Henry Lytton Earle (first Baron Dalling & Bulwer/Sir Bulwer): British. 1801-1872. Politician, diplomat & writer. Ambassador to the Porte, 1858-1865.

Caique: Ottoman. Watercraft similar to London's water taxis. Used in the Golden Horn.

Canning, Stratford (First Viscount Stratford de Redcliffe/Lord Stratford Canning): British. 1786-1880. Diplomat & politician. Ambassador to the Porte 1842-1858.

Cetate: Ottoman. North of Kalafat. Part of present-day Romania.

Corstown: Irish. Located in County Meath.

Croutier, Alev Lytle: Harem: the world beyond the veil. Abbeville Press. 1989

Crumlin Road Gaol: Irish. Located in Belfast and opened in 1841. Eugene O'Reilly is held here. In the 1960's the Northern Irish hunger strikers were held here at the tail end of its life as an active prison.

D'Aragon, Stanislas (count de Bentivoglio): French. French consul at Beirut in the 1860's. A personal friend of Eugene O'Reilly/Hassan Bey.

Devak, Istvan: The Lawful Revolution: Louis Kossuth and the Hungarians 1848-1849. Phoenix Press. 1979.

Digby, Jane (Lady Ellenborough): British. 1807-1881. Married to a Bedouin sheik & died in Damascus in 1881. Collateral ancestor of Pamela Digby Churchill Harriman.

Dublin Evening Mail: Dublin, Ireland. March 28, 1875. Obituary of Eugene O'Reilly. Reprinted from the London Times.

Edward VII, King of Great Britain and Emperor of India (Albert Edward): British.1841-1910. Private journal covering the time period of his 1862 official tour of the Levant, including Damascus. April 28, 1862, entry detailing the prince's ride into Damascus and towards the British consulate, escorted by Colonel Eugene O'Reilly/Hassan Bey. Cairo to Constantinople – the Prince of Wales's journal. 6

February – 14 June 1862 spread 59.

Elliot, Henry George (Sir Elliot): British. 1817-1907. Ambassador to the Porte 1867-1877.

Eyalet: Ottoman. Name for a provincial subdivision.

Fenton, Laurence: The Young Ireland Rebellion and Limerick. Mercier Press. 2010.

Figes, Orlando: The Crimean War: a history. Picador Press. 2012.

Fuad Pasha (Mehmed Fuad Pasha): Ottoman. 1814-1869. Ottoman statesman & diplomat. Appointed special governor of the province of Syria in 1860 following the Druze massacres of the Maronites.

Gaza: Ottoman. Port city. Before the breakup of the Syrian province, goods from the southern part of the Syrian province were shipped from here.

Giurgevo (Giurgiu): Ottoman. Located on the Danube in present day Romania.

Golden Horn: Ottoman. The body of water that constitutes the main harbor of what is now known as Istanbul.

Ghouta (al-Ghouta) Oasis: Ottoman. Oasis formed by the Barada river. Surrounds Damascus.

Great lady: Ottoman. Title of an Ottoman gentleman's first wife. She was in charge of her husband's junior wives and odalisques along with the children, slaves, and all other residents of her haremlik.

Haremlik: Ottoman. The women's section of a house.

Homs: Ottoman. A city in modern-day western Syria. Camel caravans from as far as Afghanistan terminated here.

Hornby, Mrs. Edmund: British. In and Around Stamboul. James Challen & Son, Philadelphia. 1858.

Kabul: Ottoman. Capitol of Afghanistan.

Kalafat: Ottoman. Located on the bank of the Danube in present day Romania. Directly across the Danube from Vidin.

Kilmainham: Irish. Main Dublin jail at the time of the Young Ireland Rising. Now a museum. Many members of the Young Ireland rising were held here.

Lancers: British & Ottoman. Specialized cavalry.

Litani River: Ottoman. Important water source for what is now southern Lebanon. It rises in the Bekaa valley, emptying into the Mediterranean sea.

London Times Digital Archive: British. Issues with reference to Eugene O'Reilly's involvement in Young Ireland April 4, 1848; July 10, 1848; and October 12, 1848. Issues with reference to his later career in the Levant: March 4, 1854; August 31, 1860; September 18, 1860; October 6, 1860; January 20, 1862; November 8, 1862; July 11, 1868 and October, 1868. Many of these, especially in respect to his service under the Turks, were reprinted in many other newspapers elsewhere in the British Isles and Australia. Translated into German for Prussian and Austrian papers. Items detailing his career also ran in American newspapers as far apart as New York City and Sacramento, California.

Lyons Richard Bickerton Pemell (first viscount Lyons/Lord Lyons): British. 1817-1887. Ambassador to the Porte, 1865, succeeding Sir Henry Bulwer. Ambassador to France, 1867-87.

Lovell, Mary S: A Scandalous Life: the biography of Jane Digby. Richard Cohen Books. 1995. Please see Lady Ellenborough.

Luby, Thomas: Irish. 1822-1901. Revolutionary, author and journalist. Involved in the Young Ireland rising.

Meagher, Thomas: Irish. 1823-1867. Leader of the failed Young Ireland rising.

Medjidie, Order of: Ottoman. A military and knightly order of the Ottoman Empire. Instituted in 1851. Awarded to members the British and French armed forces who came to the aid of the Ottoman Empire during the Crimean War.

Menshikov, Prince Alexander Sergeyevich: Russian. 1787-1869. Lead Russian general during the Crimean War.

Nation (The): Irish. Newspaper founded by three leaders of what would become Young Ireland. Published 1842-1849.

Novi Sad: Ottoman. Located on the banks of the Danube River in what is now Serbia. Second largest city in that nation which was formerly the Ottoman province of Serbia. Eugene O'Reilly's first post is located south of it across the river.

Odalisque: Ottoman. Concubine/slave. Ranked below the great lady and junior wives.

O'Gorman, Richard: Irish. Involved in the Young Ireland rising and friend of Eugene O'Reilly.

Omar Pasha (Mihajlo Latas): Ottoman. 1806-1871. Born in Croatia. Commander of Ottoman forces in Moldavia & Wallachia on the Danubian front forces from 1848 through the end of the Crimean War and beyond.

Rose, Hugh Henry (First Baron Strathnairn): British. 1801-1885. Senior British army official. Military advisor to General Omar Pasha in the province of Syria 1840-1848. Appointed charge d'affaires in the absence of Lord Stratford Canning in Constantinople January 1851. Fought in India. Became Commander in Chief of British Forces in Ireland in 1865.

Russell, John (first earl Russell/Lord Russell): British. Prime minister 1865-66.

Schatkowski Schilcher, L: The Hauran Conflicts of the 1860's: a chapter in the rural history of modern Syria. Int. J. Middle East Studies 13 (1891). Cambridge University Press 1891 0020-7438/81/020159-21 & JSTOR. Much detailed information and background concerning conditions in 1860's Hauran, which surrounds Damascus.

Silestra (Silistra): Ottoman. Now part of Bulgaria. A Danubian port city close to Romania. Ottoman stronghold on the Danubian front during the Crimean War.

Smith-Brien, William (William Smith-O'Brien): Irish. 1803-1864. Member of Parliament and leader of the failed Young Ireland rising.

Sloan, Robert: William Smith-Obrien and the Young Ireland Rebellion of 1848. Four Courts Press. 2000.

Smith, Albert: Customs and Habits of the Turks. Higgins, Bradley and Dayton. 1857. Descriptions of Ottoman baths in Constantinople and Stampa's store which catered to western customers.

Stamboul: Ottoman. Nickname for the city of Constantinople, now called Istanbul.

Shipman, Pat: To the Heart of the Nile: Lady Florence Baker and the exploration of central Africa. Perennial Press. 2004. Background information on the town of Vidin and on being sold into a harem, Lady Baker having been a Hungarian refugee child who was auctioned off for this purpose.

Tarazi-Fawaz, Leila: An Occasion for War: civil conflict in Lebanon and Damascus in 1860. University of California Press. 1995.

Temple, John Henry (3rd Viscount Palmerston/Lord Palmerston): British. 1784-1865. Anglo-Irish politician. Prime minister 1855-1865.

Trinity College, Dublin: Irish.Founded in 1592.

Varna: Ottoman. Now part of Bulgaria. Located on the Black Sea coast.

Vidin: Ottoman. Now part of Bulgaria, a port town on the Danube. One of the two great strongholds along the Danubian Ottoman front during the Crimean War.

Wadi: Ottoman/Arabic. A valley, ravine or channel that is dry except in the rainy season.

Wheatcroft,Drew: The Ottomans: dissolving images. Penguin Books. 1993

Young Ireland or Irelander rising: Irish. 1848. Failed rising against the British crown. Eugene O'Reilly played a small role.

ABOUT THE AUTHOR

Sarah B. Guest Perry was raised in suburban Boston and holds a Bachelor's degree from Franklin and Marshall College in Lancaster, PA. She has worked in many creative fields including, at one juncture, helping to build costumes for the world premiere of John Updike's *Buchanan Dying.* The eldest child of a Harvard-educated historian she was reared with history in the air she breathed. These are her first books.

CPSIA information can be obtained
at www.ICGtesting.com
Printed in the USA
FSOW01n0908310516
20989FS

9 781519 793911